THE DENIM DOM

Tymber Dalton

SIREN SENSATIONS

Siren Publishing, Inc.
www.SirenPublishing.com

A SIREN PUBLISHING BOOK
IMPRINT: Siren Sensations

THE DENIM DOM
Copyright © 2013 by Tymber Dalton

ISBN: 978-1-62242-917-2

First Printing: April 2013

Cover design by Harris Channing
All art and logo copyright © 2013 by Siren Publishing, Inc.

ALL RIGHTS RESERVED: This literary work may not be reproduced or transmitted in any form or by any means, including electronic or photographic reproduction, in whole or in part, without express written permission.

All characters and events in this book are fictitious. Any resemblance to actual persons living or dead is strictly coincidental.

Printed in the U.S.A.

PUBLISHER
Siren Publishing, Inc.
www.SirenPublishing.com

DEDICATION

This one's for Mr. B, who is Sir, Daddy, Pack Alpha, and pup all in one. With love, for His inspiration, His instruction, His love of perverting innocent kitchen implements and other common household items, and His own special brand of…eh, motivation. I am a *very* lucky pet.

AUTHOR'S NOTE

Yes, I *finally* wrote Tony's story! LOL. For those of you who don't know, he also makes appearances in *The Reluctant Dom* and *Domme by Default*. While this book and those two are all standalone books, the events in this book take place following the others. Leah and Seth also appear in *The Reluctant Dom*. Tilly, Landry, and Cris, and Ross and Loren, appear in *Cardinal's Rule*. Clarisse, Mac, and Sully appear in *Safe Harbor*. All of these releases are available from Siren-BookStrand.

Some people don't realize this, but it's no secret that I am actively involved in the BDSM lifestyle. That's one reason why I enjoy writing about it so much. While sometimes I draw characteristics for characters or inspiration from real-life events from my own experiences, everything I write is fictionalized to protect the…eh, guilty, so to speak. However, the kind of play I write about is the same kind of play I witness at nearly every party or private club outing I attend. Or is even play we engage in ourselves.

As of this writing, the FetLife.com screen names I invented do not exist. So if they ever do show up, please don't bug the poor people about this book because they likely won't have a clue what you're talking about.

This book took me a long time to write for several reasons. Life got in the way, my health got in the way, my own paranoia of screwing it up and letting down my readers after the tremendous response for *The Reluctant Dom* got in the way…and we lost a very dear friend and mentor in the lifestyle to cancer. Quite frankly, that took my heart away for writing this for many, many months. *The Reluctant Dom* was my way of dealing with my grief over my grandmother's death, and I knew I couldn't handle recreating that experience with a ten-foot pole at this time. So I had to wait until I felt ready to write Tony's story with the energy and heart and clarity of mind to give him the undivided attention he deserved.

My friend will one day get her own story, but this book isn't it. It was never meant to be. It held its own set of experiences and emotions, and I hope it doesn't disappoint those of you who've waited so long for it.

While Sarasota and some of the landmarks mentioned in the area do exist, I use them fictitiously. FetishCon (called FetCon by many) is a real event held every year in Tampa, but I've taken literary license with the event for my own purposes. The organizers of the convention have in no way endorsed or participated in the writing of this book. (But if you ever get a chance to go, you should. It's a pretty rockin' good time!) Characters in this book are completely fictitious and creations of my own warped imagination.

THE DENIM DOM

TYMBER DALTON
Copyright © 2013

Chapter One

Sunglasses…check. Coffee…check. Laptop—
Shayla Pierce glanced over her shoulder at the backseat. *Check.*
She'd been damn lucky to fall into this job. Last thing she needed was to mess up her first day by forgetting something important.
She put her Civic into reverse, then hit the brakes.
Crud.
Shifting back into park, she shut the car off and pulled the keys from the ignition. *Might help to have my purse today.* She jogged back to her apartment and found her purse sitting on the kitchen counter where she'd left it. She grabbed it and returned to the car.
One more try.
This time she made it out of her apartment complex and down the street. She turned onto Clark Road and headed west toward US 41. She'd timed her drive already. She should make it to her new office in downtown Sarasota in under forty minutes.
Tropical Sarasota was a far cry from her snowy Minneapolis childhood, college days spent in Athens, Ohio, at the Scripps School of Journalism, and a year on the copy desk at *The Plain Dealer* in Cleveland before being promoted to reporter, when she got to write her own copy.
Now, at thirty-three, she was starting her life over again. Or at least that was what it felt like.
No more snow. No more ice. No more turtlenecks.
Her fingers tightened around the steering wheel. *No more backstabbing,*

lying sack-of-monkey-shit bastard ex-fiancés named James I wasted eight years of my life on.

The publisher and editor in chief of *Sunshine Attitude Magazine*, Bill Melling, waved her into his office when she arrived ten minutes before eight.

He stood and offered his hand. "Glad to see you didn't back out on us, Ms. Pierce."

"You can call me Shayla, or Shay, Mr. Melling."

He smiled. "Bill's fine. We're casual around here. We've got a morning editorial meeting at nine. We have them Mondays, Wednesdays, and Fridays." He glanced at his watch. "That's in an hour. When Suzanne gets here, I'll have her show you to your desk and get you up to speed." A woman appeared in the office doorway. "Oh, there she is."

Twenty minutes later, Shayla was seated at her new desk in a large cubicle with a window overlooking Ringling Boulevard. Not too bad. Not an office, but the only one with an office in this organization was Bill Melling, so that was fair. At least she had tall divider walls and more floor space than some of her coworkers.

She took a few minutes to quiet her nervous stomach. *This has really happened. I did it.*

The day after the discovery three weeks ago, she'd been drowning her sorrows at a hotel bar with Allison, an old high school buddy. Finding out her fiancé had robbed her of over fifteen thousand dollars to pay for Internet porn tended to upset a girl.

Allison had been supportive, sympathetic, and more importantly, had called Shayla two days later with a proposal.

Fortunately, Shayla's killer hangover had gone away by then.

"I was talking to my brother about what happened," Allison said. "His best friend's uncle has a magazine down in Florida, dead-tree and web editions. Pretty popular. It's been around a long time. They're looking for someone to replace one of their staff who's leaving. A writer. You interested? I've got the info. He called him already and asked if he could refer you."

Was she interested? *Hell* yes.

She'd called Bill Melling, talked with him over the phone, flew down three days later to meet with him in person, and got herself hired.

While in Sarasota she arranged to rent an apartment, and her whirlwind move began.

Shayla fought the urge to fidget while waiting for the editorial meeting to start. Instead, she rearranged her desk several times.

New job, new apartment, new life.

She smiled to herself as she looked out at the beautiful, sunny spring day. Palm trees swayed in the gentle breeze washing over the town from the Gulf of Mexico. This was, literally, a tropical paradise.

It's a whole new start. A whole new life.

A whole new me.

* * * *

Fifteen people, including Shayla, gathered around the long conference table. As Bill introduced her to the rest of the staff, she nervously smiled and nodded to everyone. It didn't take her long to feel like part of the team even though she mostly sat back and listened.

The print magazine went out once a month, but they updated web content every week with exclusive Internet-only stories to help draw more readers and advertisers. They covered everything from local to national stories, from politics to entertainment, never shying away from controversial topics.

Toward the end of the meeting, Bill stood and walked over to a whiteboard on the wall. "Brainstorm time. Let's get some good ideas cooking."

People tossed out ideas for stories and Bill listed them without question, regardless of how outlandish they sounded. He looked at Shayla. "This is just something to help us keep the creative juices flowing. Feel free to shout out anything. Whatever comes to mind, no matter how off the wall."

She nervously smiled, a little embarrassed to be the center of attention again. "Kinky sex practices?" She wished she could call the words back as soon as she said them, horrified she'd even uttered the phrase. She'd been thinking about how to pay off one of the credit cards James had maxed out on porn charges.

He'd taken the cards out in her name without her knowledge or permission.

Everyone laughed at her suggestion, but Bill wrote it on the board, nodding as he did. "Actually, that's pretty good. The county commission is doing battle with a strip club right now. Zoning ordinance lawsuit pending. Anyone else?"

Some more ideas were floated, including a few X-rated ones along the lines of Shayla's idea. When the meeting broke up fifteen minutes later, Suzanne was busy tapping on a laptop.

Bill offered Shayla a smile. "Don't be embarrassed. That was tame compared to some of the stuff we've tossed around in here before." He nodded toward Suzanne. "She copies down the list every week and sends it out through e-mail for staff. We've come up with some of our best stories this way. Probably a little different than you're used to doing it at the newspaper, huh?"

Shayla shrugged. "Different's good."

Bill nodded. "We think so. It's what's kept us competitive and in business for so long."

* * * *

It turned out Suzanne wasn't just an administrative assistant, although that was her title. She was the glue that held the organization together. Assistant editor, nerve-soother, proofreader, den mother, referee, research—she did it all.

She spent the morning with Shayla familiarizing her with their server system and workflow process, getting their IT crew to install needed software on her new work laptop they assigned her, and taking her around to introduce her to staff in the other departments like advertising and production.

The business didn't rely solely on the magazine for income. They also did production work, printing, and graphic arts preparation for hire, which helped support the entire enterprise. The magazine made money, but the largest profit margin came from the side work.

At lunch, Shayla walked with Suzanne and a couple of other editorial employees to The Tropical Tavern, a local restaurant a block away. They served a huge lunch buffet for a reasonable price, and Shayla soon found herself warming to her new coworkers as they chatted.

One woman, Kimberly, had close-cropped, bright orange hair and large brown eyes. "That was a wicked suggestion at the meeting. I'm glad you said it. I've been too chicken to say anything like that."

Michael, the man sitting on her right, snorted. "You? Chicken? Since when? Weren't you named Queen of the Pervs or something?" Michael was handsome, with blue eyes and black hair.

Kimberly slapped his shoulder. "That's the last time I take you to Gasparilla with me, jerk."

Suzanne leaned in and in a stage whisper said, "We're still wondering when to plan their wedding."

Shayla laughed.

By late that afternoon, Shayla had helped edit three articles and taken on an assignment to write a piece for the website about movies filmed or set in the local area. Bill insisted he wanted her eased into the job and not overwhelmed her first day there.

After two weeks, Shayla felt comfortable with her coworkers and relaxed in the atmosphere. A new running joke emerged at the thrice-weekly editorial meeting. Someone always piped up at the brainstorming session with "kinky sex practices" as their idea. On Shayla's third Monday, Kimberly came to the meeting with a handful of papers, printouts from a website.

She handed them out. "We keep talking about this, so I thought you'd be interested in knowing more. Looks like this area, from just north of Tampa down to Naples and even over to Orlando and Ft. Lauderdale, has a pretty large kink population of various kinds. Did you know one of the largest and oldest fetish trade conventions is held in Tampa every year in late summer?"

Shayla read the paper. It was a printout from a site for a local BDSM group called the Suncoast Society. Very plain, without a single naked person anywhere on the page. It contained a few announcements about their monthly Munch, whatever that was, calendar updates for a play party—she wasn't sure she wanted to know what that was—and links and contact information.

Bill sat back in his chair and read the paper. "Okay, now let's talk about this for a few minutes. This is giving me a few ideas. Some of you remember we did a profile on Joe Redner, that strip club owner up in

Tampa, when he ran for a seat on the Hillsborough County Commission a few years ago. That was one of our best-selling issues ever. The web article received a ton of hits, too." He went quiet for a moment before looking around the room. "Ideas?"

Now that the boss was seriously considering this, some of the staff went silent.

"Oh, don't go all chicken on me now." He looked at Shayla. "What do you think? You've been here long enough to see how we run things. Feel free to chime in."

She shrugged. Frankly, she'd seen too much sex of the kinky kind to last her a lifetime. Especially when it cost her a hundred dollars to have her computer wiped clean of the crap after James downloaded porn to it the first time. In addition to the credit cards she'd be paying off for too damn long from the second time, thanks to him. And all the other related niceties that went along with that.

Like cancelling her wedding and having to face her family and friends and tell them why. She had refused to let James off the hook for the pain he'd caused her the second time. She'd been honest that she was dumping him due in no small part to all the money he'd cost her...and exactly how he'd spent it.

"There's a lot of roads to explore," she eventually hedged. "You could do a running series." She hesitated. "Porn addiction." That was a subject she knew all too well. "Internet hookups." She held up her copy of the printout. "Kinky lifestyle stuff."

Bill scrunched up his face and turned his gaze to the ceiling. Everyone went silent, recognizing his "deep in thought" face.

After a moment, he spoke. "I like that." He still stared at the ceiling. "I like that a lot," he said with a nod. "An ongoing series." He looked at everyone at the table. "Let's seriously consider this for a few minutes. We've hit a plateau on web hits over the past few months now that the elections are over. Housing market's still in the tank, bad news there. Economy sucks. Jobs are down. People aren't really paying that much attention to the fancy high-end lifestyle stories right now. Our biggest web hits the past few months are for the stories on entertainment and anything remotely related to sexual issues. There's also that *Fifty Shades* trilogy that's so popular."

He looked at Suzanne. "Can you pull up those web stats Barry sent you?"

She nodded and did it, then hooked her computer to the projector. Bill stood, dimmed the lights, and walked over to the wall where the figures were displayed. "Right here," he pointed. "See the trend? Every time we run a story remotely having to do with sex we get a spike in traffic. Doesn't take a rocket scientist to figure out why." He looked at his staff. "Now, I'm not saying we need to turn into *Playboy* or *Hustler*, but let's chew on this for a while longer. Anyone have anywhere they need to be right now?"

Everyone shook their heads.

"Good." He stared at the numbers again as he slowly nodded. "Very good."

* * * *

Two hours later they broke for lunch with a fairly detailed list of potential topics, ranging from local swinger groups to BDSM clubs. With the fetish convention being held in a few months, Bill wanted enough lead time to tap into that potential market. Suzanne would contact the promoters and secure an interview with them, the staff member to be assigned later.

Shayla avoided Suzanne's gaze. *Please don't let it be me.*

Shayla wasn't a prude by any stretch of the imagination. She had no problem with people's sexual preferences running more toward chocolate than vanilla. But after finding out that James was turned on by, among other things, anorexic, silicone sluts with breasts the size of watermelons getting the crap beat out of them, and that he regularly jerked off to them instead of her at times when she'd begged him to sleep with her, her self-confidence had taken a beating it hadn't quite recovered from yet.

She knew she didn't possess a Hollywood starlet's artificially enhanced, top-heavy body, but she wasn't ugly or obese. She didn't consider a size sixteen "fat" especially when she was a lanky five-eight and it was distributed all over and not in any one area. Her pale northern complexion hadn't seen enough of Florida's tropical sun to tan yet, and her hazel eyes matched the rims on her glasses. She didn't want contacts, not when she really only needed her glasses for reading or long stints on the computer. She wasn't bat-blind without them.

Yet.

She'd chopped a few inches off her hair after moving down here though. Now it hung a little below her shoulders, a blasé brown that usually did what it was supposed to when she asked it to without it bowing too much to humidity's wrath. Long enough to pull it into a ponytail, or wear it down in long layers.

Still, it stung to know James had preferred to sink into an artificial fantasy than to seek her out when there were times she begged for his attention. Rationally, intellectually, she knew it was his problem and not hers.

But her pride still suffered the aftereffects.

Adding to the sting, the additional betrayal of him taking out credit cards in her name and using them to charge his porn.

Bill accompanied them to lunch. After passing through the buffet line, he seated himself at the end of the table, next to Shayla.

Her senses on high alert, she recognized a setup when she saw it.

"I wanted to talk to you about this, Shay," he started.

Oh, boy. Here it comes.

He speared a piece of raw carrot in his salad with his fork. "How would you feel about doing a hands-on investigative piece about the local BDSM lifestyle scene?"

She tried not to choke on her broccoli soup. "How hands-on?"

He chewed his carrot for a moment. "Something beyond the crap people normally see on the Internet. Separating fact from fiction. Is everyone doing like what's on the porn sites, or is that the exception? That kind of thing. How do people get into this sort of lifestyle? Day in the life of someone. I've got Pete doing a report on the nudist colonies up in Pasco County. Alice is going to cover transsexuals, and we've got leads on strip clubs and swingers groups."

Shayla felt her face redden. She studied her food. "What are you asking me to do, exactly?"

"Get to know some of these people. Write an article, hell, even better, a series of articles about them. What makes them tick, something fair and balanced. You could even interview mental health professionals and get their take on what they do, talk to law enforcement, that kind of thing."

Shay's appetite had faded. "BDSM?"

"I won't require you to do it. If you want to say no, I understand. We can get someone else to do it. But I really think, after talking to some people locally and doing a little poking around of my own, that it'll be one of our biggest series. A way to get your name well known on our site. I'm not talking about a sensationalized T&A piece. I'm talking seriously looking at it from the inside out. It'll be a web-only series, but we'll promo it in print."

Serious writing. She did want to do serious writing. On her résumé, she'd highlighted some of the IR pieces she'd written, and that in-depth reporting was one of her loves.

She just didn't know if she could be unbiased on *that* particular topic.

"Can I think about it?"

"Of course."

She nodded. "Okay. Let me have a few hours. I'll get back to you before the end of the day."

* * * *

She knocked on Bill's open door later that afternoon. He was alone and on the computer. "Hey, what's up?" he said.

"Can I talk to you privately for a few?"

He sat back and nodded. "Sure. Close the door if you want."

She did.

Shayla sat in one of the chairs in front of his desk. It took her a moment to compose her thoughts. "About the story idea. The BDSM one."

"Don't want it?"

"I honestly don't know if I can be unbiased."

She'd found out in her few weeks of working for the magazine that Bill Melling wasn't just a good boss, he was a nice guy. Fair, easy to talk to, and was considered a friend by many of his employees.

"Need to talk about it?" he asked.

She took a deep breath. "As long as it's just between you and me."

He nodded.

"I have ex issues. The reason I left my ex was because he downloaded BDSM porn behind my back. Well, that wasn't the only reason, but that sums it up nicely."

He sucked in a breath. "Yowch."

"Yeah." She studied her fingernails. "It was the second time I'd discovered he'd been downloading porn. The first time, I found it on my computer and he swore he'd stop. It turns out, after the final accounting the second time, he'd downloaded over fifteen thousand dollars' worth of porn. Using credit cards he took out in my name." She picked at her cuticles. "I believed him the first time when he said he'd stop. He did seem to change. Got more attentive. I had no reason to doubt his word that he'd stopped and wouldn't do it again."

"He didn't stop?"

"Nope. He got sneakier, proposed, and asked me to set a date for our wedding."

He winced. "Double yowch. Bastard."

She managed a wan smile at his tone. Bill was obviously on her side. "So we spent months shopping for a dress and rings and ordering invitations and a cake. All that crap. Then I found out how sneaky he was when he'd borrowed my car. I found a stack of mail in it that he'd forgotten he left there. Including some envelopes with my name on them. That's when I learned it wasn't the one thousand dollars of the first go-round. It was over fifteen thousand, and it was six different credit cards he took out in my name without my knowledge. Most of it for sites showing that BDSM stuff."

"Well, I appreciate your honesty. I understand that it would be too much for you. I'll go ahead and reassign—"

"I'll do it."

He tilted his head as he studied her. "I was expecting you to say no after hearing about all of that."

It surprised her, too. "I want to find out why he wanted that stuff more than me. Why he was willing to lie and steal and throw away what we had for it."

She chewed on the inside of her lip to keep from crying. "We were together eight years. Lived together five of those. He swore I was the only woman he wanted. That I was the love of his life. His soul mate."

She took a deep breath. "Then I found the first batch of porn. And you know the rest of the story. I want to know why it was more important than me." She met his gaze. "I want to see if I can figure out what it was he destroyed my trust for and why, because *he* damn sure never could answer the question."

* * * *

Why the hell did I say yes? She sat on her screened-in lanai and stared out at the green space behind her apartments. A small flock of some sort of ibis walked along, checking the ditch for insects as they moved.

She still didn't know for sure. She sipped her beer and contemplated it for a while, until it grew dark outside and she felt a slight buzz from her empty stomach combined with the effects of the beer.

Inside her apartment, she settled on a toasted cheese sandwich, easy to make and easy to eat. Part of her relished the freedom of living a peaceful life, never wondering where or when—or for how much—the other shoe would drop.

Part of her cursed James for putting her in this position. Being alone with no one to rely on. All she'd wanted to do was make him happy. Was it too much to ask of him to be honest with her? To not go behind her back?

To not put her in frigging debt over his Internet porn?

Hell, after the first discovery, she'd even offered to explore kinky stuff if he wanted to. He'd flat-out refused the offer, leaving her even more confused than before.

I need to quit thinking about it tonight. This isn't helping.

Instead of the TV she opted for music. She thumbed through her iPod and found Michael Hedges. Mellow and soothing guitar instrumentals that never failed to settle her nerves. She curled up on the sofa with a book and read while she ate.

Finally, when she couldn't stop yawning, she shut off the music and headed to bed. But she lay there, her mind racing about the article she had to write.

Why the hell did *I say yes?*

Chapter Two

Tony Daniels stared at his computer monitor. He loved his job, but he hated some of the people he had to work with. More than once he'd envisioned punching his boss, Darren, in the face.

Or tying him up and beating the crap out of him with a cane.

He scrubbed his face with his hands. Not to mention there were more than a few people working under him who would greatly benefit from spending the day in a ball gag.

He smiled. Such evil daydreams were a way to amuse himself during a usually long workday. Like envisioning an employee strapped into a straightjacket, with a butt plug up their ass, a ball gag in their mouth, and tied to their chair.

His own personal form of morale improvement.

He nearly giggled out loud.

These are the kinds of thoughts that will forever keep me out of the highest levels of management in this company.

Not that he cared.

Then again, he was paid well for his long hours and the work he did. Running the computer data center at the Bradenton headquarters of Asher Insurance, a national health, life, and disability insurance company, was nothing to sneeze at. And even though he was on call twenty-four-seven, unless everything went to hell in a handbasket after he went home he could leave work at the office on most days.

When he felt his personal cell phone vibrate in his pocket, he took it out and quickly glanced at it.

A text from his friend, Leah, popped up. *Still on for tonight?*

He sent her a quick reply. *Yep. I'll be there by 8.*

Poor Leah was doing her damnedest to fix him up with her friends. Vanilla and lifestyler alike. He'd once asked her husband, Seth, to please tell her to knock it off.

Seth had simply grinned at him. "Nope. It makes her happy. I'm not going to piss on her parade."

Then again, Tony couldn't blame Seth. After witnessing firsthand everything Leah went through losing her first husband, Kaden, to pancreatic cancer, Tony didn't know if he could have denied her anything that made her happy, either.

He let out a sigh and returned his phone to his pocket. Tonight, Leah had told him, her friend Valerie was also coming over for dinner. Nice woman, worked as a bookkeeper for a local auto dealership. He supposed he could suffer through another matchmaking attempt if it would make Leah happy.

Kaden, I hope you appreciate what I still go through for you.

* * * *

Despite Leah's usual assurances that he didn't need to bring anything, Tony brought a bottle of Riesling with him. Leah met him at the front door with a hug and a kiss on the cheek before taking the bottle.

"Thank you. You know you didn't have to do that."

"You know I always will."

She laughed. It was a beautiful sound, so different from the early days after Kaden's death when they all kept watch to make sure she didn't kill herself in the deepest, darkest times of her grief. "Yes, I know. You're stubborn like that." She wore a short denim skirt, a tight tank top, and a leather collar around her neck.

That told him their guest was lifestyle-friendly, if not outright in the lifestyle. When it was a vanilla friend, she wore her silver day collar, which looked like a necklace, and less revealing, more conventional clothes.

Tony followed her to the kitchen where Seth worked on prepping the salad. "Hey, man," Seth greeted him. "Sorry I'm not shaking hands."

Tony slid onto a barstool at the counter. "No problem. I understand." Leah set a glass of iced tea in front of him, already sweetened the way he liked it.

He had to admit she was efficient.

Lucky bastard.

"So," Tony said, "based on Leah's clothes, I'm guessing tonight's matchmaking attempt already knows about my extracurricular activities?"

She grinned. "Yes. She used to be in the lifestyle, but when she dumped her ex, she got out of it. She wants to get back into the local scene here in Sarasota." She jammed her hands on her hips, her green eyes sparking. "At the very least you two would make great play partners."

"Ah. So you're not trying to marry me off this time?"

She rolled her eyes at him. "No. I'm never trying to marry you off. I'm just trying to help you broaden your social horizon a little."

He sipped his tea. "You know I work long hours. I don't have a lot of time for broadening my social horizons."

"Duh. And that's why I'm trying to help you out."

He was spared further lecturing by the sound of the doorbell.

"That's Val," Leah said, heading out of the kitchen. She turned and pointed a finger at Tony. "Be nice."

"I'm always nice," he said. "I'm the sweetest sadist you'll ever meet."

Seth roared with laughter. Leah stuck her tongue out at Tony before turning to go answer the door.

* * * *

Val, as she asked him to call her, was three years younger than him at thirty-nine, shorter than him by nearly eight inches at five-four, had short brown hair, and pale blue eyes. She loved to laugh. He found her smart, witty, charming, and friendly. They had a lot in common, including tastes in reading and music. Gainfully employed, she owned her own house and wasn't looking to jump into a new relationship without a lot of groundwork first.

He also wasn't the slightest bit attracted to her, although he wouldn't mind playing with her a few times.

Leah apparently sensed it. After Valerie left, Leah turned to Tony and scrunched up her face. "Nada? Are you sure?"

He shrugged. "Sorry. She seems like a very nice woman, but—"

"She doesn't flip your switch. I get it."

He smiled. "Never say *switch* to a Dom, Leah. In either context. I don't do one, and I'm liable to use the other."

She laughed. "Yeah, if I ever saw you switch with someone I think I'd make them haul you to the hospital for a CAT scan." She sighed. "I'd hoped you'd really like her."

"I do like her. I just don't lust after her. I'll be happy to play with her if she wants. I wish more women were like her. I'd be playing all the time if they were all nice, charming, and lacking a full matching six-piece set of emotional baggage. I'm allergic to clingy and drama. You know that."

"Yeah." She started clearing the table. "That's why I thought you two would be perfect for each other."

Leah had managed to find two types of women to try to fix him up with. Women he was physically attracted to, but he knew he could never have a relationship with. Or women who seemed to be perfect relationship material, but he felt zilch attraction toward them.

When Leah was out of earshot, Seth leaned in and whispered, "Don't worry. I think she's getting close to the end of her address book."

"Yeah, but she's got a lot of contacts putting feelers out. She won't stop until she either fixes me up or I find someone on my own."

"That's such a bad thing? A woman's got to have a hobby."

"Why can't her hobby be sucking your dick?"

He grinned. "It is, but this is her other hobby."

* * * *

Returning home a little after eleven that night, Tony put his keys and wallet in the dish on the bookcase by the front door and didn't bother turning on the living room lights. He didn't have to look at the empty house if it was dark inside.

Yes, sure, it'd be nice to have a relationship. It wasn't something he needed, however.

Missed? Of course. But not the parts with the drama. His last attempt at a relationship had been a disaster, with the woman turning into Queen Clingy the minute he agreed to being exclusive with her and had collared her as his submissive. Hell, the last two play partners he'd had, despite making it clear to them from the beginning that he didn't want a relationship with them, still tried to pursue one. Even after they assured him they understood and were fine with just being friends and play partners.

They'd both hoped they could convince him to change his mind and make him come around. The only thing they'd succeeded in doing was driving him away.

He had no room for a drama llama corral in his life, much less any interest in keeping it stocked.

The next morning, he spent his first meeting of the day idly imagining Darren naked, hands cuffed behind him, on his knees with a ring gag in his mouth while his fellow department managers used his mouth as a cum dump.

Tony rubbed his face with his hands as the image drifted away when it was his turn to speak. He hated these damn daily meetings. He didn't see why they couldn't be done through e-mail so he could spend his time actually working instead of in a corporate circle jerk. "We had a sev-1 incident yesterday when a backup server went down. Got it up and running in thirty minutes. Still troubleshooting what happened, but no customers were impacted."

Darren nodded without even looking at Tony and called upon the next manager.

Prick.

After lunch, he took a moment to thumb through his personal e-mail on his phone and found a message from Valerie.

It was nice meeting you last night. I might be at the club Saturday night. If you're going, let me know if you're interested in setting up a scene.

He stared at the message, his thumbs hesitating over the virtual keyboard. Instead of replying, he closed the message.

It can wait until later.

Upon having a night to think it over, he didn't know if he wanted to play with her. Plus he thought he might be up for a turn as a volunteer dungeon monitor that weekend. If so, it would give him a perfect excuse not to play with her. He couldn't play if he was supposed to be watching out for others.

I could always cancel. It was understood that with his job he might have to bow out of a DM stint at the last minute. He was never scheduled to be a primary DM, and they always had others working the club so his absence wouldn't leave them shorthanded.

He'd deal with it later. He wasn't poly, he wasn't interested in recreational sex or in lots of casual play, and he didn't want to lead the woman on and hurt her feelings, either.

Or end up having to extricate himself from a sticky situation if she got clingy. So far, his relationship with Seth and Leah hadn't suffered from any of the matchmaking failures, but he didn't believe in tempting fate.

By the time he got home that night and checked his e-mail on his laptop, he'd forgotten about Valerie's e-mail. After looking at his schedule and discovering that no, his DM turn was next weekend, he hit reply.

Sounds good. I won't know what my schedule is like until later in the week though. I'll have to let you know.

He hit *send*.

He stared at the screen. *You're a fucking chickenshit.* No, it wasn't a lie, exactly. Emergencies cropped up at work all the time. Meetings were added at the last minute. Critical upgrades to fix a system failure or security issues could have him going in to work in the middle of the night.

He grabbed leftovers from the fridge and nuked himself a plate of food. Eating alone sucked more and more every day. He missed companionship, conversation, the camaraderie having someone in his life provided.

Although he didn't miss drama.

At all.

He'd had enough of that to last him several lifetimes. After extricating himself from a nasty divorce from a woman whose apparent mission in life was to drive him crazy when she realized he'd really meant what he'd said before they got married about him not wanting kids, he was loathe to enter anything remotely resembling a drama-filled relationship. Queen Clingy had only cemented that resolve.

It didn't hurt that after the divorce he'd discovered he wasn't the only person who had dark, delicious fantasies about tying women up and spanking them. Once he'd learned he wasn't alone, he wasn't a freak, and that there were women out there who enjoyed being tied up and spanked, he'd refused to settle for vanilla.

Although after ten years of not finding the right long-term partner, he admitted it was difficult not to just give up on the prospect.

He knew it was doable. Ross and Loren were a prime example. And Seth and Leah. Before Seth, she had Kaden. Then there were Tilly and her guys, although many of their friends, himself included, thought at first she was nuts to welcome Cris back into her life after the way he'd dumped her.

Those were just the couples and triads he could think of off the top of his head. He had lots of friends who had found happiness in the lifestyle. He knew it was perfectly possible for lightning to strike, for the heavens to open, and to find one's perfect, kinky mate.

Living close to the lightning capital of the world, however, he found it ironic that lightning had yet to strike him.

Chapter Three

Shayla began her research for the article series on BDSM the next day despite how tempting she found it to procrastinate.

The sooner I do it, the faster I can move on to something else.

She looked at the printout Kimberly had shared from the local BDSM group's webpage. They advertised a monthly Munch at a local restaurant, in addition to having parties every month.

Sounds like a good place to start.

She sent an e-mail to the contact address on the page before turning her focus to other projects.

Part of her hoped no one would get back to her. That maybe there was some sort of code of silence. Like in the mob.

She silently swore when she checked her e-mail an hour later and found a polite reply from the leader of the group, a man named Ross.

Sure, I'll be happy to answer your questions and put you in contact with people to interview. I can also arrange a tour of a local club, and interviews with instructors, if you'd like.

She stared at his response.

Instructors?

She had no idea there were such things.

There went my easy excuse.

She tapped out a quick reply detailing what she was looking for and hit *send.*

Deliberately ignoring her e-mail until just before lunch, she found another reply from Ross. He and his wife, Loren, were a Master and slave couple.

First of all, I'm going to state what's probably obvious, and that is while we don't mind you quoting us, please do not reveal our real names, or any information that would out us to the general public. I'll do my best to answer some of your questions, but it might be better if we meet to talk in person. Some of this doesn't make sense unless you can actually discuss it face-to-face.

What we do is completely consensual. Although Loren is my collared slave, she does have limits, which I respect. We are not poly. While I sometimes do play with others, it's nonsexual in nature. We've been married for over twenty years, and our BDSM dynamic is nearly as old. There is a very active BDSM community in the Tampa Bay area. The local club we're a member of here in Sarasota has frequent classes anyone can pay to attend, although to come to dungeon playtimes you must be a vetted member. I've included a list of classes for you, one of which is taking place this week. My cell number is 941-555-1246 if you're interested in setting up a time to talk in person. Feel free to call or text.

Ross.

Her rapidly pounding pulse caught her by surprise. Quickly, she punched her mouse button to close her e-mail.

I'll deal with it after lunch.

* * * *

Shayla had packed her lunch that morning. She took it to the meeting room, along with a book to read.

Bill Melling stuck his head in the door. "Not going out with us?"

Shayla held up her sandwich. "No thanks. I'm good."

He glanced down the hall before stepping inside and pulling the door closed behind him. "You okay? You look a little… My grandmother would have called it 'vexated.'"

Crap. "I'm fine. I already started my research on the BDSM piece. I got an e-mail from a guy who runs a local group. He's going to put me in touch with some others to talk to."

He nodded. "Good. So you're okay working on it?"

"I wouldn't be doing the research if I wasn't." She hoped that didn't come out as snarky as it felt in retrospect.

Must not have, because he smiled. "I'll leave you alone with your vexation, then. See you later."

She tried to lose herself in the book, a quirky, lighthearted vampire romance, but couldn't. Her mind bounced back and forth between the porn images she'd discovered James had downloaded, to the seemingly harmless and forthright e-mail exchange she'd had thus far with Ross.

Classes? It made it sound like a community college course.

After ten minutes of rereading the same three paragraphs, she dog-eared the page she was on and closed the book. She slowly munched on grapes from her zippy bag full of them and thought about how to approach the article.

How could any woman want *to be a slave?* It didn't make sense. Women had struggled for decades to gain equality and independence. What made them want to throw all that away?

Then again, she'd been willing to forgive and forget James the first time around in exchange for what she thought would be love and security.

She gathered her things and headed back to her desk. Before she did anything else, she put on her big-girl panties, pulled up her e-mail, and replied to Ross.

When can we get together in person to talk?

* * * *

Shayla had spent the better part of the night before doing web searches on BDSM and trying to come up with something more substantial than the porn sites or sensationalized news articles about the *Fifty Shades of Grey* books that wanted to show up. She also didn't want to rely on fictional books for her research. She'd spent over an hour reading essays on one site she discovered, Leather and Roses, including a heartbreaking account written by a slave whose Master husband had died in the 9/11 attacks.

It put a human face on the issue she never considered before. It certainly wasn't the cut-and-dry kinky porn of the sites James had visited.

These were people. Real people, passionate about what they did.

She mentally smacked herself. *I need to forget about James and focus on my assignment.*

Despite her misgivings over accepting the assignment, she was determined to be as unbiased as possible. To that end, she looked up the classes Ross had mentioned and sent an e-mail to the listed contact e-mail address to reserve her spots. She'd be attending Submission 101, Beginning Ropework, and Whips for Fun, whatever that meant. The first, Submission 101, would be held late that Saturday afternoon. The other two were a week from Saturday, the whip class first, followed immediately by the ropework class.

She met them at the Village Inn on US 41 the next evening. Shayla waited for the couple in the front foyer of the restaurant. "Ross and Loren?" Shayla tentatively asked when a couple walked in, looking like they were waiting for someone.

The man offered her a friendly smile and a handshake, as did Loren. "Yes, that's us," he said. "Shayla?"

"Yes. Nice to meet you."

Ross looked like a regular, everyday middle-aged guy. He stood a little over six feet tall, with sandy brown hair and brown eyes and an average build. He wore khakis and a light blue Oxford shirt with the sleeves rolled halfway to his elbows. Loren, a good six inches shorter than him, wore black jeans and a pretty turquoise and magenta blouse that perfectly matched her reddish blonde hair and hazel eyes.

After they were seated and had given their drink orders to the waitress, Shayla pulled out her notebook and a digital voice recorder. "I'll be honest that I don't have any idea where to start," Shayla said. "Is it okay if I record this?"

Ross nodded. "Like I said, as long as you don't use any information that will out us, you're free to quote us."

Shayla nodded and activated the recorder, setting it on the table between them. "Okay. I did some web searches last night. I'm really in the dark here. I think everything I read left me more confused than when I started."

Ross looked at his wife. "You're usually the designated newbie whisperer," he teased with a smile. "You want to talk and let me fill in later?"

She gently elbowed him in the side. "Okay, let's start like this," Loren said. "Forget all the hype and bullshit and negative radical feminist hyperbole. And the porn. *Definitely* forget the porn."

"I wish I could," Shayla said as she reached for her glass of water. "I don't think there's enough eye bleach in the world to wash away some of the stuff I saw." Not just from last night, but some of the images she found when discovering what James had been up to were indelibly burned into her mental corneas.

"Probably not," Loren agreed. "But remember, what the porn producers put out there is designed to make money. Or it's exhibitionist amateurs getting their own kink on. There is very little in between that's an even slightly accurate representation of what the average person does when they're involved in BDSM. In other words, it's not what most people would call real. Or realistic, at least."

"Fair enough."

Loren clasped her hands together in front of her on the table and lowered her voice after glancing to a nearby table where an older couple had just been seated. "I'm going to give you what everyone teases me is my 'Newbie 101' spiel. Just like everything in life, from golf to fishing to fantasy football leagues, to any pastime you can think of, there is a bell curve.

"Now, on this bell curve, you'll have at the one end, let's call that the vanilla end, the people who only dip their feet in every once in a while. You'll have at the other end of the bell curve the really hard-core, extreme edge players who make some of the porn you watched look like a Disney cartoon. Then you'll have the hump of the curve, where the majority of participants fit.

"The biggest misconception out there is that all people involved in BDSM are sex maniacs and swingers and every gathering is basically one big free-for-all sex party. And going by the bell curve theory, yes, you'll have a few people like that, and maybe even a few gatherings like that. But they are the exception and not the norm. While sex is a big part of play for some people, for others, sex doesn't have anything to do with their play or their dynamic. And again, there are people everywhere in between."

Shayla nodded, her notepad and pen lying forgotten in front of her as Loren talked. This woman, if Shayla had to describe her, did not fit any kind of mousy, abused spouse stereotype she was aware of. In fact, if she didn't know Loren was her husband's slave, she would never have thought it. Not from the strength of her voice, or the intensity of her words, to the direct way Loren's piercing gaze didn't flinch from her own.

She didn't know what Loren did for a living, but she suspected she was a formidable opponent when crossed.

"So we get all that fantasy crap out of the way for starters," Loren continued. "There are people in the lifestyle from all walks of life and all economic backgrounds and all ages. There are professionals and blue-collar workers, everyone you can possibly think of. From college-aged to retirees."

Ross spoke up, a quirky smile on his face. "There are an inordinate number of nurses."

Loren laughed but gently nudged him again. "Yes, our local group does count more than our fair share of nurses amongst our ranks, but there are a lot of hospitals and doctor offices and senior citizens in this area. It's a retirement and snowbird haven. Meaning a high demand for nurses and other medical professionals. If you're in a large steel town, there are probably a lot of steel plant workers in the local lifestyle." She glanced at him. "Are you done interrupting me?"

Shayla caught the twinkle in his eye. "Yep."

She nodded at him and returned her attention to Shayla. "And as you can see from us, there are times we're just a normal husband and wife. BDSM is one facet of who we are. Yes, it's a large part of our lives. But first and foremost, we're people. We never lose sight of that fact."

"Why do people want to be in this lifestyle?" Shayla asked, unable to contain the question. "Why do it?"

Loren shrugged. "Why not?" She smiled. "Sorry. I don't mean to come off sounding flippant, but the truth of the matter is there are as many reasons for being in the lifestyle as there are people in the lifestyle."

"I just don't get what makes a person want to be beaten is all."

Ross burst out laughing and clapped a hand over his mouth to stifle it when the nearby couple looked at him. He lowered his voice. "Loren doesn't want to be beaten."

"Not all the time," she said with a grin.

He glanced at her but picked up his thought. "Impact play is only one part of our BDSM dynamic, a small part, and not everyone is into impact play."

Shayla tried to wrap her head around that. "Huh?"

He nudged his wife. "Use the diving metaphor."

Loren nodded. "Are you familiar with scuba diving?"

"Um, not really. A little. I've never done it. I'm originally from

Minnesota, and went to college and lived in Ohio the past several years."

"Okay," Loren said. "In scuba diving there is one common thing that unifies everyone in the sport, regardless of how or where or why they do what they do. Do you know what that one thing is?"

"Not drowning?"

Ross laughed again. "I like her."

Loren smiled. "Besides that."

Shayla shrugged. "Not really."

Loren tapped the table with her finger. "The sport of scuba diving is going under water while breathing from an external air source. Got it?"

Shayla frowned, but nodded. "Okay."

"Just go with me on this and you'll see my point," Loren assured her. "Some divers are basic sport divers, clear-weather and clear-water divers who do nothing but go out in the Gulf in the middle of summer when the water is warmest and when it's clear and when it's not rough. Okay?"

Shayla nodded.

"Then there are divers who are into spearfishing. Some of them are on the mild end of the scale and will only go out in summer, yadda-yadda. Some of them are avid spearfishers and will go out even in the middle of winter in five-foot seas."

"She used to teach scuba," Ross interjected.

"Hush," Loren said to him. "Some divers are into underwater photography. Some divers are into wreck diving. Some divers are into cave and cavern diving. Some divers are into deep diving for whatever reason and use mixed gases like Heliox, Nitrox, Trimix, or something similar. Some divers are commercial divers. Some shallower commercial divers don't even carry a tank, they have a line that runs from the surface. Some divers only do shallow dives in water they can stand up in. But what do they all have in common?"

"They have to breathe underwater," Shayla volunteered.

"Exactly." She gestured, making a circle with her hands before bringing them together again. "That's the 'umbrella' that encompasses scuba diving. Divers breathe something underwater, regardless of the reason they're underwater. You with me?"

Shayla nodded. "Okay."

"So swap that out for BDSM. It's an umbrella term that doesn't even fully describe what it is that we do. The unifying idea is that the people participating in it are kinky. Or, not-vanilla. The term stands for bondage and discipline, dominance and submission, sadism and masochism. So just like 'scuba diving' is a generic term, so is BDSM."

Loren made the circle gesture again. "BDSM is just a term with a unifying theme. But if I say 'scuba diving' with no other context to people who know nothing about scuba diving, a lot of people, depending on their age, they'll either think *Sea Hunt*, or Jacques Cousteau, or Navy SEALS, or whatever their frame of reference is. Okay?"

Shayla nodded. "Fair enough."

Loren clasped her hands together in front of her again. "There are people who, at least when writing it, use an acronym to better describe this lifestyle—WIITWD. It stands for 'what it is that we do.' Because you might have people who are kinky but who don't consider themselves into BDSM. There are some people who've known all their lives that they were 'different' in some way, but it took seeing something related to BDSM for them to put their finger on what that something was. There are people who stumbled into it and discovered they liked it and they decided not to turn back. There are people who maybe like being tied up in bed, and that's the extent of what they do. And there are people who spend their lives as dedicated service-oriented slaves, who never get tied up or beaten at all."

Loren made the circle gesture one more time. "Umbrella of kink. Anything not vanilla when it comes to sex could in some way fit under the kinky umbrella."

"Okay, now I'm confused. Earlier you said sex isn't a part of it for some people."

"Right. Let me clarify. Not just not-vanilla sex, but you could substitute 'relationship dynamic' for 'sex.' Does that help?"

"Maybe."

Loren smiled and sat back as the waitress approached with their tray of food. "Don't worry. It'll start making sense soon."

They sat and talked for over three hours. By the time they parted ways in the parking lot, Shayla was both enlightened and more confused than ever. Not because she didn't understand what the couple was saying, but because of the huge amount of information she'd attempted to digest in such a short amount of time.

One thing was for certain, she knew she couldn't just slough off and write something based on the talk she'd just had.

She needed to go on-site to the club Ross and Loren were members of, and she needed to attend classes and talk to other people in the lifestyle.

* * * *

Loren settled into the passenger seat. "I like her," she said.

Ross nodded. "She seems very nice."

She glanced at her husband out of the corner of her eye. "I think we should set Tilly up to talk with her. And Leah." A thought struck her. "Ooh!"

"No," Ross said.

"What?"

"I know that sound. You want to hand her off to Leah to fix her up with Tony. No. Talk, yes. Matchmaking, no."

Loren fought the urge to pout, knowing if she did that it would earn her at least five swats when they got home. "Just to talk, Sir."

They stopped at a red light. He looked at her, eyebrow arched.

"Hey," she said. "I just said I want to see if Leah and Seth want to talk to her."

"That's not exactly what you said. And it wasn't the tone in which you said it. You guys need to leave poor Tony alone. He's going to quit coming around if all of you don't stop trying to fix him up."

"Well, is he not someone who usually helps mentor newbies? He teaches. He's a DM. Are you saying we can't put her in contact with him at all?"

Ross let out an aggravated grunt she knew meant he was trying to figure out a way to admit she was right without admitting she was right.

She let the subject drop and sat back in her seat while hoping he didn't spot the smug smile on her face.

Chapter Four

Back home, Shayla grabbed a shower, a cup of hot herbal tea, and her notebook and pen. With her headphones plugged into the voice recorder, she played back their dinner conversation while jotting down information and making notes on points she wanted to hit for both further research and including in the article.

Despite what she'd hoped, she wouldn't be able to get away with only writing two or three articles on the topic. No way could she do it justice without shortchanging either the subject or the people kind enough to speak to her about it.

Already she spotted several different potential topics. The dynamics and differences between Dominants and submissives, or submissives versus slaves versus bottoms, Tops and sadists and masochists and rope bunnies and…

She hit *pause* on the recorder, pulled off her glasses, and rubbed her eyes. Just those topics alone could easily take up a couple of articles each to truly do them justice.

Then there were the different types of play. No way *that* could be covered in one article without glossing over everything and basically regurgitating what showed up on Wikipedia.

She thought for a moment. *Profile a person or couple and discuss salient topics?* was added to her growing list of bullet points.

Still, nothing she'd discovered gave her an answer to her own burning question.

Maybe I'll never really know why.

Hell, when she'd angrily confronted him the second time, even James couldn't give her a satisfactory answer. He'd begged for forgiveness, begged her not to leave him.

She'd waited to confront him until after she'd spent the afternoon alternating between throwing up in the bathroom, following his online trail through the different websites, and on the phone with various credit card companies after pulling an online credit report on herself and discovering the full extent of his treachery.

Until after she'd been armed with the truth.

Until after there was no way he could gaslight or sweet-talk his way out of it.

Okay, yes, so mailing copies of everything to his parents had been a tad on the over-the-line side of crazy, but after the shit James put her through, he should count himself lucky she hadn't mailed copies, along with a report of the criminal fraud he perpetrated, to his boss as well.

It would have cost him his job. Had she decided to press charges, he'd be looking at jail time.

She'd been able to reclaim most of the deposits for the wedding, which gave her nearly three thousand dollars she applied to paying for her move. James promised to one day reimburse her in full.

Not that she would hold her breath. Although before she departed for Florida, he had left her a check for five hundred at the apartment.

No note enclosed.

Asshat.

With a sigh, she hit *play* and resumed listening.

* * * *

Thursday morning didn't start well. Shayla startled awake on the couch at six o'clock, with a crick in her neck and the headphones still on after having fallen asleep listening to the interview.

"Shoot." She sat up and tried to ease the pain in her neck. She hadn't meant to fall asleep on the couch.

After briefly considering going to bed to sleep for another hour, she opted to put coffee on and head out for an early walk. Her uneasy dreams still swirled along the perimeters of her brain, images of naked women kneeling at the feet of hunky guys, bullwhips coiled in the men's hands. Of darkly lit dungeons and screams of pain and pleasure.

What the hell was I thinking taking this assignment?

She pulled on shorts and sneakers and with the sun beginning to lighten the eastern horizon, she left her apartment for the humid, cool Sarasota morning.

Part of her wondered what else she'd discover on this journey.

What if I never find the answers I'm looking for?

Everything Loren and Ross talked about the night before came full circle to the fact that the people involved with each other in healthy dynamics had trust and communication as a foundation. Different levels of trust, sure, depending on what activities they were engaged in.

How do I ever learn to trust anyone *again?*

She'd trusted James. Loved him. Had been ready to spend the rest of her life with him.

It was nearly seven by the time she returned to her apartment, sweating and breathing heavily after jogging all the way home.

It had been the only way to get the nagging, unanswered questions out of her brain for a little while.

* * * *

"You're still looking a tad vexated," Bill observed upon her walking into the break room to refill her coffee.

Shayla ducked around him. "I'm fine," she mumbled.

They were alone in the break room. It surprised her when she heard the door close. Turning, she saw he stood against it. "If this assignment is too much for you," he softly said, "I don't have a problem reassigning it."

She leaned against the counter and crossed her arms in front of her. "No. I want to do it." She reached up and nudged her glasses up the bridge of her nose.

His arched eyebrow spoke his disbelief.

"Seriously," she said as she turned to fill her mug. "I…" She took a deep breath to buy herself a second or two. "I'm just trying to digest everything is all. I'll be fine."

When she turned back to him, he slowly nodded. "Okay. But if you find it isn't, I want to know about it. I'd rather you hand it off than cause yourself distress."

"Understood."

With a nod he opened the door and left. A moment later she returned to her desk and checked her e-mail, where she found a note from Loren.

Hope we didn't scare you off last night. If you'd like, I can come to the Submission 101 class with you. We'll be there on Saturday anyway for the dungeon play following the class. Ross said he'd be happy to sponsor you so you can attend the night play session, and we can introduce you around. That way, we can answer any questions you might have about what you see there.

Shayla drummed her fingers on her desk for a few minutes as she reread the note before replying.

Sure, that sounds great. I appreciate it. I'll see you there.

Within minutes, she had a reply.

We're meeting friends for dinner between the end of class and when the dungeon session starts. You're welcomed to join us. They're all in the lifestyle.

More finger drumming.

Why am I hesitating? This is my fricking job. She needed to nut up and do it.

She replied. *Thanks. Sounds good. Any special dress code for Saturday night?*

Loren must have been sitting at her computer. Her reply arrived less than five minutes later.

Nope. Jeans, comfortable shoes, and a blouse are fine. Just no flip-flips or anything like that. Or feel free to dress up, if you want. Everyone will be street-legal for the restaurant anyway. Some people change clothes once they get to the club before they play if they aren't coming straight from home.

Shayla waited a little while to reply, to clear out some of her other e-mail first.

Thanks. I'll see you on Saturday.

She paged through notes she'd made the night before.

Now I just have to keep myself from chickening out before Saturday afternoon.

* * * *

Loren squealed and held out her phone so Leah and Tilly could both read the e-mail on the screen. Leah held it steady, an ear-to-ear grin filling her face. The three of them were at their weekly Thursday morning girls-only breakfast meet-up, before they went to get their nails done.

"You realize Seth and Ross will beat us in a bad way if they realize we're ambushing Tony, don't you?" Leah commented as she released Loren's hands.

Tilly let out a snort. "You two have to worry about that. *I* don't." She speared a piece of sausage and forked it into her mouth. "That's one of the benefits of being a switch. I keep telling you girls you need to come over to the Dominant dark side. We have *fantastic* cookies."

Loren let out a snort. "I've seen you 'yes, Sir' Landry more than once." She poked her friend in the shoulder. "And that wasn't Cris strapped down to a bench last weekend at the club, either. How's your ass, by the way?"

Leah laughed as Tilly turned pink. "Don't pick on her," Leah said. "We're all a work in progress."

Loren laid her phone down. She picked up her fork and bit back the joking reply she'd almost casually let fly. About Tilly being a lucky bitch and having two guys.

Leah, while healthy and happy with her husband and Master, Seth, was barely two years out from having lost her first husband, Master, and Seth's best friend, Kaden, to cancer. A long, excruciating process that left Leah grief-stricken. For a while, she, too, had two men of her own. The triad she'd longed for for years.

Until they lost Kaden.

"How do we handle things if Valerie is there Saturday?" Loren asked instead.

Leah considered it. "Well, she usually doesn't come until after nine, so we'd already be back from dinner by then. Unless or until she shows up, I won't know if we need to run interference or not."

"You can always set her up to play with Landry," Tilly offered.

Leah considered it. "That's a good idea. You don't mind?"

Tilly arched an eyebrow at her friend and pulled her long, auburn hair back away from her face. "Seriously? Landry's always in the mood to give out a beating. Better her ass than mine," she added.

Loren was glad Tilly had let her hair grow long again. For several years after Cris had left her, she'd cut it super short as well as had it dyed red, a look that harshened her features and added years to her appearance. Upon Landry popping up in her life almost three years earlier with Cris in tow, Tilly had once again learned how to enjoy life.

Especially since Landry was himself now cancer-free.

"We should dub this 'Operation Trap Tony,'" Loren joked.

"Or 'Operation Dom Date,'" Tilly added.

Leah pointed her fork at her friends. "The man needs a submissive. I've seen him at the club, the way he watches scenes. The look he gets. He's lonely."

"He's a DM," Tilly quipped. "He's supposed to pay attention to scenes. It's his job."

"No," Leah insisted with a firm shake of her head. "You don't understand. He gets this sad look in his eyes. He didn't used to have that look."

"What happened with that last girl he dated?" Tilly asked. "I thought you said they hit it off well. Wasn't she his submissive?"

Leah let out a snort. "They did. She hit it off too well. She gave him an ultimatum that she wanted a commitment from him, or she was gone."

Tilly winced. "Yowch. Never demand a Dom do anything."

"It was more than that. It wasn't a situation where he dumped her on principles or anything. She just wanted more of a relationship than he was ready to give. And she was really clingy. He's not into clingy. He wants someone independent, who's their own person."

"You know," Tilly said, "not to piss on this party or anything, but we don't know that they'll hit it off, or that she's even looking for a relationship. Especially a BDSM one. She might be vanilla."

Loren triumphantly smiled at them. "I'd be willing to bet you're wrong. I know for a fact that she's single because I asked her. And you didn't see the way she looked last night while we were talking. She wasn't scared off, and she didn't appear judgmental, either."

"She's writing an article, Loren," Tilly said. "It's her job."

"I'm just saying, the longer we talked, the more she had that little gleam in her eye." She took a bite of pancakes. "And all it takes is a tiny spark to start a forest fire."

* * * *

Tony felt his personal phone vibrate in his pocket during his pre-lunch meeting. He glanced at it, half expecting to see a text from Leah. It was about this time every week she started firming up weekend plans for their tight little kinky social group.

Instead, he discovered it was a series of texts from Loren. *We're bringing a newbie to dinner and the club. She's taking the Subbie class Saturday, and your whip class and the bondage class next week. Reporter. I'm sitting in with her Saturday. Can you make dinner and talk with her for her research?*

He started to reply, then decided to wait and tucked the phone back into his pocket.

His first instinct was to say no. Then again, if the woman was going to the club with everyone after dinner, babysitting a reporter would be the perfect excuse to avoid play with Valerie if she showed up.

That sounds like a plan.

He waited until lunch to respond to Loren. *Sure. No problem. Meet at the club and ride to dinner together?*

He barely had time to get the phone back into his pocket when it vibrated again. *Damn, Loren must be sitting on the thing.*

He checked. Sure enough, it was from Loren. *Sounds great! Class ends 6:30. CU there!*

He stared at the message for a minute. It wouldn't be the first reporter he'd talked to. Ever since *Fifty Shades of Grey* hit the bestseller list, it seemed reporters were crawling out of the woodwork to get soundbites about the lifestyle. Since he taught classes at the dungeon, he didn't mind talking to reporters as long as they didn't name him or take his picture.

Then it hit him that today was Thursday. Leah always got together on Thursdays with Tilly and Loren.

I wonder if I should be suspicious.

He discarded the notion. Leah wouldn't try to set him up with someone on a club night when another friend she'd already tried to set him up with would be there.

Would she?

He called Ross. If anyone knew what was going on, he would.

Or Ross could get the truth out of Loren for Tony.

"Hey, what's up?" Ross said by way of greeting.

"I just had a text from Loren. So a reporter's coming to dinner with us on Saturday?"

"Yeah, we met with her last night. She's doing an in-depth series on the lifestyle for *Sunshine Attitude Magazine*. Nice girl. She's even going to take a few classes."

Tony immediately felt his guard drop. Ross would have outright warned him if it was another fix-up attempt. Unlike Seth, Ross would rein in Loren's matchmaking attempts. "Okay. I was just curious who she was."

"We spent close to three hours talking last night. I get the impression she's determined to do a fair series and not sensationalize the crap out of it. Oh, hey, while I've got you on the phone, I told her I'd hook her up with people who could answer her questions. Mind if I forward your name and e-mail to her? She's going to be in your whip class next weekend."

"Sure, no problem. What's her name again?"

"Shayla…" He paused. "Hold on, let me look." He was only gone a second. "Sorry, had to bring up my e-mail. Shayla Pierce. Why?"

"Nothing, just curious. Thanks. See you Saturday." He ended the call and spun his chair around to his desk terminal. It took him less than thirty seconds to find the magazine's website. He'd heard of them, even bought a copy or two when an issue caught his eye in the store, but he hadn't explored their website before.

Clicking on the Staff link, he saw there were pictures of everyone, their names and e-mail addresses conveniently arranged in alphabetical order. Most of the shots were torso up, semi-candid shots as opposed to formal mugs, taken while the person sat at their desk. Halfway down the page, he stopped scrolling when he found her.

Straight brown hair to her shoulders and what appeared to be hazel eyes behind her glasses. Nothing overly remarkable, except for her smile and the way she held her arms close to her, hands clasped in her lap, as if guarding herself.

Her smile looked tentative, cautious, and didn't even begin to touch her eyes. She was cute. Could even be called beautiful if it wasn't for whatever it was she was holding back behind that sad smile.

He sat back and studied the picture, intrigued. He managed over forty people in his section of the company's IT division. In his nearly twelve years with the company, in addition to his years of experience in the BDSM lifestyle, he'd grown adept at reading faces and nonverbal cues.

He also saw that she didn't wear any rings on either hand.

Hmm.

Noting the time, he shut down the webpage and got back to work, soon forgetting about their conversation once absorbed in his daily activities.

* * * *

Shayla ate alone in the conference room again. Instead of a book to read she had her notebook and pen, sat with her headphones plugged into her digital voice recorder, and listened to more of the previous evening's conversation. That was why she jumped, startled, when someone touched her shoulder.

Bill Melling looked apologetic. "Sorry, didn't mean to startle you, but you didn't hear me when I called to you."

She paused the recorder. "It's okay. What's up?"

He nodded toward her lunch. "You all set? Or would you like us to bring you anything?"

She pushed her glasses up. "I'm okay, thanks."

He looked like he wanted to say something else. Instead, he nodded and left without another word.

She'd decided to start her series of articles with an introductory article about her own experience at the class and dungeon on Saturday. She would include very basic information about BDSM. The audience would learn right along with her.

That sounds like a plan.

She was still mulling said plan over when Kimberly popped into the conference room on her way back from lunch. "You still alive in here?"

Shayla took off her glasses and rubbed her eyes. "If brain-dead is considered alive, then sure."

Kimberly nodded toward the notebook. "Already got a lot of info, huh?"

"More than I ever wanted to know."

"I know what you mean," Kimberly said. "I read that book, you know, the *Fifty Shades* one?" She shrugged. "I don't get it. I mean, I get people want to be kinky. Heck, I'm not exactly tame in the bedroom myself. But I just don't get the whole slave thing. It's not me."

"Me either." She put her glasses back on. "I mean, what I've learned so far is not gelling with what I thought it was. That means there are a lot of people out there like me, who have no clue what BDSM really is about. So I'm glad I get a chance to write a series of articles that will be educational."

Kimberly snorted. "If sex ed had been this much fun in high school, I might have actually enjoyed it and learned something."

"You've got that right."

Kimberly left with a wave. Shayla gathered her things to return to her desk. *There might have been other things I wouldn't have suffered through, either. Like giving James a second chance.*

Chapter Five

Kimberly grabbed Shayla a little before five Friday afternoon. "You and me are going out after work today. No excuses."

Shayla tried to find one and couldn't. Not to mention the orange-haired imp's enthusiasm was contagious. "Okay, uncle. Where are we going?"

"Just over to Main Street. There's a new tapas bar there I want to try. We can walk. Suzanne's coming with."

She had wanted to make friends. This was one way to do it. "Deal."

She walked over with them. The late-afternoon sun sent golden shafts steeply slanting between the buildings and trees planted along the sidewalks, and the sea breeze had cooled the warm air to a pleasant, albeit slightly muggy, temperature.

"How do you like Florida so far?" Suzanne asked her.

"Different in a good way." A freak snowstorm had just dumped three inches of snow on Cleveland that morning. And here she was, in short sleeves and sandals, walking several blocks from the office. "I certainly can't complain about the weather."

"Do you have any family down here?" Kimberly asked.

"Nope. Took a leap of faith based on the job offer. I'm glad I did. It's beautiful here."

"Just needed a change of scenery, huh?" Suzanne asked.

"You could say that."

Kimberly looked at the addresses as they walked. "There it is." She pointed and led the way.

The small restaurant smelled heavenly. With the space nearly filled to capacity, they were lucky to get a table by the front windows. "I'm sorry we haven't taken you out sooner," Suzanne said. "I finally had a night free. I've been wanting to get together with you since you started."

"She runs Mom's Taxi Service," Kimberly teased. "Between dance classes and scouts and sports, her little heathens run her ragged."

"Oh, how many kids?" Shayla asked.

"Two boys, nine and thirteen, and a girl, fifteen. I told Hubby that either he took them out for pizza tonight and gave me a mental health break, or he'd be doing ballet practice and Girl Scouts for three months. Needless to say, he jumped at the chance."

Shayla laughed. "Gave him his marching orders, huh?"

Suzanne nodded as she browsed the menu. "I don't mean to sound bitchy. He's a good husband and a good father. There are times I just have to crack the whip on him."

Shayla fought the urge to giggle at that. Since starting her research she found herself able to turn the most innocuous of statements into something tinged with innuendo.

"Maybe he likes it when you crack the whip," Kimberly chimed in, echoing Shayla's thoughts.

Suzanne shrugged. "No, he's just a stupid guy sometimes. Has to be reminded hello, I need a life, too. Do you have any kids, Shayla?"

She shook her head. "No. Doubt I will, either."

"Biological clock's not ticking loudly, huh?" Kimberly asked.

Shayla snorted. "I think it's on permanent snooze. Right now, I'm at a happy place in my life and I'm enjoying the simplicity of it. There's little I'd change. It'd take a damn special guy working overtime to make me want to make any changes."

I've wasted too many years of my life on someone else as it is, she silently added.

* * * *

Shayla refused to listen to any more of the taped conversation or look at her notes or research BDSM online that night. She'd be attending the class in less than twenty-four hours, and wouldn't spend the night obsessing over the subject. Ross had forwarded her the name and e-mail address of a guy she'd meet on Saturday, a Dom who also taught the whip class she'd signed up for.

She'd put off e-mailing him because of the overwhelming amount of information she already had to sift through.

Hell, I'll be meeting him tomorrow anyway.

Instead, she found an old Abbott and Costello movie on TV and curled up on her couch to watch it with a microwaved chicken pot pie.

Maybe I need a cat. James had been allergic to cats. Even though Shayla had cats growing up, she didn't get one in the hectic years of college, and later going to work for the paper. By the time she'd begun thinking about getting one, she'd already met and started dating James, which put an end to that idea.

Her apartment complex allowed up to two cats per unit, with a minimum extra deposit. She could even have a small dog if she wanted, but wasn't sure she was ready for that level of commitment. A cat wouldn't rely on her the way a dog would.

And she expected indifference tempered by occasional attention from a cat. She'd be afraid of letting a dog down if she got too busy with work.

I'd feel a little less lonely when I was home, at least.

The crying jag hit her from out of nowhere. Before she realized it, a lump swelled in her throat as her eyes prickled from the sting of tears. Up in Ohio, she had friends who had lives and families. While she e-mailed and texted and Facebooked with them, it wasn't the same.

Down here, she had no one yet. Her loneliness after the nice time she'd had with Kimberly and Suzanne only exacerbated the void in her life. If she was back up in Cleveland right now, she'd be out with Allison and others.

Okay, sure, I'd be up to my ankles in snow and slush, granted.

But she wouldn't be alone.

When she'd announced her move, her parents had implored her not to make such a sudden change. Leave James and move into her own place, sure, but stay in Cleveland. Or move back to Minnesota and live with them and look for a new job there.

Neither option appealed to her at the time. Then Allison had mentioned the job to her and it seemed like a great opportunity.

Shayla had needed out and away from everything reminding her of James more than she seriously considered the ramifications of the move. Finding the Sarasota job seemed like a gift from the Universe. Her brother, who also lived in Cleveland, gave her lessons on how to drive the rented moving truck with her car towed behind it on a dolly before he and his friends helped her load what little she was taking with her. Barely enough to furnish a one-bedroom apartment. She only took what she had before she met James, or things she'd bought that wouldn't remind her of him.

Allison's brother's friend contacted two friends of his in Sarasota, where they were originally from, and arranged for them to meet Shayla at the new apartment and help her unload in exchange for pizza and beer. Both of the men were nice, but she was thirty-three and the men were twelve years younger than her and still in school at New College.

She didn't exactly feel a biological clock ticking inside her. She just wished she could meet someone to hang out with. Someone she could get to know casually at first. Maybe more later, if she felt attracted to them.

Hell, she'd settle for girlfriends to get together with to kvetch and unwind.

I'm definitely not in a hurry to get attached to someone else. Looking at her bank account and comparing that to what she owed in money she hadn't spent nearly made her sick. She could have filed charges against James, and then contested the fraudulent credit cards. That would have meant staying in Ohio and being tied to the man. He'd sworn he would repay her, but considering his lack of tenacity in sticking to his other promises, she wouldn't hold her breath.

Losing the money meant a clean break. And it would be a stern reminder to herself to keep her head firmly on her shoulders in the future. To never trust someone without a lot of proof.

If she needed an orgasm, well, she had a vibrator.

And it couldn't take out credit cards in her name without permission.

* * * *

The next morning she tackled a stack of boxes she'd shoved into the far corner of her living room after the move. Knickknacks and odds and ends, books—all the extras that made a house homey, but weren't necessary to unpack immediately such as kitchen utensils and pots and pans.

She tried not to think about the apartment she'd left behind. James had stayed at a friend's place for a couple of weeks while she moved out, agreeing he'd take over the full rent and utilities once she left. She didn't trust him to do it until she accompanied him personally and witnessed him signing the paperwork at the rental company's office, and at the offices of the various utilities.

Although in retrospect, that apartment, while larger, hadn't been in as nice a complex as she lived in now. The old complex was made up of older, brick buildings and had little green space to speak of due to its proximity to downtown.

And none of the units in this complex had burglar bars on the first-floor units, either. No trash blown into the corners. No graffiti on the back walls or fences. She also had a screened lanai all to herself, with a short privacy fence on either side hiding her view of the neighbors.

There was the added benefit of having a pool and a hot tub, both open at all hours for residents. And a workout room she had yet to explore. This unit even had its own washer and dryer, stacked in a closet by the kitchen, making life very convenient.

No more hours spent reading while sitting on the washer to keep her clothes from getting stolen.

While packing, she'd ruthlessly downsized to her pre-James days. She'd lived perfectly comfortably before him, albeit in a tiny apartment even smaller than this one. Anything having to do with the wedding planning got trashed. She left behind anything else that she didn't want.

Her opinion was he caused the mess, he could deal with it.

God help his next ex.

When she finished unpacking those boxes and broke them down to take to the recycling Dumpster later, she looked around, nodding with satisfaction.

It was comfortable, homey.

And all mine.

Now if only she could remove the traces of James from her heart and memory the same way she had from her apartment.

* * * *

Fighting a close battle with her nervous stomach, Shayla pulled up to the address listed on the information page of the club's website fifteen minutes before the scheduled start time of the class. The club was located in one of several nondescript two-story warehouse suites located in a large complex just east of I-75 in Sarasota, not too far south of Fruitville Road.

The area didn't look run-down or seedy, with other assorted businesses such as a custom automotive restoration shop, a cabinet shop, and a water softener distributor also located in the complex, but apparently closed for the weekend.

Six other cars were also parked in front of the address, which was identified only by an address number plate and a small sign reading *VENTURE* in black, block-print letters.

She double-checked the address and stared at the building again. On its surface she saw nothing that hinted at what kinky pursuits occurred inside.

Loren and Ross had assured Shayla that the Submission 101 class was the perfect place for her to begin her first-hand research and allow her to see different aspects and opinions of the lifestyle.

Not to mention they would help fill in any blanks or correct any misconceptions Shayla had in her research thus far.

Taking a deep breath, she grabbed her purse and notebook and headed inside. The blacked-out glass door opened into a large lobby. Three of the walls were filled with merchandise—collars, cuffs, canes and crops and other implements she couldn't identify. There was a section of books, both fiction and nonfiction. At the far end of the lobby, a young woman manned the desk. She looked up and smiled at Shayla's entrance.

"Welcome to Venture. Here for the class?"

Shayla nodded. "I'm supposed to meet Loren here."

"Oh! You must be the one she told me about. She's already inside." The woman handed her a clipboard with a simple form on it. "Fill this out for me real quick, please. And I need your driver's license or some sort of photo ID, and ten dollars for the class."

Shayla handed over her shiny new Florida license and a ten-dollar bill. She quickly read through the form before filling it out. It was a basic information form, privacy agreement, liability waiver, and listed the club's rules.

Three other people, two women and a man, also entered the lobby while she was filling out the form. They had to go through the same procedure with their IDs and forms.

Shayla felt comforted that all three also looked as nervous as she felt.

Inside the club she found close to ten people, all but one of them women, gathered in a cluster of round tables at the far corner of what turned out to be two of the warehouse suites. In front of them stood a middle-aged woman with her long black hair in a braid. She wore a plain, black blouse over a colorful peasant skirt that nearly swept the floor.

Shayla felt relief when she spotted Loren. Loren turned and waved her over. "Hi! I saved a chair for you."

"Thanks."

"Ross dropped me off. You can ride with us to dinner, if you want. That way we'll have more time to talk."

"Sure. That'd be fine."

Once everyone was seated, including yet an additional two women who arrived just before the start time, the instructor began the class. She used a laptop computer attached to a projector, which shone on a whiteboard behind her.

"Thank you all for coming. I'm Maria. On FetLife my screen name is Eggmans_kinky_pet." Her information appeared on the board behind her for everyone to see. "Feel free to friend me on there if you haven't already. We have a reporter with us today, Shayla." She pointed out Shayla in the group. Shayla felt compelled to force a smile and wave and wished she could slump down and hide. "She's here today to observe and learn. Please don't worry about your anonymity. She's already been briefed about our privacy rules, and she will not do anything to out anyone here. She's just here to learn like everyone else."

Shayla gave her a thumbs-up and hoped she wouldn't be asked to stand and speak.

Maria turned out to also be a married slave. In her day job, she was the accountant at her husband's legal firm. "It makes life easy when we know we don't have to worry about being fired," she explained. "But we still keep this part of our lives separate from our vanilla lives, for obvious reasons."

One surprise was the implements Maria laid out and invited the class to pick up and try out if they wanted. Shayla even let Loren smack her on the back with a leather flogger. She actually found the thuddy impact a pleasant sensation, not unlike a massage. Shayla suspected hard strikes from some of the canes and riding crops against bare flesh might hurt like hell, but Maria talked about how and where each implement should be properly used.

I wonder of OSHA has safety rules covering this? Shayla barely kept her silent snicker to herself.

Another topic Maria emphasized, especially to her female students, was how to spot and avoid predators in the lifestyle. Shayla found it particularly eye-opening. While Shayla had seen mentions of it in some of the sites she'd already explored, it hadn't accurately transferred over to a real-world concept in her mind.

A lot of the advice was common sense, but, especially, tips on how to spot red flags while negotiating hard limits and scenes made more sense explained in person with examples.

By the time the class ended, Shayla once again found herself with the conundrum of knowing way more than she had when she walked in, but having still more questions about a lot of what she'd learned.

And feeling like she knew even less than before, considering the depth and breadth of the topic.

Shayla frowned as she flipped through her notebook and nudged her glasses up a little, making a few addendums here and there to her notes. Loren must have spotted her consternation.

"It's like getting tossed down a rabbit hole, isn't it?" Loren asked. "That's the way people commonly describe it."

"That about sums it up." So far, contrary to what Shayla originally thought going into the assignment, instead of finding herself disgusted or completely disassociated from the information she learned, she found herself intrigued.

Which unsettled her in a way.

These weren't a bunch of freaks. Well, maybe some of them were. But the people sitting around the tables this afternoon, some drinking coffee or water from Styrofoam cups, could have easily been members of a book club get-together and not a class on the basics of kink.

"I feel woefully ignorant," Shayla admitted to Loren. "Like I know more and understand less than I did when I started."

"Don't worry. We can talk plenty at dinner tonight." Loren turned and raised a hand to a man who'd just walked in from the lobby area. "In fact, there's Tony now."

* * * *

Tony didn't see either Ross or Loren's vehicles at the club when he pulled up, but suspected that meant Ross had dropped Loren off earlier. He recognized the young woman working the front desk.

She waved him through. "Loren's inside. Class just broke up. Go on in."

"Thanks."

He continued through the door leading from the lobby into the main area. Over half of the dungeon consisted of equipment and play areas, including a couple of smaller rooms in the back, curtained off for patrons to change or do more private play. And upstairs, an open loft area visible from the lower floor held play spaces for more specialized activities, like wax play, electrical play, and other things, to keep them out of the more heavily trafficked downstairs play areas.

The other downstairs half of the space contained tables and chairs for patrons to sit and socialize. It also did double-duty as classroom and meeting space when the dungeon wasn't open for play. And it'd even hosted a wedding or two, such as when their friends Tilly and Landry got hitched.

He spotted Loren just as she raised her hand in greeting. She was sitting at one of the tables with the woman he suspected was Shayla Pierce. He walked over.

He'd Googled Shayla Pierce the night before and found her byline on many articles from *The Plain Dealer*, and a few on *Sunshine Attitude Magazine* articles, but not much info other than that.

He'd located her profile on Facebook, but she'd set her privacy so you had to be a friend to see any updates. Her LinkedIn profile listed her college degrees and her time spent at the newspaper. Based on her college and work experience, he guessed her age around thirty-two or thirty-three, because she didn't have her birthday or age listed.

And that was it. She didn't even seem to have a Twitter account.

Nice to see she doesn't splash her life across social media.

Loren stood to hug him. The other woman stood and turned to face him. He sucked in a breath and prayed she didn't spot the erection that suddenly strained against the front of his jeans.

As he'd suspected from the picture he'd seen on the magazine's website, she looked guarded, sad despite the practiced smile she immediately fastened into place when Loren introduced her. Her hazel eyes looked hidden behind her glasses.

"Shayla Pierce, this is our friend, Tony."

He extended his hand. "Tony Daniels. Nice to meet you."

Her grip felt light, but not weak. "Nice to meet you, too. Ross gave me your name and e-mail. I'm sorry I didn't contact you this week, but it's been busy."

He offered her a smile. "No worries." He longed to figure out whatever it was that happened to her. She didn't just look sad. It was an invisible cloak surrounding her. Something she used as armor against the world, he suspected, from the way her arms immediately crossed in front of her, hands clasping her elbows, as if to both comfort herself and throw up a barrier between herself and him. And the way she kept nudging the bridge of her glasses with her index finger.

Unconscious nervous gestures, if he had to guess. "Loren tells me you're going out to dinner with us?"

She nodded. "I really appreciate you all talking with me. As I told Ross and Loren, I won't give away any personal or identifiable information unless you specifically okay it. I'm going to let those mentioned in my articles read them first before I turn them in, just to make sure I don't get anything wrong."

"Appreciated."

Together, they walked out to the lobby just as Ross walked in. "Ready for dinner?" he asked them.

"I know I'm starved," Tony said. He extended his arm, indicating for Loren and Shayla to go first while Ross held the door for them.

Admittedly, he wanted to get a rear view of Shayla's sweetly rounded, plump ass. Her dark blue denim jeans were a blessing and a curse. They showed off her curves perfectly.

As he followed the group to Ross' car, Tony realized he no longer cared if this was a setup or not.

He wondered how much hands-on learning Shayla might be up for that night.

* * * *

Shayla blinked and quickly cut her gaze away from Tony's green eyes as she released his hand. Something about him drew her to him in what she knew could be a dangerous way. Dark brown hair with a little grey along the temples, and a full goatee and moustache neatly styled and trimmed. A few inches taller than her, probably around six feet. While not a ripped gym rat he appeared to be in shape. He wore jeans over black motorcycle boots, and a light blue short-sleeved Oxford shirt.

He had an air about him of quiet confidence. If she'd met him in any other place under any other circumstances, she wouldn't mind chatting him up for a phone number. He looked like Joe Anybody.

Albeit on the pleasing end of the scale.

As she followed Loren into the parking lot to their car, Shayla mentally smacked herself. *Duh, he's a Dom. He's probably married or dating or whatever.* Loren had a slim, trim figure Shayla knew she could never compete with. While a few of their fellow students in the class had larger builds than Shayla did, the majority of the women were younger, prettier, and thinner.

I look like a frump compared to the rest of them. She'd opted for jeans to be on the safe side, and a black, long-sleeved, button-up shirt open over a royal blue cami top.

At the car, Loren immediately headed for the backseat, but Tony stopped her. "I'll sit in back with Shayla," he offered.

"But my legs are shorter," she countered.

"I don't mind."

Shayla didn't miss how Loren looked to Ross for a ruling. He tipped his head toward the front door.

Without further argument, Loren opened the front passenger door and climbed in.

Tony opened the back passenger door for Shayla and held it while she got in. One more misconception blown to hell. She was glad to see being a Dominant didn't conflict with gentlemanly manners.

He walked around the car after closing her door and slid in behind Ross. "So how did you enjoy the class?" Tony asked her.

She swallowed, silently cursing herself for letting her gaze dart away from his green eyes again. Normally she didn't have problem maintaining eye contact with someone. She nodded. "It was good. Enlightening. Lots of information to digest." She quickly opened her notebook, as if to browse through it. "I'm not sure where I'll start my first article because there's just so much to cover."

"How many articles are you planning?"

She shrugged and made herself look at his face again. *What the hell's wrong with me?* She focused on his chin. "I don't really know. I don't have a word count limit. Since it's a web series, length and space aren't an issue." She closed the notebook and wrapped her fingers around it to have something to do with them. "My publisher gave me free rein. There's a big fetish convention in Tampa in a few months. All the articles sort of lead up to that."

"FetCon," the others said at the same time before laughing.

She blinked. "Oh. You know about it?"

Loren turned as far as her seat belt would allow, a smile on her face. "It's an annual tradition with our gang," she said. "They have a huge vendor floor."

"Lots of fetish models," Tony added.

Shayla felt a little ill and shoved a memory back into its hole. She wouldn't let thoughts of her experience with James spoil what had been an otherwise nice experience so far. "Models?"

Tony shrugged. "Not my thing. They have to make a living though, I guess. I go for the vendors, sometimes the classes, and the dungeons at night."

"Don't let him fool you," Loren said. "Tony usually teaches. And I think Seth and Leah will also be teaching this year, too. You'll meet them at dinner."

Shayla was still trying to process and interpret Tony's dismissive, yet not derogatory comment about the fetish models. "What do you teach?"

"Depends on what they need. This year I'm teaching a class on negotiations."

"Oh."

He smiled. "No clue, huh?"

She breathed a quiet sigh of relief. "Not really."

She loved his smile. "Scene negotiations. Communication skills. How to make sure everyone's clearly setting their boundaries and expectations out on the table from the start so there are no misunderstandings later."

"You'd be surprised how many people lack that basic skill," Loren said. "A lot of newbies come into this totally clueless. That's why Maria covered some of it in class."

"Ah, I see. That makes sense now."

"What does your boyfriend think of you coming out to class and the dungeon?" Tony asked.

Shayla shrugged. "Don't even have a cat waiting for me at home." She hoped it came off sounding as nonchalant as she wanted it to.

* * * *

Tony didn't miss how Loren quickly turned to face the front again. He also didn't miss the brief smile she vainly pursed her lips against.

"Same here," Tony said, trying to keep one eye on Loren. He suspected while legitimately bringing him in to help Shayla with her article, his first instinct about a setup had been right after all.

Damn sneaky subs.

Well, he was attracted to Shayla. He wouldn't deny it. *Might as well test the water.* "Have you read any of the BDSM fiction out there?"

Shayla rapidly shook her head. "No. I'm more a lighthearted, chick lit kind of girl. Well, when it comes to romance. I like a wide variety of genres."

"Good. A lot of BDSM fiction is completely unrealistic and written by vanilla writers anyway. Nothing wrong with that for escapism, but not good for education. You won't have a lot of preconceived notions to overcome when you watch people playing tonight."

Seth and Leah had pulled into the restaurant's parking lot just ahead of them. And Tilly, accompanied by Landry and Cris, arrived a moment later. With the gang all gathered, he likely wouldn't have a chance to get either Ross or Seth alone to ask them if they knew what their damn subs were up to.

It'd be pointless to ask Landry or Cris. Landry was sadistic enough to enjoy taking pleasure in any discomfort Tony might experience over a setup. And Cris probably wouldn't be in the loop anyway if Tilly was a co-conspirator. He suspected if he tried to get the info out of Tilly, regardless of whether or not it was true, she'd simply smile and give him a friendly "go screw yourself" brush-off just to have her friends' backs.

Damn switches.

Leah had called ahead to the restaurant the day before with their reservation. The hostess took them to their usual place in a far corner, where three tables had been pushed together to accommodate their party.

That was when he noticed extra chairs. "Who else is coming?" he asked Loren.

"Sully, Mac, and Clarisse said they'd be down."

"It'll be like old home night," Ross joked. "I haven't seen them in months."

"How's Mac doing, anyway?" Tony asked. Their friend had been the victim of a vicious attack by Clarisse's ex a couple of years earlier. He'd only seen him a few times since then, once going up to visit him in the hospital after he regained consciousness, and then a few times here and there, usually at private parties.

"Sully said Mac's pretty much back to his old self. Sometimes he gets dizzy spells, but all the physical and occupational therapy paid off."

Right on cue, the three walked in the front door and were brought back to their tables. Tony didn't miss how after introducing Shayla to everyone that Loren had made sure to sit her next to him.

He raised an eyebrow at Loren, who blushed a pretty shade of pink before quickly turning away and taking her seat on the other side of Shayla, next to Ross.

* * * *

Shayla found it easy to like Loren. She felt as if the woman had taken her under her wing. And Loren's friends were all nice, welcoming, and more than willing to answer her questions.

The gathered group of people was no more remarkable than any other group in the restaurant in the way that they were dressed. Although Shayla noticed Leah wore a necklace of braided silver chain that appeared to have a small, silver heart-shaped padlock on it. Anyone else might have thought it simply a pretty locket. Clarisse wore a silver choker necklace that Shayla suspected also meant more than others might think. Cris wore a heavy silver bracelet on his right wrist, as did Mac.

Landry and Tilly were married, and it wasn't until Shayla was able to talk with them for a few minutes that she was able to clarify Cris' place in their dynamic as an equal partner. Sully, who walked with a noticeable limp and used a cane, was married to Clarisse, although they were also apparently equal partners with Mac.

She filed those factoids away for future reference. She'd need an entire article dedicated just to poly dynamics to cover it properly. Even then she wasn't sure she could do it justice.

Hell, it's confusing enough trying to figure it out when the people are sitting right here talking with me.

By the time they finished dinner over an hour later, she realized all of these people were ones she could easily be friends with. They had widely varying interests. Sully, Mac, and Clarisse, who revealed they were expecting a baby in November, owned a boat and ran dive and fishing charters. Apparently more as a hobby than anything because Sully, a retired cop, was also a published and successful author and seminar teacher. Seth and Leah managed properties, but before that, Seth had attended nursing school. Both Seth and Mac were former military, although Seth seemed more open to talking about that part of his life than Mac.

"Would you be willing to let me interview you for my article?" Shayla asked them.

She noticed how both Mac and Clarisse looked to Sully for their answer. When he nodded, so did they. "We probably should do it tonight," Sully suggested. "Maybe at the club after we play. Unless you want to do it over the phone or come up to Tarpon Springs."

"Tonight would be great, thank you."

Ross owned his own business, and Loren was usually a stay-at-home wife, although she helped Ross out sometimes. Loren, Leah, and Tilly were heavily involved volunteers and event organizers for local charities. Landry and Cris ran a software firm.

"But my main job," Tilly, also a former nurse, said, "is keeping my two men in line."

For some reason, that elicited a round of hearty laughs from all at the table and prompted Loren to lean in and say, "I'll tell you later."

These people weren't sexual predators or weirdoes or people on the fringes of average society.

They were everyday people. Hardworking people. Respectable people with responsibilities and who not only contributed to society, but to their communities as well.

Nice people.

What she wished she could ignore was how quickly she felt comfortable talking with Tony.

Why would he be interested in me?

She discounted the thought. He was a handsome and apparently well-off man who likely had his pick of women. *Why even set myself up for disappointment?*

When the checks were settled, Tony turned to Shayla with a smile that nearly dampened her panties. "Ready to dive headfirst through the rabbit hole, Alice?"

She swallowed hard and nodded.

Chapter Six

During dinner, the sun had dropped into the Gulf. The last vestiges of purple light struggled to maintain a tenuous grasp on the landscape despite the holes being punched into the deep shadows here and there by streetlamps. For the return drive to the dungeon, Tony once again insisted on sitting in the backseat with Shayla. In the darkened interior of the car, she felt safer looking at his face, comforted by the illusion of insulation provided by the shadows.

He was a man who smiled readily, the corners of his eyes marked with lines attesting to that fact. He listened intently when people spoke, and had a warm laugh that he shared with friendly ease.

He also didn't strike her as a man who demanded other people defer to him, or who was an attention whore. He seemed relaxed, settled in his place in the conversation and holding his own when the situation allowed, but also content to sit back and listen to others.

He wasn't a pushy, overbearing, arrogant idiot. She didn't know what he was like with a submissive, but he certainly was blowing her preconceived notions out of the water even better than her earlier conversation with Loren and Ross. Sure, it was fine to find a couple who were happy doing…this, but Tony seemed the kind of man to validate their claims that the average person in "the lifestyle" was just that—an average person. From what little time she'd spent with him, he seemed like a genuinely nice guy.

And other than his earlier question about what her boyfriend might think of her outing, he hadn't approached discussing anything personal about her other than how long she'd been in Florida, how she liked it there, and questions about her job.

In fact, he stayed remarkably clear of any kind of personal questions.

Then again, maybe he's just not interested in me. She knew he was single, because Loren, Tilly, and Leah had all, at some point during the dinner conversation, made mention of it to Shayla.

If Shayla didn't know any better, she'd think the women were trying to hook them up together.

There were considerably more cars in the parking lot when they pulled in and parked. Before emerging from the car, Loren asked, "Did you bring your toybag, Tony?"

"It's in my trunk. But I doubt I'm playing tonight."

"Could you bring it in and show Shayla the ropes?" She giggled.

He arched an eyebrow at her. "Ha, ha. Like I haven't heard *that* one a million times." His light tone belied his words. "And no, I don't mind bringing it in."

"If it's going to be trouble," Shayla said, "it's okay, don't worry about it."

They climbed out. "No, no trouble. I'm just parked over there."

She waited with Loren near the club's door for Ross to get their things from the trunk of their car while Tony removed a large, black rolling suitcase from the trunk of his. Inside, since they already had Shayla's information on file, she didn't have to fill out another form.

She discovered however that entry wasn't guaranteed as she pulled out a twenty and prepared to hand it over.

A different woman manned the front desk. She was older, with closely cropped blonde hair, a black corset squeezing her ample breasts up and nearly out of the confining garment, and had freshly lacquered, deep red nails and makeup done to perfection. Shayla felt frumpy just looking at her.

"I see you're not a member yet," the woman observed as she looked Shayla up on the computer. "Who is your sponsor?"

"Um, sponsor?"

"Yes. You can't become a member without a sponsor. Classes are open to the public, but to come to play sessions you have to be a member."

Loren and Ross had both started to speak up when Tony stepped forward. "I'm her sponsor."

The woman's carefully plucked eyebrows sailed skyward. "Really? I was under the impression Valerie was here with you tonight."

From somewhere behind them Shayla thought she heard Leah mutter, "Crap," before she darted through the doorway into the play area.

Before Shayla could process that, her attention immediately returned to Tony and the Hydra at the desk. He leaned in, his voice dropping to a low, dangerous tone.

"Unless *I* personally tell you someone is with me, Lydia," he said, "you do *not* assume anything. Do I make myself perfectly clear?"

The woman's eyes widened. Shayla wanted to laugh as she watched the woman swallow, suddenly not as sure of herself as she was a moment earlier. "Yeah. Uh, sorry."

He straightened and handed her a twenty of his own. "You'll see I have three membership credits on my account. Apply one to Shayla for her membership. And since this is her first play session, I believe she gets in free tonight. Correct?"

The woman's red lacquered nails flew across the keyboard. "Yep, sure, you're right. Sorry, Tony. I didn't mean to… I just thought—"

"Are we done here?" he asked.

She blinked up at him. "Yes. Of course. No problem. Go on in. Have a good night."

Shayla still stood there, trying to process what had just happened, the twenty for her fee still clutched in her fingers. Tony grabbed the handle of his rolling bag with one hand and with the other gently caught her elbow and propelled her along with him.

"I'll explain inside," he softly whispered in her ear. They headed to the door, which he grabbed first and held open for her.

Upon walking through the door, the music, barely noticeable in the well-insulated office, soared to near anti-conversational levels. At least twenty-five people were scattered throughout the large space, some at the tables and some near equipment.

He steered her toward an alcove where several couches were grouped. "Sorry about that," he said.

Shayla began to wonder if she'd liked Tony too soon. *I should have Do Not Trust People tattooed on my wrist as a reminder.* "What the heck was her problem? And I take it Valerie is a girlfriend of yours?" At that moment she spotted Leah speaking with a woman on the far side of the club.

"No, she's not a girlfriend. I just met her this week at dinner at Leah and Seth's house. But Lydia, the lady out on the desk tonight, is a self-appointed social director with a huge-ass chip on her shoulder when it comes to single submissive women."

"Huh?"

"She got burned big-time by an asshole. Now she's hypervigilant about anyone she worries might get taken advantage of. Including inserting her nose into business where it not only doesn't belong and wasn't invited, but, as in this case, with completely wrong assumptions."

Leah was leading the woman over to where Tony and Shayla stood. Shayla thought Leah looked extremely relieved and wondered what piece of the puzzle was glaringly missing from the picture.

"Shayla, this is my friend Valerie."

The woman's warm smile certainly looked genuine. When she extended her hand to Shayla, her grip felt friendly.

"Hi," Valerie said. "Nice to meet you." She offered Tony an apologetic smile. "Honestly, all I told Lydia was that you said you might be here tonight. I swear I didn't tell her we were playing together or anything else."

Tony dismissed her apology with a wave. "It's okay. I put her in her place. Again. I'm going to have a talk with Derrick this week about permanently taking her off desk duty. She needs to get her head on straight. She's going to piss off the wrong person some night and get her ass kicked."

"She needs to get her head out of her ass is what she needs to do," Valerie said. She returned her attention to Shayla. "Seriously, everything's copacetic. Leah told me you're a reporter. I think it's very cool you're doing a story on BDSM."

"And Tilly said feel free to ask Landry to play, if you want," Leah offered.

"Oh?" Valerie turned to look at where Tilly and her men had set their bags on the far side of the area, closer to the play equipment. "Hmm. I might just take them up on that." She smiled at Shayla. "I hope you enjoy tonight. Tony's a really nice guy. You couldn't be in better hands." She waggled her fingers at them and headed off, apparently to go talk to Landry.

Tony, however, still seemed to look concerned. She caught him watching her. "Are you okay?" he asked.

"Yeah. Sorry, I just wasn't expecting to get embroiled in a dungeon drama."

"Sorry about that," Leah said.

Loren walked up at that moment. "Everything okay? Did Lydia strike again?"

"It's all settled," Tony assured her. He turned to Shayla. "I'm all yours for the evening."

* * * *

Because they were still full from dinner, they skipped the buffet offering laid out along the far wall in the table area.

"Since it's not busy yet, let me take you on a tour," he said. They started up in the loft area, where no one was playing yet. As they climbed the stairs, he explained the club's rules as well.

"No pictures can be taken in the club without permission from the DMs first. And even then only if no one else is in the background. No one touches people or their things without permission. If someone says *red*, their play stops immediately unless they've talked to a DM ahead of time and arranged a different safeword if they're going to do edge play. Violating those three rules is the easiest and fastest way to get kicked out and banned."

"Seems pretty straightforward. Is that a problem, usually?"

"No, not normally." He turned to her when they reached the top of the stairs. "But in a lot of the BDSM fiction out there, one of the favorite tropes vanilla writers use is the innocent female submissive who somehow accidentally stumbles into a club and then some big, bad Dom slaps a collar around her neck and starts to play with her despite her protests."

"Really?" She thought about Lydia the gatekeeper in the lobby who nearly didn't let her in. "Just accidentally stumbles in, huh?"

"You wouldn't believe how many newbies honestly worry that might happen to them. Sure, if you go to a fetish night held at a bar you might get hit on like you would anywhere else, but someone tries to grab you against your will, you just scream and bouncers take care of them. In all my years in the lifestyle I've never seen someone forced to play in public against their will with no one helping them. Now I have seen asshats get grabby and get kicked out. Helped escort a few of them out when I've been DM'ing. But it happens far less frequently than you'd believe if you read the fiction."

"But you have seen some people forced to play?"

"No. One time I saw a scene where the bottom called *red* and the Top didn't stop. DMs stepped in to end the scene. If some douche doesn't respect a safeword and doesn't stop when a bottom calls a scene, that's not BDSM. That's assault. And it's prosecutable."

From up in the loft area, they could view the entire space. She also realized Loren, Tilly, and Leah had disappeared. "Where did they go?"

"They probably went to change out of their street clothes. Unless they're coming straight here from home, they usually change after they get here."

She looked at him, dressed as if going to work. "Do you change clothes?" she asked.

"Nope. This is what I wear."

"I thought Doms like to wear leather and stuff." In fact, several of the male Dominants in the club were dressed in either leather pants, a leather vest, or both in some cases. Many of them were dressed either all in black, or in some combination of black and red.

He nodded. "Some do, yes. But leather is hot and hard to move around in and I'm more comfortable in my jeans and a regular shirt. I'm not a leather kind of Dom when it comes to practicality." He smiled. "I'm much more a denim kind of Dom."

Shayla arched an eyebrow at him. "A denim Dom, huh?"

He nodded. "Better than a sweating-my-ass-off Dom." He let her go down the stairs first. "Any questions so far?"

She gave silent thanks for opting to wear flats and not heels tonight. "Oh, I've got plenty of questions. I just have no idea where to start asking."

"This is why, as you can tell, I'm not particularly fond of most BDSM fiction," he said. "Not if it's written by someone who hasn't done plenty of research first, or who isn't in the lifestyle. I've had several women approach me this year with completely unrealistic expectations based on their choice in reading material. One of them actually got pissed at me when I laughed at her."

At the bottom of the stairs, Shayla turned to him. "Why'd you laugh at her?"

"She informed me that I would help her duplicate a scene from one of her favorite books, and that if I was a 'real' Dominant, I would do it."

"You didn't like that, huh?"

He grinned. "I suppose no one had told her that while subs might set the limits, the Doms make the rules. She spent the night kneeling on the floor while I talked to friends. When she got pissed off at me for not doing what she wanted, I laughed and told her she must not be a 'real' submissive then." He smirked. "The irony was lost on her."

He showed her around and explained the different equipment to her. Some she recognized from her online research, and some she didn't.

Some of it looked more dangerous and painful in person than it had on her computer.

He also introduced her to quite a few people. Everyone was friendly and more than a few offered to answer any questions she might have. She accumulated FetLife IDs and e-mail addresses at an incredible rate.

I can see I'm going to have to join that site.

This seemed to be the magic hour, because the slow trickle of people arriving turned into a flood as several dozen entered the space within about fifteen minutes. Tony led Shayla back to the area with the sofas to retrieve his bag.

"Come on," he said, leading her toward one of the far tables in a corner. He laid the bag flat on the floor and unzipped it. When he opened it, she realized it was completely full of different implements. Paddles, floggers, riding crops, canes, even what looked to be a whip or two.

And other things, like vibrators.

She shivered.

"I normally carry my canes and riding crops in a blueprint tube," he said. "I didn't bring it with me tonight, though. I left most of them at home."

"How many canes do you need?" she asked.

He laughed. "As many as it takes."

* * * *

Tony watched her face as he showed her everything, explaining each item's use and the differing sensations it provided.

"What is this?" She held it up.

"That's a silicone tasting spoon." He took the dense, double-ended orange cooking implement from her and smacked the cupped side against his palm. Its deceptive heft always surprised people.

She frowned. "Tasting spoon? As in something you cook with?"

He smiled. "Yep. Get some of my best toys at a cooking supply store at the flea market. This baby might not look like it'd hurt, but if you use the convex side of it and hit hard enough with it, it'll put bruises on a person." He rummaged around in his bag and found a pair of long, bamboo spoons. "These are great as a matched set." He tapped out a rhythm against his thigh. "You can drum with them."

That got a smile out of her. "Sadistic drumming, huh?"

"The best kind." He laid those aside and picked up another matched pair of items.

"And what the heck are those?" she asked as he handed the metal objects to her. A little less than a foot long each, the handles branched out into lots of wire arms topped with metal balls on the ends.

"Cooking whisks. You know." He mimed mixing something in a bowl.

She tested them in the air, a look of doubt on her face.

"Go ahead and try them on your leg."

She did. "Doesn't seem like they would hurt very much."

"They won't. Unless you hit someone wrong with them, like smack them on the nose or poke them in the eye or something. Not every implement is meant to inflict pain. Some of them are meant to create a certain sensation. These are great along the back and shoulders, or along the arms. Because they are so light, you don't have to worry about damaging someone's spine or shoulder blades. And if they're cold, it's another sensation. Or they can be used in a transition phase of play, either stepping up or down the intensity. Or even just as a massage." He took them back, stood, and stepped behind her. "May I?"

"Okay." She turned a little in her seat to give him access to her back and shoulders.

He gently drummed up and down her back and across her shoulders. He stopped when he noticed her eyelids slowly dropping shut. When he stepped away, she reacted almost startled, as if she'd really been enjoying it. "Like that."

She blinked, looking up at him. "That felt pretty good."

He put them away and noted how she looked moderately disappointed. "Like I said, not everything is meant to induce pain. There are plenty of implements that, depending on how they're used, can bring pleasure or pain. That's another common misconception, that all Tops are heavy sadists, and all bottoms are masochists."

"So you're not a sadist?"

"Oh, I'm absolutely a sadist. But the person I'm playing with has to want that kind of play. Or want to take it to please me when I'm topping them. I have no desire to force someone to do something against their will. That's sociopathic behavior, not sadism. I can grab a cane and the heaviest pain slut in the room and probably have them code after three hits. Is that a good thing? No. But I can just as easily get my sadistic jollies by making someone dress up in something they hate to wear as I can by topping them in a scene. A scene is like a dance. There are many different steps, many stages. Everyone has their own way of playing. What might look like a vicious beating to the uneducated is most likely a carefully choreographed routine on the part of the Top."

"That makes sense."

"A good example is Landry over there. When he plays with Cris, he beats the ever-loving crap out of him. And it's not that Cris is a masochist, either. But Landry is a heavy sadist. Cris derives satisfaction out of pleasing Landry. He also takes pride in pushing himself physically to the limits of his endurance. So while he doesn't enjoy the pain, he enjoys the act of taking it.

"Now Tilly, when she's in her Domme mode, watch out. She's pretty sadistic herself. On the other hand she's not a masochist, but she will sometimes switch with Landry and let him top her. When Landry plays with her, which they don't do a lot of in public, you'll see a completely different side of Landry. The tender Dominant topping his wife with a lot of sensual and sensation play as opposed to sadism."

"I guess that's a good thing for Valerie's sake if she's going to play with him, huh?"

Tony nodded. "Landry is one of those people who enjoys being a service Top. He won't play with everyone, but he can play with someone with far less of an emotional or mental connection than some Tops can. He'll also play with men or women."

"What about you?"

"What about me?"

"Are you a service Top?"

"Not really. I prefer a much deeper connection with a person. If I'm not in a dynamic with someone or know them very well, the first couple of times I play with them I'm really holding back and making sure I'm not going too far."

"I thought Doms liked to push their subs."

"True, but if someone is just bottoming to me and they're not my submissive, I don't feel I have a right to push them unless they've specifically told me what they want done."

"That's confusing. I thought you said the Dominants made the rules."

He laughed. "Welcome to the irony inherent in the lifestyle."

Chapter Seven

More people began playing. With Tony as her personal guide, Shayla got to witness impact play of various styles and severities, wax play, a violet wand session, knife play, fire play, and forced orgasm play.

And that was within the first hour.

When Landry began playing with Valerie, Tony led Shayla to a vantage point near the spanking bench Landry had bound Valerie to with rope. They stopped a respectable distance away, along the fringes with other observers, to watch the play.

He leaned in, his breath warm in her ear. "Watch how he plays with her, and then compare that later to how he plays with Cris."

"How do you know he'll play with Cris later?"

"He made him dress out." He tipped his head toward where the other man now knelt on the far side of the spanking bench. He'd changed and now wore a leather collar and cuffs, as well as a leather jock. And nothing else.

Shayla glanced around and found Leah, Clarisse, Tilly, and Loren talking with another woman Shayla hadn't met yet. She returned her attention to the scene before her where Landry was running his hands up and down Valerie's back. She was naked, except for a black thong, and had a towel under her.

Shayla tilted her head toward Tony again so she could whisper and be heard. "That would make me jealous."

"What?"

"That. I don't think I could let my husband do that to another woman."

"You have to remember, Tilly was a pro Domme for several years. And she doesn't let Landry just play with any woman. She has to know the woman, or the woman has to be known and approved of by one of her close friends. Tilly still tops other men, too. Sometimes she co-tops them with Landry."

A loud *smack* broke over the music as Landry slapped both of Valerie's ass cheeks at the same time, leaving red handprints on her flesh. Valerie let out a squeal and struggled against the ropes binding her to the padded wooden bench, but Landry had securely tied her. He continued spanking her with his bare hands as the woman twisted and struggled and cried out.

Just when Shayla thought the woman appeared at the end of her endurance, Landry stopped and grabbed a handful of Valerie's hair. He yanked her head up and back, looking into her eyes.

"Are you coding?" he demanded.

Despite the tight grip on her hair, she shook her head. "No, Sir!"

"Where are you?"

"Green!" she gasped.

"Good girl." An evil smile filled his face as he released her hair and went back to spanking her with his bare hands.

After a few minutes of that, he bent over a toybag, a black rolling suitcase much like Tony's, which lay open on the floor. He removed two leather floggers and started rhythmically working his way up and down her shoulders, back, ass, and legs with them.

Tony leaned in again. "Those give a thuddy sensation, but they're made out of very soft suede. Unless you poke the bottom in the eye with a handle or a fall, or snag a piercing with them, you can't hurt someone with them."

Shayla only had pierced ears, but she winced at the mental picture that invoked. "Yowch."

"Yeah. I once saw a guy lose a nipple piercing to a singletail that wrapped around him from behind."

Landry continued as Valerie squirmed on the bench under his attention. From the look on her face, it was obvious she enjoyed it.

After a few minutes of that, he returned to the toybag and swapped out the floggers for a riding crop. Valerie froze when he placed it across her ass, obviously letting her feel what was in his hand.

Landry drew back his arm and a *thhwip* preceded the strike to her ass. Valerie let out a shout of shock and pain. The welted imprint of the riding crop left clearly visible marks in her already reddened flesh.

"Color?" Landry barked.

"Green!" Valerie gasped.

He nodded and continued striking her, stopping every few strokes to smooth his hand across her ass, soothing her before continuing. Down the backs of her thighs, especially in the crease where her ass cheeks met her upper thighs, with new marks left by every stroke.

From there he switched back to a flogger, a different one than he'd used before. Shayla didn't get a good look before he started swinging it, but Tony offered up helpful commentary.

"That's a heavier flogger than the last time. The falls are braided leather. He's not hitting her hard enough with it to do any damage, but that is an implement that could seriously injure someone if used the wrong way."

Shayla smoothed her hands up and down her arms to soothe the ripples of gooseflesh. Valerie seemed to be enjoying it, however.

Then Landry stopped, hauling off and smacking her ass hard with his bare hand. "Hold still. I didn't give you permission to rub yourself."

Beside Shayla, Tony chuckled, even as they heard Valerie let out a disappointed moan. But she fell still on the bench.

"What was she doing?" Shayla asked.

"She was trying to get herself off. That's why she looked like she was humping the thing."

"Oh." Shayla had thought she was just trying to reposition herself or wiggling to avoid the strikes.

Landry went back to the toybag to get something else and leaned in to speak with Cris. While Landry returned to Valerie with a wooden paddle, which he applied to her ass and upper thighs, Cris rummaged around in the toybag, apparently getting something ready for Landry. Shayla couldn't see what he had in his hand when he finally stood and walked over to Landry, apparently waiting for some signal for him.

The paddle made a loud *crack* with each impact against her flesh. Valerie began sobbing, her fingers clenched around the ends of the padded bench. Each stroke Landry took sounded harder than the next. Shayla realized she was digging her own fingers into her upper arm as she uncomfortably watched the scene play out.

Then, when Shayla was sure the woman would have to code, Landry made a swap with Cris and stuck something between the woman's legs.

"Come!"

Valerie let out a loud wail. Her back arched as far as the ropes would allow, her fingers and toes flexing and clenching.

That was when Shayla realized it was a vibrator in Landry's hand.

Her throat suddenly felt dry as she watched Valerie writhing on the bench, in pleasure this time. When the bound woman tried to wiggle away from Landry's hand, he placed his free hand on top of her lower back and held her down. "Come!" he ordered again.

She let out another wail that dissolved into more sobs of pleasure. After keeping her in that state for several minutes, he finally relented and pulled the vibrator away. He switched it off and handed it back to Cris.

Then Shayla got a better look at it and realized the top of it had what looked like a condom covering it.

Tony proved very perceptive. He leaned in again as Cris returned to the toybag and, with his back to them, started doing something. "The condom helps keep it cleaner. He'll still wipe it down with alcohol and disinfectant wipes."

Meanwhile, Landry stood next to the sobbing woman and stroked her back. After a couple of minutes, he looked over at Leah, who had been paying close attention toward the end of the scene. When he nodded to her, she hurried over and knelt in front of the woman and started talking to her while Landry began untying her. When they had her freed and sitting up on the bench, Landry draped a fleece throw around her and spoke to her too softly for anyone else to hear.

Valerie smiled and nodded, then gave him a kiss on the cheek. Landry and Leah helped her to her feet. Once insuring she was steady, Landry fully turned her over to Leah, who led her across the area to one of the couches, where they sat together.

As the observers dispersed, Landry walked over to Tilly, leaving Cris to clean up the bench and put away their toys

"Well?" Tony asked.

Shayla blinked. "Wow."

He grinned. "Good wow?"

"Maybe. She's going to have a sore ass tomorrow."

He glanced over to where Leah and Valerie sat. "Likely. And that's probably exactly what she's hoping for."

* * * *

The next big scene up for viewing was Sully and Mac. Mac, who wore more than Cris in that he had a leather hood in addition to a leather jock and his collar and cuffs, had been strung up on a bar suspended from chains. His feet were held far apart by a spreader bar connected to the cuffs at his ankles, and he stood with his arms stretched high above him by the restraints.

"What are those things on his hands?" she asked Tony. They looked more like mitts than they did regular cuffs.

"Suspension cuffs. They're made especially for this kind of play, where the arms are over the head. You can't bear weight with regular wrist cuffs because you risk causing damage to nerves and tendons. And you can never use handcuffs for suspension work. But with those, they have a built-in handle inside he can hold on to. I have a pair in my bag, but they're made differently than that brand."

"Oh."

Sully had positioned Clarisse, who had changed into a short, black sundress and a leather collar, on a comfortable-looking pillow in front of Mac. Her pregnancy wasn't far enough along yet for her to be showing.

Sully blindfolded Mac and put a ball gag in his mouth. Shayla wasn't sure what Clarisse's job was other than to offer moral support to the man. She stroked his legs while Sully began their scene. He started out with bare-handed slaps and pummeling Mac's back and shoulders with his fists, which quickly progressed to other implements.

He used a riding crop before quickly switching to a paddle, followed by canes. When he paused and stepped close behind the other man he made a gesture to Clarisse. She reached up and unsnapped the front cup of Mac's jock, exposing his cock.

Shayla's eyes widened. Despite the beating he'd already taken, his cock was semi-stiff and definitely nothing to be ashamed of in terms of size.

Sully reached around Mac's front and grabbed him by the throat, forcing his head back. They couldn't hear Sully's words, but whatever he said had an effect on the restrained man. His cock grew and stiffened, fully erect now.

Stepping back, Sully grabbed a whip and uncoiled it. The first strike made a loud *pop* in the air and to Mack's left. He flinched, rattling the chains and metal bar he was affixed to, but didn't struggle.

"He's gauging his distance and giving Mac a little mindfuck," Tony softly explained.

Sully took two more test strikes on either side of Mac before taking aim and beginning in earnest. The lash landed first between Mac's shoulder blades.

And Clarisse leaned in, sheathing Mac's cock with a condom before she began stroking it with her hands. Mac's head drooped forward as his hips thrust in the air.

Sully landed a hit on Mac's right ass cheek. "Don't come until I tell you to!" Mac's head popped up, his back arching at the pain from the strike.

"This club doesn't allow penetration or oral sex because of zoning regs," Tony explained. "But I've seen them at private parties where she goes down on him during this part of the scene. The condom keeps the mess to a minimum. I hear you signed up for my whip class next Saturday."

She nodded, unable to take her eyes off the scene before her. "And the bondage class." Clarisse appeared to be doing her best to get Mac off while Sully had clearly ordered him not to.

"Good. You'll learn a lot in the bondage class. Seth and Leah teach that one. Kaden taught him well." His melancholy tone of voice caught her attention and pulled it from the people they were watching. She noticed Tony wore a sad expression.

"Who?"

"Kaden. Leah's first husband and Seth's best friend." He gave her a strained smile. "Long and sad story. Not one for tonight."

Another *crack* caught her attention. Sully had landed another strike between Mac's shoulders. Not every strike made a sound. She suspected he only did it to startle Mac and get his attention. But every lash made Mac jump, his hips wildly trying to thrust against what Clarisse was doing with her hands while still trying to obey Sully's order.

"Depending on how you strike and what kind of fall is on the whip," Tony said, "you can tickle someone or cut them to the bone."

That little tidbit quelled her throbbing clit. "Yikes."

He tipped his head toward Sully. "He's good. Really good. I wish he'd teach classes on whip technique."

"Why doesn't he?"

He shrugged. "He just doesn't have any interest in it. But as you can see, when they play they draw a crowd." She glanced around and realized over half the club patrons had gathered to watch the trio.

"Does everyone here play?"

"Not usually. A lot of people only come out to watch and meet with their friends."

"Why would they come here then? Why not get together somewhere else?"

He shrugged. "Why not? If people didn't want to be watched, they could do this stuff in their living room or bedroom. I'm not saying everyone who plays is an exhibitionist or anything. Some people don't have access to equipment like this at home, so they scene here or at a party. Or they have kids or other family at home and don't have the privacy to play there. Some like to scene and don't care who watches. Some like to be watched. Some people only do certain kinds of scenes in public and leave the rest for at home. And the voyeurs get their fix by watching."

* * * *

Tony watched Shayla's face as the scene played out before them. He didn't know if she was fascinated or horrified by what she saw.

Or perhaps a mixture of both.

The scene ended when Sully began a crescendo of whip strikes along Mac's ass before yelling, "Come!"

Mac's body went rigid as Clarisse stroked him to completion. After a moment, he went limp in his restraints and looked like he could barely hold himself up. Clarisse used a paper towel to remove the condom and wipe him up before snapping the jock back in place. Sully brought Mac down and, with Clarisse's help, led him over to a quiet corner where Clarisse first put down the pillow and a blanket before helping Mac to the floor. He curled up with his head in her lap while Sully went to pick up their toys and clean the station.

"Want something to drink?" he asked Shayla.

He noticed her blinking, as if confused, before turning her focus to him. "I'm sorry, what?"

"Water? Tea? Coffee? They usually have sodas, too."

"Oh. Water's fine, thanks."

He led her over to the buffet area and fished a bottle of water out of a cooler. He twisted the cap loose before handing it to her.

"Thanks." As she took a swig, she looked pensive.

"Thoughts?"

"I'm just trying to figure out how to conduct an interview with them after what I just saw."

"So how are you liking the rabbit hole, Alice?"

She let out a soft laugh. "It's nothing like what I thought it'd be."

"What'd you think it would be like?"

A dark look flitted across her features for a moment. Grief, perhaps? Maybe anger? He didn't know, but part of him really wanted to find out even though he suspected tonight wasn't the right time for that kind of in-depth discussion with her.

"I really don't know," she finally answered. "I mean, yes, everything fits perfectly with what Ross and Loren talked about the other night."

She took another drink from her bottle. He suspected it was to give herself a moment to think. Then she looked up at him, and he realized she was the perfect height. She could wear stilettos and still be shorter than him.

He'd swear deeply ingrained pain flared in her hazel eyes. "I'm thinking there are some questions I'll probably never get answers to."

Tread lightly, Daniels. "I can't speak for anyone else, but I'm happy to try to answer anything I can."

Her gaze dropped to the floor. "I think no one here can answer those questions for me."

He studied her but suspected she wouldn't elaborate. Not tonight, at least, and perhaps never, unless he developed a deeper relationship with her.

He also suspected the answers she sought were a key to the reason she tried to wall herself off from others.

And maybe even tied to the fact that she was single, considering her abrupt relocation from Ohio to Florida.

* * * *

Shayla tried to stay objective as she watched other scenes unfold. As Tony predicted, Landry did scene with Cris. It was a hard and heavy scene completely unlike the way Landry had topped Valerie. And she found it every bit as sexy as the scene between Sully and Mac earlier.

The brute force, the clear sadism in Landry's movements, the way Cris responded to him, all of it mixed together to take her breath away and wish she could experience some of that herself.

Ross then scened with Loren, a sensual scene that ended with a round of forced orgasms for Loren and left Shayla's panties damp just from watching them. Seth scened with Leah, a mix of pain and pleasure different yet from what she'd witnessed.

Part of Shayla's brain recoiled at what she saw, the impact play, tears, marks and welts and actions that looked completely contradictory to what made up loving, caring relationships.

Tilly scened with a man who, it turned out, was a former client of hers. She was sadistic, every bit as brutal with him as Landry had been with Cris. And yet even Shayla could sense the way Tilly seemed to read the man's body language, how she raised and lowered the intensity throughout the scene until she finally ended it after what Tony called a warm-down.

And despite the man being in tears and obvious pain a few minutes earlier, he was left smiling and even gave Tilly a friendly hug and kiss on the cheek when he recovered.

That was the part Shayla found difficult to reconcile. The contradiction of the bottom appreciating what the Top did for them.

Landry's third scene of the night—Tilly. As Tony had predicted, the tender, loving hubby came out. Less impact play than with Valerie, but a lot more sensual sensation play.

And far more forced orgasms.

By the time he finished with her, Tilly was a limp puddle who could barely stand. He wrapped a blanket around her and carried her over to one of the couches where he sat with her while Cris cleaned up the bench and put away their implements.

Part of her envied the women—and a few men—being topped. She knew they had a trust in their Dominant that she didn't have. She felt a sensual, visceral emotion she didn't know how to label, and watching the scenes that ended in orgasm for the bottom wasn't a hardship, for sure.

She didn't know if she'd ever again have the trust they had in their Tops with anyone. Not after what she'd been through.

Sully approached her and Tony a little after midnight. "Did you want to sit down and talk?" Sully asked her.

"Oh, yes. Please. If you don't mind."

"No, we don't mind. We'll be leaving soon, and Mac's feeling up to talking again."

Shayla was glad Tony trailed along behind without her having to ask as Sully led her to the sofa area where Clarisse was curled up in Mac's lap. Mac had gotten dressed again. Except for the leather collar buckled around his neck, and the cuffs around his wrists, he looked like any other guy. He wore jeans and a black, short-sleeved collared knit shirt.

She pulled her notebook and pen out of her purse. "I honestly don't even know where to begin," she admitted. "I'm pretty brain-fried at this point."

Sully smiled. "I can give you our contact info," he said. "We can always do a phone interview, or by e-mail."

She handed over the notebook and pen. "That would be great, thanks."

Clarisse smiled at her from Mac's lap. "It's a lot to take in at first."

"Everyone keeps telling me that. I'm still trying to wrap my head around it."

"Don't worry," Clarisse assured her. "The more you see, the more it makes sense. No two dynamics are the same." She looked up at Mac. "It took me a while watching my guys doing their thing together before I could accept it wasn't abusive."

Mac smiled at her. "We wore you down."

"Not exactly," Sully said as he handed back the notebook. "Clarisse's ex was…let's just say he was a piece of work. After she came to live with us and watched our dynamic, and saw that Mac willingly stayed with me and that it wasn't all about the Master and slave stuff, she was able to accept what she saw."

Shayla looked at the information he'd written down to make sure she could read it. "Isn't it a lot of work living with all those rules?"

The three of them burst out laughing. "There aren't as many rules as you might think," Mac said.

"I have too much to do," Sully added, "to micromanage them. They know how I like things to be done, and they do them. Real life always takes priority. Anyone who thinks an absolutely strict twenty-four-seven dynamic is practical or doable has obviously never tried it, or they're so rich they can spend their time doing nothing but BDSM."

"I don't mean to be insulting," Shayla warned, directing her question at Clarisse, "but do you get sick of him bossing you around?"

She shrugged. "No, because it's not like that. He's my husband. They both are. He has to work. Mac and I run the boat and have stuff to do with that. We're like any other relationship. We have boundaries and roles and responsibilities." She sat up and looked like she was thinking how to phrase her next statement. "I love making them happy. Isn't that the ultimate goal of any relationship? To make your partner happy? I mean, it is for me. As long as there is a mutual give-and-take," she added.

"For me," Clarisse continued, "making these two guys happy makes me happy. That's what it boils down to. I love them. We have a great life together. I trust them. I know if something's wrong I can speak up and tell them, and together we'll take care of fixing it. And it's the same for them."

Shayla studied her notebook as she jotted down a few things. Her mind reeled. Back to the issue of trust.

How can I write about trust when I can't even feel it myself? When I don't know if I'll ever feel it again? "That must be scary, though. Putting yourself out there like that."

"It can be," Clarisse agreed. "And that's part of the fun. Part of the thrill. I know they'll both push me to try things I might be scared to try, but I also know they'll never cross my hard limits. It's freeing to just let go and trust them and experience things."

"I never thought I'd hear slavery described as freedom," Shayla said.

"It's one of the most freeing feelings in the world," Mac responded.

Chapter Eight

Shayla couldn't sort out her conflicting thoughts about everything she'd learned and seen. Upon getting home from the club, sleep did not come after she went to bed Saturday night.

Rather, Sunday morning.

Even after she'd used her vibrator to reach orgasm twice, which was a record for her. It wasn't uncommon for her vibrator to be useless getting her off, especially since her breakup.

That was something James had in his favor. Despite his failures as a decent human being, he'd been great in bed. At least, he had in the beginning before the porn took over his life and attention.

Damn sure the only thing I miss about him.

Another obvious sign she still mentally kicked herself for missing. As his sexual attention waned, she hadn't thought much of it at the time. They'd both been busy with work, and didn't all relationships eventually reach a plateau where sex became secondary and not a primary part of the dynamic? She never dreamed it was due to the fact he had a severe porn addiction.

Nothing Shayla had learned in the class, or the things she'd seen in action at the club, had been even remotely like the hard-core, sadistic, humiliating bondage and abuse videos James had been so fond of. Even the scene between Landry and Valerie had enough tenderness and consideration between the participants to make some little part of Shayla sigh with satisfaction.

Yes, Landry had delivered some pretty hard blows to the woman's ass, but in retrospect, after Tony's educated commentaries, she could see the care Landry took not to cause harm or overstep Valerie's limits.

Then there was Sully and Mac's scene. That definitely left her panties damp, and she'd never thought she'd be turned on by watching two men together. The thick, delicious sexual tension in their scene was hotter than any raunchy porno she'd ever viewed despite the apparent brutality of some of Sully's actions.

Clarisse is a lucky woman.

Watching Landry top Cris later had been even sexier.

She lay in bed, tossing and turning until seven Sunday morning when she finally admitted sleep was out of the question.

She got up, put on shorts, a T-shirt, and some running shoes, and headed outside. It still felt relatively cool compared to how hot the afternoon would turn. With thin shadows still draped across the green space, she headed north along a path. It led to a county trail made out of a converted railroad bed.

Trying to escape her thoughts, she walked for nearly an hour. By that time the sun had fully risen and chased away the last of the cool shadows.

And still, answers eluded her.

She didn't understand why part of her responded so viscerally, so positively, to what she had seen. Every time she thought about Landry jamming the vibrator into Valerie's crotch and forcing her to orgasm, she felt her own clit throb a little with longing.

Thinking about how Ross made Loren come during their scene. And Seth and Leah.

Pain and pleasure, irrevocably mixed together. Even when Tilly had scened with that guy…Bob? No orgasms there, but when they finished, the gratitude in his eyes as he hugged her, how her tenderness with him contradicted the vicious, hard-edged Domme she'd been only moments before.

Then how Landry took that same dominant, sadistic woman and turned her into a melted pile of submissive jelly.

It proved impossible to reconcile in her mind.

After heading home, she grabbed a cool shower and donned a large T-shirt and nothing else. It was tempting to use the vibrator on herself, but she had work to do and wanted to sort out her thoughts.

With her damp hair pulled back into a ponytail, she sat on the couch with her laptop and started compiling her notes. She wasn't sure if she had enough information, or maybe too much to sort through, to write her article yet, but maybe putting everything down would help her focus.

The problem was she still had more questions than answers at this point.

Certainly a ton more questions than when she started.

It's not like I can ask anyone for their opinion, either. She didn't want to admit to any of her friends or family what she was working on, much less that she'd volunteered to take on the project when she could have asked it be assigned to someone else. She didn't want to have to explain herself to them after all the outrage they'd expressed on her behalf.

And still, the answer she wanted most of all and the one she'd likely never get—why hadn't she been good enough for James? Had he wanted to dominate her like the women in the videos he watched? Why didn't he feel he could talk to her? Why had he refused her offers to dabble in it with him after the first revelation?

As she studied her notes, she remembered everyone had given her their FetLife.com user names last night. She logged on to the website, hesitating as she had to think about what user name to create.

Shayla, and quite a few variations thereof, were already taken. After thinking on it for a while, she tried *SaraShayla,* since she lived in Sarasota. That user name came up as available.

Why not? It wasn't like she'd be giving out any personal information other than the fact that she lived in the area, along with her age. And anyone she met last night, duh, already knew more about her than she'd give out online.

She filled out the profile, listing herself as *just curious right now* when it asked how active she was, and *friendship* under the "looking for" option.

Then, after thinking about it for a few moments, she checked the *mentor/teacher* option as well. For her BDSM role she waffled between *vanilla, unsure,* and *not applicable* for a while before eventually checking the last of the three.

Faced with the blank window to add to the *About Me* section, she opted to go short and sweet.

Journalist learning about the lifestyle for a series of articles.

She looked up and sent friend requests to everyone she'd gotten to know and realized how bare and boring her profile looked compared to everyone else. Unable to think of what else to put as a picture, she dug out a meme of Grumpy Cat bearing the simple caption, "No."

Maybe that will keep the creepers away.

She spent over an hour looking through the site. Some of the images she saw scared her, and admittedly, a few intrigued her. The intricate shibari ropework in some of the pictures looked more artistic than sadistic.

She joined a couple of the local groups her new acquaintances had recommended, including the Suncoast Society Munch group. While browsing through different discussions, she encountered everything from thoughtful discourses on current events to sexual trolling. Looking through the lists of groups her friends were members of, she found everything from political forums to health issues to book groups.

And there were even LOLcats pictures posted, although some of them with captions that would likely never be allowed on more vanilla social media sites.

Hmm, it really is *a kinky Facebook.*

And still, she had no answers to her questions.

Maybe I do need to read some of the fiction. It couldn't hurt, right? Grab some of the popular books of the genre, now that she had a grasp of the basics, the realities of the dynamics, and see why this was so popular. Or at least take a look at the popular fallacies in contrast to the realities.

After searching Goodreads for reader recommendations, Shayla realized her best bet would be buying e-books. She resigned herself to getting dressed and headed out to Best Buy. There, a salesman gave her a tour of the different brands and models. She finally settled on a Kindle and returned home.

At least the covers are hidden. She'd seen numerous readers report that the privacy afforded by an e-reader was one of the big draws, in addition to the instant gratification.

Once it was charged up and she had the device added to her Amazon account, she ordered her first e-book. Popular according to reader reviews, it was a novella that took her less than an hour to read. Admittedly, the sex scenes were hot enough to make her want to grab her vibrator for some relief of her own, but from what little she'd already learned the story's setup was so unrealistic as to be laughable.

Using the site's recommendations of similar books, she bought three more novellas by the same author and started reading.

By the time she finished she was both hungry to eat dinner and had damp panties.

She also understood why Tony had asked her about her reading habits and if she'd read any BDSM fiction. Had she gone into this with nothing but fictional expectations, she would have assumed Tony and the others were lying down on the job as Doms. On the other hand, she now suspected she saw the attraction so many women had to the genre. A hunky, Alpha Dom to love and protect and train her. To take the reins so she could just *be* for a while.

To make mad, crazy-sweet monkey-sex love to her.

Someone to lay absolute trust in.

She let that stew in her brain and congeal with what she'd witnessed, combined with the information she'd gleaned from her talks with locals in the scene and stuff off the Internet. She didn't want to write a sensational series of stories just to titillate.

She wanted to do the people she wrote about justice and fairly portray them. Especially since they'd been so welcoming and friendly to her. She also knew what she had to do.

I need to talk to Tony again.

* * * *

Tony glanced at his phone when it rang. He almost let it go to voice mail until he realized it was Shayla. He answered. "Hello?"

She sounded hesitant. Nervous. Tentative. "Hi, Tony? It's Shayla. We…ah, from last night."

He smiled. "Of course. How are you?"

"I'm fine. Can we talk?"

He picked up the TV remote and hit *mute*. "Sure. What's up?" She had his interest. She sounded nothing like she had last night.

Now she sounded almost timid.

"I meant in person."

"What about?"

"This."

When she didn't elaborate, he fought the urge to laugh. "I need a few more details than that."

"BDSM. Can we talk more about it?"

When his cock stirred again at the thought of looking into her sweet, hazel eyes, he shoved that distraction away. This wasn't pleasure, it was business.

So to speak.

"When did you want to get together?" He imagined fisting his hand in her hair. And about her deliciously spankable ass. A perfectly rounded figure that got his motor running. A woman who could take what he gave her without him having to worry if she'd break on him.

He shook that thought out of his mind, too. He had no idea if she was even interested in dipping a toe into the lifestyle, much less whether or not she was interested in him.

"I don't know what your schedule is like," she said. Yep, her voice definitely sounded timid. He didn't understand why, but her tone more than anything stirred his curiosity. "I know you said you're busy. I could meet with you tonight, if you wanted. I haven't had dinner yet and was just trying to decide what to do."

He did want to meet with her again. Alone.

He wanted to very much.

He just didn't want her to know how much he wanted to. "That sounds good." He reached down and adjusted his semierect cock through his shorts. "When and where?"

"Would you like to meet at the Village Inn on 41?"

"Sounds good. Give me an hour."

"See you then."

He hung up and smiled. *Don't get your hopes up. She probably wants to talk more for her article.*

Still, as he got up to grab a quick shower, he couldn't help wondering what Shayla looked like without her clothes.

* * * *

Shayla arrived just before Tony did. She'd nervously changed clothes three different times before settling on a black sundress she hadn't worn since the previous summer. It hit her just above the knee and with her black sandals, it didn't look too dressy.

Once they were seated and the waitress took their drink orders, Tony leaned forward with his hands clasped on the table in front of him. "What did you want to talk about?"

Shayla realized she was probably using her notebook more as a crutch at this point and left it lying unopened on the table next to her. "I don't understand," she finally said, knowing it explained nothing but with lack of a better place to start.

One of Tony's eyebrows slid up in a delicious way. "You're really having a tough time with this, aren't you?"

She breathed a sigh of relief. "More than you'll ever know."

"BDSM is very difficult for someone vanilla to understand unless they recognize deep within them some of those same urges. Even then, it's something hard to explain. Just like someone who likes vanilla ice cream but loathes strawberry might have a hard time explaining to someone why they loathe it. They might answer, 'I just do.' That doesn't make their answer wrong, and it might not fully explain their reasoning. They might not even know the reason. It might be a legitimate preference, or it could be based in some deep-seated prejudice stemming from an incident that happened in their childhood that they might not even remember.

"Maybe they were eating strawberry ice cream when they heard a loved one died, and since then they've loathed it, but don't remember that connection. Maybe they once got sick soon after eating strawberry ice cream, but while the two had nothing to do with each other, they became entwined in the person's mind.

"Maybe it's simply a preference and nothing more. Sometimes, a cigar is just a cigar, and not some Freudian symbol. Does that make sense?"

"But people letting someone beat the crap out of them isn't a simple flavor preference."

He leaned in and tapped his finger on the table for emphasis. "But that's just the point. It is. It might not be your thing, but it doesn't make it any less valid a choice."

"How is someone enjoying inflicting pain on someone else a valid choice? Isn't that sociopathic?"

"Not if it's consensual, no. Have you ever had a massage so painful it hurt, but later felt great?"

"I've never had a massage."

His lips pressed together for a moment as he apparently sought another approach. "Usually the strawberry ice cream metaphor works."

"Sorry."

He leaned back and waved away her apology. "No, it's all right. I know it's a difficult subject for some people to wrap their heads around." He thought for a moment. "Are you against gay marriage?"

"No. I could care less what people do with their love lives."

"Exactly," he said. "Think of it like that. There are people who object to consensual BDSM on nonlogical grounds, because it conflicts with their feelings, just like they object to gay marriage because it conflicts with some religious or moral point of view they hold. Not because there is any legitimate reason to object to it."

She chewed on that. "Okay, that makes sense, but I'm still having trouble with it."

"See, that's the thing. It's okay if you have trouble with it. You don't need to understand it to agree it's okay for consenting adults to engage in it."

"It's not okay when I want to write a fair article about it that can educate others. How am I supposed to educate anyone when I feel like I can't even educate myself?"

His green gaze seemed to study her. He looked like he needed a shave, stubble filling in the areas around his mustache and goatee. He slowly scratched at his chin for a moment.

"I think," he said after a moment to gather his thoughts, "that if you are truly dedicated to doing the topic justice, you will. You don't necessarily have to understand the whys of it. Maybe it even makes you a better choice to write the article, because you don't have an axe to grind and you are deliberately trying to give it a fair treatment."

She swallowed a little nervously at that. She did have an axe to grind. A battleaxe of barbarian proportions, as a matter of fact. But she also knew these people had nothing to do with that and she didn't hold it against them, either.

"Do you think next weekend's classes will help me any?"

"Probably. You'll get to see more things, learn more, meet more people. I'm sure Loren gave you her newbie 101 talk the first time you guys met, right?" Shayla nodded. "She's absolutely right," he continued. "There are so many different flavors and ways people practice BDSM that it's impossible to lump them all together. They can't even lump themselves together without someone inevitably pissing in the pool because others aren't doing it 'their' way. I call them 'won twue wayers,' because they can't accept that there are many ways to do things the 'right' way in BDSM.

"If the individuals in the dynamic are consenting adults, and happy with the way things are, and no one's being harmed, that's all that matters."

"That's almost verbatim what she said."

"Well, that's because despite what the won twue way asshats think, it's all that matters."

"I feel woefully unprepared and unqualified to write this." She ran her finger down the spiral spine of the notebook. "I'm scared I'm going to screw it up and piss everyone off that I've just met."

He smiled kindly at her and reached across the table to squeeze her hand. "You'll do fine. I don't mind reviewing it for you before you submit it, and I'm sure Ross and Loren won't mind, either."

"I'm glad you feel so confident."

* * * *

Tony once again got the feeling there was more to it, some deeper issue that she wasn't ready to reveal. He wouldn't press her about it, but he wished she'd open up to him. He'd carefully observed her the night before while she watched scenes play out. If he wasn't mistaken, he'd spotted more than a bit of longing on her face.

And a bit of fear, too.

Fear of what, he wasn't sure. He knew from years in the lifestyle that people sometimes feared the part of themselves that desired the BDSM lifestyle. It usually flew in the face of what had been drilled into them about how "good" people behaved in life. It was shocking and shameful and a disgusting display of sexuality and against all moral behavior, or so they'd been told.

It was also the most fun some people ever had in their lives.

He did not want to scare Shayla off. "You said you were writing a series of articles, right?"

She nodded.

"Why not start with a general overview, using quotes from me and Loren and Ross, and then lead into deeper topics in later articles? At least it will buy you a little time and breathing room."

She finally met his gaze. "That's not a bad idea."

"You can always feel free to bounce stuff off me. And we'll have next Saturday to talk more during and after class." Their waitress returned to take their meal orders. "Deal?"

She rewarded him with a tentative smile. "Deal."

Their conversation ranged wide afield from the topic of BDSM for the rest of their dinner. He suspected she hovered dangerously close to an overloaded mindset, one where she could easily tip to either side of all-in or fuck-it-all if pushed too hard in one direction or the other. He desperately didn't want it to be the fuck-it-all side she landed on.

He found himself far too attracted to her to allow that to happen if he had any say in the matter.

Chapter Nine

Shayla wasn't sure her talk with Tony had helped her comprehension any, but it hadn't hurt. At least now she felt more relaxed about how to approach the initial article. It would be a jumping-off point to the rest of the series, one inviting the reader to come along for the ride without making any conclusions one way or the other.

A little before lunch on Monday, Kimberly stopped by Shayla's cubicle. "We're heading out to eat. Want to come with?"

Shayla stared at her computer screen where another article stared at her. She hadn't even tried to start her first BDSM article yet. "No. I really need to work."

"Tell me about the club," Kimberly said. "What was it like?" Kimberly had been the only one she'd told about going to the class and club. Mostly as a backup in case she didn't show up at work on Monday, although she rationally hadn't expected any problems.

Shayla shrugged. "Everyone was really nice. It wasn't anything like I thought it'd be."

"Did you try anything at the class?"

"I didn't get naked, if that was your question."

Kimberly grinned. "That wasn't my question, but it was going to be my next question. So what did you try?"

The memory of Tony working over her shoulders with the wire whisks flashed into mind. She hoped she didn't blush. "I didn't really try anything like what you're thinking. I tested a couple of the implements on myself. There's a lot more pleasure than pain in what I saw people doing. Does that make sense?"

Kimberly shrugged. She grinned and dropped her voice. "Makes sense to me, but then I'm kind of a spanko." The other woman left as someone called her name, leaving Shayla to wonder about her statement.

Tuesday morning, Shayla managed to turn in an article about a local art exhibit going on at New College without thinking once about riding crops, or whips, or Tony Daniels' delicious green eyes.

Bill Melling stopped by her cubicle. "Good article. Thanks."

She nodded. "No problem." When he eyed her for a moment she knew what he wanted to ask. "And the other assignment is coming along fine," she said before he could. "But it's probably going to be several articles more than I originally thought."

"Okay. Good. We'll take them all."

She finished her day by clearing out her inbox and handling edits on another article. Her drive home was spent thinking about what to add to her grocery list. She hated shopping, but was nearly out of milk. *I'd rather go home and make a list and make one trip than stop for stuff and have to go back later.*

She parked in front of her unit and left her stuff in the car, locking it. She had a short walk down to her mailbox and enjoyed the exercise. Not to mention the grounds were lovely, and spending a few minutes outside in nature helped relax her. She felt pretty good when she reached the sheltered alcove holding the mailboxes and opened hers with the key.

That feeling exploded as she shuffled through her mail, her gaze falling upon the return address of one envelope buried amongst advertisements from businesses welcoming her to the area and her regular catalogs and bills.

James Tavery.

She didn't realize her hands shook until she tried to slip her thumb under the flap and rip it open. She finally managed it. Inside, she found a check wrapped in a sheet of paper, upon which he'd handwritten a note in black ink with his tight, economical script.

Rather than read it there with her breath coming in gasps, her legs shaking, and on the verge of tears, she hurried back to her apartment and slammed the door shut behind her before she unfolded the paper.

Dear Shay,

I don't know if you'll read this or not, and I won't blame you if you don't. I know I screwed up. I'm sorry. I have a problem. I admit it. You were too good for me and instead of going and getting help the first time I fucked up even more because I thought I could control it.

I'm not stupid enough to think you'll believe me when I say I'm really changing this time. I found a group meeting I've started going to twice a week for porn addiction. I'm looking around for a psychologist who maybe can help me get my head on straight.

I don't know what I'm asking for other than forgiveness. I've taken a second job, on nights and weekends, to repay every dime I owe you. I know you could have pressed charges against me and didn't, and I won't make you sorry for deciding that.

I'm sorry for what I did and wish I could take it all back. I lost the best thing to ever come into my life and I'm going to regret it for the rest of my days with every breath I take.

Love,
James.

She held the check in trembling fingers and looked at it. Another five hundred dollars.

Her knees unhinged. Unable to hold herself up, she slid down the door and cried.

* * * *

She pulled herself together and went to retrieve her stuff from the car. She'd already downed her first beer when she remembered she'd wanted to go to the store.

Too late now. She never drove after drinking, even if it was only a little bit.

Now, all she felt like doing as she stared at the envelope, letter, and check on her counter was drink and cry.

Fuck it.

She pulled another beer out of the fridge, and a turkey pot pie from the freezer. She'd go to the store tomorrow after work.

By the time she was settled on her couch with her notebook and laptop on the coffee table in front of her and beer number three ready to consume, and a steaming pot pie on a paper plate, she'd nearly managed to forget about James.

Although the third beer more than anything was the catalyst for that.

She put the TV on Cartoon Network and stared at her notes as she worked on the pot pie. She needed a good opening hook for her lede. That was what she was focused on when her cell phone rang.

Dammit.

She'd left it on the counter. She reached it before it kicked over to voice mail, but her eye caught sight of the envelope from James on her counter as she answered. "Hello?" She spun around and returned to the couch.

"Shayla? It's Loren."

"Hi." She drew her legs up under her on the couch. "How are you?"

"I just wanted to check in and see how you were doing after the other night."

"Good. I'm good. I actually had a sit-down with Tony Sunday night."

"Oh? How'd it go?"

"He seems like a really nice guy. Very patient with my questions. Thank you for introducing me to him."

"Awesome. Listen, I know you work, but Leah, Tilly, and I usually get together on Thursday mornings for a girls' day. We're going up to visit Clarisse this week to take her out to brunch to celebrate the baby. We wanted to know if maybe you could get the time off to come with us?"

It was on the tip of Shayla's tongue to say no. That she had too much to do, too many things on her plate. But it would be a lie because she knew Bill Melling encouraged his staff to take exactly these kinds of opportunities if it meant their assignments would benefit.

"Let me check with my boss in the morning, but I think I can make it."

"Great! Just send me a text and I'll let you know when and where to meet up with us. You can ride with us if you want."

Something about Loren's hopeful tone stayed any hesitation on Shayla's part. "Sure. That'd be great. Thanks."

Shayla got off the phone and stared at her laptop, where she'd opened a blank document. With the pot pie growing cold, she leaned forward and typed.

Last weekend, a group of friends gathered around a table at a local restaurant and discussed their week, their jobs, their lives, graciously inviting this writer into their inner circle. Nothing distinguished them from anyone else in the restaurant.

Except that an hour later, after dinner ended, they all met up at a local private BDSM dungeon club to continue their evening.

She grabbed her beer and took a long swallow as she reread the opening. Slowly nodding, she set her beer aside and started typing again.

Two hours later she had a thousand words, a cold pot pie, and her beer buzz was a thing of the past. Happy with the rough draft, she carried the plate and empty beer bottle to the kitchen.

Her feet stopped cold at the sight of the letter on her counter.

Dammit. I really need to get the fuck over that.

She dumped the trash and scooped the letter and check up. The check she stuck in her checkbook after filling out a deposit slip for it. She'd drop it by the bank in the morning. The envelope she ripped into tiny pieces and threw away.

The letter...

She left it folded but couldn't bring herself to rip it up.

Instead, she shoved it in her kitchen junk drawer and slammed it closed before heading to her bedroom.

Maybe it was the beer, or perhaps James' letter had triggered it, but Shayla found her sleep plagued by sexy, seductive dreams.

Mostly of Tony Daniels tying her to a bench and using a flogger and his hands on her bare ass before forcing a vibrator between her legs to make her orgasm. Knowing it was a dream didn't lessen the impact on her. Various scenarios flashed through her brain at warp speed. One minute he had her spread out, naked, on the suspension bar while he used a singletail to raise welts on her ass. The next, she was spread-eagle on her back while he used a large dildo to fuck her dripping cunt.

She awoke Wednesday morning dazed and horny and without enough time to try to get herself off before she had to get ready for work.

What the hell have I gotten myself into?

Chapter Ten

"But you know, if you don't think I should be out of the office that long—"

"Nonsense," Bill said. "I think it's a great idea. They obviously like and trust you or they wouldn't have invited you along." He stared at Shayla. She'd snagged his attention upon arriving at the office that morning, wanting to get it out of the way as soon as possible. "You're a big girl. You don't need me to make your decisions for you. As your boss, I'm fine with you taking the day to go with them. If you're looking for a reason not to go, that's on your shoulders."

Shayla swallowed. In the sober light of day, that was exactly what she was looking for. The journalist in her rationalized spending a day candidly talking with the women would likely bring insights for several articles.

Some deep part of her hesitated. She knew her dreams the night before played no small role in her newfound reticence.

Her alarm had awakened her just as her dream-self began to scream with pleasure, and she wondered as disorientation faded if she'd actually started to climax in her sleep.

The fact that she'd discovered her panties were soaked contributed to that possibility.

The dream unsettled her on a number of levels. That she'd yearned for the freedom to let go to someone she trusted with her health and safety. That she felt viscerally attracted to the hard edge in the man's green eyes as he pointed at the floor and she sank to her knees.

That her heart raced at the feel of a heavy leather collar being buckled around her throat.

Unfortunately, the dream wouldn't vanish by the time she finished her first cup of coffee, as most of her dreams usually did. This dream tenaciously hung on, solidifying in her mind the more she tried not to think about it.

"Shay?"

Bill Melling stared at her from the other side of his desk.

"Oh, sorry."

"You look lost."

She slowly nodded. "I'm beginning to feel a little that way."

"The offer to reassign is still open."

Despite her dreams the night before, she shook her head. "No. I'm going to see this through to the end. They're nice people who've agreed to open up to me and share an intimate part of their lives. I'd rather not pawn it off on someone else at this point."

He smiled. "Then have a good day tomorrow."

Shayla returned to her desk and texted Loren. Within a minute, she had a reply text from Loren with the time and address.

Accompanied by a smiley face.

* * * *

Dream Tony returned to her that night. She knelt on the floor at his feet as he buckled a black leather collar around her neck and snapped a leash to it.

"Come."

Without hesitation, she crawled on all fours behind him, feeling her pussy tingling with anticipation at what was to come.

Hopefully, her.

He led her to a bench like the one at the club and bound her to it, hand and foot. A blindfold slipped over her eyes.

As her pulse spiked, she felt a hand between her legs, fingers unerringly finding and stroking her clit, working harder, faster.

"Why don't you come for me?" he whispered into her ear.

The fingers wouldn't stop, relentlessly pushing her toward the edge of climax until, finally, her body arched...

And she awoke to find her hand buried inside her panties as the last vestiges of her orgasm waned.

Gasping for breath, she tried to swim out of the hold of sleep on her system. As what happened finally sank home, she let out a harsh laugh. It was still four o'clock in the morning and she suspected she wouldn't get back to sleep.

Damn, I need to get laid.

* * * *

After her restless night, Shayla was anxious for a distraction. *Any* distraction. She was grateful for the chance to spend the day with the women. They met at Loren's house before piling into Tilly's SUV to make the trek north to Pinellas County, where Clarisse lived.

Shayla, sitting in the backseat with Loren, had a chance to get to see some of her adopted state as they headed north on I-75. When they reached the Sunshine Skyway Bridge, Shayla sucked in a breath. "Wow. That's beautiful."

"Want me to pull over for a minute?" Tilly asked. "There are rest stops at either end. Great views."

"No, that's okay." The waters of the Gulf of Mexico and Tampa Bay met at the bridge. Today the wind was low, the water looking nearly glassy except for low rollers and the occasional boat wake breaking the surface.

"You've never been here before?" Loren asked.

"No. First time I'd ever been to Florida was when I came down to interview for the job in person. And then I was too busy, between that and finding an apartment, to do any sightseeing."

"Why did you decide to move to Florida?" Leah asked.

Why indeed? Hell, these women had been more than open with her. She suspected they would hold her confidence if anyone could.

Not to mention she'd seen them naked and vulnerable.

"Well, and I'd appreciate if this didn't get spread around, but I needed a fresh start." She took a deep breath and spilled the story, surprised at how relieved she felt at the end of the telling.

"You're a better woman than I am," Loren said. "I would have had his ass put *under* the jail."

Shayla shrugged. "That wouldn't have gotten me anywhere except saddled with the apartment and utilities and a long fight to get the credit card companies to forgive the debt and go after him. Where I am now, my monthly bills are nearly fifty percent cheaper, there's no state income tax, he has paid back some of what he owes me, and I don't have to worry about him showing up at my front door."

"Well, there is that," Tilly agreed. "Can't say's I blame you there."

"What'd your parents say when you told them?" Loren asked.

"They were supportive. My dad wanted to go beat him up and wring his neck."

"I like him," Tilly snarked.

Shayla smiled. "Fortunately, they were safely up in Minneapolis and not in Cleveland. So James' neck was safe. They didn't like that I wanted to move all the way to Florida, but they did support me when I convinced them it was the best thing for my mental health."

"How do you like Florida so far?" Leah asked.

"It's different. Good different," she added.

"Why the hell would he pay for porn?" Tilly pondered.

Leah looked at her. "Seriously, Til? *That's* your question?"

Tilly shrugged. "Guy's got to be pretty damn stupid to pay that much for porn when so much of it is readily available for free." She glanced in the rearview mirror and made eye contact with Shayla. "I mean, yes, obviously it's pretty shitty for him to rob you like that in the first place. But to me, that just piles stupidity onto his criminal asshattery."

Shayla laughed. "I hadn't thought about it like that. I guess you're right. And I appreciate you letting me talk about this. All my friends and most of his wanted to kill him when they found out what he did. It's nice to be able to just talk about it. I lost a couple of friends when I took him back the first time. I hadn't told all of them what he'd done, just a few. They told me I was an idiot to forgive him then. I guess they were right. But I loved him. I didn't think he'd do it again. I definitely didn't think he'd rip me off the way he did. I didn't know how badly he'd destroyed his credit the first time around."

"Love makes us do things against our better judgment sometimes," Tilly said. "And we all do stupid, silly stuff in our lives in the name of love. And, eh, not to sound like a bitch, but you might want to get tested for STDs in case he's lying about more than you know."

"Oh, believe me, I already did that. I did that before I left Cleveland," she said, remembering the humiliation she felt having to ask her doctor for the tests.

"Good. I mean, not good that you had to get it done, but good they were negative."

Shayla smiled. "I know what you meant."

Clarisse and her men lived in a small, upscale private gated community on a bayou in Tarpon Springs. When Shayla got out of the car and stared up at the large stilt home, she realized just how tiny her apartment was in comparison.

Their master bedroom is probably bigger than my apartment.

Tilly led the way upstairs, where Clarisse greeted them with smiles and hugs. "Ready for brunch?" Tilly asked her.

Clarisse patted her stomach. "The morning sickness has settled, so that's a huge *yes*." A tiny Yorkie ran into the foyer, where he screeched to a halt before he began barking.

"Bart! That's not nice." Clarisse scooped him up, quieting him immediately. "Sorry. He thinks he's lord and master of the place and we humans are here to serve him."

"Has he stolen any more butt plugs?" Tilly asked.

Shayla laughed. "What?"

Clarisse rolled her eyes. "We've lost more butt plugs to this little dog than I think we've even owned." She set him back on the floor. "He's a klepto. Don't worry, he only steals clean ones. But I'm seriously beginning to wonder if some of our friends aren't bringing butt plugs with them and sneaking them to him as a joke. I've found butt plugs stashed in his bed that I know we didn't buy." She directed her next comment to Shayla. "He likes them as chew toys."

"He's Dom dog," Tilly joked.

Leah joined Shayla and Loren in the backseat, while Clarisse took the front passenger seat. She gave Tilly directions to a restaurant on the Sponge Docks. Shayla couldn't help feeling like a tourist as she tried to take everything in.

"Don't worry," Clarisse told her. "We'll take a stroll up and down the main street to walk off the meal."

The restaurant wasn't very crowded due to it being early in the day before the lunchtime crowd arrived. They were seated at a large, round table in the back of the restaurant.

Clarisse hungrily eyed the menu. "I think I need one of each."

Leah laughed. "Are your guys harping on you to eat healthy?"

She laughed. "Are you kidding? They're close to tossing food at me to keep me happy. Apparently I've had a few tiny mood swings, as Mac called them."

"Where are they this morning?" Shayla asked.

"They departed early to go look at nursery furniture. They're researching everything. You've never seen two men so obsessed with making sure everything is perfect and safe."

"They're not giving you a say in it?"

"Oh, they will, once they narrow their choices down. Nothing but the best, as far as they're concerned. They won't let me look at price tags because they know I'll want to go for the cheap end of the scale." Clarisse put down her menu. "I spent a lot of years scrimping and saving before I met my guys. Old habits die hard."

"How did you meet them?"

Clarisse smiled. "I was a stowaway."

"What?"

"Yep. I was on the run from my ex. He beat the crap out of me, and I was convinced he was going to kill me. I thought my uncle still owned the boat, so I hid out there."

Shayla managed to stifle a shudder. At least James hadn't beaten her. Then again, she suspected if he had, she would have left him the first time it happened.

At least, she hoped she would have.

"I thought Landry was going to cry when I made him sell his McLaren," Tilly said. She looked at Shayla. "It was a ridiculously expensive Mercedes that he owned before I met him."

"Why'd you make him sell it?" she asked.

"Because it made me nervous. It was worth several times over more than my house, and the insurance on it was outrageous. It had to stay parked in the garage because I was freaked out a bird might poop on it. I countered with the fact that if he was willing to send Cris packing on my say-so, then selling a car should be no big deal." She grinned. "He finally did sell it. Besides, it wasn't practical for the three of us. I told him if he wanted a substitute penis, he could buy a friggin' strap-on and ditch the fancy car. I did let him buy a Mercedes SUV though. At least the insurance was reasonable."

"So how did you get involved with Landry and Cris?" Shayla asked. "Tony said you were a pro Domme. Is that how you met them?"

Tilly nodded. "In a way. You sure you want to hear the full story?"

"If you want to tell it."

Tilly played with her straw for a moment with a faraway look in her eyes. "I'm not real proud of myself for some of the things I did," she eventually said. She met Shayla's gaze. "You know what it's like to be hurt by someone you thought you could trust with your life."

Shayla's heart pounded, her throat going dry. She nodded.

A sad smile crossed Tilly's face. "Then you might understand some of what I'm about to tell you." She stirred her tea for a moment. The pensive look on her face told Shayla she was trying to gather her thoughts. Loren, Leah, and Clarisse didn't speak.

Finally, Tilly continued. "I was Cris' slave," she softly said. "I thought I was going to spend the rest of my life with him. He's the man I would have considered marrying if he'd asked me. He helped me through a lot of emotional pain and scars that I've carried since I was a kid. I would have died for him to save his life."

The faraway look returned. "Then, *poof*, one day he disappeared. He left me a note and a bunch of paperwork signing everything over to me. Said he had to leave and couldn't tell me why, and he was sorry, but he had to release me."

Tilly's jaw tightened and she nodded toward Loren. "If it wasn't for her and Ross, I don't know what I would have done. I fell apart. Literally. They had to hospitalize me for a couple of days. When I finally got my head out of my ass, I decided never again. Never again would I open myself up like that."

She stirred her tea some more without drinking any, the straw and ice making slow rounds in the glass. "I finished nursing school."

"How did the pro Domme gig happen?"

"Well, it paid a lot better than being a nurse. I sort of fell into doing it. I was helping a friend out one night, and it went from there. Someone said I should start charging for it, and I did it to help pay the bills. Eventually, even though I was only taking pro Domme jobs on my off days, I was making twice the money doing that as I was as a nurse." She smiled. "No sex. That was a hard and fast rule."

Tilly focused on the glass and the slow revolutions of the ice inside. "After a couple of years I realized how dead I felt inside. One of my clients and I went out on a vanilla date and I realized how lonely I was. I hadn't dated anyone since Cris left. Hadn't slept with anyone. I was a vicious bitch. It was how I protected myself. My heart hurt too bad, felt too raw. I spent years after Cris left wondering why I wasn't good enough for him to stay. Or if he'd lied about how he felt for me. You name it, I thought it."

"Then in walks this guy one night while I'm at the club with the client I went out on a date with. He wanted to talk to me about training his male slave. We met a couple of days later to talk, and he tells me he's got cancer and wants to make sure his slave will be able to respond to another owner."

"Landry?"

Tilly nodded as she met Shayla's gaze again. "He shows up at my house with his slave for the evaluation session. I don't see the guy's face at first because his hair was long and he kept his head down and turned away from me. Then Landry spills the rest of the story. That his slave was someone else's Master. That when Landry was in a wreck a few years before and nearly died, they discovered his cancer and the slave came back to him. But the slave left behind a slave of his own. Abandoned her."

"Hell!"

Tilly nodded. "Yep. I tell you what, I could barely breathe as he told me the story. Then he makes this crazy proposal to me, literally. To marry him and help him through his cancer treatments, and he'd pay me well for doing it. And if he died, I inherited everything." She smiled. "That's when I found out he was a multi-millionaire."

Shayla didn't know what to say, so she just nodded.

"Then Landry said he'd be back at the end of the hour session and walked out, leaving his slave behind."

"How'd that go?"

"Not well. At first Cris didn't even want to look at me." Her face reddened and she looked back down at her glass of tea. "I screamed at him. Beat the crap out of him. Wanted to kill him. But I agreed to Landry's crazy scheme and somewhere along the way, I fell in love with Landry."

"How do you live with a guy who hurt you like that?"

She shrugged. "Landry told me if I said the word that he'd order Cris gone." She snapped her fingers. "Like that."

"Why didn't you?"

She finally sipped her tea. "I couldn't. He loved Landry, and Landry loved him. And deep down inside me, I still loved him, too. Like I said, I'm not proud of some of the things me and Landry put Cris through in the beginning. I did it out of pain and anger. Landry did it just because he's a sadist, but that's still no excuse." She sighed. "Fortunately, I was able to forgive Cris and move on."

"But how do you ever trust Cris?"

Tilly slowly nodded. "I don't. Not like I used to. Not in the same ways. Forgiving him was for *me*, for *my* sanity, not for his sake. He did beg for my forgiveness. And I love him. I never stopped loving him, even through the pain."

"I can't reconcile that," Shayla admitted.

Tilly put down her glass and stared at it for a few moments. "I'll never have the same trust bond with Cris that I used to have," she said. "Ever. Not possible. But over the past couple of years, as I've healed I've formed a new trust bond with him. During the rough times with Landry's treatment, we learned to lean on each other. To work as a team. No, he's not my Master. He'll never be my Master again, unfortunately. But I love him and to be honest, once I knew the full story and calmed down and got some perspective, the slave part of me understood why he did what he did, and respected him for it."

"I'm not trying to be disrespectful by asking this, but how can you respect a man who abandoned you like that?"

"Because yes, he did love me. He had some misconceptions, that if he revealed the truth to me about Landry, I wouldn't respect him anymore and couldn't deal with him being someone else's slave. Not saying I agreed with him for doing it, but on the back side of it, I understood."

"You didn't know about Landry when you were with Cris the first time?"

She shook her head. "He didn't talk about that part of his past. I knew he had a rough family history. So did I, so I could understand why he didn't want to talk about stuff. He never lied to me about Landry. He just never told me about him."

"How did Cris feel about you marrying Landry?"

She shrugged. "He's Landry's slave. He had no choice in the matter.

Landry gave him two options—stay or go. And since Cris stayed, it meant he wouldn't oppose or resent the marriage. He loves Landry, and he loves me. All he cares about is the people he loves are happy. I'm just glad he put up with me in über-bitch mode for a while until I got it out of my system."

"That must have been hard on you, helping Landry through his treatments and dealing with Cris."

"You have no idea. It was hard dealing with my friends, too."

"Why?"

Loren snorted. "Most of us wanted to castrate Cris with our bare hands. When we found out he was back in her life, we thought she'd lost her mind."

Tilly smiled. "I think it was harder on them seeing Cris come back than it was me. I took my retribution in private." Her smile faded. "And looking back, like I said, I'm not proud of everything I did. But it's what I needed to do to be able to put it behind me and move on. And now the three of us are happy together in our weird little way. What's past is past. We have today and the future together, and I won't waste it. Life's too damn short and way too precious for that."

"Amen," Leah softly said as she raised her glass in a toast before taking a sip.

Shayla thought about watching Tilly scene with Landry the previous weekend. "What do you consider Landry then? Besides your husband?"

She shrugged. "Neither of them are my Master or Owner or any other term like that. I choose when I want to submit to Landry. I'd say our default mode is more of a Daddy Dominant kind of dynamic, although I don't consider myself a little. I also don't consider him my Dominant. I'm a switch. When I need to, I can…let go to him. But he doesn't order me around or expect my service, if that makes sense?"

Shayla nodded.

"When I need a little more structure as a mental break, he slips into a dominant role with me. Usually in bed or in play, not as an everyday thing the way he is a Master and Owner to Cris."

"What about Cris and you?"

Her gaze returned to her glass of iced tea. "I don't top him. I…just can't. I can't bring myself to do it. Sometimes in bed I let him get toppy with me, but not as a scene. I can count on him in ways that both fulfill his need to be of service as a slave, and his need to take care of me like a Dominant might, and my need to be taken care of without bringing a D/s dynamic into it. Make sense?"

Shayla pulled her glasses off and rubbed her eyes. "Not really, no."

Leah laughed. "Don't worry. We've known them for years and it still throws the rest of us off at times. Labels don't work with them. We don't expect you to understand it all in one lunch."

Clarisse snorted. "I guess I have it easy. I'm submissive to both my guys. Mac's the switchy one, although Sully lets Mac get toppy with him on the boat. As long as I keep saying, 'Yes, Sir,' everything's good."

Leah jumped in to change the subject. Sort of. "I saw you're coming to our shibari class on Saturday."

"Yes. And the Whips for Fun class before that."

"Oh! Tony teaches that."

"That's what he said Saturday night."

"Busy day," Leah said. "Will you stay for the play session later? Come to dinner with us."

"Sure. Why not? Not like I have any other plans."

"Watch out," Clarisse playfully warned. "This is how we suck you in to the dark side. With rope and whips."

"And good cookies," Tilly added.

Chapter Eleven

They spent the day in Tarpon Springs with Clarisse, shopping and talking and even catching a late lunch before heading back to Loren's house around four. She spent time working on her notes about the day before she grabbed a shower.

The things they'd talked about wouldn't leave her mind. How happy each of the women seemed in their relationships. Sure, Tilly had a slightly different dynamic than the others, but she was happy. By her own admission, happier than she'd ever been in her life.

And it felt damn good to have a group of women she could open up to and not worry about them judging her for what she did by forgiving James and giving him a second chance, and then not having him prosecuted the second time.

She liked Kimberly and Suzanne, but despite knowing Kimberly was a little wilder than Suzanne, she still didn't feel…well, totally comfortable opening up to them the way she was with these women. Shayla didn't want anything she said to accidentally make its way around the office.

After the good day she had with Loren, Leah, Tilly, and Clarisse, she wanted more than ever to do more than just talk about BDSM.

She wanted to experience it.

After waffling about it for nearly an hour, she called Tony a little before eight o'clock and was pleasantly surprised when he answered instead of his voice mail.

"Hello, Shayla."

"I hope it's not too late to call."

"No. What's up?"

She took a deep breath and took the plunge. "I know this is short notice, but are you available tomorrow night to get together for dinner or something and talk again?"

There was a moment of hesitation she was positive meant no, but then he surprised her. "Sure. How about someplace other than Village Inn?"

It was one of the few places she actually knew in the area. "Oh. Okay. Sure. Wherever you'd like."

He named the restaurant and she wrote it down. When she hung up with him a few minutes later, she realized her hands were trembling.

Crap.

* * * *

She spent another restless night with sexy dreams of Tony and his green eyes running through her brain. The next morning, Bill Melling stopped by her cubicle. "How'd everything go yesterday?"

"Really good. Thank you for letting me go."

He shrugged. "You need to be able to research."

"I should have the first article ready by Monday."

"Good."

"It's going to be a long one."

His smile broadened. "Even better."

She stopped by home to grab a quick shower and change before heading to the restaurant. There, she stood and fidgeted in the foyer, unable to just sit and wait. When she saw Tony's car pull in five minutes before their meeting time, she couldn't deny the little thump in her chest as she watched him smoothly climb out of his car and stride toward the restaurant.

He's just a guy. He's just a normal, everyday guy.

Who's now haunting my dreams.

She felt heat rise in her cheeks and pressed her palms against them to try to rid herself of the embarrassing flush before he walked in.

His eyes met hers through the glass door as he reached out to push it open. Unable to help it, her gaze dropped to her feet for a moment before she looked up again. He wore a friendly smile and extended his hand.

She'd reached out to hug him, and they did the awkward hug-handshake dance before settling on a hug. "Nice to see you again," he said. "Glad we didn't scare you away last weekend."

"Everyone's been really nice. That's why I want to make sure I write the best story possible. I don't want anyone getting the wrong impression about what you all do. I want to make sure I'm accurate."

He held out his arm, indicating for her to go first, and they approached the hostess stand. He held up two fingers and they were led to a booth.

Once settled, with their drink orders placed, he leaned back in his seat and smiled at her. "So what did you want to talk about tonight?"

* * * *

Tony admitted his curiosity had run overtime after her phone call the night before. Over the phone Shayla sounded more timid than ever, a woman wanting to ask something and apparently afraid to spit it out. He'd found her discomfort amusing and endearing.

Not to mention the sadist in him got a little twist out of it in the bargain.

He knew she'd spent the day before with Leah, Loren, Tilly, and Clarisse. He wouldn't be nosy and ask what they talked about, but he couldn't help wondering if her call to him was a result of it.

She laced her hands together in front of her on the table, her eyes trained on them. When she spoke, her voice sounded so soft he had to sit forward to hear her.

"You said you've trained submissives before," she said.

He slowly nodded and folded his arms on the table in front of him. "Yes?"

"And you teach, too? I mean, I know you teach the whip class, but you teach other stuff."

"Yes?"

"How much do you charge?"

He thought maybe he'd misheard her. "I don't understand."

She still wouldn't look at him. "How much do you charge to train a submissive?"

"I don't."

That forced her gaze up to his before it dropped to her hands again. "But I thought you said—"

"When I train a submissive, it's because myself and the person have reached a mutual agreement to pursue that. That's personal, not a business transaction. I've never charged to train a submissive. I don't hire myself out to do that. Now, I've taught private sessions on technique with rope bondage, whips, that sort of thing. But the relationship between a Dominant and their submissive is a personal one. At least, it is for me. I know there are people out there who claim to make a business out of training submissives and slaves, but I'm not one of them. What I do in my personal life is for pleasure. The only reason I even accept money for my classes is to cover expenses and time, not to make a profit."

"Oh." She sounded disappointed. Her hands disappeared from the table into her lap. "Okay. I'm sorry. I misunderstood you."

He took a chance and dropped his voice. "Shayla, look at me."

Her eyes fluttered everywhere and anywhere but where he wanted them until she finally met his gaze. He waited until her eyes were steadily focused on him and nowhere else.

"What exactly is it you're looking for?" he asked in the same soft, even tone.

He didn't miss the way she swallowed, the way her throat worked, the pulse point clearly visible under her flesh.

I'd love to pull her head back and nibble all the way down her neck.

He forced himself not to budge as his erection painfully sprang to life in his pants.

"I want to go through training as a submissive. To see what it's like from that side firsthand. I...I think that's the only way I'm going to really understand all of this for my articles."

He let her soft words hang in the air for a moment as he tried to process what she'd said. He couldn't move, couldn't sit back. The urge to adjust his pants would be too great, and he suspected what she'd just said had taken every ounce of her courage. He didn't want to make a wrong move and scare her off.

"You want me to train you?"

Her eyes flickered away, but he waited her out. Her hazel gaze eventually returned to his again. "Yes. If you're interested," she quickly added. "I mean, I know you're busy and if you don't have the time, or don't want to, it's okay. I understand and it won't hurt my feelings."

Part of him wanted to reach out and pull her into his arms. A thick layer of insecurity lay behind her walls, of that he was now certain. She'd been rejected somewhere down the line and had taken a massive hit to her self-esteem as a result. He didn't know exactly how or why, but he'd seen it plenty of times before in others and recognized it all too well.

Of course, he knew he could be wrong, but he doubted it.

"Is this really just for your story? No other reason?"

She nodded.

"Is any of it for you personally?"

He thought at first she wasn't going to answer him. Then she softly said, "I don't know. Maybe."

He allowed himself to slowly lean back in his seat, his palms flat on his thighs under the table. He studied her, noticing the way her gaze dove away from him, down and to the side again, to the dessert menu propped up at the end of the table by the window.

I'll have to work on that first. She would have to learn to accept direct eye contact with him, to hold and maintain it no matter how uncomfortable it might feel to her.

He realized what he'd just thought and knew regardless of the outcome, he'd probably already made up his mind the other night when they were talking at the club.

He'd just never thought he'd have a chance to make some of those fantasies come true.

"Okay," he said. "I'll do it."

Chapter Twelve

Shocked because of her certainty he'd say no, she looked up at him. His even, steady gaze never wavered from hers. Heat filled her cheeks again as her dreams about him came rushing back to mind.

In her dreams, he'd born that same intense look.

"Really?"

Instead of answering he looked away from her as the waitress returned with their drink order. "Ready to order?" she asked. "Or do you need a couple of minutes?"

He picked up his menu, which had lain unread in front of him. "Just a couple more minutes, please."

When they were alone again, he tipped his head toward her menu. "Let's get our orders put in and then pick up this conversation in a few minutes."

She nodded. As she reached for her menu, she realized her hands trembled. She opted to lay it open, flat on the table in front of her, and stare down at it. She didn't want him to see how badly his acceptance had rattled her.

Part of her truly had expected him to say no. Well, that had been the fantasy best-case scenario. Worst-case, she'd anticipated her reaction if he'd laughed in her face at the suggestion. Not that she'd honestly expected that from him, but she wanted to be prepared regardless.

After the waitress returned for their orders and left with their menus, Tony leaned forward again. "What are your expectations?"

"I don't understand."

"Are you looking for just an afternoon to experience stuff, or did you mean you wanted me to train you the way I normally would a submissive, or what?"

"How would you normally train a submissive?"

He smiled. "Normally, she would be my girlfriend and the process would involve lots of sex and orgasms. I would, of course, remove that option from the table for you under the circumstances. Unless you didn't want it removed."

Her pussy fluttered at the thought. She reached out for her water glass to take a sip and had to use two hands because they trembled so badly. "Oh," she managed.

She couldn't read his expression. "And I want to confirm there isn't a boyfriend or significant other in your life who might take umbrage with this process. If there is, I need to have a sit-down with him before we do anything."

"No. I'm single."

"Okay."

"Would I need to sign a contract or something?"

His lips pressed tightly together as if he was trying not to laugh. "No. If someone's not adult enough to hold their end of a deal, a contract certainly won't keep them in line. Besides, they're not legally binding."

"I thought some people use them."

"Some people do. I don't. I never have. If someone's word isn't good, I'd rather not be in a relationship with them if it takes a piece of paper to keep them honest."

"Okay." She buried her hands back in her lap. "Where do we start?"

When he smiled, she realized how handsome he was. "Right here."

"I don't get it."

"Unlike the idiots who think submissives and Dominants magically bond together on the basis of labels and common kink, I am a firm believer that if you can't be friends with someone, then you surely can't be in a D/s relationship with them. There's two-way trust that must be established. I won't top someone I don't have some sort of an emotional connection with, and I don't want someone submitting to me who doesn't trust me."

"Oh." She nodded and took a deep breath. "Okay."

"You look relieved."

"I…I just didn't expect it to be so…" She didn't know what word her brain grasped for to insert into that statement.

"Boring?"

She could tell from the way the corner of his mouth quirked up that he wasn't upset. "Normal," she said.

He reached out for his iced tea. "I think the word you're looking for is 'vanilla.'"

* * * *

It'd taken every ounce of his will not to burst out laughing. She was so cute and so naïve. She had no preconceived, desperate desires to act out. No "do me" demands to make upon him.

If nothing else, it'll be a way to have some fun.

And drive away his loneliness for a while.

While they ate, he purposely kept the conversation light and away from anything remotely resembling BDSM. He wanted to know about her tastes in reading, music, TV, movies. What she enjoyed about her job. Her past.

When he tried to guide her toward discussions about previous relationships, she nimbly danced around it.

Opting not to force the issue, but adding it to a mental checklist of topics he wanted to pursue later in private, he let the subject drop. "So about tomorrow's whip class."

"Yes?"

"It starts at two. I'd like you there by one."

"Why so early?"

"Because I have things I want to go over with you in private. I have a key to the club, don't worry."

"Okay."

He stared at her until it became an uncomfortable silence. She finally caught on and asked, "What?"

He raised an eyebrow at her. She'd have to learn sooner or later if she was serious about going through this process with him.

Either that, or she'd quickly come to enjoy spankings.

She frowned. "What's wrong?"

"'Okay' isn't the answer I wanted."

She looked confused. Somehow, he kept from rolling his eyes at her. "The correct answer would be, 'Yes, Sir.'"

"Oh. Sorry."

He cleared his throat.

"Yes, Sir," she said.

He smiled. "Good girl. And tomorrow, I want you to wear the black sundress you wore Sunday night when we met at the restaurant. No bra, and no panties unless you have a thong to wear under it."

He barely held his amusement in check as her cheeks flushed with color. "No panties?"

"Like I said, you can wear a thong. But no, no panties. Unless you're on your period."

Her mouth opened and shut like she was trying to decide whether or not to argue. If she was going to balk at his orders, this would be the first one she'd challenge.

"Yes, Sir," she finally whispered.

He broadly smiled at her, delighted to a nearly giddy level that she agreed to his demands. "Good girl."

* * * *

Part of her bristled. Then she realized she'd asked for this. *Duh.*

She didn't have a thong. *I'll have to go shopping for one tomorrow morning.*

"I can't and won't make you submit to me," he continued. "That's not something that holds any interest for me. Either you want to, or you don't. If you want to then I expect you to respond not with *yeah*, or *okay*, or anything else like that. Yes, Sir. No, Sir."

"Anything you say, Sir?"

He arched an eyebrow at her. "There is a term for submissives who like to mouth back. They're called SAMs."

"What's that mean?"

"Smart-assed masochist."

"Does this mean I'm expected to keep my mouth shut and do as I'm told?"

"No, not at all. It simply means there are, within the context of our D/s dynamic, proper ways to express yourself and your opinion. I'm not saying this is the way everyone does it, but it's the way I do it. I don't mind disagreement. It's how that disagreement is presented. I expect a submissive of mine to behave in a respectful way toward me at all times regardless of whether they agree with me or not."

"Hold on. You're not going to pass me around to other Dominants or something, are you?"

"No." He smiled. The damn, sexy smile that dampened her panties. "I do not share well with others. I should say, I don't share at all. Not my desserts, not my implements, and damn sure not my submissives. The only time I will allow a submissive of mine to play with another Top is if that Top is skilled in something I'm not, I trust the Top not to harm my submissive, and the submissive must ask me for permission. I will never volunteer my submissive to do something like that. I'm a Dominant, not a douche."

"I have a feeling there are a lot of things I'm going to have to learn."

"Since I'm pretty busy, and since I prefer an independent submissive over a clingy person, I don't think you'll have any trouble with my requirements. One requirement I will not bend on is I do not like drama."

"What do you mean by that?"

He shrugged. "We're both adults. What I expect from you is if you have a problem with something at any time that you code and talk to me about it. You don't pitch a hissy fit, you don't give me the silent treatment, you don't play mind games, you don't get passive-aggressive. And in return, I will give you the same respect." He smiled. "The only mindfucks I engage in are in the middle of a scene. But I don't have time or energy to deal with drama. I won't hesitate to walk away from drama without a look back."

"Sounds fair enough." *It'll be a relief compared to James.*

"By code, I mean you call *red*. It's that simple. Whether it's in the middle of a scene or like now, in the middle of a restaurant. You say *red*, and we stop and talk about whatever it is."

"That simple?"

He nodded. "That simple. As for rules, for the basics, I want you to text me every morning when you get up, and every night before you go to bed."

"Why?"

"Routine. We don't live together. I want my submissive to have a routine to stick to when she can't be with me."

"Fair enough." She took a sip of her tea.

"And you do not masturbate without texting me for permission first."

She nearly spewed her tea over the table. "You're not serious?"

She spotted his sly smile. "Oh, I'm absolutely serious. You want to do this or not?"

She blinked and studied him. His gaze never wavered from hers. "Why?"

"Because I said so."

"But what if I don't want you to have control over that?"

"Then you need to take that off the table now. But if you want orgasm play to be part of what we do, that's one of my conditions."

She swallowed hard. Her mind flashed back to the scenes she'd witnessed last weekend. And to the sexy, hot dreams she'd been having of Tony Daniels and his wicked, wicked ways.

As the seconds ticked by, his smile widened until he eventually said, "You're not taking it off the table?"

"I'm thinking."

"That's not a no."

"It's not a yes, either," she shot back. "Sir."

He smiled. "Good girl."

Her pussy clenched. *I'm single. He's single.*

Why the fuck not?

"Okay," she whispered. "Sir."

"Okay that orgasm control and play is on the table?"

She nodded.

* * * *

Damn. And I'd just gotten my cock under control, too. Not that he was complaining. A chance to have this woman squirming under his hands?

Yes, please!

He would go slow with her, though. He didn't want to scare her off. He damn sure didn't want to pressure her to do anything she might regret later.

"Let me tell you my thoughts," he said, "and you correct me if there's anything you want to change. Okay?"

She nodded.

He'd let the lack of a verbal answer slip this time because he could tell she was still wrapping her head around the situation.

"Orgasm play. Not the first night out, perhaps, but once you're comfortable. I'll keep my clothes on and only use hands or toys on you. And I won't let anyone else touch you."

She nodded.

"The reason I want you to hand over control of your orgasms to me is psychological," he explained. "If you can't have them when you want them, you want them all the more. That makes you more receptive during training to the reward phase."

"Reward phase?"

He smiled. "Yes, reward." He reached across the table and gently touched his index finger to the center of her forehead. "I'm going to show you how easy it is to rewire a brain to crave pain with pleasure."

He noticed she didn't lean away from his touch before he finally drew back.

"I'm not a dog," she said.

"No, but I do enjoy puppy play." When he spotted her frown, he quickly added, "*Human* puppy play. It has nothing to do with bio-dogs. I enjoy it from a training and discipline aspect."

"I read about that. I think." She looked unsure.

"It's okay. That's something we can talk about more tomorrow. Tell me about your hard limits."

She looked like a deer in the headlights. "No choking. And I don't want to have any of my limbs cut off. Sir. No bleeding. Not on purpose, at least."

He liked her snarky sense of humor. "Well that's a good thing, because I don't like amputations myself. Normally, if I was in a relationship with someone, I'd go through an extremely exhaustive list with them, more than once, to find out what their likes and dislikes are. Since this is a slightly different situation and there isn't any sex involved, and since you want to experience various things, we're going to take a different approach."

"I thought we were going to do orgasm play?" She almost looked slightly panicked.

Hmm. "Sex and orgasm play are two different things," he told her.

"Huh?"

"Yes, we'll be doing orgasm play. Meaning I get you off if I so choose. You are not responsible for my orgasms."

"What if I want to be?"

His cock throbbed again. *Down, boy.* "I appreciate that, but I'd rather not muddy the waters right now with sex. Nothing personal, and yes, I do find you attractive. But as a Dominant, I refuse to be a douche. That means until I feel the time is right, regardless of a sub's thoughts on the matter, I keep sex off the table. That's for your protection. Okay?"

She eventually nodded. "Okay. Thank you. Sir," she added.

"Let me also add that I won't renegotiate in the middle of a scene. If I have you tied down and you beg me to do something outside of our original negotiation, it will not happen. I want you to be able to trust me, which means under no circumstances will I violate a boundary mid-scene. Trust can never be completely rebuilt once it's shattered. I will stop a scene and wait until I feel you're able to rationally discuss something if that's what it takes, but I will not take a scene farther than our preset limits."

He noticed she flinched a little during all of that. "What's wrong?"

"Nothing. Sir." He noticed she was working to try to remember to add that to her answers.

"You reacted to something I just said. I saw it."

She shook her head. "It's all right. It doesn't matter."

He mentally replayed what he'd just said. "No, I saw you reacted. I need you to tell me."

* * * *

Dammit. It was spooky how tuned in he seemed. She took a deep breath. "You probably should know up front I don't trust easily. It's not you. Nothing personal."

He nodded. "All the more reason for me to take things slowly." He wouldn't take his gaze off her. "Is that what you reacted to? Me talking about trust?"

After a deep breath, she slowly nodded.

"Something you want to talk about tonight?"

"I'd rather not. Not here and now."

"Understood. So how long do you want to continue doing this?"

"Doing what?"

"Being trained as a submissive."

"I don't know."

"Well, with my work schedule, most of my available time is on the weekends. The less time we have to do this, the less I'll be able to teach you. It'll be cramming a ton of stuff into a very short amount of time."

"Oh. Yeah." She considered it. "I should probably have my last article in by the second week of June. It's almost the end of March. How about until the last day of May, unless we decided to stop sooner?"

He nodded. "Sounds good to me. I'm going to be away for a couple of weeks in early June anyway. I have to go out to Denver to oversee the equipment installation in a new data center my company is building out there. Construction is on track. As long as there aren't any delays, we start installs on June second. Once I'm out there, I need to be fully focused on what I'm doing. It's going to be a monster pain in the ass to get it up and running in the time allotted. I'll barely have time to eat and sleep, much less be social. So that's perfect timing. A little over eight weeks." He nodded. "That's reasonable. And of course you're free to alter the timeframe up or down if you want. It's just my schedule might get in the way."

"Yes, Sir." It felt more comfortable every time she said it.

"And that's another thing. Our professional lives have to come first. I won't knowingly give you any orders that will interfere with your job, and there might be times we have plans that I'll have to change or cancel if work issues come up. If any orders I give you cause you problems with work, you have to code and tell me that up front."

"Yes, Sir."

He smiled. "Good girl. What we do needs to be tempered with a good dose of common sense. If I give you an order that you cannot in all practicality perform, use your best judgment and talk to me about it when you can."

"Yes, Sir."

By the time they called for their checks an hour later, Shayla realized she'd had a more in-depth conversation with Tony in that short amount of time than she'd ever had with James in eight years. Including Tony initiating a frank, and thankfully brief, discussion about STDs and their sexual health histories even though they wouldn't actually be having sex.

It reinforced her opinion that she could trust him to be a man of his word. She also knew more about Tony as both a person and as a Dominant, vanilla and kinky things, than she realized in retrospect that she'd ever known about James.

How could I have been so blind?

Yes, she'd dated a few guys before James, even slept with two of them. *Why did I settle for someone who, in retrospect, was a tight-lipped, secretive, deceitful sack of monkey shit?*

Yes, it was pointless to keep kicking at that dead horse. She could second-guess herself until time ended and she likely wouldn't have any answers.

It also wouldn't change anything.

Moving the fuck on.

With the bills settled, Tony walked her out to her car. "I'm looking forward to tomorrow, pet," he said, looking down into her eyes.

She blinked. "Pet?"

She suspected that damn smile of his would be her undoing. "Yes. Objections?"

She shook her head. "No, Sir."

"Good girl." He held her door open as she climbed in. "Be on time tomorrow, pet. I hate tardiness."

"Yes, Sir."

With that he closed her door and stepped back. She started the car and drove off.

* * * *

He waited until she drove away to get into his car. He immediately called Leah.

She sounded concerned. "What's up?"

"Talk to me about Shayla."

Her tone turned guarded. "What do you mean?"

"I had dinner alone with her tonight—"

"Oh? That's good."

"And I know you, Loren, Tilly, and Clarisse spent the day together yesterday. Talk to me about what's going on with her."

"I don't know what you mean."

"Bullshit. I'm guessing she had a dick for an ex."

He heard Leah's sigh on the other end. "I can't tell you."

"Why not?"

"Because she confided in us and asked us not to tell anyone."

Fuck. "Am I stepping into a landmine with her? Tell me now before I get too involved with her."

"What? Involved with her how?"

"She asked me to train her as my submissive."

"Oh. Oh! That's good, right?"

He rolled his eyes. "Quit screwing around, Leah. I'll ask Seth to put you on chastity lockdown for me."

"Tony, please. She confided in us something that happened. Yes, her ex was a dick. Not abusing her, as far as I know. But what he did that caused her to leave him hurt her badly. You need to ask her about it."

"I plan to. I just wanted to go in armed with as much knowledge as I can get."

Leah hesitated, no doubt trying to figure out how to answer him without breaking Shayla's trust.

"Is what happened related to why she moved to Florida?" he asked to give her an opening.

"Yes," she said.

Okay, so twenty questions it is. "Is her ex a psycho who might hunt her down and I'll end up in the middle of it?"

"No. I don't think so. She didn't say anything to that effect. She got the job through a friend of a friend or something. Came up fast and she jumped at the chance to get out of Ohio because of the timing."

"The timing of what happened between her and her ex?"

"Yes."

He chewed on that. "You can't give me any clues, huh?"

She hesitated again. "You know how sometimes people ask you to bring DVDs to the private parties?"

He frowned. "The porn?"

"Yeah. I mean, I know it's not a big deal to you, and I know it's not like you substitute that for reality or anything."

He snorted. "No. Most of it I don't even watch. It's just for background. I'm in IT so I'm automatically everyone's go-to guy for good porn. Well, watchable porn in terms of video quality. I wouldn't say a lot of it's very good."

"Right, exactly," she said. When she next spoke, she kept her voice slow and deliberate. "Some people…might not…have the same…*feelings*…about that."

"About porn?"

"I didn't say that," she quickly said.

"Then what did you…" He thought about it. "Oh. That's your hint."

She cleared her throat. "I didn't say that either."

"Keep my computer locked down?"

"I didn't say that, but it wouldn't be a bad idea."

"Okay. I'm tracking. Her ex was a porn addict?"

"You did *not* hear that from me."

He smiled. "No, I didn't, but it gives me a starting point to avoid the minefield."

"Oh, and Tony?"

"Yeah?"

Leah sounded worried. "She's got some big trust issues. Legitimately. Okay? There's more to it than that, but she needs to be the one to tell you."

"She did tell me that little bit, which is why I'm talking to you now. And no, I'm not going to throw her naked into a puppy pile Saturday night at the club if that's what you're worried about." A couple of friends of his from the Tampa area, who were into pup and pony play, would be at the play session Saturday night.

Shayla would make a cute puppy.

She snorted, amused. "No, that's not what I was worried about, smart-ass, but thank you. I know she's in good hands with you."

He thought about Shayla's rounded hips, how her ass moved in her jeans.

I'd love to have my hands on her bare flesh. "Thanks, Leah. I appreciate it." He hung up and drove home, deep in thought.

* * * *

Shayla drove home, deep in thought. Her pulse raced. *Ohmigod…ohmigod…ohmigod!* She couldn't believe she'd agreed to this.

Then again…not much about her life had changed.

Had it?

How much different was it, really, than dating a guy? At least Tony spoke his mind and decisively told her what he did and didn't want. No mind games. Not about their dynamic, at least.

But she felt different. She wasn't able to put her finger on it, but she did.

No doubt Tony would eventually force a discussion about James, but she hoped it'd be later rather than sooner before she had to talk about it.

She undressed and started to put her phone on the charger when she realized she hadn't texted him yet as ordered.

Well, I was just with him a few minutes ago. He didn't mean tonight, did he?

She stroked the screen for a moment, undecided.

Hell with it. She pulled his number up from her contacts and sent him a quick text. *Better safe than sorry.*

She typed, *Good night, Sir.*

A moment later, her phone vibrated in reply. *Good girl. Good night, pet.*

She blinked as she read and reread it. That little thrill ran through her again.

Pet.

She couldn't help the smile. She liked it.

She put the phone on the charger and lay down to try to sleep. That was when she realized how horny she was.

She'd even rolled over to get the vibrator out of her drawer when she remembered Tony's admonition about needing his permission to orgasm.

Dammit!

She thought about it. *I could do it and not tell him.*

But then again, that would be violating the spirit of their agreement.

Conflict ran through her mind. She'd left James for what boiled down to the fact that he couldn't control his libido.

That washed over her desire like cold water. She wasn't like James. She was far better than James. And she would be with Tony tomorrow. Maybe he'd even take care of her itch for her.

She closed her eyes and willed herself to sleep, praying dreams of Tony would fill her night.

Chapter Thirteen

Shayla gave herself plenty of time Saturday morning. She was up, had texted Tony, got herself caffeinated, showered, dressed, and out the door by nine o'clock in search of a thong. Fortunately, they had them on sale at her first stop, Target, so she bought an array of colors.

Including several in black in preparation for any similar orders Tony might throw her way.

Returning home, she tried a pair on and remembered why she hated thongs. The back piece immediately slid between her cheeks.

Maybe I should just go commando.

Her face heated as she thought about that. If Tony ended up bending her over one of the spanking benches later that night, she'd be flashing everything for the world to see. Not that a thin wedge of ass floss uncomfortably digging between her cheeks was much in the way of cover, but it was the principle of the matter.

Which brought her to another thought.

Hmm. She kept her bush trimmed close, hating to let it get long and shaggy. But she wasn't shaved down there. She'd noticed most of the women at the club had been either totally devoid of carpet, making matching the drapes a moot point, or had the barest landing strip of hair down there.

Back to the shower it is.

When she emerged, she'd left a small landing strip surrounding her clit for modesty more than anything. Again, not that it would conceal much, but she preferred to think of it that way. By the time she fixed herself some lunch, changed into her sundress and thong, put on the lightest of makeup, and styled her hair, she had forty-five minutes to get to the club.

Plenty of time.

Curbing her anxiety, she tossed a pair of jeans, a blouse, a bra, a pair of real underwear, and a sweater into a tote bag to take with her.

Just in case.

She could wear the sandals with the jeans or her sundress. Grabbing her purse, notebook, and pen, she took a deep breath and headed out to her car while fighting the urge to dig the thong out of her ass.

This will take some getting used to.

Tony's car wasn't there when she pulled up to the club ten minutes early. In fact, no cars were parked outside the club.

She texted him. *I'm here.*

He replied in seconds. *ETA 5.*

Sure enough, his car pulled into the lot five minutes later. He parked next to her and got out wearing that panty-melting smile of his.

This thong won't be any help.

If anything, the way it rubbed between her legs was just making matters worse, although the distraction from the way it dug into her ass tempered the sexy effect somewhat.

She hoped she didn't end up with a wet spot on her dress.

He removed the toybag from his trunk along with an additional bag, and a blue plastic tube about a yard long that had a strap he slung over his shoulder.

"What's that?" she asked.

He grinned. "Your doom." When her eyes widened, he laughed. "Sorry, I've always wanted to say that. It's my cane and crop tube." He locked his car and headed to the front door. After finding the right key, he opened it. "After you."

"No alarm?"

"Nope. He doesn't keep cash on the premises."

She walked into the office as far as the daylight drifting into the room allowed for her to see. He left the two bags just inside the front door and walked over to a wall switch, hitting it. The office lights came up.

"Let me get the ones inside." He disappeared through the play space door. A moment later, he returned without the tube. "All set. I should probably ditch the 'come into my parlor' line of jokes, huh?"

She smiled. "I'm all right. Sir," she added.

He laughed. "You're a quick study. I like that."

She followed him into the larger area. He'd brought all the house lights up, which brightly lit the entire area. During the play session last week, softer lights and individual, colored lights illuminated the play area, adding a feeling of intimacy to the setting, while the lights over the social area were much dimmer. He took his bags over to a table at the front of the social area, where she saw he'd also left the tube. He opened one of the bags and rooted around inside it for a moment. When he straightened, he had a couple of items in his hand.

"Put your things on the table," he said, his voice slipping into a lower, more serious tone. "Including your glasses."

Without hesitation, she did.

"Good girl. Arms out in front of you."

She did, struggling against her nerves. He buckled a black leather cuff around her left wrist, then her right one. "Not too tight, are they?" he asked.

She shook her head even as her pulse raced. *Well, I asked for this.*

He pointed at the floor. "When I do this, I expect you to kneel in front of me. I shouldn't have to say a word about it."

She knelt on the floor.

"Good girl. Hold your hair out of the way."

When she did, he buckled a matching leather collar around her neck, inserting a couple of fingers between it and her flesh to check the fit. "Too tight, or good?"

She let go of her hair and swiveled her head around. "It's good. Sir."

He laughed. "I like how you remember to add it on. Don't worry, it'll become a habit soon enough." He stood in front of her and her heart pounded as she recalled her dreams. "Hands on your knees," he quietly said.

She did.

He stood there for a moment, not speaking. As the air conditioner kicked on, the silence in the immense room deafened her, made her acutely aware of how vulnerable she was.

And the fact that she hadn't thought to tell anyone what she was doing. That she would be here alone with Tony.

Don't be stupid. Everyone trusts him.

She flinched a little when he rested one hand on the top of her head. "It's all right, pet," he softly soothed. "I just need to go over a few things with you. For starters, when we're alone, you will give me a greeting before we start our play. You will kiss my feet—the tops, not the bottoms—the backs of my hands, and then…" He laughed. "I guess we'll modify the last part. You'll nuzzle my cock through my pants. Understood?"

"Yes, Sir."

"No objections?"

"No, Sir."

"Good girl. Greeting, pet."

She leaned forward and kissed each motorcycle boot, on the top of his foot. Then she sat up and pressed her lips against first his left hand, then his right. His height and her position put her at the perfect position to lean in and rub her nose against the zipper of his jeans.

She didn't think it was her imagination that the bulge there grew a little.

"Good girl. Stand up."

She did, a little disappointed to know nothing else was going to happen, and amused to see him adjust himself through his jeans.

"Skirt up."

She swallowed. "What? I mean, Sir?"

He cocked his head at her. "I gave you specific instructions on how to dress. Show me."

"Oh." She looked at the floor, her face blazing hot as she lifted her skirt.

"No. Look me in the eye."

It took her longer to force her gaze up to his than it did to hold her skirt up.

"Keep your skirt up until I say put it down," he sternly said when her hands had started to lower.

She jerked her hands up again, forcing herself to maintain contact with his green eyes.

He looked amused. "How do you feel right now, pet?"

"Exposed," she squeaked.

He chuckled. "Good. That's the way I want you to feel. Exposed and vulnerable. I want to force you out of your comfort zone. I need you to be able to trust me. I need my commands to become second nature in your brain. Where you respond to me, not to anything around you. Where your focus is solely on me and you can trust me and let go regardless of what else you might feel."

She nodded.

He walked around her. "Hike the back of your dress up, too, pet. Let me see."

Swallowing again, she adjusted her grip on the fabric until the skirt was gathered around her waist.

"Spread your legs. More," he ordered when she didn't spread them to his liking.

Now her face felt like a neon beer sign in the window of a bar next to a dry county.

His soft voice in her left ear startled her. "How do you feel now, pet?"

"Extremely exposed, Sir," she whispered.

"Good. Stand like that until I say otherwise, with your skirt up and your feet spread." He turned his back on her and walked over to his bag and grabbed a couple of items. When he returned, she saw he had the metal whisks from the other night, a short, leather strap with a solid handle she knew was called a slapper, and a…

"Is that a spatula, Sir?"

He grinned and held the black object up. "Yep. Good for scraping batter out of bowls, or smacking subbies' asses." He stepped in close and hooked a finger through the front D-ring on the collar. "I'm not going to hurt you," he said. "And as I told you, you can always call *red*. I want to give you a little taste of what I have in store for you later tonight, so you have something to look forward to. Any objections?"

She shook her head. "No, Sir."

His grin did dangerous things to her reserve. "That's my good girl. Keep that dress up and those feet apart."

He released her collar and walked around behind her. She flinched again when she felt his hands on the thong's waistband.

Then she realized he was pulling it down her legs.

She closed her eyes and pressed her lips together as she felt what little covering she'd had disappear.

He put an arm around her waist to steady her and tapped her right leg. "Step up, pet."

She lifted her foot and felt him pull the thong off her leg and drop it to the floor, where it puddled around her left ankle. "Foot down, pet."

She complied.

"Legs apart, like I told you." This time he nudged her right foot out with his. The boot leather felt warm against the side of her foot through the sandal.

He stepped away again. She heard him move in front of her. "Do you want a blindfold, pet?"

"Yes, Sir." The words slipped from her lips without even needing to think about them.

"Ah, my poor, bashful pet. I should make you watch this time, but I won't. I'll go easy on you." She heard him walk away. Then he rummaged through his bag, his boot heels making solid sounds on the painted concrete floor as he returned. She felt him slip a soft leather blindfold over her head and buckle it.

"How's that, pet?"

She nodded. "Good, Sir."

Even the word "pet" had taken on a new connotation for her. It felt like a new name. She was his pet, his toy, his plaything.

She heard him pick up one of the items he'd left on the floor next to her feet. When the plastic touched the skin of her inner right thigh, she twitched but didn't draw her legs closed.

"Keep that skirt up, pet," he said in a low warning tone when she'd let it slip. She yanked it back up again, bunching it in her hands so she could keep her elbows at her sides and not drop the fabric.

He lightly slapped her ass and thighs with the slapper first, just barely enough to be stingy in a pleasant, scratching-an-itch kind of way. After a few minutes of that he switched to the spatula.

He caressed up and down her inner thigh with the spatula, down to her calf, behind her knee, with both the flat side of it and the edge. Then up her thigh, just between her legs where he skipped her clit and pussy altogether and repeated the teasing on her left leg.

"You're wet, pet. I can smell you." He sounded amused.

He didn't chide her for not replying, so she remained silent.

He did that for long minutes, back and forth.

Then a stingier slap, against her inner right thigh, making her yip in surprise more than pain.

"Legs apart!" he barked. It startled her, and she forced them apart. He started slapping the insides of her thighs with the spatula, up and down, the backs of her legs, her ass. Not as hard as she suspected he could hit, but in a few moments she felt the stinging all over.

He stopped, which shocked her almost as much as when he'd started.

His warm breath blew across her clit. "My poor, wet pet." He lightly brushed her clit with the spatula.

She froze, which didn't escape his notice. "Good girl. Hold very still." He slipped the edge of the spatula back and forth through the folds of her labia and up the seam of her ass, teasing her. She pressed her lips together to try to hold back her whimpers.

It seemed nothing escaped his notice. "Make all the noise you want, pet. It's just us."

He dragged the edge of the spatula across her clit. That made her moan and involuntarily thrust her pelvis forward, wanting to maintain contact with it.

"Good girl," he cooed. "That's exactly what I want you to do." He repeated the motion, tormenting her with the spatula, making her clit swell and throb even as her pussy began to dully ache with a cramping need she knew only an orgasm would take care of.

When was the last time I felt like this?

That would be never.

Even James, in the best of days, had never inspired this much desire, this much blatant need in her.

Suddenly, all contact ceased. She moaned.

"Patience, pet. You gave me control of this. That means we do it my way." Then cool metal touched her inner thighs.

The whisks. He slid them up and down her legs, occasionally brushing against her clit in the process and tormenting her even more.

"How do you feel, pet?"

She had to lick her lips. It took every ounce of will to speak. "Horny, Sir."

"Good girl."

Something else touched her clit. She didn't have time to process what it was when he sternly ordered, "Come for me, pet." A strong, vibrating buzz filled the air and her clit at the same time.

She cried out, surprised, but even more shocked when her body responded and an orgasm pulsated through her. Her knees went out from under her, but Tony's arm appeared around her waist to catch her. He kept the vibrator firmly pressed against her pussy with his other hand. "You can do it, pet. Give me another."

She sobbed as another one did, in fact, roll through her. Her legs felt like they couldn't support her at all. He slowly eased her to the floor before pulling the vibrator away and shutting it off. As she lay there recovering, she realized she was curled half in his lap and half on the floor.

It took her a couple of minutes for her breathing to slow and her wits to return. He unbuckled the blindfold and carefully removed it. She blinked against the sudden intrusion of light and looked up into his face.

His serene, satisfied smile beamed down at her. "I think you have achieved at least partial comprehension."

She closed her eyes and nodded as she let her head fall to his lap again.

He laughed. "Poor pet. Two orgasms and you're worn out already."

He helped her to her feet after removing the thong from around her ankle. He led her over to the couches, grabbing a clean, folded towel from a basket next to them. He spread it out for her before easing her down onto the couch.

He knelt in front of her so he could look her in the eye. "We've got about twenty minutes or so before anyone arrives. Take a few minutes. Okay?"

She nodded. He reached out and stroked her hair. "You all right?"

She nodded and closed her eyes. *I'm better than all right.*

And he was right.

Now she did understand at least part of the attraction of BDSM.

* * * *

He studied her face for a moment before standing and leaving her. *Dammit*, now his cock felt like it was going to explode.

He grabbed the vibrator, spatula, and whisks he'd used on her and took them into the men's room. How long had it been since he'd had that much fun giving a woman an orgasm?

Too damn long.

He hadn't planned on doing orgasm play with her that soon, but when he'd laid his hand on the vibrator in his search for the second whisk, the temptation had just been too great. He wasn't even sure he would use it on her, until the way she arched her back to push her clit out against the spatula.

She hadn't shied away from him at all. He washed the implements and the vibrator with soap and water and left them on the edge of the sink. He walked into one of the three stalls, locked the door behind him, and unfastened his jeans.

He already had a wet spot on the front of his briefs where his cock strained against the material.

Freeing it, he spit in his palm and started stroking, hard, with his eyes closed. It didn't take more than a few seconds before jets of cum exploded from him and left him shaking so hard he had to lean against the wall of the stall for support.

Fuck. No one had ever affected him like that before. Taking him dangerously close to a loss of control. He hadn't expected her to agree to nuzzling him through his pants. He would have understood if she'd refused to do it.

But she hadn't. It didn't take any great leap of imagination to think about sinking his cock into her throat between those delicious lips of hers as she nuzzled his bulge.

Not that he would have forced himself on her, but he had come dangerously close to coming in his pants toward the end of their play.

He opened his eyes and let out a snort. *I made a bigger mess than she did.* One splash had hit the tile wall at the back of the toilet. Another string had landed on the seat.

He snickered. After he relieved himself into the toilet he cleaned himself and the stall up, flushed, and went back out to wash his hands and gather the implements.

Shayla still lay on the couch where he'd left her. She'd felt so good in his arms. If the damn floor hadn't been so hard and cold he could have easily sat there for hours with her nestled in his lap.

Don't rush things. You've already rushed enough.

He put the implements away and went to check on her. "How's my pet?"

She opened her eyes and smiled. "I think I need a nap."

"That would be nice, but unfortunately we have a class now."

She sat up. He wondered if that same, sweetly dreamy look she now wore was the same post-orgasmic look she always wore.

He also wondered how deep into subspace he'd driven her with that play session.

He reached out and tucked a strand of hair behind her ear. "Go get cleaned up, pet." He handed her the thong. "You might as well keep that off for now until we go out to dinner." He smiled. "I suspect it won't do you much good anyway."

Her face reddened again as she took the sodden thong from him. "Thank you, Sir," she mumbled.

"And you can take the cuffs off. Leave the collar on, though. I want you to wear it during both classes."

"Yes, Sir."

"When I introduce myself, I will be introducing you as my submissive. All right?"

She nodded. "Yes, Sir." She wouldn't meet his gaze.

He reached out and tipped her chin up, forcing her to look at him. "Another rule. When I speak to you, unless I've instructed you not to, you will look me in the eyes. Understand?"

He noticed she swallowed hard. Another nervous tic, he suspected. He'd noticed her doing it several times during the course of their previous conversations and today. "Yes, Sir."

"Good girl." He kissed the top of her head. "Go clean up."

He watched her get up, carefully observing her to make sure she was steady on her feet. As she walked toward the bathroom, he laughed. "You can straighten your skirt and put it down now, pet."

She looked at him over her shoulder. "Thank you, Sir."

Although the view is nicer when your ass is bare.

* * * *

Shayla looked at herself in the mirror. Her hair was mussed and her face still pink. *I should have skipped the makeup.* She washed her face and patted it dry with a paper towel. Then she took a couple of dampened paper towels into a stall with her. After using the toilet, she cleaned herself up as best she could. She patted her pussy as dry as she could with yet another paper towel and washed her hands.

I look like I've just been fucked.

The burping laugh escaped her.

You were just fucked. Sort of.

Holy crap, if he could do that to her with just that little bit of play, what else did he have in store for her tonight?

She realized she didn't care, and that she was eager to feel every last bit of it.

Chapter Fourteen

Shayla walked over to the table and tucked her thong into her bag. He was right. It was pretty useless.

Add to that the fact that she'd be plagued from there on with the memory of the feel of him slowly removing it from her, and she might as well have a vibrator strapped to her clit as wet as it threatened to make her.

Maybe I need to grab that towel from the couch to keep on my chair during class.

"How are you doing, pet?" Tony asked.

She noticed while she was in the bathroom he'd opened the other bag he'd brought inside. Two tables were covered with different kinds of whips in various colors and configurations.

"Good, Sir," she said.

He grinned. "Ready for more?"

Why fight it? She smiled. "Yes, Sir. I think so."

"Good girl." He started to say something else when the door opened and a woman called out. "Tony?"

He looked around Shayla and held up a hand. "Over here, Jenny."

The woman stepped into the area. "Oh, good. I thought that was your car. You need anything?"

"Nope. We're all set up."

The woman's brow furrowed. "'We?'"

"Yes. I'd like to introduce you to Shayla. My submissive."

Shayla felt heat fill her face…along with a thrill she couldn't place.

The woman walked over and smiled at Shayla. Shayla didn't remember seeing her the previous weekend. "Nice to meet you. I'm Jenny."

Tony let out a laugh. "You can shake hands with her, Jenny."

Shayla sent him a puzzled glance as Jenny smiled again and stuck out her hand. "I always like to make sure first," Jenny said.

As they shook hands, Shayla noticed Jenny wore a rainbow-hued collar made up of what looked like a small-gauged rod. "I'm new at this. Shayla. Or Shay. Nice to meet you."

"She's a reporter," Tony said. "She's doing firsthand research for a series of articles she's writing. Loren and Ross hooked us up."

"Oh!" Jenny brightened. "Okay. Leah did mention that. Let me know if you have any questions. I'm happy to answer. You've got a great teacher, here." She motioned toward Tony. She was going to say something else, but they heard a noise in the office. "Oops, sounds like the students are arriving. Talk to you later." She hurried back to the office.

Shayla looked up at him. "What was that about? The hand shaking?"

"Some people are ultracautious about protocols. Some Masters have strict rules about their slaves and submissives not having physical contact with others. Some slaves and submissives just aren't comfortable with contact with others. When in doubt, it's easier to just wave hi and not risk accidentally pissing someone off."

"Is that really a problem?"

"Not a huge one. But all it takes is one mouthy won twue wayer to get bent out of shape and a community feud can arise. Obviously, if the submissive offers to shake hands or moves to hug you first, it's all right."

"That sounds complicated."

"Not really. You'll see what I mean."

Tony had a full class of twenty-five students. Her initial unease at briefly being made the center of attention by Tony's quick intro soon faded as she found herself immersed in his class. His talk about whips, how they were made, the different styles and materials was not only instructive, but entertaining as well.

Once he'd gone through the basics, he moved the class over to the play side of the space, where he hung a paper napkin from one of the suspension bars. He'd used a black marker to draw a small circle on the napkin, toward the bottom edge.

Uncurling one of the whips, a four-foot kangaroo-hide signal whip, he demonstrated the proper stance and technique.

"Your first concern is accuracy, not trying to make it crack. If you make it crack too loudly too many times in an enclosed space like this, someone's liable to ask you to stop or leave. Remember, consent is one of the core values of what we do, and making everyone in the room deaf without their consent is generally frowned upon."

Shayla found herself chuckling with the group.

He showed the class how to judge distance and how to properly throw the whip. The fall of the whip caught the napkin exactly at the circle, leaving a slight rip in the paper.

He turned back to the class. "You also have to worry about who and what is around and above you. I know some people think they need a six- or eight-foot whip, but good luck finding indoor venues who'll let you use it. You'll clear a room. Literally, because of the space they require. We have a couple of members of this club who can properly use a whip like that and who are sometimes granted permission to use them inside during play sessions. But again, it goes back to consent. You don't have a right to inconvenience others with your kink. So stick to a three- or four-foot whip to start with. Three is better. If you plan on doing a lot of outdoor play, or your house is large enough to allow you to play with a longer whip, sure, go longer. You will, however, get more use out of a shorter one."

He let all the students take a try with the whip, including Shayla. She liked that she was the only student he pressed his body up against as he guided her through the motions.

"Another reason not to start with a longer whip," he explained as he uncoiled one, "is that you're more likely to hurt yourself with it. You can easily have it come back and wrap around you, or put out an eye. In fact, wearing eye and ear protection when you're first learning isn't a bad idea." He shook the whip out to its full length. "This one's eight feet long. Everyone stand way back, and plug your ears with your fingers."

They did.

He slipped a pair of foam ear plugs into his ears. Shayla guessed he considered his glasses adequate eye protection. Then he changed his position, judged the distance to the target, and threw the whip.

The loud *crack* exploded through the play space like a gunshot. The target, which he'd reset with a fresh napkin, barely moved.

But a fresh slice had appeared in the bottom of it.

He looked at them as he removed his earplugs. "Like that. Yes, shorter whips can make loud cracks, too. Usually, however, they aren't that loud. But how would you like to be scening and be deep in subspace just to be blasted out of it by that?"

Everyone nodded.

"When you're using a whip on a person, make sure you've done plenty of practice on inanimate objects first. It's way too easy to cut a person with a whip. You can snag piercings, wrap it and dig into flesh, cause permanent injury and scarring. Not exactly the kind of pain and marks most bottoms are looking for. If in doubt, stand farther away, and always throw gently until you can absolutely control every swing."

He coiled the whip and put it away. "Any questions?"

He spent the next half of the class working with students. Some had brought their own whips with them, some used ones he had available as loaners. Shayla's job was to go around and keep everyone supplied with fresh napkin targets, in addition to keeping track of the loaner whips. Every available piece of play equipment that was at least four feet tall had been put into use as target holders.

Leah and Seth arrived five minutes before the class was scheduled to end. She walked over to Shayla and gave her a hug. "How's it going? Looks like a full class, huh?"

She nodded. "Indiana Jones makes this crap look easy."

Leah laughed. "Seth, Tony, and Sully make Indiana Jones look like a damn puss."

At the end of class, Shayla helped Tony retrieve and account for all his loaner whips as well as make sure all the little bits of napkin targets were picked up.

"So does she get volunteered as a demo dolly today?" Seth joked with Tony.

He smiled. "Nope. I'm going to play along with the class and tie her up myself." He winked at her, sending her heart into an overdrive of fluttering. "I'll stick a ball gag in her mouth if she starts moaning too much."

"Good deal. I'm going to get my rope bag. I'm guessing you have your own?"

He smiled. "Yep. I packed the pink rope especially for her."

* * * *

The rope class was just as full as the whip class. Five of the students from the whip class were also taking the rope class. They moved a giant wooden A-frame off a large carpeted section to use the carpet to sit on, everyone gathered on the floor in a wide semicircle around Seth and Leah.

"Today's class is literally a basic overview," Seth told them. "I don't want to hear about any of you going out and trying to suspend someone tonight. We're starting a biweekly series of rope classes if anyone's interested in taking things further. Suspension without proper training and practice can be downright dangerous, if not deadly."

He started by demonstrating a basic series of wraps which, surprisingly, didn't involve any knots. Each student wound up creating a short wrist gauntlet that ended halfway up their forearm.

Except Shayla. She found her arms bound together in front of her in an arm binder tie using the same series of wraps Seth had explained to the class.

Seth laughed and pointed it out to everyone. "This is an example of what you can do with that same technique. I should add, for those of you who don't know him, Tony's advanced beyond basic rigging and has been doing it for a while."

Shayla marveled at how comfortable the tie felt. Unlike what she'd thought from some of the pictures she'd seen on the Internet, while restrictive, it didn't cut off her circulation or even cut into her skin. It felt firmly wrapped around her flesh, warming to her skin the longer it stayed on.

Tony had left a tail of rope by her hands. He grabbed it and raised her hands above her head. Leaning in, he whispered into her ear, "Now, just imagine being bound like this and me doing to you what I did earlier."

She let out a soft whimper she hoped the rest of the class couldn't hear.

He quickly unbound her as the class moved on to a different skill. By the time they finished with that, Shayla wore an intricate chest harness over her sundress. The ropes pushed and pinched her breasts, making them stand out and strain against the fabric.

Tony once again leaned in. With his body blocking her from view of the class, he brushed his fingers against her nipples where they stood out in stark relief through the fabric. "Poor, bound pet," he whispered. "Imagine if I had you tied like this, naked, and could torture your breasts and nipples. Along with a nice hip harness, with a couple of ropes rubbing against your clit."

She let out another soft whimper. Her pussy already cramped, aching for another round with the vibrator.

* * * *

Tony hoped he didn't end up with a wet spot on the front of his jeans. He enjoyed the glazed look that had returned to Shayla's eyes upon starting the rope class.

It was like Christmas had arrived and brought him a shiny new toy to play with.

One he didn't ever want to let go.

Patience.

Not necessarily one of his strong suits when faced with something he badly wanted. He hated it when people were labeled, by themselves or others, as a "natural submissive." Yes, some people took to certain aspects better and more quickly than others.

Shayla, he could see, had readily taken to sensual play. He suspected their night in the dungeon would bring a lot of eye-opening experiences for her. If all went well, he planned on asking her over to his house for more private play on Sunday.

He'd already told Jenny he wouldn't be able to DM that night because of Shayla, so his time was free.

By the time the class ended, he'd put her in two more basic ties, mercilessly teased her sexually until he knew she had to be hornier than hell, and suspected he might need to run to the men's room again to rub another one out when they finished.

Why did I take sex off the board? Oh yeah, because I'm an idiot, apparently.

No, he wouldn't ask her to put sex back on the table. Wouldn't even mention his condition to her. Tonight was about her and letting her experience what the BDSM world had to offer while building her trust in him. Patience was hard, but worth it.

She was most definitely worth it.

No one he'd played with in the past several years made him feel like this regardless of the level of play. The pure wonder on her face as she discovered new things, and he got to experience them along with her, reminded him of all the good there was in this lifestyle he'd chosen.

And for the first time in a long time, he realized he didn't feel the aching loneliness that had plagued him for so long.

Chapter Fifteen

Seth slung the rope bag over his shoulder and headed out to their car. "Are you guys coming to dinner with us?" Leah asked.

"Yes," Tony said before Shayla could answer. "We're taking my car. We'll be along shortly."

"Okay. See you there." Leah left the play space.

Tony looked at her. "How are you feeling, pet?"

She nodded. "Good, Sir."

"You don't mind we're driving over alone, do you?"

Shayla suspected he wanted to talk in private. "No, Sir. I don't mind."

"Good girl. Go get cleaned up. I'll get my bags loaded."

She headed to the bathroom, marveling at the already fading ligature marks left on her flesh from the pink rope. It hadn't been frightening at all. Not with Tony's skilled hands winding the rope around her...and teasing her into a sexual frenzy.

She looked herself in the eye in the mirror.

I'm going to take this all the way. No matter what else he wanted to do to her that night, she'd do her best to go along with it. His enthusiasm had proven infectious, and she didn't want it to end.

She gathered her things, including her glasses, which she'd almost forgotten, and met him out at his car, where she found her hunch had proven correct.

"Why did you move to Florida so suddenly?" he asked once they were underway.

She took a deep breath. "I needed a fresh start."

"A breakup?"

"Yeah. Yes, Sir, I mean."

He didn't take his eyes off the traffic. "I need you to be able to talk to me. To confide in me," he said. "No matter how uncomfortable it feels. I need to know these things so I don't accidentally do something douchey along the way and trigger you."

She was letting him have unfettered access to her lady parts. If she couldn't talk to him, she was seriously fucked in the head. "I caught my ex downloading porn. Most of it extreme BDSM porn. He downloaded it to my computer at home. He used his laptop for work and apparently didn't want to risk it. He thought since he'd set up a different user account on my computer that it wouldn't show up. I found out he'd spent about a thousand dollars on it.

"He swore he'd stop, that he'd never do it again." She picked at her cuticles. "He even proposed to me after being together nearly eight years at that point. I was stupid enough to believe him and we planned our wedding. The whole nine yards."

"But he did it again?"

"Yep. Yes, Sir."

"Tell me what happened." They pulled up to a red light and he looked at her.

"I caught him, only this time it was over fifteen grand, and on credit cards he secretly took out in my name. I called the wedding off, told everyone what he did, and left his ass. Moved to Florida after a friend of mine put me in touch with Bill Melling and he offered me a job."

"I'm surprised you're doing this story."

"Believe me, so am I. I thought maybe it would give me some answers."

"What did you feel?" he asked.

"What do you mean?"

He arched an eyebrow at her.

Inwardly, she sighed. This discussion had yanked her out of the emotional happy place she'd blissfully existed in since turning herself over to Tony hours earlier. "What do you mean, Sir?"

"When you found out what James did the second time?"

The muscles in her abdomen tightened dangerously as she fought back a rising rush of anger, turmoil, and bile in her gut. She remembered every second of that afternoon. Finding the mail on the back floorboard of her car, where he'd forgotten it behind the driver's seat after borrowing it. The PO Box address she didn't know about, but her name was on several of the bills. The way she got a paper cut sliding her finger under the first envelope's flap to open it. How her hands trembled when she pulled the credit card bill, several pages long, out of the envelope and tried to make sense of the charges.

Tried to make sense of line after line of charges to the same few websites.

How her body felt like it simultaneously burst into flames of rage and grew deadly cool at the same time as her brain struggled to process what it was she read.

The list, the all-too-familiar list of charges.

The credit card she damn well knew she'd never applied for, even though the bill was in her name. Repeating with the other envelopes, other credit card bills.

The way she collapsed, crying, at the latest check she received from James just days earlier.

Fuck.

"I really don't want to talk about it," she quietly replied. "Sir," she added. "Not right now. I want to enjoy tonight. I've had too good an afternoon with you to let that talk spoil my mood."

"Fair enough, pet. I do, however, want to talk about it at some point. Soon."

"Yes, Sir."

"I need to ask you this. If he was to show up on your doorstep tomorrow with the money to pay you off and asked you to take him back, would you?"

She shook her head. "Not a snowball's chance in hell. Fool me once and all that crap."

"You don't think he'll ever come down here and get violent with you, do you?"

"No. Part of me wishes he had hit me, as sick as that sounds. I'd like to think I would have left him sooner if he had."

"Don't blame yourself, pet. We all do silly things in the name of love, sometimes."

She let out a little snort.

"What?" he asked.

"I told the others. Leah and Tilly and Loren and Clarisse the other day when we were together. They pretty much said the same thing."

"Well, then. That should tell you something, right?"

"Yeah, but every time I look at how much I now owe because of him it makes me sick to my stomach."

"Yeah, I guess that is rough. He's paying you off though?"

"A little at a time. I don't know how long it'll last. I won't count on him following through."

"Can I ask one more thing and then I'll let it drop for tonight?"

"Yes, Sir."

"Why didn't you press charges? That's not meant to sound judgmental. I'm just curious."

"I keep asking myself that same question. I only wanted gone. Out of there. Either he was going to pay me back or he wasn't. He damn sure couldn't if he lost his job and was in jail."

"What does he do?" He glanced at her. "Sorry, I did say one more thing. You don't have to answer that."

"No, it's okay, Sir. He's a CPA, if you can believe that. Works for a pretty large firm in Cleveland."

"Wow. Okay, again, sorry, but have you checked your taxes to make sure they're okay?"

She smiled. "I always filed separately from him and I did my own. He always offered to do them, but mine were so simple I used the software. I'm actually looking forward to not having state income taxes to file now."

"Smart pet."

"I didn't know how smart at the time, but yeah, I'm glad I stuck to my guns on that one."

He reached across the seat and laced his fingers through hers. "No more questions about that. I'm sorry. Anything you want to ask me? Fair's fair."

She looked at him, studying his profile as he drove. He was a handsome man. To her, at least. "Tell me about your divorce."

He shrugged. "I didn't want kids. I told her that from the beginning. I made no secret about it. She said she was okay with that."

"She wasn't?"

"Nope. Apparently not. She spent the first several years hinting and trying her best to get me to agree to it. I refused. When she realized I really meant it and that I had scheduled an appointment for a vasectomy, she turned into three gallons of crazy in a two-gallon bucket."

Shayla laughed. "And that's why you're allergic to drama?"

"I had a low tolerance for it before that, but yes." He gently squeezed her hand. "I mean it when I say I don't want to be a douche. This is supposed to be fun for both of us." He glanced at her before returning his eyes to the road. "I need you to talk to me. I can't read minds. I expect you to call me out if you think I'm out of line. I want a submissive, not a doormat. I expect you to have opinions and to express them. I want to be worthy of your trust."

She felt the lump grow in her throat and swallowed it back. She squeezed his hand. "I don't think you're a douche, Sir," she quietly said. "And a lack of trust is because of me, not because of anything you've done. You've been great." She laughed. "This afternoon was fantastic."

He pulled into the restaurant's parking lot. "I feel honored that you've put what trust you can in me."

"Well, Leah, Loren, Tilly, and Clarisse all speak highly of you." She smiled. "I got the impression that Tilly isn't someone who trusts people lightly."

He laughed. "No, she's not. She's been through a lot, which you've probably already heard from her."

"Yes."

Loren and Ross had also arrived and stood with Seth and Leah in the restaurant's foyer, waiting for them. Tony gently grabbed Shayla's arm to stop her.

"Hold on, pet." She looked up at him and spotted his devilish grin. "I'm not going to force you to wear a leather collar in a vanilla restaurant on your first outing with me."

She felt her face heat immediately as he reached to the back of her neck to unbuckle the collar. She had forgotten all about it.

Loren giggled, but Shayla sensed it wasn't mean spirited. "Don't worry, I do that all the time. Ross is always having to remind me to take my collar off."

Tony handed it to her to slip into her purse before they found their way to their group of tables.

* * * *

Tony had almost let her go into the restaurant with the collar, but decided against it. He'd built her trust in him to a certain extent. He didn't want to go blowing that, no matter what sadistic little jollies he'd get over her wearing his collar in public. At least now he had the bulk of the story from her about what happened.

He felt outraged on her behalf. She was taking this a lot better than he would in her situation. He could understand her logic about not pressing charges despite it making her liable for the money.

Didn't mean he agreed with it.

Tilly, Landry, and Cris also joined them for dinner. Tony noticed after putting in their orders that the women disappeared en masse to the restroom.

"I think you're about to get graded, buddy," Seth teased him.

Tony nodded as he sipped his iced tea. "I believe you're right. They're going to make sure she's doing okay and get the dirt on this afternoon. Damn sneaky subs." He grinned.

Landry cleared his throat. "Speak for yourself. It's not the sub I have to worry about," he said as he cast a glance at Cris. "It's the switchy bitch I married." His playful smile belied his words. "She can be a holy terror, can't she, Cris?"

He let out a laugh. "You've got that right."

Ross shook his head. "They've adopted Shay into their ranks." He arched an eyebrow at Tony. "God help you if you piss those women off."

"Not in my game plan, believe me." The women returned from the bathroom at the same time a few minutes later. When Shay retook her seat next to him, he asked, "Interesting chat?"

She blushed a little. He doubted she was a good liar given how easily her skin took on that sweet, pink flush. "Just catching up, Sir."

He carefully watched her throughout dinner. She seemed more relaxed and engaged than she had last week, now that she was familiar with the other women.

When he started to think about what a nice tradition this would be, he snapped that line of thinking off at the source. There was an expiration date on this dynamic, unless she decided she wanted to make it a permanent one.

He knew if things continued to go as well as they were, he wouldn't mind that at all. Unless something cropped up, it would seem lightning had finally struck him and delivered his unicorn into his lap without him even looking.

Funny how that works.

He found her physically attractive, fun to play with, and interesting to talk to. They had similar interests in reading, movies, TV, and music. He hadn't seen her apartment yet, but unless she was a nominee for her own episode of *Hoarding: Buried Alive*, he didn't see anything that threw up red flags for him.

She was obviously an independent woman. Leaving behind everyone and everything she knew to move across the country to a state she'd never been to before to take a new job had to be a huge step for her.

When it was time to settle the checks, he picked up hers and refused to let her argue. "Leave it, pet. It's my treat."

Her face flushed a little. He could tell from the way her gaze kept trying to drift down to her lap that she struggled with his order to look him in the eye. "Thank you, Sir. I wasn't expecting that."

"It's not a problem. I can afford it, and I want to do it."

He draped an arm around her shoulders for the walk out to his car. *She fits me perfectly.*

It wasn't any large stretch to imagine what her body would feel like next to him in bed. However, that thought made his cock ache again, so he nipped it in the bud. He liked the way she leaned in against him as they walked.

"How are you feeling, pet?"

She smiled up at him. "Good, Sir."

"Ready to play?"

"Yes, Sir."

He stopped next to his car and took both of her hands. "I meant it when I say if something happens that you don't like, safeword immediately. I don't want to push you past your limits and have you hate me later. I'm not a douche."

"I don't think you're a douche, Sir."

"You're really okay with everything we did earlier? You won't hurt my feelings if you say no."

"I'm really okay, Sir."

"Good girl. I'm very proud of you for how you handled today. You did very well."

She blushed. "Thank you, Sir."

He opened the door for her and held it. "Take your collar out of your purse." She did and handed it to him. She held her hair out of the way while he buckled it around her neck. "Now let's go play."

Chapter Sixteen

Butterflies multiplied in Shayla's stomach at an alarming rate as they drew closer to the club. Armed with the confidence that she could stop events at any time, and with the support of the other women, she was determined to see the evening through to its conclusion.

I hope I don't embarrass him.

She blinked, glad for the darkness of the car's interior to hide her red cheeks. *Where'd* that *come from?*

The warm thrill from his praise still rolled through her.

I'm very proud of you.

When was the last time she'd heard those words out of anyone's mouth since she graduated from college?

James had damn sure never said them to her. A memory flashed to mind, of the day two years earlier, when she'd received word about an IR series she'd written about Medicaid fraud in Cleveland receiving a state journalism award.

She'd picked up the phone and called James about it before telling anyone else.

His response?

"That's nice. I'll talk to you when I get home."

How she'd bit back disappointment at his disinterested tone, swallowed her pride, and not mentioned it again to him.

Neither had he.

How could I have been so fucking blind for so long?

Yet the man never hesitated to crow about his work accomplishments, even getting a tad petulant with her if she didn't stroke his ego.

Maybe she was the crazy one after all, and the women and men she'd met in BDSM dynamics were the sane ones. They all asked for what they wanted and didn't settle. She'd spent eight years settling. Even before she moved in with James, once they'd started dating, she recalled times she'd changed things around in her apartment to please him regardless of how she felt about it.

How when they moved in together, it was easier for her to go along with what he wanted than to put up with his whining and badgering until she gave him his way.

She'd spent the first several weeks of her time in Florida doing her best not to think about James or what she'd been through, with the exception of the good times. She hadn't wanted to come to the conclusion that she'd flushed eight years of her life down the toilet.

Now, that realization slapped her in the face. When piled upon her mental scales, she couldn't ignore any longer that the good times she'd had with James were far outnumbered by the bad. Especially when she realized how much of her own personality and needs she'd put aside to make room for James and what she'd previously thought women were supposed to do in a relationship.

Then add in the mental anguish and money he'd caused, and cost, her.

It's a lesson I won't soon forget.

Tony's voice cut through her thoughts. "Are you all right, pet?"

They sat at a red light. The dashboard lights illuminated his concerned glance.

She reached over, found his hand, and squeezed. "I think," she softly said, "that I'm better than I've been in a long time, Sir."

He squeezed back and rewarded her with a smile. "Good. You looked pretty consternated there."

She laughed. "My boss calls it 'vexated.'"

He nodded as the light turned green and they started off again. "That's another good word, too. I hope I'm not the one vexating you."

She settled back in her seat. "No, Sir. I think you're the one *un*vexating me."

* * * *

It would be a busy night at the club. Shayla saw that nearly two dozen cars already sat in the parking lot when they pulled in behind Leah and Seth.

Before they got out, Tony patted her on the thigh. "Remember, pet. All you have to do at any time is say *red* and everything stops. Understand?"

"Yes, Sir."

She watched as his eyes seemed to search her face. "I don't want to push you too hard."

"I'm all right, Sir. I want to be pushed."

The corners of his eyes crinkled in amusement. "Be careful how you say that. You might find yourself coding sooner than you realize. But seriously, I don't want to be a douche—"

"Sir, please stop saying that. You're not a douche." She blew out a long breath. "Believe me, I know douches, and you've been anything but that."

The pity she read in his expression nearly made her burst into tears. "I'm sorry, pet. He did put you through the bad kind of mindfuck, didn't he?"

She nodded. "I really don't want to think about him anymore tonight. I'd rather spend the time letting you disengage my brain again, Sir."

As she said it, she realized that was exactly what it had felt like earlier.

He cocked his head. "What just went through your mind, pet? You look like you had an epiphany."

She ran her tongue over her front teeth as she considered it. She nudged her glasses up on her nose. "I think I did, Sir."

"Tell me."

She had no trouble meeting his gaze. "What we did earlier...it's like my brain just shut off."

"I hope that's a good thing."

She slowly nodded. "All I could focus on was what you were doing to me. Nothing else." A sense of wonder flowed through her. "I've never felt like that before."

He smiled. "I've heard subspace will do that to a person."

"Is that what it was?"

"From what I saw on my end, I think so."

She took a long, deep breath and let it out again before grinning. "I'd like to experience that again, Sir."

His grin probably matched hers. "You don't have to ask twice, pet. It'll be my pleasure, believe me."

She locked her glasses and her wallet in her car after getting her driver's license and a twenty-dollar bill from her wallet. Tony left his whip bag in the trunk and only got his cane case and toybag. She followed him inside the lobby and felt anticipation expanding in her chest.

She did want to do that again. Hit that blessed plateau where the only thing in her world that mattered was what Tony Daniels did to her.

She also thought she might have taken one step closer to comprehension.

They got checked in and found a place for their things near the play equipment. "Can I ask a stupid question, Sir?"

He grinned. "Sure."

"Why do you all go out to eat when the buffet is included in the price?"

He shrugged. "We've been doing it for years. It started as an offshoot of the Suncoast Society Munch group." He lowered his voice as people walked past them. "You know how you have different kinds of friends, like office coworkers, and good buddies you've known for years, and people you're socially acquainted with but aren't really friends with, like that?"

She nodded.

"It's the same for us here. I've got friends, like Seth and Leah, who I've known for years and consider good friends, even outside the lifestyle. I know plenty of people on a first-name-only basis through the scene that I usually only see here, but I wouldn't necessarily want to associate with them in vanilla life. If that makes sense?"

She nodded.

"I don't mean to come off sounding like an asshole by saying that. But those of us who come to the weekly dinner, we're all friends first, outside of the lifestyle and in it. We met through the lifestyle, but our friendships became something more, something solid and lasting. While there are a lot of nice people in the lifestyle, some of them are, to me, like coworkers. It's okay to socialize with them in certain settings, but I don't necessarily want to broaden that contact to other areas of my life. I keep the boundaries firmly in place."

"That makes sense, Sir."

"We like that restaurant. It's nice being able to sit down and chat with them. We can talk about our vanilla lives and we can talk about our BDSM lives. They're very close friends I can trust in either situation not to reveal my secrets to others. Most of the people here in the dungeon who know me, if they even know what I do for a living, it's that I'm in IT, and that's it. I don't give my last name to most of them. They don't know the company, they don't even know what city I work or live in. And that's the way I want to keep it."

She frowned. "Are you afraid of someone trying to blackmail you?"

"Not really. I'm more afraid of what I do here as play getting back to my employer and it causing trouble for me with them."

"Do you think it would?"

"I don't know. The teaching, that's different. No one's getting naked and I'm not teaching anything overtly sexual. So I'm teaching a negotiation class at FetCon. My last name isn't listed anywhere on the program, and neither is my picture." He shrugged. "It's a human relations and communication class. The skills can be applied to a variety of situations. They'd be hard-pressed to use that against me. Ditto the whip and rope classes. But I'd rather not have curious employees showing up here out of the blue in numbers to see if there's anything else I do."

"Have you ever run into any coworkers here?"

"No. I did once at an event in Tampa, but he was also an upper manager and more than happy to look the other way. We've never talked about it, and won't talk about it."

"Could you lose your job for this?"

"Only if it caused problems at work. The more separation between the two, the happier I am. I don't talk about my private life at work at all. There are people who can and have lost their jobs by being outed, though."

He accurately interpreted her sudden nerves. "Don't worry, pet. I wouldn't take a chance if I thought there was a concern." He placed his hands on her shoulders and looked her in the eye. "You let me do all the worrying tonight," he quietly said. "I want you to relax and let go. I want you to take off your reporter's hat and let me be in charge. All right?"

Something about his low, steady tone proved damn near hypnotic to her. "Yes, Sir."

He smiled. "That's my good girl."

* * * *

Tony wasn't sure if he wanted to scene early with her, or wait and tease her for a while and do it later. The former would mean less people around to potentially make her nervous.

The latter meant the evening might end sooner if he wore her out and she wanted to go home.

That was something he didn't want to happen. He wanted to steal as much time with her as he possibly could.

He pulled the leather cuffs from his bag. "Wrists, pet."

It tickled him that she held out her hands without hesitation.

After quickly buckling the cuffs around her wrists, he pointed at the floor. She immediately knelt in front of him.

I'm going to be in damn misery all night. Her immediate compliance had hardened his cock again. "When I ask you for a color tonight, regardless of what we're doing, even if we're standing and talking, I want you to give me either *green*, *yellow*, or *red*. Understand?"

"Yes, Sir."

"Good girl. Where are we now? Give me a color."

"Green, Sir."

He couldn't resist stroking the top of her head. Her eyes fell closed and she rested her forehead against his thigh, a content look on her face.

If it wasn't for the fact that it was a concrete floor and he didn't want her knees to start hurting, he'd gladly stand there all night just like that, with the warmth of her flesh melting through his denim jeans and scorching his flesh. Her hair felt silky slipping through his fingers.

"Such a good girl," he softly said. Reluctantly, he gently tapped the top of her head. "Stand up, pet."

She did.

"For tonight, pet, here are my other rules. If you need to go to the bathroom, or you need a drink, or you get hungry, you ask me for permission first. Understand?" He watched her eyes for any sign he was pushing her too hard, too fast, being too strict.

His cock wanted him to scruff the back of her neck and drag her home for sexy, private play.

He shoved that thought away.

She nodded. "Yes, Sir."

He opted to wait to scene with her. He tried to tell himself he wanted to give her a chance to watch other people scening, maybe see a few things she might like to try, but he knew that was a lie.

He didn't want to see the night end any sooner than it had to.

He laced his fingers through hers and they made the rounds of both the play area and the social area. He introduced her as his submissive and made no mention of her job. He didn't want her slipping back into a work headspace when he could see how much she obviously enjoyed subspace

After two hours, they'd watched Seth and Leah play, as well as Ross and Loren. Apparently Tilly and Cris weren't playing that night, but Landry topped a couple of different people. Tony checked in with her and got nothing but *green* in reply. He paid close attention to how she watched other scenes play out, what she seemed interested in, what seemed to turn her off, and made sure to pick her brain about her feelings.

When his preferred bench in the far corner came up available, Tony decided he'd delayed enough. He led Shayla over to it and had her sit down. "You stay here. I'll be right back with my bag."

Chapter Seventeen

Shayla's throat suddenly went dry. *This is really happening.*

She felt her cheek with the back of her hand. She knew as hot as her face felt, it had to be bright red. But barely anyone seemed to pay attention to her sitting there.

Tony returned with his things and pointed at the floor.

Running on instinct, she dropped to her knees and resisted the urge to stare at the floor.

He stroked her hair. "How's my pet?"

"Green, Sir." *If a racing pulse, cold sweat, and dry throat are* green, *I'm peachy.*

"Good girl. I'm going to get my things ready. Do you need to use the bathroom?"

She'd gone maybe ten minutes earlier and didn't feel right using that as an excuse to stall. "No, Sir."

"Okay."

He opened the bag and cane tube. He rearranged a few things in his bag and laid out several implements from the cane tube on the inside of the open top of the bag. He also draped a large towel over the bench and pulled out several lengths of pink rope.

Once he had everything ready, he held out a hand to her to help her to her feet. In his other hand he held the blindfold he'd used on her earlier. He led her over to the end of the bench and rested his hands on her shoulders. "Give me your thong, pet."

Her cheeks still ablaze, she reached under her sundress and pulled it off and handed it to him.

"Good girl." He buckled the blindfold on her and placed her hands on the bench. "Climb on." He helped her get positioned the way he wanted her. Then he quickly bound her arms to the bench with the rope, using the cuffs as well. He followed by binding her ankles and calves to the bench.

When he told her to test the restraints, she could barely move.

She sensed him squat in front of her. "Remember, I will be the only one touching you, pet. The only hands you'll feel on you will be mine. Understood?"

"Yes, Sir," she whispered.

"How are you?"

"Green, Sir."

He kissed her forehead, sending a gentle shiver of anticipation through her. "Good girl."

She sensed him move away again. She startled a little at the feel of him working her skirt up, pulling it out of the way and bunching the material on her back, leaving her bare and exposed from the waist down.

And still she knew her cunt was wet, embarrassingly so. Her clit throbbed and from her position on the bench she now understood why Valerie had been trying to rub herself into an orgasm the week before.

Shut. Brain. Off.

He started massaging her with his strong, warm hands, simultaneously relaxing her and driving her need even higher. Now she comprehended why he'd said he would refuse to broaden the limits of a scene in the middle of it.

Hell, if he asked to fuck me right now, I'd gladly let him.

The thought scared and thrilled her at the same time.

The first light, stinging slap brought her mind sharply back into focus on the scene and what Tony was doing to her. He alternated slapping her ass cheeks, back and forth, gradually increasing in force until the warmth turned into an itchy sting that soon transitioned into a borderline-painful smack.

He stopped, rubbing her ass, kneading her flesh with both hands. "Where are we, pet?"

"Green, Sir," she mumbled.

"Good girl."

He disappeared for a moment. When he returned, she felt him drape something along her ass and legs. "Floggers, pet. Relax and enjoy it." He apparently had two of them and soon set a rhythm that made her want to melt into the bench. The definition of *thuddy* completely clarified in her mind as he worked up and down her body with them.

She suddenly wished she was totally naked on the bench, so she could feel the suede falls all over her back and shoulders and not through the fabric of her sundress.

After several minutes of that he switched to a different set of floggers. She immediately felt the difference. While still thuddy, the falls on these were heavier, stiffer, and delivered a little more bite with each impact.

That ceased. Both his hands made contact with her ass cheeks at the same time, a hard, stinging blow that made her *yip* and strain a little against her bonds.

His voice had grown deeper, commanding. "Color, pet."

"Green, Sir."

"Good girl."

She felt something flat and cool against her ass. "Time to step things up a little, pet." One of his hands pressed down in the center of her back at the same time he delivered a stingy blow with what was obviously a paddle. She let out a startled screech, but he pressed down harder on her back. "Take it for me or safeword, pet." The blows continued, varying in location all over her ass and the backs of her thighs, ranging in strength from light to hard and stingy enough to make her cry out and try to twist away from him.

He started a crescendo of blows she thought she'd have to safeword over when he suddenly stopped, leaving her gasping for breath and trying to process it.

His hands returned. He gently stroked her flesh, soothing the sting away. Cool air from the room brushed against her pussy and she realized just how wet she was. If it wasn't for the towel, she'd likely have a puddle forming under her.

She sensed him walk around in front of her again. His voice whispered in her ear. "Such a good girl. I'm so proud of you. You're doing great."

Inside her, a switch she'd never been aware existed flipped open. A wave of desire to please him, to make him happy and keep the praise coming flooded through her entire being. She no longer cared what he did or how much it hurt, if it meant he'd keep saying that to her in that same, damn, delicious tone of voice.

She'd take every last bit of it.

He kissed her forehead before disappearing again. A moment later he laid something hard and thin across her ass. "Riding crop, pet."

He started lightly at first, working up and down her ass and thighs and even the backs of her lower legs. He increased the impacts until she was yelping with every blow, straining and pulling, her struggles only serving to increase the friction against her clit.

He stopped, a laugh reaching her ears. "Squirmy pet. Give me a color."

"Green, Sir," she gasped.

"Good girl." He paused and she felt him circling her midsection with several loops of rope, tightening it and securing her even more firmly to the bench. "That will keep you still."

Then he picked up where he left off with the riding crop. His strokes came from everywhere, keeping her guessing where he'd strike next, even a few of them lightly flicking her clit and making her jump as well as gasp with pleasure.

He stopped and she wondered where the next blows would land.

Then, they didn't.

She had a few more seconds to wonder about this when she felt something pressed against her labia, stroking up and down. She groaned and tried to lift her hips but the rope held her down.

He laughed. "Pet likes this. It think pet will like it even more in a minute." Whatever it was, it wasn't the same vibrator he'd used on her before. It felt larger, like a dildo. He slowly pressed it forward, deeper, back and forth until it slid between her lips and she let out a moan of pleasure at the feel of its size stretching her. He took his time fucking her with it until it was deeply buried inside her.

"How's my pet?"

She had to lick her lips to speak. "Green, Sir," she whispered, not trusting her own voice.

He chuckled. She felt him holding the dildo with one hand, but sensed he changed position.

Then he smacked her with a different paddle, definitely a heavier one than the first one he'd used, but kept the strokes on the pleasant side of pain.

And he started fucking her with the dildo.

Pleasure and pain danced together in her body, her mind unable to separate the two and finally deciding it didn't matter. She moaned as he stroked harder and faster with the dildo, the strokes from the paddle also increasing in strength until she didn't know if her moans were from pleasure or pain.

Then he hit a switch and the dildo turned into a buzzing vibrator and he stopped with the paddle.

She felt like her body would come unglued. Her back arched, straining against the ropes as the orgasm ripped through her.

"That's it, pet," he said, his stern tone only increasing her pleasure. "Come for me." He fucked her hard with the vibrator, relentlessly, until tears rolled down her face from the force of the climax shattering her body.

Then came the strokes from another implement. "Take these cane strokes, pet. Take them for me."

The hand holding the vibrator slowed down, but each slash from the cane left a streak of fire across her already tender ass. She lost count how many cane strokes he gave her, but she cried out in pain at each one.

Then he rolled out his next trick—he turned up the speed on the vibrator and began fucking her hard with it as he delivered several more excruciatingly painful cane strokes to the backs of her thighs. The pain kept her climax at bay, barely, until suddenly the cane was gone and only the vibrator was left, fucking her hard and deep.

A loud cry rolled out of her. She clawed at the air with her hands, the ropes keeping her in place so Tony could continue fucking her with the vibrator.

"Such a good girl," he cooed. "Look at how hard you're coming for me."

She sobbed as another orgasm bubbled up from deep inside her. Tears ran down her face and she was glad for the blindfold hiding the world from her. Her existence had shrunk to his voice, his hands, and pleasure so mind-bogglingly strong it bordered on pain.

He yanked the vibrator from her, making her yelp in surprise as he started spanking her with his bare hand again. No quarter given, the hard slaps shook her entire body and left her brain scrambled as her greedy cunt and throbbing clit begged for more from the vibrator.

Somewhere, she still heard the vibrator buzzing, but the pain in her ass had started outweighing the residual pleasure from the orgasms. She twisted, sobbing, squirming, and unable to escape the blows.

Then he rubbed the vibrator up and down her pussy again. "Is this what you want, pet? Is this what you're missing?"

"Yes, Sir!" she sobbed, trying to arch into it as he kept it tantalizingly out of reach.

"You have to pay the piper, pet. Pleasure doesn't come without pain."

She felt a hard, deep, thuddy blow on her ass that made her cry out. The vibrator returned. Another blow, on her other ass cheek, and more vibration. Then he slowly inserted the vibrator, timing his thrusts with it, hard and deep ones, with each blow from the newest implement.

"The infamous silicone spoon, pet. Let's see how much you like it."

The vibrator clicked into a higher speed.

He fucked her hard and fast with it, each stroke earning her another hit with the spoon until reality upended yet again. She let out a loud, long cry when the climax exploded through her. She fucked herself back against the pleasure and the pain until he delivered a crescendo of strokes inside and out before the spoon disappeared.

Leaving only the vibrator in her pussy on high.

She felt him stand behind the bench, the denim of his jeans rough against her sore ass, his hip pressed between her thighs and holding the vibrator inside her. His fingers sunk into her hips just below where the rope had her immobilized. "Fuck it, pet. Fuck that cock."

She frantically rocked herself against it and him, his hands helping her, pulling her, the toy bottoming out at the bottom of each stroke and making her scream in pleasure as one more orgasm took her breath away until she lay shuddering on the bench, all strength gone.

His body disappeared. Then the vibrator was gently removed from her, and she heard it shut off.

He pulled the skirt of her dress down over her ass and moved to her head where she still sobbed, unable to process anything.

He kissed her forehead. "Color, pet," he whispered in her ear.

"Green, Sir."

His lips pressed against her forehead again, lingering for several long, tender seconds. "Such a good girl. You made me very proud."

This brought a new round of tears she couldn't and didn't want to understand. She lay there while he quickly worked to untie her. She felt him drape a light throw over her. "Don't move yet, pet."

Not that she could if she'd wanted to.

He disappeared for only a moment before returning again. His arms enveloped her, helping her stand, then scooping her up, blanket and all, when her knees gave out.

"I'll get the bench for you, Tony," she heard Leah softly say somewhere to their left. "You take care of her."

"Thanks."

He carried her, still blindfolded, through the play space. She draped her arms around his neck and kept her face buried against his chest. He smelled warm and musky, no cologne, just laundry detergent and soap and shampoo.

She felt him turn and sit and realized he'd carried her over to the couches.

"It's all right, pet," he whispered against the top of her head. "We have plenty of time. Take as long as you need."

Curled in the safety and warmth of his embrace, she cried.

* * * *

Tony closed his eyes and kept his cheek pressed against the top of her head. *Jesus, please don't let me have gone too far!*

She'd have some nice marks. Already, angry red welts and bruises from the crop and cane striped her ass and thighs. And the silicone spoon was guaranteed to leave her with deep-tissue bruising she'd feel for days.

Some submissives didn't like marks. Some craved them. She'd have to tell him her preference on the back end of this, once she'd recovered. Although he had been careful not to mark her anywhere it would be readily visible, unless she had some bruising from where her wrists had pulled against the leather cuffs.

The crying didn't shock or surprise him. It wasn't an uncommon reaction from some people. In fact, some submissives used scenes to induce cathartic crying they normally couldn't achieve any other way.

Eyes closed, he listened to the sounds of the dungeon around them. People talking, the music, the sounds of other scenes underway.

All he cared about was currently nestled in his arms, her tears turning to soft sniffles.

He couldn't remember the last time he'd had that much fun in a scene. If they'd been at home in his private playroom he would have used a strap-on to fuck her while using another vibrator pressed against her clit.

I hope she gives me another chance to do just that.

He also hoped she turned out to be a submissive who liked marks. He could have easily kept her flying all night, balancing her on that fine razor's edge between pleasure and pain.

He let his mind wander, about how nice it would be to sink his cock into her while she was tied to a bench, or to let her have her aftercare while sucking on his cock.

Stop it, Daniels. That's way too far, way too fast.

She eventually quieted in his arms. "Ready for the blindfold to come off, pet?"

She nodded.

He didn't correct her over not speaking. He suspected she was still deep in subspace. With one hand he carefully unbuckled it and watched as she slowly blinked against the light.

Her hazel eyes slowly focused on his as he stared down into her face. The urge to lean in and kiss her was great.

She looked vulnerable, sated.

Beautiful.

"How's my pet?" he softly asked.

She slowly blinked and nodded a little.

He smiled. Yep, she was definitely still deeply out of it. "Good?"

She nodded a little, then closed her eyes and snuggled against him again.

He rested his chin on top of her head and breathed in deeply. She smelled like floral shampoo and sex, with just a hint of leather from the collar and cuffs she still wore.

I could get used to that scent.

He almost didn't hear her when she finally spoke. "How long did we play?"

"Thirty, maybe forty minutes."

"Okay."

He stifled a chuckle. She sounded like a sleepy little girl with a full tummy.

I could get used to that sound.

* * * *

She felt like a deep-sea diver slowly making her way to the surface.

Eventually, the sounds of the dungeon finally penetrated her cocoon and she opened her eyes again and looked around. It felt like she'd been gone for hours, but around them not much had changed from when he'd blindfolded her, except different people now occupied play equipment.

When she looked up at him again, his green eyes searched her face. "How we doing, pet?"

"Green, Sir," she said.

The corners of his eyes crinkled when he smiled. "Feeling okay?"

"Yes, Sir." *Except that I don't want to leave your arms.*

She couldn't remember ever feeling so safe and secure, so cared for.

Protected.

"You feel ready to sit up so I can go get you a bottle of water?"

She wanted to say no, to stay curled up there forever, but she pulled the throw around her and nodded.

He helped her sit up and waited until she was settled again to get up and retrieve two bottles of water from a cooler by the buffet table. She didn't take her eyes off him the entire time, longing for the solid warmth of his body to once again anchor her to reality.

Already the experience felt hazy in some ways, like a fading dream. She suspected she'd feel it in her ass in the morning, but for now all the sensations had blended together into a delicious warmth encompassing her entire backside and pussy.

He returned to sit beside her and handed her one of the bottles after opening it for her. She didn't think she was thirsty until she drained half the bottle in just a few swallows.

He draped an arm around her. "Better?"

She nestled against his side. "Yes, Sir."

"I think Tilly, Loren, and Leah are dying to come over and check on you."

"Why don't they?"

He laughed. "They know the way things work. You don't harsh someone's subspace buzz. I'll wave them over when you're ready to receive visitors."

She snickered at that. "Thank you, Sir."

"No, thank *you*, pet. That was a lot of fun." He kissed the top of her head. She tipped her face to his and wished he'd kiss her, really kiss her, but instead his eyes met hers. "I hope you still like me tomorrow."

"I'm sure I will, Sir."

"You say that now. I apologize in advance for the marks if they freak you out."

"They won't freak me out." In fact, she was curious to see what they would look like in the morning. She was used to always having bruises somewhere on her body. First growing up and roughhousing with her older brother, then as puberty hit and she grew congenitally klutzy. If she didn't bang into something at least once a day, it was a miracle.

It took another twenty minutes for the brain fuzz to dissipate enough she felt ready to talk to her friends. But she still wanted to stay nestled against Tony's side on the couch.

He waved to the three women. They hurried over, smiles on their faces.

"Well?" all three of them asked at once.

Shayla laughed. "I'm okay."

"Did you have fun?" Loren asked.

She smiled up at Tony. "That would be a definite yes."

They chatted for a few minutes until an unexpected yawn hit her.

Tony chuckled. "And I think that signals the beginning of the end of our evening."

Come to think of it, she was really tired.

He stood and held out a hand to her. He helped her up, making sure she was steady on her feet. "Are you going to be okay driving home?" he asked.

She nodded. "I think so, Sir. I'm okay."

She followed him over to his things, where he dug the vibrator out. He'd wrapped it in a towel and stuck it in a side pocket of the bag. "I'll be right back. Going to go wash this off."

While he was gone, she folded the throw and placed it on the bag. She wasn't sure where he wanted it. He returned a few minutes later. After saying their good-nights to everyone, they went out to the parking lot. He locked his things in the trunk and then walked her over to her car.

"You're sure you're okay to drive?"

She nodded. "Yes, Sir."

"Do you want me to follow you home?"

"I'll be okay, Sir."

He motioned for her wrists. He unbuckled the leather cuffs and then engulfed her in a hug she never wanted to end. "I had fun tonight, pet. I hope you did, too." He placed a kiss on the top of her head.

"I did, Sir. Thank you."

"Wear the collar home. And text me as soon as you get home so I don't worry."

"Yes, Sir."

"Don't forget to text me when you wake up tomorrow and let me know how you are."

"I won't forget, Sir."

"What's your afternoon look like tomorrow? Any plans?"

"No, Sir."

"Then wear your collar while you're at home. Unless you're in the shower or go out or something like that."

"Yes, Sir." He took her keys from her and unlocked her door, holding it open for her and waiting until she was safely inside and had found her glasses.

"Drive safe, pet. And good night."

"Good night, Sir."

He closed the door and watched her drive away.

It wasn't until she was halfway home she realized he still had her thong. She giggled at the thought, her hand going up to the collar. When she got home, another large yawn hit her as she tried to unlock her door.

Realizing she wasn't long for the land of the conscious, she quickly texted him that she'd made it home. She pulled off her dress and crawled into bed, crashing almost immediately into sleep before her head hit the pillow.

Chapter Eighteen

Shayla awoke from a sleep of the dead a little after three o'clock Sunday afternoon. When she rolled over, she groaned at the aches in her muscles. When she sat up, her bruised ass caught her attention.

She also felt a not-unpleasant ache in her pussy from where Tony had used the vibrator on her.

Wow. If last night was even a fraction of what other submissives felt on a regular basis, she could easily understand why they did it. Hell, she'd readily volunteer to do *that* again anytime.

As long as it was with Tony.

She still wasn't sure she could wrap her mind around why the heavy masochists did what they did, but Tony had clearly driven home the point that not all pain was painful…some of it was damn pleasurable.

And subspace was a blessed place to escape from reality.

With another groan she stood and headed to the bathroom. When she walked in she caught sight of herself in the mirror. The leather collar was still buckled around her neck.

I forgot to take it off.

Then she stopped that thought. No, she hadn't forgotten. Tony had instructed her to wear it at home unless she needed to take a shower or go out for errands. Her fingers stroked the leather, remembering how it felt the night before when he'd hooked a finger through the D-ring on the front and pulled her head up so he could look into her eyes.

A hot flush ran through her body. She'd had the best orgasms of her life last night, in front of a room full of mostly strangers, with a man she barely knew who hadn't even taken off his clothes.

Wow.

She knew she'd do it again in a heartbeat, and not for any story, either. She'd loved it.

Turning, she looked at her ass in the mirror. Instead of chiding herself for her weight, she marveled at the marks there. The imprint of a riding crop was clearly visible in several places, as were his handprints, and several stripy cane marks. She imagined the round, isolated marks were from the wicked silicone spoon. The marks ranged in color from pinkish red to beautiful shades of purple and blue.

A smile curled her lips.

She ran her fingers over the welts and remembered how he had skillfully mixed pain and pleasure, taking her up the scale to a point where she'd thought she'd have to code before he applied the pleasure of the vibrator.

By the time he'd finished with her, she knew she wouldn't safeword unless he absolutely didn't stop the pain. The reward for holding out each time was too great.

Snickering, she remembered his playful warning to her the other night in the restaurant, of how easy it was to rewire a brain to scramble pain and pleasure together.

He got that right.

She finally used the bathroom and went to the kitchen to make a pot of coffee. As it brewed, she had a thought and retrieved her cell phone.

Good morning, Sir, she texted him.

She was curled on the couch with her coffee and her laptop ten minutes later when he replied. *Good morning, pet. How's the ass?*

She giggled. *Pleasantly sore, Sir.*

Still wearing your collar?

She'd pulled on a T-shirt, but yes, the collar was still buckled around her neck. *Yes, Sir.*

Good girl. I just woke up. I want you to meet Me here at My house at five. I'm cooking dinner.

Her heart raced. It wasn't like she had anything else better to do.

Yes, Sir.

After a few minutes, his reply. *:) Good girl. Wear your collar.*

Another thrill ran through her. Would she ever get sick of that feeling?

Probably not. Not anytime soon, at least. *Yes, Sir,* she texted back.

She caught up on her e-mail and was heading back to the kitchen for her second cup of coffee when her cell phone rang. Part of her hoped it was Tony, but her throat dried when she saw it was her parents' home line.

"Hello?"

Mom. "Well, glad to see you're alive."

Shayla cringed. "Sorry I haven't called lately. I've been busy."

"Busy doing what? You haven't even updated your Facebook status in a week."

That was true, although she had commented on some friends' pictures. "I've just got a lot going on. Work, friends—"

"Friends? So tell me about your new friends."

Shayla felt the blush coloring her cheeks even though she wasn't face-to-face with her mom. "Just some really nice people I met while working on a story. They've...sort of adopted me."

"James called us yesterday."

Out of the blue, Shayla's heart sank. Her good mood faded. "What the hell did he want?" she snapped.

She could tell from her mother's tone she wasn't happy about receiving the call, either. "He was asking about you. If we'd heard from you."

"So that's why you called me? Great. Thanks."

"No, but I did want to talk to you and make sure you were doing all right."

"I'm fine. What else did he want?"

"He told me he's paying you back."

"He sent me a check for five hundred last week, yes. I won't say he's paying me back until he's completely paid me back in full. Considering his craptacular track record in keeping promises I won't hold my breath. What did you tell him about me?"

"I chewed him out for trying to use us to get information about you. That if he wanted to talk to you, he needed to talk to you himself."

Her heart soared that her mom was still taking her side. "I don't want to talk to him."

"That much I figured. I wouldn't want to talk to him, either, if I were in your shoes." She sighed. "I just wish you hadn't up and moved so suddenly. I'm worried about you."

Shayla looked around her apartment. "Mom, honestly? I'm fine. I'm better than I've been in a long time. It's cheaper living down here than up there. I'll be okay."

"Your father was talking about taking a weekend to come down and visit you."

"And check up on me?" She smiled despite her tone.

Her mom laughed. "Yes, of course. He's worried, too."

"I don't have a big apartment, Mom. You guys would have to stay at a hotel."

"I know. You know your father. He won't take a vacation, but a chance to check up on his little girl, he'll jump at that. He didn't worry as much when you lived in the same city as your brother."

Shayla reached up to scratch at her throat and remembered the collar. She blushed despite her mom not being able to see her.

Thank god we don't Skype! "I'll look around and find a couple of good hotels to choose from. Summer's their slow time down here."

"Thanks, sweetheart." She paused. "You're really okay?"

"I'm really okay, Mom. Honestly. I'm done keeping secrets." *Well, okay, except about getting my ass beaten last night. They damn sure don't need to know about that.* "I wish I had told you guys what James did the first time."

"Quit beating yourself up over it."

"That's what everyone keeps saying, but I don't seem to be able to do it."

* * * *

She didn't have any trouble following the directions Tony e-mailed her.

Along with his address and how to get to his house, he'd included two instructions.

No panties, and to wear a sundress or skirt.

Both instructions had left her clit throbbing and her pussy wet.

He lived off Bee Ridge Road, east of I-75. He lived in a community of large homes situated on even larger pieces of land, most of them several acres each, and many of which held grazing cattle or horses. He met her at the front door.

"Looks like you found it all right, pet," he said, his gaze traveling to her collar before meeting her eyes.

"Yes, Sir."

"Come in." As she stepped through the door, he rested his hand on the back of her neck, on the collar. Not roughly, but firmly.

Authoritatively.

Possessively.

He shut the door and led her into the house. Tastefully decorated, it didn't look like a Dom lived there, if she had to guess. And something smelled delicious.

"Let me give you the tour," he said, his hand never leaving the collar as he showed her throughout the house.

Four bedrooms, three and a half baths. Huge eat-in kitchen, with separate dining and family rooms. A home office. Tile throughout, with gorgeous throw rugs scattered here and there.

If she had to venture a guess, the house alone was probably worth over half a mil.

He saved the best for last, leading her through the kitchen, through a utility room, to a door locked with an electronic combination lock. "The playroom."

He punched a four-digit code into the lock. It let out a beep and he led her into what turned out to be his personal dungeon. It held a St. Andrew's Cross, two different spanking benches in different styles, a suspension bar similar to the one at the club, and racks of implements, among other things.

He pointed at another door. "That just leads out to the rest of the garage. I used to have a classroom area in there, but after Kaden died, Seth and I both lost the heart to teach here. Too many memories, for me at least, of Kaden. That, and frankly, liability. It's easier for us to teach at the club." He turned to her. "What do you think, pet?"

She knew her racing heart had nothing to do with fear. "It's very nice, Sir."

He chuckled. "Turn around and show me your marks, pet."

She turned and hiked up the skirt of her sundress. She didn't move when his hand caressed her flesh. "Very nice. What do you think? Too much?"

She shook her head, her cheeks burning. "Not too much, Sir."

"Keep that skirt up." He gently pulled her glasses off and put them on a shelf. Then he took hold of the back of her collar and led her over to one of the spanking benches. He pushed her down and over it, her ass exposed. "I really enjoyed spanking your ass last night, pet. So another rule is that when we're together, I will be giving you a greeting spanking. As long as we're not in public, of course."

Her throat felt like it might close up from the rush of moisture that had fled her mouth for her cunt. "Yes, Sir," she squeaked.

He chuckled. "Good girl." He wasted no time, holding her pinned by the collar as he spanked her hard and fast. She didn't bother keeping track of the strokes and he didn't seem to mind her crying out as he stepped up the spanking. Then he stopped, his hand soothing her ass. "Such a good girl," he softly cooed. "I'm very proud of you for taking that, pet."

She didn't move, could barely breathe. She knew she'd let him beat her all night long to keep feeling like this, to keep hearing that tone of voice from him.

Is this subspace again? If it was, she never wanted it to end.

His hand stopped in the center of her ass, fingers pointing down the seam, almost but not quite brushing her pussy. "Well, pet certainly enjoyed that."

Her face couldn't get any hotter, could it? "Yes, Sir," she whispered.

He chuckled. Then one finger probed between her labia, easily slipping inside her. "Oh, pet is very, very wet. I have something I think you'll enjoy."

She couldn't suppress her disappointed groan when he removed her hand.

He patted her ass. "Don't worry. You stay right here. Do not move a muscle."

She froze as he released her. She didn't move her head to look but could hear him open a cabinet and rummage around for something. He softly hummed while he searched for what he wanted before returning a moment later.

"Don't move, pet." He belted something around her waist and cinched it snug. More straps encircled her upper thighs, and the last went between her legs. Before he buckled the last strap, however, he inserted something into her pussy. Something large and round. She moaned as he slowly worked it back and forth between her labia, coating it with her juices before fucking it into her a little at a time.

Then he pushed it all the way inside her. She felt her body greedily suck it into her cunt. He secured the last strap, which rubbed against her clit and didn't help her situation.

Walking around in front of her, he knelt so they were eye to eye. He held up a small remote control. "You don't come unless I give you permission. If you come without permission, it's five hard and painful strokes with this." He held up a rattan cane in his other hand. "Understand, pet?"

She nodded, a little fearfully now.

He must have sensed it, because his eyes crinkled in amusement. "Either way, it's win-win for us both. The sadist in me is thrilled, and the masochist wanting to come out in you will be happy."

Then he thumbed a button on the remote. She jumped as what turned out to be a vibrating egg sprang to life inside her. She whimpered and thrust her hips uncontrollably as he played with the settings, working it back and forth from high to low, different pulsation patterns, until he settled on one he was happy with. "That should be just uncomfortable enough to keep you distracted, pet," he said as he stood. He put the remote in his pocket and held out a hand to help her up.

On shaky legs, she stood. Her skirt fell down.

He chuckled. "Okay, pet. I think the dress needs to go. Don't you?"

She nodded. "Yes, Sir." Her arms trembled as she struggled to pull it over her head while the deviously evil egg continued throbbing inside her.

Fuck.

She also realized she didn't care if coming without permission earned her strokes.

Although she did want to obey him.

He took the dress from her and hung it over the back of a chair so it wouldn't wrinkle. "Shoes off, too, pet."

She had to hold on to him for support as she removed one sandal, then the other.

When she was naked, except for her collar and the harness keeping the egg from sliding out of her pussy, he hooked a finger through the front ring of her collar and pulled her close. "How's my pet?"

"Green, Sir," she whispered.

"Good girl." He kissed her forehead.

"Sir?"

"Yes, pet?"

She belatedly realized her question sounded silly. "Why haven't you kissed me on the lips yet?"

He cocked his head a little to the side as he met her gaze. When he answered, his voice sounded quiet. "As silly as this might sound," he gently said, "I consider that a very intimate part of sex. Of making love. Like I told you, I don't want to be a douche. As your Dominant, unless or until you decide you want to put sex on the table, I won't do that. I consider what we do, like this, not to be sex. It's play. Sexual, yes. Sex? No. Making love? No. I don't even consider oral sex to be the same level of intimacy. Or strap-on play."

He stroked her cheek with his thumb and she had to fight to concentrate and keep her eyes open as she nuzzled him. "Kissing," he continued, "to me, is intimate. It's saved for when two people have made a commitment to each other. Does that make sense?"

She nodded. It made perfect sense.

It also made her want him to kiss her even more.

He smiled. "How's my pet?"

"Green, Sir."

He reached into his pocket and adjusted the egg's pattern. She let out a moan and struggled not to come as her body finally acclimated to it.

He grinned. "That's my good girl."

He released her collar and pointed to the floor. "Greeting, pet."

She slowly sank to her knees, trying to angle her body in such a way that the despicable egg didn't press directly on her G-spot and send her spasming into an orgasm. He laughed as he watched her kiss his feet and the backs of his hands, well aware of the discomfort she was in. "Problem, pet?"

"No, Sir." Somehow, she managed.

And when she nuzzled the front of his jeans, there was no mistaking the iron bulge pressing against the inside of his zipper.

At least I'm not the only one who's horny.

Chapter Nineteen

Tony struggled not to laugh at her predicament. She was adorable, trying so hard to obey him. He reached into his pocket and adjusted the egg's remote again to slow it down and give her a little respite. He stroked the back of her head with the other, enjoying the feel of her warm cheek pressing against his engorged cock through his jeans.

"Pet, do you realize I came home and rubbed not one, but two out, after you left the club last night?"

"Sorry, Sir."

"Oh, don't apologize. I'm just returning the favor," he teased. "I'm sure I'll be rubbing more out later on. I haven't felt this horny in a long while." He belatedly realized what he'd said and wished he could take it back. It was okay for him to think and feel that way.

He just didn't want to admit it to her and scare her away.

Luckily, she didn't seem put off by that. "I could help you with that, Sir."

"Ah, what a good pet. But not tonight. Maybe one day. Tonight, after dinner, I'm going to give you another spanking to warm that sweet ass of yours, and then I'm going to introduce you to my stunt cock."

She laughed. "Stunt cock?"

He grinned. "Yep. Some men are afraid of sex toys. I, for one, love using a strap-on on a woman. I can buy them in any size I want, and they never go soft."

Her eyes widened a little.

He leaned in close and hooked a finger through the ring on her collar again. "Tonight I'm introducing you to the sadistic world of forced orgasm torture."

She swallowed hard. "Yes, Sir. Thank you, Sir."

"Don't thank me yet, pet. It's called torture for a reason."

He led her from the room and back into the kitchen. "Oh, shoot. Stay here, I forgot something."

She didn't move while he retraced his steps to the playroom. He returned with a small fleece throw similar to the one he'd used on her the night before, and a large pillow. "I want my pet to be comfortable." He put the pillow on the kitchen floor. It looked like a large dog bed.

When he pointed at it, she carefully sank to her knees on it.

He handed her the throw. "You don't have to stay on your knees, pet. But you do need to stay on the pillow. If you need something, you ask for it and I'll get it. Only use the throw if you're actually cold. I can adjust the thermostat if you need it warmer. I want to see your body. Are you cold?"

"No, Sir."

One side effect of the vibrating egg was that her nipples stood out like hard, aching peaks. He reached out and lightly pinched one, then the other.

She whimpered, broadening his smile.

"Poor pet. Are you horny?"

"Yes, Sir."

When he did finally let her come, he suspected she'd be screaming her head off.

He almost giggled with sadistic glee. It'd been over a year since he'd been able to have a good, long, uninterrupted forced orgasm scene with someone. He actually didn't like doing those kinds of scenes in front of others. He preferred to do them in private, where the bottom could feel more relaxed and uninhibited.

And so could he.

What he'd done to her at the club last night was only the tip of the iceberg. He expected by the time he finished with her tonight, she'd be a melted puddle of goo.

He gently patted her on the head. "I need to finish preparing our dinner, pet. You stay right there."

"Yes, Sir."

He set about putting their salads together, glad to find out she also liked bleu cheese dressing, his favorite. The turkey noodle casserole he'd put together earlier only had five more minutes in the oven.

He'd given serious thought to making her eat her dinner on the floor out of one of the stainless steel dog bowls he had stowed in his cabinet, then opted not to. He didn't want to push her too hard, especially not after the night she'd had.

And the evening she was about to experience.

She would eat on the floor, on her pillow, but he'd let her use utensils. This time.

* * * *

Shayla did her best not to come throughout dinner, although getting up from the pillow to move from the kitchen out to the living room, where they would eat in front of the TV, and then back down again onto her pillow once there, proved problematic. He was nice enough to lower the speed and pattern of the egg, but the crotch strap on the harness rubbed against her aching clit and made moving difficult.

Dinner was delicious, but she had difficulty concentrating on the conversation and eating at the same time.

When they finished, Tony grinned. "Are you having problems there, pet?"

"Um, trying not to, Sir."

"Such a good girl. Considering the walloping you took last night, I wanted to introduce you to a different form of sadism."

"Thank you, Sir. You're too good to me."

He laughed and reached for the remote, which he'd put on the coffee table next to his plate. "Ooh, sarcasm. That means pet needs a little more distraction."

Her protest turned into a plaintive moan as she struggled not to orgasm when he bumped the setting higher on the vibrating egg.

"You can always safeword," he reminded her with an evil grin.

Truth be told, she didn't really *want* the torture to end.

She shook her head.

Now gave her another look she loved besides his playful smile. This grin, almost like a little boy with a toy, made him look practically giddy. She loved it.

She loved that she was the reason he smiled like that, the source of his amusement, even if at her own expense.

Then again, it was no large sacrifice to endure.

He didn't let her help clean up. He moved her back to the kitchen on the pillow where he could keep an eye on her and keep her mentally off-balance with the vibrating egg. When he had the leftovers put up and the dishes clean, he crooked a finger at her.

Carefully, oh so carefully, she got to her feet without orgasming.

Barely.

He smiled. "Such a good pet. I think you're ready for the next part of our night." He turned the egg off. She found that to be both a blessed relief, and that she missed it.

He picked up her blanket and pillow, hooked a finger through the front ring of her collar, and led her back to the playroom.

Working quickly, he removed the harness and pulled the egg from her. After wiping down the harness, and then washing the egg in a sink in the far corner that she'd missed before, he draped a towel over one of the spanking benches. He adjusted it to his liking, so the head was higher than the feet. Rolling up another towel, he put it at the head of the bench.

"On your back, pet. Ass at the lower end."

She did. He quickly used clips on the base of the bench to attach the wrist cuffs so her arms were down and immobilized. "Comfy, pet?"

"Yes, Sir."

He grinned. "You won't be for long."

He grabbed another set of leather cuffs and attached them to her ankles. Then came a two-foot-long, smooth metal rod less than an inch in diameter with eyelets at each end.

"Spreader bar," he said in response to her unasked question.

He clipped the ankle cuffs to the spreader bar, then made her draw her knees up to her chest.

It left her wide open and exposed.

"Oh, it gets better, pet," he assured her. He used ropes, tied to the ankle cuffs and the base of the bench above her head, so that she couldn't put her legs down if she wanted to. "And I don't want you to fall off, either." He used more rope, securing her waist to the bench.

"There. That's better." He actually clapped his hands and rubbed them together. "Questions, pet?"

She shook her head.

He pulled a chair over, and a rolling tray that reminded her of a hospital bed tray.

She watched as he assembled a variety of implements, dildos, and vibrators before he appeared satisfied.

He sat down in front of her and leaned to one side so she could look him in the eye. His expression grew serious. "Same rules apply, pet. Green, yellow, red. If at any time there's bad pain, or you get a leg cramp or something, then you safeword. All right?"

She nervously nodded. She was so horny, and now apprehensive, she didn't dare speak.

"Good girl." His grin returned.

The first item on his agenda was introducing her to nipple clamps. He stood and stepped beside her, holding them up. "These aren't too bad," he said as he flicked one of the clamps, which resembled long tweezers. "I want to work you up to the heavier, vibrating kind."

He gently rolled her left nipple between his thumb and forefinger, making it hard and aching from the attention. She yelped when he quickly attached the clamp to it.

The clamps were joined by a length of light, jewelry-weight chain. He repeated the attention to her right nipple before attaching the clamp.

Aaaand now her clit really throbbed like crazy.

He hooked one finger under the chain and lifted it, applying just a little tension to her nipples. "How's that, pet?"

"Ye–Yes, Sir."

He laughed. "Just think, maybe one day I'll be able to have your nipples pierced. Then you can wear a pretty, jeweled chain joining them and a ring through your clit hood. I could attach a leash to it and lead you around by it."

Her cunt throbbed at his words and the visual they painted.

His eyes narrowed as his gaze speared her. "Would you like that, pet?" he quietly asked.

She discovered yes, she thought she just might. "Yes, Sir."

The grin returned. "Such a good girl. You are in for a treat. I was going to start training you for anal tonight, then thought no, we'll save that for next weekend. You were so good last night I'd rather just give you a night of pure pleasure."

Her heart raced. *Anal?* Yes, they'd talked about it. And yes, she'd agreed to it, but she'd never actually done it before in her life. Until now, that orifice had always been exit-only.

She suspected if he worked her up the way she felt now before trying it, he'd have her begging for the biggest butt plug he had in minutes.

He returned to his seat.

If going to the gynecologist had ever been this fun, I'd have appointments every month.

"From this point on, pet, you have permission to come as much as you want. In fact, I'm counting on it because that's sort of the whole point." He leaned to the side so he could look her in the eye. "If we were in a relationship, by the way, there would be no red allowed for this kind of scene." He smiled.

"Wh—Why not, Sir?"

He laughed. "That's a benefit of being in a relationship. Orgasms don't hurt. Yes, I realize after a while you can get raw and chafed. I'm not talking about that. Then the code is *black*, meaning medical, all play stops immediately. That is never taken off the table. But if a woman wants to safeword after two or three orgasms just because they're intense, not painful, that sort of defeats the whole purpose of 'forced orgasm torture.'"

She nodded. Her brain found it difficult to speak with the nipple clamps distracting her.

"You, however, can of course use the codes I gave you. I just wanted to let you know how I do it under circumstances where I have full control. Now, let's get busy."

He reached over to the tray and grabbed something. She didn't even bother looking to see what it was. She closed her eyes and took a deep breath, trying to calm her racing heart. Impossible, because it felt like all the blood in her body was now located in her cunt and clit.

Is this what blue balls feels like?

He rubbed the dildo up and down between her labia. When he slowly started working it inside her, she gasped. It was larger than the one he'd used on her last night.

"This is my favorite rabbit," he told her. "Never fails to deliver." Once he'd worked a majority of the length inside her, she felt the forked arm of the clit stimulator rubbing on either side of her engorged nub.

He turned it on. She jumped, surprised, as it started swirling around inside her. "It rotates and vibrates." He hit another button and the vibration started. "By the way, this room is pretty well soundproofed. Feel free to scream."

It felt like someone lit a propane tank in her clit. He turned the vibrator up to high and held it still as she let a shriek fly. The ability to form conscious thought fled as she twisted and struggled to move away from the intensity of the sensations. Between the dildo part inside her hitting her G-spot and the clit stimulator directly thrumming against her, all she could do was lie there and suffer through wave after wave of the most powerful orgasms she'd ever felt in her life. Even as she struggled to move away from it, her bonds securely held her to the bench.

He laughed. "That's right, pet. You can't get loose. You're here for the duration until I decide you've had enough. And we've just gotten started." He started fucking her with the vibrator, temporarily allowing her to get her breath back just to press the rabbit back into position so her clit was once again under attack.

Tears rolled down her face as she tossed her head back and forth. It was too much, too intense—

"Such a good girl," he cooed. "Look at you, all tied up and coming for me."

She pried her eyes open to see him smiling at her.

Nothing short of unbearable pain would make her safeword now.

After a few minutes he turned off that vibrator, leaving her panting and gasping for breath. He didn't let her rest for long, however.

"I think you'll like this one, too," he said.

When he pushed it into her pussy, her body greedily sucked it in the way it had the vibrating egg earlier. Then she heard the sound of pumping and realized the dildo was inflating inside her.

"Let me know if it's too big," he sternly ordered as he inflated it.

Just when it got to the point she wasn't sure she could take it anymore, he stopped. "That's good," he said.

Then she heard buzzing of a different kind and he pressed a vibrator directly to her clit.

She would have come up off the bench if not for the restraints. She cried and pulled and twisted, but he forced more orgasms out of her until they all seemed to roll together into one red-hot climax she could barely breathe through. As he did that, he tugged on the base of the dildo with his other hand, pulling and pushing it just a little, rapidly, hitting her G-spot and everywhere else inside her at the same time, it felt like.

Torture...holy crap, it is torture...

And she never wanted it to end.

He soon tired of that one. He gave her a few moments to rest while he deflated and removed the dildo. He reached between her legs and up her body to the nipple clamp chain and gently tugged it. "How we doing, pet?"

She softly sobbed as the stimulation made her buzzing clit throb again. "Green," she managed to whisper.

He tugged the chain a little harder. "What, pet?" he sternly asked.

"Ow! Green, Sir!"

He laughed and released the chain. He rested his warm palm flat on her tummy. "Such a good girl for me," he said. "I'm so proud of you."

He stroked her belly. "Just think how much better this will be next weekend when I have a butt plug up your ass at the same time. Maybe I'll even put one of my penis gags in your mouth. I have a small one. Then you can have all three holes filled at the same time while I'm buzzing your clit. Would you like that, pet? I know I'd love it. I could put you on all fours on the other bench, move it out to my living room, and sit there and watch TV while you lie there all night, helpless to do anything about it except come. I'll even put the weighted, vibrating nipple clamps on you so that every time you move they swing around and add even more torment."

She whimpered, almost ashamed to admit it when the mental image made her pussy throb again. "Yes, Sir," she whispered.

Right now, hell, she'd agree to anything he asked. The blessed endorphins had returned with a vengeance. Nothing in the world mattered to her besides what they were doing at this moment. She wanted to please him and keep feeling like this.

"Good girl. Consider it added to next weekend's agenda." His hand disappeared. Then another dildo slowly started fucking her. Thicker than the rabbit, he quickly had it buried as far inside her as it would go. He held it in place with one hand, using his fingers to spread her labia far apart.

Then she howled as a pinching pain attached itself to the top of her left outer labia.

"Just a clothespin, pet," he scolded. "Are you safewording?"

She thrashed her head back and forth. "No, Sir."

"Give me a color!" he barked.

"Green!" she sobbed. "Green, Sir!"

"Good girl," he cooed, then a matching pinch clamped down on the right side. She let out a cry, but that turned into a moan as he started fucking her with the dildo and he pressed another vibrator against her clit.

He added more clothespins until she lost count, tempering each one with more fucking and buzzing until the whole orgasm-pain cycle melded into one long, searing quicksilver of sensations she both hated and never wanted to stop.

He turned up the vibrator and started fucking her harder with the dildo. "Come again for me, pet. Now!"

Pulling against the restraints was futile, but it was all she could do. She screamed as more liquid fire seemed to consume her cunt and clit, no longer able to tell what was pain and pleasure.

"Good girl!" He kept the vibrator going, leaving her gasping and sobbing as more aftershocks robbed her of strength. The clothespins disappeared one by one though, and even as he kept vibrating her clit he soothed her flesh with his other hand, gently rubbing her folds and taking the pain away until only pleasure was left.

She flexed her hips as much as she could in time with his thrusts with the dildo. She could no longer tell which orgasms started within and which ones were triggered by her clit.

He shut off the vibrator and removed the dildo at the same time. Shocked, she gasped, relieved and disappointed at the same time. She shivered a little as the fine sheen of sweat now covering her body chilled her.

"Such a good girl." He reached up and freed her nipples. She yelped again when they stung as blood rushed back into them. He soothed them with his fingers though, until his touch was pure pleasure.

Keeping her eyes closed, she let herself relax as all she felt was his hand, working back and forth between her nipples until that, too, ceased.

She should have known better.

"Let's see how you like this, pet." She felt him press something over her clit, something round, and before she could raise her head to see what, she heard a pumping sound.

Lightning exploded in her clit. Or, that was what it felt like. "This is clit pumping, pet. I'll only leave it on for a minute or two." She howled as her swollen and sensitive clit was sucked into the cup and he disconnected the hand pump.

Then the *click* of a vibrator, which he placed against the side of the cup.

She thrashed against her restraints as pain and pleasure struggled for dominance until she didn't care anymore. She was about to safeword when she felt the suction disappear at the same time she heard a soft *whish* as he released the valve on the cup.

It took every last ounce of strength to suck air into her lungs as the soft sound of his chuckle came to her. He knelt next to her and stroked her hair. "My poor pet. That was almost too much, wasn't it?"

She closed her eyes and nodded.

"Don't worry. We can work up to longer times on that." He stroked her forehead. "But I will be trying the cups on your nipples next weekend. For as long as you had the nipple clamps on tonight, I expect you'll be able to tolerate them for a while."

She shivered and forced her eyes open. His gaze looked concerned, his face inches from hers. "Where are we, pet?" he softly asked.

She couldn't close her eyes. She wanted to drown in his gaze.

A scary thought struck her. *I'm falling in love with him.*

She shoved it away. "Green, Sir."

"Good girl." He leaned in and kissed her forehead. "You were a very good girl for me tonight. We're done. Now, we're going to go cuddle on the couch and watch TV and you can even take a nap if you want."

She closed her eyes and nodded as the tears started.

He quickly unbound her and wrapped a blanket around her. "Hold on to me," he said.

She wrapped an arm around his neck as he scooped her up. She rested her face against his chest and kept her eyes closed as he carried her out to the living room. Only after he had her settled on the couch with her head in his lap did she open her eyes and look up at him.

He gazed down at her. His hand kept stroking her hair, something she hoped he didn't stop doing. "Are you all right, pet?"

She nodded, too tired to say anything. As her tears faded, she felt darkness closing in and gave in to it.

* * * *

It wasn't until he was sure she'd fallen asleep that he threw back his head and closed his eyes. His body thrummed with tension, adrenaline, desire.

He'd never had so much fun in his entire life. If he could, he'd put her in his bed, get undressed, and curl his body around hers all night long.

Jesus, I'm in love with her.

By all rights he knew he should end their agreement now, and tell her exactly why.

But it wasn't her fault he couldn't keep his heart corralled.

I can do this. I can handle this.

He hoped.

He'd only had her on the bench for about thirty minutes, but she slept nearly two hours. He dozed off and on, starting awake anytime he felt her move.

He was awake and watching her when she finally rejoined the land of the lucid.

He smiled down at her. "Sleep well?"

She nodded. "Thank you, Sir."

"It was definitely my pleasure, pet."

"How long was I out?"

"Nearly two hours. It's all right. I wore you out." She looked sad for a moment. "Are you all right?" he asked.

"I'm not going to want to go to work tomorrow," she said. "I feel like I've run a marathon."

"I'm really impressed by how well you did. You took everything I threw at you like a champ. You probably would have tolerated the clit pumping better if I'd done it early on, but you kept up with me."

She blushed. "Thank you, Sir."

"Any questions?"

She stared up into his eyes again. He loved her hazel eyes, little flecks of amber and green and brown giving her a sweet look. "Are you still horny, Sir?"

His cock throbbed in his jeans. "Yes, pet. That's my problem, not yours."

"May I watch you…" She blinked. "You know, can I watch you rub one out?"

He pressed his lips together, tempted to say no, that it was pushing boundaries too far and fast considering she was still likely in subspace.

But the longing in her eyes, he couldn't resist that.

"Okay." He extricated himself from her and went to the bedroom, where he grabbed a towel from his bathroom and a bottle of lube from the bedside table. Upon second thought, he opened the drawer again and grabbed a spare double-ended snap clip out of it before returning to the living room.

She had the throw wrapped around her and was sitting up. "Hands behind you," he ordered.

She complied immediately, even though she looked confused. He quickly snapped the clip to her wrist cuffs, keeping her immobile. "That's so you don't tempt me too much," he said, brushing the tip of his finger down her nose.

She smiled.

He draped the throw around her again so she didn't get chilled. He kicked off his shoes and unzipped his jeans. He pushed them and his briefs down his legs. His shirt joined the fabric on the floor. After spreading the towel out, he sat at the other end of the couch, turned sideways and facing her. He braced his feet against the side of her leg. "You stay there," he said, pointing at her. "I'm going to consider this a pet reward since you were such a good girl for me."

Hell, he could lie to himself and her about that, use it as an excuse.

The truth was, he wanted her to watch. To see what she did to him.

* * * *

She unconsciously licked her lips as she watched him settle into position. He had a beautiful body, athletic and trim, but not overly muscled. A light dusting of dark hair tapered down his chest into a treasure trail that ended in the short nest of hair surrounding the base of his member. His cock was gorgeous, at least eight inches, cut, that put James to shame. His eyes locked onto hers as he squirted lube into his left hand and slowly started stroking.

"I thought you were right-handed—"

"Shh," he said. "Quiet, pet."

Her lips clamped closed. She realized how smart he was to clip her hands behind her back. If she was free, she'd be crawling between his legs, eager to lick and suck his cock.

Pre-cum already oozed from the slit at the engorged head. He kept his eyes on hers as he stroked, the hard edge to his gaze fading and softening as his breath came in shorter gasps.

The first orgasm came in maybe two minutes with a soft grunt that made her pussy clench when she realized that was how he'd sound if he was fucking her. Pearly jets of cum exploded out of the end of his cock and all over the towel. But he only slowed his strokes, didn't stop, never taking his eyes from her. After another moment, he was fully hard again.

"You do this to me, pet," he whispered, stroking harder and faster now, a little twist of his wrist at the top of each stroke swiping across the head of his cock before sweeping down his shaft again.

Her lips parted. An image flashed in her mind, of her kneeling before him while he did this, his cock pointed at her open and eagerly waiting mouth.

She blinked and was back on the couch, his green eyes holding hers.

"Get ready, pet," he whispered.

This time, his whole body tensed. His eyes fell closed as his chin dropped. He stroked harder, faster, the light slapping sound audible over the TV as his strokes turned into short, hard, jabbing motions.

He threw back his head and let out a loud groan as his cock exploded. The load of cum exploding from his cock didn't look any smaller than the first. This time he fell still, breathing hard and leaning against the back of the couch as he caught his breath.

She was still staring at him when he opened his eyes. He let out a soft laugh. "Well?"

"Wow."

He cleaned himself up with the towel before standing. She couldn't take her eyes off him. She wished she could beg him to fuck her right then.

He looked amused. "Are you all right, pet?"

She nodded. "Thank you, Sir."

His gaze softened. He pulled on his shirt, briefs, and jeans before leaning in and kissing her forehead. He reached behind her and unclipped her wrists. "No, thank you, pet. As you can see, playing with you like this seems to have given my decent libido a boost. Usually I'm good for one." He grinned. "You've set my sadistic motor running and that always makes me horny."

He could have taken advantage of her at any time that night. He could have asked her to let him fuck her, or to suck him off, or anything. He had her trussed up tightly and so deep in subspace that she would have gladly begged for him to do it if he'd suggested it.

But he didn't.

He'd kept his word.

Is this what trust feels like?

He led her back to the playroom, where he removed the wrist and ankle cuffs, but had her keep the collar on. She put her dress and sandals back on and he brought her glasses.

He stood in front of her by her car door, his hands on her shoulders. "Thank you for tonight, pet. It was wonderful."

He's thanking me? "I had a great time, Sir," she said.

"Any answers yet to those questions you're puzzling over?"

She nodded, wishing she could tell him what was on her mind and afraid it would mean the end of their arrangement if she did. "Maybe. I don't know."

"I'm glad I can be the one to help you find them."

She wanted to rise up on her toes and kiss him on the lips, to feel his goatee and moustache rubbing against her cheek. "Me, too, Sir."

Chapter Twenty

Monday morning, Shayla crawled into the shower after sending Tony a good-morning text and starting her coffeepot. She stood under the hot spray to loosen her aching muscles.

How can pain feel so damn good, and pleasure feel like pain?

Every pang and twinge reminded her of the things that happened to her over the weekend.

She had no idea how to explain it to others, but at least she felt miles closer to understanding it on an instinctive level.

Note to self, never mention to Tony when I'm horny. She had to laugh, because while she'd witnessed forced orgasm play last weekend, she never imagined in her wildest dreams it could feel like…

That.

She also never imagined she'd ever reach a point of pleasure so acute it almost felt like pain.

Hence the term "orgasm torture." Duh.

When she emerged from the shower, he'd returned her text.

How do you feel, pet? :)

She laughed, knowing that was a loaded question if she ever read one.

Wrung out like a wet dishcloth, Sir.

She was getting dressed when she heard her phone go off again.

:) Good. Can you keep Wednesday open for Me? We'll do pizza at your place. I'll take it easy on you.

She smiled as she noticed in text or e-mail, he'd started capitalizing his pronouns. She liked it. It made her feel…

Owned.

She shoved away her feelings for him and locked them up tight. She didn't want to ruin this by getting clingy and needy and having him pull the plug.

Yes, Sir.

His reply came as she was getting into the car to head to work. *Good girl. I'll be there by seven.*

It was hard to force herself into work mode. Her mind kept drifting to the events of the past forty-eight hours. She admitted it was clichéd, but it felt like her world had been upended, yet everyone else still acted the same.

After the Monday morning editorial meeting, she opened the document containing her story and went through it. She still needed to add some to the end of it. After what she'd experienced, she now knew how to write it. She included basic information she'd learned in the submissive class the week before, the whip class, and the bondage class, before writing her conclusion.

I invite you along on this journey of discovery with me. In a very short amount of time I've had many stereotypes pulverized, met wonderful, welcoming people, and realized that the saying about normal being nothing more than a setting on a dryer is more true than I ever knew. This series of articles will examine different facets of BDSM, and the real, everyday people who practice it. It might make some of you realize you aren't as "weird" as you thought you were. It might also give some of you a welcomed insight into questions that have run through your own mind.

I know I, for one, will never be the same. And I think in my case that's a good thing. (Apologies to Martha Stewart.)

After one more read-through, Shayla selected the entire article and copied it into an e-mail that she BCC'd to Loren, Leah, Tilly, Clarisse...and Tony.

She added a note at the top.

Sorry for the short notice, but I'm turning this in this afternoon. If you all have any suggestions or corrections I need to make, please let me know. I should be able to make edits to it until late Tuesday.

She hit send and sat back in her chair.

Tony texted her a short while later. *Got e-mail. Busy with meetings. Later?*

She smiled. *Yes, Sir. Later is fine. Thank You.*

For him she'd do her damnedest to hold the thing until the absolute last minute on Tuesday afternoon if she had to.

Loren called her within an hour. "The article's great. So? How's the ass?"

Shayla laughed. "Doing good." She'd texted back and forth with Loren a few times Sunday afternoon before going to Tony's.

"Aaand? Tell me what happened last night."

She lowered her voice. "He introduced me to forced orgasm torture."

"Oooh, lucky bitch." She giggled. "Defies description, doesn't it?"

"Um, yeah, that's one way of putting it."

Tony called her after lunch. "I read the article, pet. It sounds good. I don't have any recommendations."

She felt herself blush. "Thank you, Sir." Leah, Tilly, and Clarisse had also weighed in via text, e-mail, and phone, also giving their endorsements.

"So you liked the suggestion I had about what to do during our next private session, hmm?"

Her face felt like a supernova. Her gaze dropped to her lap. "Yes, Sir," she whispered. *Damn*, she'd have to clean up after this phone call. She felt how wet his voice had already gotten her.

"We'll do more talking than play on Wednesday," he said, "but I want you to be naked except for your collar when I get there. Understand?"

She sucked in a breath. "Yes, Sir," she whispered.

"Is anyone listening to you right now?" he asked.

"No, Sir, but I'm in a cubicle."

"You're such a good girl to remember our protocol," he said. "Calling me Sir while at work. Such a brave, good pet."

Her insides felt like mush. She knew if she didn't get to the bathroom soon to clean up, she'd definitely end up with a wet spot on her slacks. "Thank you, Sir."

He chuckled. "I'll let you get back to work. I'm looking forward to Wednesday night."

"Me, too, Sir. And thank you."

"You're welcome, pet. It is most definitely my pleasure."

* * * *

Tony ended the call and fought the urge to giggle. Instead of imagining torturing his coworkers or boss, now he could recall the real-life torture he'd inflicted upon Shayla. He'd already started the morning by rubbing one out in the shower.

He spent the day trying to focus on his work and constantly found his mind drifting back to the events of the weekend. That wasn't like him. At work, he never had a problem being all business.

No one had ever affected him like this before.

Ever.

I'm just going to have to spend the next eight weeks showing her how good it can be and hopefully she won't want to end it.

* * * *

Tony mercilessly teased Shayla via text all day Tuesday. She couldn't wait for Wednesday evening to roll around. The thought of a spanking, or of whatever things he would do to her, kept her in a constant state of horniness.

By the time he texted her as he left work Wednesday night, she was more than ready for whatever he wanted to dish out.

On my way. ETA 25. Order pizza.

She grinned and called it in, thrilled to know he'd be there shortly. As ordered, she was naked and wearing her collar when Tony arrived.

He wasted no time. After their greeting, he hooked a finger through her collar and led her over to the couch. "Over my lap, pet."

She felt her juices flowing already as he spanked her with his bare hand. She cried and sobbed as the stinging pain grew more intense, but she didn't safeword.

When he stopped, she gasped for air and closed her eyes, relaxing as he rubbed her ass.

"Such a good pet. Spread your legs."

She did. He inserted two fingers inside her and slowly fucked her with them, turning his hand so he could also rub her clit with his thumb.

He reached in front of her and stuck two fingers of his other hand into her mouth. "Suck my fingers, pet."

She did, eagerly, holding on to his wrist as he finger-fucked her through two orgasms, her cries muffled by his fingers.

"Sit up, pet."

On shaky legs, she did.

"Open."

She complied.

"Suck my hand clean, pet. You made a mess."

She closed her eyes and took her time, laving her tongue up and down his fingers as she licked every last drop of her juices off his hand.

He smiled. "Such a good girl."

A knock on the door interrupted them. Her eyes must have grown wide because he laughed. "Relax, pet. I'll get it."

Fortunately, she couldn't be seen from the front door. She heard him talk with someone, then he returned carrying the pizza. "Dinner's here, pet. Perfect timing."

He washed his hands as she finally got her legs to start working again and joined him in the kitchen. "Where are your forks?" He glanced at her and laughed. "You can go clean up if you want to, pet."

"Thank you, Sir. Over there." She pointed at a drawer before heading to the bathroom.

* * * *

He didn't bother hiding his amusement. Yep, she was already in subspace. He loved playing with her, how responsive she was, how cute she looked when she realized a spanking had made her wet.

Good thing I'm not an evil scientist.

He opened a drawer, but it wasn't full of utensils. It looked like a catchall drawer. On the top lay a folded piece of paper. He picked it up and, before truly thinking about it, looked at it.

A letter from her ex.

Even as his brain screamed at him not to, he read it.

Why would she hold on to this?

Unless she's not really over him.

He put the paper back and closed the drawer, ashamed of himself for the violation of her privacy. He was better than that.

Yeah, but you don't want to lose your heart to someone who will turn around and leave you, do you?

Dammit.

The seed of doubt grew into a strangling vine at light speed.

Quit being stupid.

By the time she returned, he'd found the forks and paper plates and had the pizza ready to serve. They settled on the couch and even the sight of her naked and collared and still looking freshly fucked couldn't erase from his mind the image of that letter in her drawer.

"Have you heard anything else from your ex lately?" *Subtle, Daniels. Really subtle.*

Shayla tensed a little. "Not since the last check he sent me." She picked at her pizza.

Don't do this. Do not *do this!* "You haven't demanded a repayment schedule from him?"

She shook her head. "He either will or won't repay me. And even if he gives me an answer, I can't trust him to stick to his word." She glanced at him. "He lied to me. Destroyed my trust. If he told me the sky was blue, I'd stick my head out a window and check. I'd rather expect the worst from him than get my hopes up that he'll make good just to give him the power to disappoint me again."

He charged ahead anyway, wanting it cleared up. "What kind of porn was it you said he was into, again?"

"BDSM porn." Now she wouldn't look him in the eye.

Why are you doing this? He put his plate down, well aware the next few minutes might be the end of their evening, or even the end of their time together. "I need to ask you something, and I want an honest answer. Look at me, pet."

She did.

"You're not using this, what we're doing, as a way to better understand it in hopes of trying to win him back or something, are you?"

Her mouth gaped. *"No!* How could you even *think* such a thing?"

"I'm not proud of this, but I accidentally found his letter to you in your junk drawer. I couldn't help wonder why you saved it. I'm sorry, I shouldn't have read it, but it's a legitimate question."

"No, it's *not* a fucking legitimate question!"

"He put you through a lot. I'm not accusing you, but I need to know for sure. I'm just trying to make sure we're on the same page."

She stormed over to the kitchen, where she yanked the drawer open and pulled the letter out before stalking back over to him. She waved it in front of him. "This is what I think of him!"

She ripped it into tiny pieces and threw it in the air. "It shocked the hell out of me when I got it, all right? It was wrapped around the check. At the time I got it, it upset me and I couldn't think, so I stuffed it in there and forgot about it. Okay?"

He felt both relieved and like shit that he'd snooped. He also belatedly realized, from the tension in her body and the tone of her voice, that he'd inadvertently ripped the scab off her fresh emotional wound. "Okay."

She angrily wiped at her eyes. "I trusted him. I loved him. And he took that and threw it away. You don't think I know how that feels? Do you honestly think so little of me that you think I'd turn around and do that to someone else? Have I given you any reason not to trust me?"

"No, you haven't."

"Then what the hell?"

"I'm sorry, pet. I was out of line."

"Damn right you're out of line." She dropped back down to the couch, a scowl on her face.

He tried again. "I should not have read it. It was wrong."

She glared at him. "He fucking put me through the goddamned wringer. I thought you understood that. I trusted you with that information. I thought you understood what I went through, but I guess I was wrong."

He sensed her winding up into an epic tantrum and felt helpless to diffuse it. "You have to understand what it looked like from my end."

* * * *

Shayla saw red. In an instant she'd gone from feeling blissfully subbie to feeling like she'd just been tossed, naked, out of a moving car onto a gravel road. Her fragile, newfound trust once again felt sliced into jagged pieces that cut into her heart and soul.

She wanted him to hurt the way she'd been hurt.

The way James had hurt her.

Even worse, to have a beautiful, sweet taste of trust, of something she'd never thought she'd ever have again, just to have it brutally yanked out from under her was more than she could bear.

Am I really that crappy a judge of character? Maybe I don't deserve to be in a relationship if I can't manage to pick a decent guy. "You men are all alike, aren't you? Everything's so cut and dry? It doesn't matter what we do, we're always going to get questioned for it. You're all fucking assholes."

"Pet, calm down, please. Let's talk about this."

"No, I'm done talking." She stood up and took her plate to the kitchen. "I fucking talked my heart out to James and thought he'd changed and it turned out he was just using me. Are you just using me, too, asshole? Huh? I know I'm not built like one of those goddamned porn models, but I'm good enough to get your jollies off over, aren't I?" Her rapidly fraying control barely hung on by a thread.

"*Pet.*" She heard his warning tone, the way he drew the word out, and ignored it.

She felt the tears rolling down her cheeks and was helpless to stop them. She turned on him again. "No, fuck this shit, fuck men who just use women. So I kept a letter. Big fat hairy deal. I'm still trying to deal with all that shit, you know. And I would think you'd be a little more understanding about it instead of an asshole."

All the pain and rage she'd tried to hold back bubbled like a toxic stew to the surface. She felt as helpless to hold it back as she was to control what her body did in Tony's hands.

He stood. "Last warning, pet," he quietly said. "Calm down and let's talk this out. I'm very sorry I invaded your privacy, and I'm sorry I questioned your motives. You have every right to be angry with me for that. I was wrong. But we can leave the dramatics out of it—"

The last thread snapped. "No, I'm *not* going to fucking calm down! How can you be so fucking calm, huh? I guess life is happy in Dom town where everyone does what they're told when they're told. Well in my world it didn't work like that. I was made a chump by a guy who many of my friends warned me would hurt me again. And they were right, he did. I'm an idiot for trusting, and I'm beginning to think you're all alike. That you're all assholes."

"Good night, pet. When you can discuss this calmly, we'll talk."

She watched as he left. After a minute, when he didn't return, she raced to the front window and realized he had, in fact, driven off.

What the fuck did I just do?

Yes, she had every right to be angry at him, but as all the pain and anger flowed out of her, as control began to seep back into her brain, she realized what she'd done, what she'd said.

He had apologized. He had tried to calm her down, and she would have nothing to do with it.

Her appetite gone, she shoved the pizza, box and all, into the fridge and went to bed where she cried herself to sleep.

Chapter Twenty-One

Stupid, stupid, stupid.

All day Thursday, she felt like crap. She didn't text Tony that morning when she got up, and she didn't hear from him at all.

Man, I fucked this up.

All she knew was that she had to try to find a way to fix it. It felt like a huge sinkhole had suddenly developed in her life.

Like a large piece of her had dropped out of existence.

Maybe this was just an arrangement to him, but she realized she couldn't lie to herself about how important it was to more than just her series of articles.

She wanted Tony in her life. If the only way she could have him was for this short amount of time, she'd take it and be glad of it.

Late Thursday evening, she swallowed her pride, pulled up Tony's number on her contact list, and dialed it.

By the third ring she was certain it would go to his voice mail. That was why it startled her when his voice came on the line. "Hello."

"Um." She cleared her throat and tried again. "Hi. It's, uh, Shay."

"I know. I saw your number on the screen."

She realized he wasn't going to lead her through this. She'd have to nut up and spit it out. "I wanted to call and say I'm sorry."

"Thank you. I appreciate that."

She blinked, waiting. When he didn't continue, she said, "Aren't you sorry?" She regretted the words as soon as she said them.

"I'm sorry we fought, yes. And I apologized to you several times last night, if you'll recall, for reading the letter and for doubting you. If you're expecting an apology for me leaving when you started throwing a tantrum, I'm not going to apologize for a fight I didn't escalate."

She wanted to blast him, except for there being one teensy weensy problem with that.

He was right, and she knew it.

Dammit.

She let out a breath and tried again. "I'm really sorry, Tony. I shouldn't have lost my temper. Can I have another chance? Please?"

"I warned you that I'm not into drama. I don't tolerate it at work, and I damn sure won't tolerate it in my private life. I was doing you a favor. I don't appreciate being called an asshole for my efforts."

"I didn't agree with you."

"That's fine. You have every right to disagree with me. Even to be angry with me. You can, however, be respectful when expressing your disagreement and anger. I'm not perfect. But I'm also not your ex and I don't deserve to be treated like him just because you're still not finished dealing with your pain and anger over what he did to you."

Dammit. He was right.

Again.

"Look, I said I'm sorry. Please?"

She heard him let out what definitely sounded like a sigh on his end of the line. Although she didn't know if it was one of aggravation or acceptance. "What do you want from me, Shayla?"

She felt a wave of dismay at him calling her Shayla instead of Shay.

Or pet.

"I told you. I want another chance."

The pause before his answer seemed to last a year. "I usually don't give second chances when disrespect is involved. I made that perfectly clear to you in the beginning. I thought we had the start of a really good dynamic going and you pull something like that. It makes me reluctant to want to invest more time in it."

She felt like crap and took the plunge. "I'm sorry, Sir," she softly said. "I have issues, all right? I warned you about that, too. Sir."

This time he laughed. She hated that the sound made some place deep inside her feel good. "You don't have issues. You have subscriptions."

"Ha-ha, yes, pick on the vanilla chick who's diving headfirst into all this. Very funny. I said I'm sorry." She felt desperation setting in at the thought of never feeling his hand on the back of her neck again. In a whisper, she begged. "Please, Sir? May I have another chance?"

She didn't realize she held her breath awaiting his response until she let it out when he finally replied. "Fine. No more chances after this one. Not for that. You have a problem, you handle it like an adult and not a brat. You code and talk to me. You don't act out. You don't be disrespectful. Yes, I screwed up. But when I'm standing there admitting I screwed up and apologizing for it, it's time to back down and talk, not throw a tantrum."

She struggled to hold back tears of relief. She spit it out before she lost her nerve. "I'm sorry, Sir. I was scared."

That made him pause. "Of me?"

"No," she softly admitted.

Another pause. "Tell me."

"Can we please do this in person? It'd be a lot easier on me."

The pause was deafening and felt like forever. "Do you think you can still trust me?"

"Yes. This wasn't about you, it was about me. And you were right. I think there's stuff I need help dealing with."

"Seven o'clock tomorrow evening. Meet me at The Pig and Pint on Ringling. You know where it is?"

She could almost see the pub from her cubicle window at work. "Yeah, pretty sure I do."

"What was that?"

She closed her eyes. "Yes, Sir. Sorry, Sir."

"Good girl. I'll see you tomorrow evening, pet. Have a good night, pet."

"Good night, Sir."

She closed her eyes, trembling at the echoes of his voice in her head. His tone had changed, back to smiling and warm.

Good girl.

Pet.

Part of her hated what those words, and the way he said them, did to her insides.

And the rest of her loved it.

Craved it.

Needed it.

Dammit.

* * * *

Tony hung up with her and let out a long, relieved breath.

Thank god she broke down first. If he hadn't heard from her by Sunday, he'd planned on calling her and asking for a sit-down. And at that point he was going to take the chance and admit his feelings for her. Either get things out in the open, or get the finale over and done with.

Either way, it would be a resolution.

Now, at least, they could step back into their dynamic and let it continue. After their time was up, if they made it that long, he would confess to her how he felt and let things shake out however they would.

He'd hated fighting with her, but he'd recognized the sharp, shrill edge of panic in her voice when things blew up last night and knew anything else he said then would only make things worse.

The landmine he'd stepped on had blown up in a huge way. Yes, she had major triggers regarding her ex and what he did to her. He just hadn't realized how big they were.

Or how she obviously hadn't faced her grief over the issue.

She needed an out. She needed permission to face her demons, grieve, and move on.

She needed a safety valve.

He'd seen it before and suspected with events so fresh and raw in her mind, combined with the sudden move and now all of this, that it had festered to a point she didn't want to process it.

He was pleasantly surprised when he received a text from her just a few minutes later.

Good night, Sir.

He smiled as he read it before he replied, *Good night, pet. Sweet dreams.*

Seconds later, her reply.

Thank You, Sir.

He didn't miss that she capitalized the *Y*.

* * * *

He arrived at the pub early only because he'd managed to catch every light green from Bradenton. She walked in a couple of minutes after he got there, and still twelve minutes before their agreed-upon time.

I wonder if I point at the floor if she'd kneel? If she'd give me our greeting here in front of all these people?

From the desperate look on her face he suspected she would. Which was all the more reason he remained seated and kept his fingers laced together on the table in front of him.

She sat across from him. He patted his hands on the table. When she held out her hands, he laced his fingers through hers and looked into her eyes.

"I'm very sorry, pet. I'm sorry I violated your privacy, and I'm sorry I questioned your motives. There will be times I screw up. And I screwed up."

Her lower lip trembled and a tear spilled from her left eye. "I'm sorry I blew up, Sir," she whispered. "I'm sorry I called you names. I'm sorry, I…" Her head dropped and her eyes closed as she softly cried.

He quickly switched seats and tucked her against his chest, his arm around her shoulders as she cried. She took off her glasses and laid them on the table after he pressed a napkin into her hand.

"Shh, it's all right, pet. We'll get through it together."

"I trusted him," she whispered, her pained voice ripping at his heart. "I believed him. Why would he do that to me? I gave him a second chance and it's like he didn't care."

"I don't know, pet. Some men are just assholes." At least she snorted a little laughter through her tears.

She finally looked up at him. "How do I get over this? How do I know I won't screw up somewhere down the line and misjudge someone again like that?"

He tucked her hair behind her ear. "I don't have an answer for you there, pet. Sometimes, people suck. Fortunately, not everyone is like your ex."

"But what if they are?"

"I'm not." He made her look at him. "I feel horrible about the other night. I feel rotten that I made you feel bad. And I hate that we fought."

"Thank you, Sir."

"But."

She wore an expression of anticipation.

"You were disrespectful. I think punishment is in order, don't you?"

She nodded.

"We can move on from this point, but there will be punishment. Tomorrow, not tonight because you're too upset, before we go to dinner and the club. You have to understand that I don't mind disagreements or anger or any of that, as long as it's handled in a respectful, drama-free manner. You need a reminder of that. Deal?"

"Yes, Sir."

He kissed the top of her head. "Good girl."

* * * *

They talked for over an hour before they ate. She managed to pull herself together, but he still sat on the same side as the booth with her, allowing her to sit cuddled against him, his arm around her.

After dinner, he followed her back to her apartment where she quickly stripped and put her collar back on before giving him their greeting.

And she received a spanking over his lap on the couch.

Followed by three orgasms.

And another round of tears he held her through.

Before he left, he gave her instructions for the next day. "I want you to wear your hair in a ponytail tomorrow. Be at my house promptly at two, understand?"

"Yes, Sir."

"Sundress, no panties. Sandals. Punishment will happen first and then we'll move on and put this behind us. I also promise I will not violate your privacy again. But you have to promise to talk to me and not blow up. Code and talk. Okay?"

"Yes, Sir."

When she finally crawled into bed Friday night, emotionally drained but happy, she was almost asleep before she remembered she hadn't checked her mailbox since Wednesday.

Dammit. Add that to the list of things to do tomorrow.

Chapter Twenty-Two

Shayla was so eager to get to Tony's on Saturday that she rushed out before remembering to check her mail again. He'd told her to meet him at his house at two and not to be late, and that was what she'd do.

She suspected the punishment he had in store for her was something he didn't want to deliver at the club in front of others.

She didn't care. She'd take it.

As her mind wandered, she realized no matter what the punishment, she'd be glad to have a chance to make amends. She hadn't irretrievably fucked up their quirky little whatever it was they had, and that was all that mattered to her.

She pulled into his driveway at five minutes 'til two and felt relief wash over her that he wore a smile when he opened the door for her.

"Come in, pet."

"Thank you, Sir." She put her purse, phone, and glasses on the counter and turned to face him, ready to drop to her knees at his signal.

Instead of the expected gesture to kneel, his hand shot out and grabbed her ponytail.

Now she knew why he'd ordered her to wear her hair that way.

He forcefully pulled her head back, so she had to bend her knees to follow the movement. It forced her to look up into his eyes as he leaned in so close she could feel his breath.

So close she could kiss him if he'd just lean in a millimeter closer.

His voice dropped to a deep growl. "You were a very disrespectful pet Wednesday night."

Her juices flowed as fear and desire struggled for domination in her body.

Unfortunately, desire fought dirty and kicked fear in the balls before locking it in a closet.

"I'm sorry, Sir," she whispered.

"I know you are. Not as sorry as you will be. You agreed to punishment, correct?"

"Yes, Sir."

"Punishment does not include a safeword. Not this time. You have two choices. You accept my punishment, or you leave and we part amicably."

"Punishment, please, Sir." The words left her without hesitation.

The hint of a smile returned. "Good girl." He marched her by her hair, still bent over, to the playroom.

He took her to one of the spanking benches and forced her across it. "Stay." When he released her hair, she froze in place, barely breathing and wondering if he could smell how wet she was.

He buckled the leather cuffs around her wrists and ankles and then grabbed her hair again, pulling her back into a standing position. "Dress off."

She lifted it up. He switched holding her ponytail with his other hand so he could take the dress from her. He tossed it onto the floor, then bent her over the bench again.

"Hands down, and hold on to the bench."

She reached down and grabbed the base on either side.

"Legs spread apart."

She did.

Only then did he let go of her ponytail. He knelt next to her. "You are accepting your punishment. I will not restrain you. If you fight me or get up, the session ends and you leave. If you really want to continue, you will take every stroke I give you. I will not force you to take them. You will choose to take them. That's why you have no safeword, because you are free to get up and walk away. Understand?"

Her fingers tightened around the bench. "Yes, Sir," she whispered.

He stood and walked behind her. She couldn't see where he went, but when he returned and she heard the first *zwip* cut through the air, she knew exactly what he held in his hand.

Only a rattan cane made that sound.

"Twenty-five for disrespect. Count every one out aloud. If you miscount, I start over. We will stay here as long as it takes, even if it means missing dinner and the club, for a full count of twenty-five. Understand?"

She felt the endorphins kicking in already. "Yes, Sir." She tightened her grip on the bench even more, knowing these would hurt like a motherfucker.

And she'd show him she could take it.

She'd show him how sorry she was.

She'd prove it.

"Here we go."

She closed her eyes as she heard the cane's path even as it struck her squarely across the ass. She let out a cry as a stripe of fire seemed to follow in the same breath. "One, Sir," she said with a shaky voice.

She was sobbing by the time he hit five, and suspected the endorphins had really driven her deeply into subspace because every stroke, while painful, felt lighter than the last from number ten on out, although they all hurt like a son of a bitch and drew a loud cry from her with each impact.

By the time they reached twenty-five, she hadn't missed a single count and she was sobbing so badly a puddle of snot and drool had formed under her cheek where it pressed against the bench.

He grabbed a towel and walked over to her, tenderly tucking it under her face. His hand lightly stroked her ass and thighs where she knew there would be welts and marks visible to the whole dungeon that night.

But she'd done it. She'd taken them for him. The fire in her ass from every stripe he'd laid in her flesh was worth it.

He gathered her against him. "That's my good girl," he softly said, rocking her in his arms. "There's my very good pet. All the bad gone. The board's reset, and my pet's all good again."

She sobbed even harder, so relieved to hear the tenderness return to his tone. She clutched at him. "I'm sorry, Sir. I'm so sorry."

He pressed his lips to the top of her head. "All's forgiven, pet. In the future, you will code and talk to me, no matter how uncomfortable it feels. I will be patient with you, but you cannot fight me like that. You have to talk to me."

"Yes, Sir."

* * * *

Tony wondered how long it would take her to discover the ruse. She'd howled like she'd taken a hell of a beating, and in her distress that was what she thought she had.

She had two, maybe three cane stripes on her ass that would probably fade by the end of the night. The rest were light strokes he delivered with a thin metal rod he'd grabbed from the freezer in the utility room just before he started. In her deep subspace, she'd processed the cold as pain, especially when he'd combined it with swishing the real rattan cane in the air with his other hand to make the sound as he'd touched the cold rod to her ass.

When he saw she genuinely wanted to atone, he'd gone for the mindfuck, glad to be able to use it and not having the heart to truly whip her ass. Mark her head to toe in fun?

Sure.

Punishment?

He hated having to do it. She'd obviously beaten herself up mentally far more than he could ever in good conscience beat her physically.

And she hadn't let go of the bench once. Not even after the first couple of blows from the rattan cane, which were physically the hardest strikes he'd delivered.

When she finally calmed, he waited until she blew her nose in the towel to point to the floor. She slid to her knees.

"Greeting, pet," he softly said.

She immediately bent to kiss his feet, the sight of her rounded back as she did stirring his cock. Then she kissed the backs of his hands.

Then she nuzzled the front of his slacks before looking up at him, eyes red and puffy from crying.

She was beautiful.

He helped her to her feet and handed her dress to her. "Good girl. Go clean up, pet, and meet me in the living room."

"Yes, Sir."

He was sitting on the couch when she walked in a few minutes later looking confused.

That didn't take long. "Problem, pet?" He patted the couch next to him and had her curl up with her head in his lap.

"I'm confused, Sir."

He bit the inside of his lip to stifle the laughter. "Why?"

"You gave me punishment."

"Yes?"

"And I counted out twenty-five strokes."

"Yes?"

"I only have a couple of marks, Sir. Not that I'm complaining," she rapidly added.

He laughed. "Oh, my sweet pet. Let me tell you about the art of a truly fine mindfuck."

* * * *

Shayla awoke late Sunday morning with a sore ass and a happy heart. She'd laughed along with Tony when he explained the various ways to mindfuck someone in a scene. Including relating a firsthand anecdote he'd read from someone who'd been convinced they'd had chunks of their flesh taken from their body, which was then cooked and fed to them, only to find out a few minutes later they didn't have a scratch on their body.

Obviously, that had been the extreme end of the scale, but after having been through it she could understand it.

Then they'd had another talk. About James.

About the emotional debris she still worked to clear from her heart and soul despite knowing what he'd done wasn't about her as much as it was about him.

She also resigned herself to the fact that she never would understand why he did what he did. There would never be a clear-cut absolute she could cite with any certainty.

"The *only* thing for you to keep in here," Tony said as he looked down at her and touched his index finger to the spot between her eyes, "is that *nothing* you did or could have done would have changed what he did."

"If I hadn't given him a second chance—"

"*Stop*, pet." He tapped her forehead. "You're giving him rent-free space in here when he damn sure doesn't deserve it. I know you can't turn emotions and pain off like a light switch. But the first step to getting over it for good is accepting it's not your fault. And in this case, it isn't. You're a good woman, with a good heart, and at the time, for you, it was the right thing to do. Maybe it wouldn't have been the right thing for someone else. But tell me this, had you left him the first time, do you think maybe you would have been tempted to keep agonizing over the 'what if' option of giving him a second chance?"

She hadn't thought about it like that. She had considered leaving James the first time around.

Then he'd proposed.

And she'd felt too much shame the first time at the thought of admitting to her full circle of friends and extended family why she was leaving him, didn't know enough about porn addiction at the time to understand it.

Never dreamed he'd rob her blind, or that he'd already taken out the first credit card in her name without her knowledge.

She stretched and grabbed her phone from the bedside table to text Tony. *Good morning, Sir.*

He texted her back a little while later. *Good morning, pet. How's the ass?*

She smiled. Later at the club, he had put marks on her ass. As she studied them in the bathroom mirror that morning she could see imprints from a riding crop, the dastardly silicone spoon, and more cane marks.

Real ones, this time.

Good, Sir.

Excellent. How soon can you be over here?

A delicious shiver ran through her. He'd detailed all the things he planned to do to her today. Anal training was first on the list.

Along with more forced orgasms.

One hour.

He replied a few minutes later. *Don't be late.*

She was already in her car thirty minutes later when she remembered she hadn't checked the mail yesterday. *Screw it, I'll drive past it.*

In a hurry not to be late, she grabbed the handful of mail that had filled her box and didn't bother sorting through it. She threw it on the passenger seat and headed for Tony's, her heart light even as butterflies created a hurricane in her stomach.

When she reached Tony's driveway with eight minutes to spare, she was going a little faster than she meant and had to brake hard as she made the turn. The mail on the seat, along with her purse and phone, went flying.

"Dammit."

She parked in her usual spot and shut the engine off. Tony appeared in the front door as she leaned over to grab everything.

That was when she spotted the envelope with a Cleveland return address.

From one James Tavery.

She sat there staring at the envelope, not realizing she was crying until the knock on her window startled her. Tony stood there, concern on his face, but he looked blurry through her tears.

He opened her car door. "What's wrong, pet? What happened?"

She couldn't talk. With a trembling hand, she held out the letter.

He took it, frowning as he read the return address. "This is from him?"

She nodded.

"When did you get it?"

"I forgot to check my mail Friday and Saturday. I stopped by when I left, but I didn't look through it. It...everything just fell on the floor...I picked it up..."

Then he had her seat belt unfastened and his arm around her shoulder and was leading her into the house where he sat with her on the couch.

"Shh, it's all right." He pulled her head into his lap and rocked her as she cried.

When she finally got her wits together, she stared at the envelope, which he'd put on the coffee table. "Will you please open it for me, Sir?"

"Are you sure?"

"Yes, Sir."

He stretched to reach it and finally grabbed it without having to make her get up. He ripped it open. Inside, nestled in a folded sheet of paper, was a check. He handed it to her.

She read the amount. Three hundred dollars.

She snorted. "He's getting cheaper. The last one was for five hundred." She showed it to him. "I wonder how long until they trickle to nothing."

He hadn't read the paper. He held it up. "Do you want to read it?"

She considered it. "No. Would you please read it for me and tell me if there's anything I need to know?"

"Of course." He scanned it for a few minutes. "He's sorry, he's changing, and he's asking your forgiveness. And he's hinting he wants a second chance even though he doesn't have the balls to come out and say it."

She snorted again. "That sounds familiar. Same shit, different day."

"What do you want me to do with this?"

"Do you have a shredder?"
"Yes."
"Please shred it and the envelope."
"Done." He carefully repositioned her so he could get up. He walked out of the room, and a moment later she heard a shredder briefly grumble to life in another room. He returned empty-handed.

"Are you feeling up to playing?" he asked.

She nodded. "I think I need it more than ever, Sir."

He laced his fingers through her hand, helped her off the couch, and led her to the playroom.

He lifted her dress up and over her head and draped it over a chair. Then he got her wrist and ankle cuffs and buckled them around her.

He pointed at the floor.

She sank to her knees and gave him their greeting. When she finished, she pressed her forehead against his thigh and closed her eyes at the feel of the warmth of his body through the denim of his jeans.

He always felt warm. Comforting. She'd come to love this simple moment, the blessed calm washing through her.

Just able to *be*.

He stroked her hair. "I had a pretty energetic agenda for my pet. You sure you're feeling up to it?"

"Yes, Sir. Please." She didn't know how to vocalize her need. How in a short time she craved every session, every dip into the blessed abyss of subspace.

The peace it brought her mind and heart and soul even as her body was put through the wringer of pleasure and pain.

"All right. Stay here." He stepped away from her. She didn't open her eyes, choosing instead to listen to him move round the playroom. Once he'd assembled his items, he returned to her. "Up, pet."

She opened her eyes and stared into his green gaze. He cupped her cheeks with his palms and seemed to search her face for…something.

"You really do enjoy this, don't you?"
"Yes, Sir."
"It's not just about the story anymore, is it?"
"No, Sir."
He kissed her forehead. "Such a good pet," he whispered.

He led her over to one of the benches and had her straddle it facedown, on all fours. She could rest her torso on the top piece, but it was narrow enough her breasts were exposed and freely accessible on either side.

He worked quickly, using clips to attach her wrists and ankles to the bench. He also buckled a leather strap around her midsection, firmly holding her to the bench. And he clipped a short piece of rope to her collar, the other end which clipped to the bench as well. She could only raise her head an inch or two.

He began stroking her back, her legs, her ass with his hands. Strong, warm hands that had seemingly unlocked every secret of her body. "Very little pain today, pet. Only enough to add to the pleasure. I want you to relax and experience this. Turn your brain off."

Gladly. "Yes, Sir."

His hand stroked between her legs, which were spread wide open by her restraints and left her cunt exposed. "You're already wet, pet." He chuckled. "That's good."

He put the soft leather blindfold on her before she heard him return to the end of the bench. He picked something up. The sound of a glove being snapped onto his hand, followed by the sound of something viscous being squirted, made her heart race.

Then his hand returned to her ass. "I'm going to take my time, pet. Relax. You'll be here for a while."

She felt his other hand touch her virgin rim and her whole body tensed.

"Breathe, pet. Yes, this will feel uncomfortable at first. But I have every confidence that you'll take to it like you've taken to everything else so far. Relax and trust me. You have permission to come as much as you want."

Cold goo smeared around her rim. Then he slowly began rubbing the puckered muscle with one finger, not attempting to breach it yet.

The hand on her ass disappeared. It returned holding a small dildo, which he slowly fucked into her cunt.

A soft moan escaped her and she tried to flex her hips in time with his motions.

"Good girl." He began pressing his finger against her rim, applying more pressure now as he kept her distracted with the dildo in her pussy. By the time he had one finger worked into her ass and was slowly fucking her with it, she was rocking in time with his motions, not able to get over the edge though.

The finger and the dildo both disappeared at the same time and the sudden emptiness made her gasp.

"Don't worry, pet. We're barely getting started." He drizzled more lube along the seam of her ass and apparently on his hand. The dildo returned to her cunt and the finger to her ass. He fucked her ass harder with his finger, making her moan at the strange sensation.

Then he withdrew and started pressing a second finger for entrance.

Her body stiffened, anxiety breaking through her blissful haze of need.

"Relax, pet." The dildo disappeared, quickly replaced by something else. When he turned it on and it started buzzing and rotating, she realized it was the rabbit.

He kept it turned on low, slowly fucking her with it as he worked the second finger into her ass. At first it felt strange, uncomfortable having both his fingers penetrating her rim. The stretching sensation struggled to dominate the pleasure she felt in her cunt until after a while, both felt really, really good.

He chuckled as she tried to rock back and forth. "Good girl. Now three."

He added more lube and then began working a third finger into her. She froze, whining, unsure now if she could take it.

His voice turned stern. "Code or take it, pet."

She hesitated only a moment. "Green, Sir."

"Good girl." He took it slow in her ass while he fucked her cunt with the rabbit, careful to keep the clit stimulator away from her nub.

She suspected he wasn't trying to get her over yet, just to tease her to the point where she could barely think. More operant conditioning of his pet, getting her used to something new with a whole lot of pleasure to light the way.

When he had all three fingers buried as deep inside her as he could get them, she was gasping, rocking, whining, desperate for release and desperate to have the intrusion removed from her ass, and also desperately hoping he wouldn't.

There was something wonderful about the full feeling in her cunt and ass at the same time, made only better by the little bit of discomfort she felt.

Then everything disappeared. She tried to rear up and complain but her restraints held her down.

"Stay, pet." She heard the glove being pulled off, then the sink ran briefly. She heard another glove being pulled on and then the sound of more lube being squirted.

He inserted something into her cunt. She softly moaned in pleasure when she heard the familiar sound of him inflating the dildo. He kept inflating it until she whined as it reached the upper threshold of pleasure.

He patted her ass. "Good girl. You'll appreciate that being there." She heard a low buzzing and a vibrator brushed against her clit. Too lightly to get her off, she tried chasing it with her hips but he kept teasing her, tormenting her with it.

Then she felt something press against her rim.

"Breathe, pet. It'll get big and probably uncomfortable as the large part goes in, but the base is narrower." He slowly worked the butt plug into her ass as he continued tormenting her clit. Drawn between pleasure and discomfort, the plug did get bigger, almost to the point she thought she might have to code.

Then he held the vibrator to her clit. She moaned as the first blessed orgasm finally broke free. In the middle of that, he pushed the butt plug home, fully seating it inside her.

She didn't care. He kept her coming for several minutes until she could barely catch her breath. When he removed the vibrator, she went limp on the bench, only then able to fully process how large the butt plug felt.

"Don't worry, pet. It's only a medium one. But it will stay there for a while, so get used to it." He deflated the dildo and removed it.

As she lay there, softly whining at the intrusion in her ass and missing the vibrator and dildo, he walked around to her head. "Next part." His fingers took hold of both her nipples, slowly rolling and tweaking them until she was whining again, each pull sending another bolt of need to her clit.

"Good girl." He clipped something to her left nipple, making her let out a yelp. "Patience, pet." It felt like a little weight hanging from her nipple. He repeated it with the right, and now she was squirming again. "You can take this. Take it or code, pet."

She didn't want to code. She struggled to process the new sensation when she felt him reach out to both nipples at the same time.

She heard two soft *clicks*, followed by vibrations that rolled through her.

His pleased laugh as she cried out stirred her passion. "Good girl.

Vibrating nipple clamps, I knew you'd like them."

She hovered between pain and pleasure, her ass temporarily forgotten. She learned the more she moved, the more they moved, and it was better to hold still.

"Such a good girl," he cooed in her ear. He stroked her hair, immune to her plaintive whining. "Look at you, taking a butt plug and vibrating nipple clamps. I'm so proud of you."

A soft sob escaped her as her struggle to process the sensations continued.

She wasn't aware he'd moved until she felt him between her legs. His fingers played with her clit, not enough to get her off but more than enough to tip the scales toward pleasure again.

"Poor, poor pet. Does my pet need to come again?"

Her face burned. "Yes, Sir."

His voice turned stern. "Ask me, pet. Tell me what you want."

"Please make me come again, Sir."

"Does pet want me to use the strap-on on her?"

"Yes, please, Sir!"

"Such a good girl."

She heard him getting something ready. It surprised her when something touched her lips. "Open, pet. Worship it."

The dildo was large, not the largest he'd used on her, but it got her attention as she tried to open her mouth wide enough to take it. He firmly held her head in place while slowly fucking it in and out of her mouth. She eagerly devoured it, pretending it was really his cock and not a fake one.

He sucked in a sharp breath. "Damn, pet. You really like that, don't you?"

She whined a little in agreement, unable to answer because the strap-on was now almost down her throat.

He withdrew and returned a moment later with something else. "Open, pet."

She did, wide, making him laugh. "Penis gag, pet. It'll keep your little mouth busy. If you need to code, give me three loud grunts. Understand?"

"Yes, Sir." She opened her mouth again.

He slowly worked the gag into her mouth as if it was a real cock, making her clit throb even more. Before he finally buckled it around the back of her head, she was eagerly licking and sucking on it as if made of living flesh.

"Such a good pet."

He stepped between her legs. She felt his jeans rubbing against her inner thighs as he pressed the head of the dildo between her labia, rubbing it up and down through her juices. She tried to arch her back a little to urge him on, but that made the nipple clamps move too much so she fell still.

"Such a slutty little pet you are for me. Look at you, ass stuffed, mouth stuffed, nipples tortured, and you're about to have your pussy stuffed by my stunt cock." He delivered a light, stingy swat to her right ass cheek with his bare hand as he pressed forward a little. Then to her left ass cheek. He alternated slaps as he slowly worked the strap-on inside her until it was buried completely within her cunt and she felt the harness pressing against her flesh.

"Now, pet. Start moving."

She whined as she slowly did, as much as her restraints would allow and trying not to jostle the nipple clamps.

He slapped her ass hard, making her yelp around the penis gag. "I said move, pet. You asked for this. Start fucking that cock."

She did, tears now spilling from her eyes behind the blindfold as the pleasure-pain in her nipples increased with each stroke.

"I think you need some motivation." He reached around her and pressed something against her clit. When the vibrator turned on, set to *high*, she jumped, causing more pain in her nipples. "Move, pet."

She had to. She wanted to come and she couldn't resist the draw of the vibrator on her clit. As the next orgasm hit her, she let out a long, loud moan. He pushed on the base of the butt plug. "That's it, pet. Suck that cock in your mouth."

His voice drove her deeper into that blissful realm where even pain felt good. She no longer cared about her nipples, only about the liquid heat spreading all through her body from her clit and cunt. He pulled and pushed on the butt plug in time with her writhing.

"That's it, pet. Show me what a good little fuck toy you are."

Drool ran from the corners of her mouth as she slurped on the penis gag, trying to lave her tongue around it as much as she could while rocking back and forth against the dildo and the vibrator. Everything blurred. Time disappeared. Her world shrank to nothing but sensations and the sound of his voice.

She never wanted it to end.

Shayla let out a shocked whine when the vibrator shut off. He laughed as his fingers closed around the waist strap. "Don't worry, pet. We're not close to being done." He started fucking her with the strap-on, drawing grunts out of her with every stroke as the nipple clamps kept her clit throbbing and begging for the vibrator again.

"Suck that cock, pet." She did in earnest, earning her another laugh. "Such a good girl."

When he withdrew, she gasped at the sudden emptiness. The nipple clamps were removed and she whined again at the sting as blood flow returned. He rubbed them, which soon turned into tormenting pinching.

"Suck that cock!" he ordered.

In her discomfort she'd forgotten. She began slurping on the gag again, making him laugh. "Damn, that's cute."

She'd also forgotten about the butt plug. Until he began removing it, that is. The mix of pain and pleasure as he pulled it out reset her brain a little, bringing her up from the depths of subspace. He wiped her bottom clean with what felt like paper towel and disappeared.

The sink ran for a moment. She heard some noises she didn't understand, and then the rabbit returned to her cunt. She was able to sink back down again, freely flexing her hips and fucking herself against the toy even though he wouldn't let her reach the clit stimulator.

"Okay, pet. I've been dying to fuck that sweet ass of yours tonight. Don't worry, I changed out the dildo. It's not any bigger than the butt plug. I promised you'd be full in all three holes, and you have been. Now it's time to break in that virgin ass of yours. Get used to it, because it will be part of our new routine during our private sessions. I'm going to train you to crave anal as much as you love pain now." He worked more lube into her ass.

She froze, but he cranked up the rabbit's speed and repositioned it so the clit stimulator hit her perfectly.

She howled as the climax slammed into her, barely aware of him slowly fucking the dildo into her ass as she was too busy humping the vibrator.

"That's it, pet. Fuck yourself onto my stunt cock."

To get one, she had to have the other. She didn't care anymore, her body possessed by the sensations flowing through her. She felt him grab hold of the waist strap with one hand while the other held the rabbit in place. He started fucking her in time with her motions until she felt the dildo buried all the way inside her ass.

Sobbing, she fucked harder, faster, rocking back and forth as much as she could against her restraints and needing more, wishing it was an even bigger dildo in her ass now.

That was when the vibrator cycled to high.

"Fuck it, pet!" he barked. "Don't you dare stop fucking that cock in your ass."

Frantically she did, blissfully lost in the pleasure as his thighs slammed against hers. She was vaguely aware of his pleased laughter as another wave of pleasure hit her. She didn't care what she looked like, didn't care what anyone thought of her, she didn't want to stop. With abandon she rode wave after wave of orgasms until she wasn't sure how much more she could take and her jaws ached from where the penis gag kept them apart.

The rabbit shut off, and he slipped the dildo from her ass. Winded, she collapsed onto the bench and tried to catch her breath.

He wiped her down again. She didn't even flinch when he slid another butt plug into her, maybe smaller than the first one, maybe the same one, she didn't know and didn't care. The burning pinch had long ago disappeared and now all she was left with was her throbbing clit.

He removed the waist belt, but then she felt him insert something into her pussy, and he buckled an all-too-familiar harness around her hips.

When the egg clicked on, she whined a little, unable to resist.

He chuckled. "Yes, pet. I plan on keeping you coming off and on all evening."

He left her blindfolded and the penis gag in her mouth but unclipped her wrists, ankles, and collar from the bench. He had her sit up, and she whined again as the pressure pushed the butt plug deeper inside her and the egg rumbled in her pussy.

It sounded like he giggled. "Aww, poor pet. Come on, let me cook you dinner." He led her, still blindfolded, out to the kitchen and helped her down onto her pillow. He covered her with the throw. "Feel free to take a nap if you want to."

Despite the egg vibrating in her pussy and keeping her on edge, she dozed off.

After dinner he stretched her over his lap on the couch and gave her an over-the-knee spanking while he cranked the egg up to high. Each stroke jostled the butt plug in her ass until she couldn't resist any longer. The egg pushed her into an orgasm as he kept spanking her until she finally stopped coming.

She didn't know what was better, his pleased laughter or the climax she had.

After that they lay on the couch and watched TV while she recovered. He made her keep the egg inside, and the butt plug, but at least he turned the egg off. It was nearly eleven o'clock by the time she made it home. The drive home proved interesting, the way her ass as well as her asshole both felt used, with every vibration from the road jolting through her.

As she worked her aching jaw, the thought of the penis gag in her mouth sent a flood of moisture to her pussy.

I don't want this to ever end. The thought shocked her. Thinking back to what she must have looked like strapped to the bench, she realized she didn't care.

I want this. I really do want this.

Chapter Twenty-Three

Time blurred and flowed by way too fast for Shayla's liking. Every session they had, at the club or privately, was more intense and passionate than the next. And when she received two more checks from James, one for one hundred dollars and one for three hundred, both accompanied by notes, she'd immediately called Tony.

Both times, he'd come over to her apartment that night to hold her while she cried...followed by an over-the-knee spanking that always left her wet and anxious for their next weekend session.

Their fourth Saturday together, he took her to the club and had a no-holds-barred scene with her that she was pleased to learn later had drawn quite a crowd as well as left her sore and sated in all the good ways. In fact, the scene had left her with a tingling sensation that seemed to vibrate straight to the core of her soul and wouldn't go away.

The way he'd made her open her eyes and look at him. The way his serious expression changed to a sexy, pleased smile when she'd tipped over the edge and lost all control as the orgasms ripped through her, one after another without even a chance to catch her breath between them. The way his eyebrows had raised as he pushed her through "just one more" until she thought she'd melt.

Sex had never been that hot with James.

Ever.

Not even in the beginning, in the good times, or what she'd thought were good times, when they weren't able to keep their hands off each other.

Hell, Tony hadn't even taken off any of his clothes to make her come. He was stuck getting his own rocks off after taking damn good care of her.

In a way, she felt a little guilty over that. Here he was doing all the work and she got to have all the fun. Not once had he even hinted at asking her to help get him off despite what had to be a painful erection he always seemed to sport during their play sessions.

When she arrived at his house the next evening for another private Sunday session, her panties were already damp at the thought of what he might have in store for her. She was more than ready, after four weeks of teasing and torment, to take things to the next level.

Once inside, naked, collared, and kneeling on her pillow in the playroom, she waited for him to give her his full attention. When he walked up to her and she gave him their usual greeting, she felt a peace settle over her as he stood close so she could rest her cheek against his thigh.

It felt like home, like every stress and worry could melt away replaced by his quiet, secure strength taking care of her.

"So how are you doing tonight, pet?"

"I'm fine, Sir."

"Last night didn't wear you out?"

"Only in the good ways. I would like to talk to you about something before we get started."

"Yes?"

This time, she couldn't make herself look up at him. Instead, she felt her fingers curling into anxious fists on her knees as she forced out the words. "I want to do something for you."

"Look at me, pet. You know our rule."

She closed her eyes before tipping her chin up toward his voice. Only then was she able to command her eyelids to open and stare at him.

He stood over her, patiently waiting. "Tell me."

Her mouth went dry and she found herself unable to swallow. "I'd like to amend our agreement, please, Sir."

"How so?"

"I'd...I'd like to be able to reciprocate, Sir."

One eyebrow slowly arched. "Please be clear, pet. You're trying my patience. If you can't even talk about it, I won't consider doing it."

"I want to give you a blow job." The words rushed out of her so fast she wasn't sure he'd be able to understand her.

She damn sure didn't know if she'd be able to say them again.

He studied her for long minutes that made her nearly want to cry. *He doesn't want to. He's not really attracted to me. I'm a stupid idiot.*

The words he next spoke took her breath away. "This is a limit I can't agree to unless you agree it doesn't end up in your articles. This takes our dynamic to a very private and personal level that is no one's business but our own. Since neither of us have significant others, I'm okay with it if you are."

Blinking, she tried to comprehend what he'd just said. She nodded. "I mean, yes, Sir. It won't be part of the articles. I promise."

He continued to study her. After another seemingly endless moment, he nodded. "No penetration. Except fingers and toys, of course."

She nodded, although in retrospect, she realized putting intercourse on the table wouldn't be bad at all.

I won't rush it.

"Yes, Sir."

"Am I allowed to reciprocate?"

She eagerly nodded. "Yes, Sir. If you want to."

"All right then, pet. But only after I'm finished with you. If at the end of our play session you still want to, then we will. Deal?"

She nodded.

He strapped her down to one of the benches and quickly had her deep in subspace. He used the vibrating nipple clamps to distract her while he inserted a large butt plug. She felt her face heat as she realized he had quickly succeeded in training her to enjoy anal play. He'd made her beg for the butt plug the last time before doing anything else to her, making her realize she was wet and horny at the thought of it stretching her rim and filling her ass.

He's an evil genius.

Next came the strap-on. He fucked her pussy with it while using a vibrator on her clit, until she lost all track of time and felt the world shrink as orgasm after orgasm stole conscious thought from her.

She loved that feeling.

Craved it.

Needed it.

Once she was left spent and panting on the bench, he removed the nipple clamps and unfastened her restraints and helped her up.

She noticed the butt plug remained.

He pointed at the floor. She dropped to her knees, praying this was the moment she'd hoped for.

He considered her for a long time, as her clit throbbed with ghostly memories of the vibrator and her ass clenched around the butt plug buried inside her.

"You asked me earlier to do something, pet."

"Yes, Sir."

"Say it."

"I want to give you a blow job, Sir."

"You still want to?"

"Yes, Sir. Please, Sir."

"There is a price to pay for that."

"Yes, Sir."

"Do you care what it is?"

"No, Sir. I trust you."

He reached out and stroked her hair. "Such a good pet. Stand up."

She did, as he kicked off his shoes. He held out his arms. "Undress me, pet."

Her fingers trembled with anticipation as she worked the buttons on his shirt. She barely managed his belt and the button on his jeans. His hard cock made pulling the zipper down difficult, but she managed.

As his jeans slid down his hips, she couldn't help pressing her face against the front of his briefs, where the rigid outline of his cock strained for freedom.

She could smell him, warm and sensuous, and she couldn't wait to have his cock in her mouth.

Once he was naked, he hooked a finger through the front ring of her collar and put her back on the bench, where he clipped her wrists and ankles to it.

It put her at perfect height to take his cock.

He stood in front of her as she opened her mouth, but he kept his cock tantalizingly out of reach. "Patience, pet. When I come, you will hold it in your mouth without swallowing until I tell you. Understand?"

"Yes, Sir!"

He fisted his cock and moved closer. She reached out with her tongue, but he seemed to derive evil pleasure tormenting her like that as well. She could smell him, see the drop of pre-cum already pearling at the slit.

"Beg me, pet. Beg me to worship my cock."

"Please, Sir! Please let me suck your cock. I want to suck your cock. I want you to come down my throat."

The soul-melting smile returned. "Such a good girl," he cooed. "Now that you love anal so much, maybe I'll train you to be my cock slut. Would you like that?"

"Yes, Sir!" Now her pussy clenched, nearly cramping with need.

He slowly fed his cock to her. She eagerly lapped at it, hungrily, moaning at the taste of his juices. He took his time, slowly thrusting, his hands resting on either side of her head until she realized, like that night with the strap-on, he was driving and fucking her mouth.

His cock felt like silken steel against her tongue, warm and thick and musky and sweet, everything she dreamed and better. She relaxed her mouth and let him use her, his praise sinking her deep into subspace again.

He went harder, faster. "Get ready, pet," he grunted. "Remember, hold it. Do not swallow."

His cock went rigid against her tongue and she felt jets of hot cum streaming into her mouth. His body went rigid and he groaned, making her groan with him as she finally got to taste him.

It wasn't until he went soft that he pulled out. "Show me, pet."

She opened her mouth, careful not to lose any of it.

He smiled. "Good girl. Mouth closed and hold it until I say so."

He walked behind her. Then she sensed him kneel between her legs and felt his hot breath on her clit. She whined when his hands spread her labia, opening her wide to his view.

She almost forgot to keep her mouth closed when his tongue flicked out and stroked her clit. He took his time the same way he did everything else, driving her desire harder, faster, higher, until she didn't think she could take it anymore.

"Swallow, pet," he ordered. Then his teeth clamped down on her clit.

She was mid swallow when the orgasm hit. He didn't stop either, using his lips and tongue and teeth and sucking, nipping, licking her through several orgasms that left her sobbing with relief when he finally finished. He kissed the insides of her thighs and stood. "Such a good girl."

She lay there with her eyes closed, basking in the post-orgasmic bliss. She didn't know how he did it. How he managed to make her come over and over, and when she was sure there was no way in hell she could come again, he blithely revved her motor and sent her on another cycle of climaxes she never dreamed possible.

She heard the sink run briefly. Then he was standing in front of her again. "Want seconds, pet?"

She opened her eyes, eye to eye with his erect cock.

She met his gaze as she opened her mouth wide.

"Such a good girl. You can swallow this time." He used her hard and fast. Deep inside, she felt more than pleased and satisfied. He was using her for his pleasure. She was making him feel like this.

She'd let him use her however he wanted if she could keep feeling that good.

He came a lot faster that time. When he finished, he let out a happy sigh before unfastening her restraints. "TV and cuddle time, pet."

She smiled and nodded. "Thank you, Sir."

* * * *

He got her settled on the couch. "Want a drink, pet?"

"Yes, please."

A few moments later, Tony returned from the kitchen with a glass of water for her and her phone. "I heard it vibrating on the counter," he said. "I didn't know if you wanted to check it or not."

"Thanks." She drank several long swallows from the glass and waited until her head was once again securely snuggled in Tony's lap before checking her phone.

She'd missed two text messages from her mother. When she opened them, she swore.

"What's wrong, pet?"

She stared at the screen. "My mom just sent me flight and hotel information. They're arriving late Friday night in Tampa and driving down to Sarasota." She looked up at him, nearly in tears that she'd have to give up their Saturday afternoon session, and maybe their Sunday one, too.

"You don't want to see them?"

"I..." She hesitated, not wanting to appear clingy or needy. And definitely not wanting to admit the full truth of her feelings to him. "I'd really looked forward to our Saturday is all."

He laced his fingers through hers and rubbed his thumb across her knuckles. "It's all right, pet. I'll go with you, if you want. Feel free to tell them I'm your boyfriend."

"Really?" She sat up and threw her arms around him. "Thank you, Sir!"

* * * *

He had to bite back the urge to laugh. A chance to meet her parents? *Hell, yes.*

A chance to spend a relatively vanilla day with her and give her a chance to see what it could be like between them in a relationship beyond their agreement?

Fuck, yeah.

Like hell he'd give up a chance to spend time with her, period, as long as work didn't interfere.

Maybe I can win them over, he idly thought.

He smiled. *A chance to get her used to calling me her boyfriend?*

No-brainer.

Chapter Twenty-Four

Shayla had another reason to feel less than enthused about her parents' visit.

That reason smacked her in the face Tuesday morning as she sat at her desk, chin propped in her hand, and she stared at her computer.

But if Mom and Dad were reading my articles, wouldn't they have said something? Anything?

She hadn't told them about the series she was writing for the magazine, although the job of weeding through her work e-mail every morning grew longer as the series went on. She deleted without reply the few e-mails blasting her for the series, usually preachy missives telling her she would burn in hell for her sinful activities.

She also deleted, without reply, the blessedly few creepy e-mails asking her out.

The rest of the e-mails were either from people in the lifestyle praising her accuracy and the positive spin she gave BDSM practices, or from people asking questions about how to find out more information to get involved themselves.

It didn't hurt that their website hits for the series had spiked to an all-time high.

After thinking for a few more minutes, she returned her fingers to the keyboard and added to the copy she'd already written that morning.

It's difficult to explain to someone what it's like to dislike pain and yet crave the act of receiving it for another's pleasure. It's certainly not something I ever thought I would find myself doing.

And it's definitely not something I ever thought I would enjoy.

She sat back and stared at the article, reading it once again from the beginning. Her time with Tony seemed to be moving far too fast, and yet it felt like he'd been in her life forever.

Part of her wanted to ask him to extend their agreement, or ask him his opinion of changing it from just an arrangement to a formal relationship.

But she also didn't want to appear clingy, or torpedo things with him before their full time was up, either. On top of that, he'd had several crazy weeks at work and several times stated how he enjoyed their time together as a way to put work out of his mind.

She didn't want to ruin that for him.

I should wait until the end of things. If he wants to change things up sooner, he'll tell me. He's the Dom.

* * * *

Shayla nervously paced her living room Saturday morning until she heard Tony's car pull up next to hers and shut off. She didn't even let him reach the front door before she had it open and was waiting for him.

He smiled as he stepped in and shut the door behind him.

Then he pointed to the floor.

Without hesitation she dropped to her knees and kissed both of his feet then the backs of his hands before nuzzling the front of his slacks.

As always, his bulge hardened immediately, making her smile.

She looked up at him, his smile making her wet. He stroked the top of her head. "Such a good pet," he softly said.

"Thank you, Sir."

"We have fifteen minutes before we need to head to their hotel. Panties off."

She swallowed hard but complied immediately, standing and pulling them off. When he held out his hand for them she placed them in his palm.

He took hold of the nape of her neck the way he always did, gently but firmly, and marched her over to the couch. He sat, then patted his lap. "Face down, pet."

More moisture flooded her pussy as she knew what was coming. *Damn him!* But it wasn't anger churning her guts, it was need.

When she was settled on his lap, her head toward his left so he could spank her with his right hand, he carefully balled up her panties. "Open, pet."

She did. He tucked them into her mouth before his left hand settled firmly on the nape of her neck, his fingers hooked around her collar. His right hand pulled up the skirt of her sundress, exposing her ass and thighs.

His smooth, low tone helped stoke her desire. "I think my pet needs a nice, warm, red ass before she takes me to meet her parents," he said. "Because I want my pet to remember who she belongs to. I think my pet wants that, too. Don't you?" His right hand stroked her ass.

She desperately fought the urge to rub herself against his thigh. She'd be wet enough as it was after the spanking. She mumbled, "Yes, Sir," around the panties.

"Ask me for it."

If she didn't leave a wet spot on his slacks, it would be a miracle. "Please spank me, Sir," she mumbled around the makeshift gag.

His warm chuckle only fanned the flames. "That's my good girl." When his right hand fell still, she braced herself for what would come next. Sure enough, the first blow fell, hard and fast and stinging and making her glad for the fabric in her mouth to chew down on to stifle her cry so she didn't scare the neighbors.

He spanked her hard, stopping every few strokes to squeeze and soothe and caress the flesh of her ass before starting again, over and over, until she sobbed into her hands, which she'd tightly clenched together against the pain.

And yet safewording didn't cross her mind.

When he stopped and gently patted her rump, she gasped, relieved and disappointed that it was over so soon. "Sit up, pet."

She did, the panties still in her mouth.

"Hold up your skirt for me."

She did, and he immediately laughed. She felt her juices running down the inside of her thighs. He reached between her legs and coated his fingers in them. Then he pulled the panties out of her mouth and replaced them with his fingers.

She eagerly sucked them, wishing it was his cock in her mouth, wishing she could spend all day worshipping his cock and that they didn't have to go meet up with her parents.

What is wrong with me? She craved it, wanted it.

Needed it.

"Such a good girl." She looked into his eyes and wished she could melt into them. He seemed to pierce through to the center of her being with that look.

Be a slave? Hell, she'd give up everything just to spend the rest of her life receiving that look from him. To please him.

To make him happy.

To hear him tell her she was a good girl.

His good pet.

I understand.

He cocked his head a little. "Are you all right, pet?"

He pulled his fingers from her mouth so she could answer. "Yes, Sir."

"Why do you look sad?"

"I'm not sad, Sir. I just wish we had more time so I could take care of you."

He looked down at his lap, where his slacks were tented. "I'm sure I have a wet spot of my own," he said. "But that's okay. I'll be sure to make you work extra hard for it later." He caught the front of her collar with his finger and pulled her down so he could kiss her on the forehead. "Go clean up, pet." He handed her the panties. "And you may pick out a fresh pair of those to wear."

She hurried into the bedroom to grab another pair of panties. Then into the bathroom to clean up. She couldn't help but turn and hike her skirt to look at the marks.

Yep, the sweet, hot stinging she still felt in her ass was displayed not only by red handprints, but by little purple and blue blood welts, too.

She caught sight of her pleased grin in the mirror and froze. *What is wrong with me?*

She thought about it. *I'm the happiest I've been in my life doing this.*

"Three minutes, pet," he called from the living room.

That shook her from her thoughts and she hurried to get ready.

He had to stop by the bathroom too before they left. At the front door, he unbuckled her collar and handed it to her to put in her purse. "Ready, pet?"

"Yes, Sir."

"How's the butt?"

She smiled. "Warm and tingly, Sir."

"Good. Just what I was going for. I'm sure your clit is nice and warm and tingly now, too, isn't it?"

"Yes, Sir. I'm horny."

He grinned. "Say it for me, pet. You know I love hearing you say it."

She blushed, but didn't look away from his gaze. "When you spank me, Sir, it makes me horny."

"Aw, such a good girl. I know it does, pet. Spanking your sweet ass makes me horny, too. Don't worry. If you're a good girl today, I'll give you another spanking later, before I use the strap-on on your freshly spanked ass. You'll like that, won't you?"

She sucked in a breath as a new flood of moisture pooled between her legs. "Yes, Sir," she whispered.

He laughed. "What's the matter, pet?"

"I'm horny, Sir."

"I know." He waggled his eyebrows at her. "That's the point."

She settled into his passenger seat, fully aware of her freshly warmed ass. He glanced over at her with a grin as he backed out of the parking space.

"Doing okay there, pet?"

"Yes, Sir." She wiggled a little into her seat.

He noticed and let out a little laugh. "Good girl."

* * * *

Shayla decided it would be easiest to introduce Tony as her boyfriend. Which, to her, surprisingly felt right. She felt nervous about seeing them, worried what they might think.

Not that it matters. He's not really my boyfriend.

Even though I wish he was.

She blinked. *Where'd that come from?*

She needed to remember to keep her head on straight. Which might be hard to do with her freshly spanked ass distracting her. She wouldn't be one of those clingy, needy women Tony didn't like. If he wanted to keep things going, no doubt he'd speak his mind.

He had no problems telling her what he wanted. And she didn't want to risk ruining what she had if he didn't feel the same way about her.

Best to let sleeping dogs lie, isn't that what they say?

It didn't take long to make it to their hotel. Her parents were waiting in the lobby, where they offered smiles and hugs.

"This is Tony Daniels," Shayla said. "My boyfriend."

"You didn't tell us you were seeing anyone," her mom playfully scolded.

"We've only been seeing each other for a few weeks."

"It's nice to meet you, Tony," her dad said, but Shayla spotted the guarded look on his face even as he reached out to shake hands with Tony.

"Tony's going to play tour guide for us today, if that's okay with you guys?" Shayla said. "He's lived down here all his life."

"So what do you do for a living?" her dad asked.

"I'm in IT. I run the data center at Asher Insurance."

Her dad frowned. "Asher? Isn't that a pretty big company?"

Tony offered up the smile that could easily part Shayla from her panties. "Nationwide."

Donald Pierce looked impressed. "You must make good money."

Tony shrugged. "I do okay. I certainly don't have to take out secret credit cards in my girlfriend's name."

Karen Pierce laughed out loud. "Oh, I like this one, honey," she said.

"Okay, if we're done playing 'Interrogate Our Daughter's Boyfriend,'" Shayla suggested, "I'd like to go eat. I'm starving."

He took them to a restaurant on St. Armand's Circle. He also scored brownie points with her parents by picking up the check and refusing to let them pay. Then the four of them spent time walking the circle, browsing through the shops.

"You should see this place around Christmas," he told them. "Everything's decorated. It's beautiful."

"I bet it's warm down here at Christmas," her mom said.

"Sometimes. The only white Christmas we have is on the beaches, though."

"You guys should come down for Christmas," Shayla said. "Rent a condo for a week. We can have Steven come down, too. Have a Florida family Christmas." It'd be nice to have her parents and her brother around for the holidays.

Her mom stopped walking and looked up at her dad. "What do you think, Don? I like that idea. It'd be nice to escape the snow. You were going to take two weeks off at Christmas and New Year's anyway."

"I think I'm outnumbered," he said to Tony.

Tony nodded. "Looks like it."

They walked into a small gift shop to browse. A small rack of pewter amulet necklaces caught Shayla's eye. Sitting on the counter, each artisan amulet looked hand-stamped and hung from a black cord.

One in particular, with a design of quarter moon, stars, the sun, and hearts, caught her eye. "Ooh, that's cute." She looked at the price tag and immediately let go of it. "Not that cute."

"What?" Tony looked at it. "You like it?"

"I love it. My budget, however, doesn't." Her mom called her over to look at something. When they left the shop a few minutes later, Shayla didn't understand Tony's sly smile. As much as she loved that smile of his, she wished he'd stop it. Her panties were already dangerously close to being soaked through as it was.

He drove them to Mote Marine, where they spent a couple of hours touring the exhibits, before heading down to the world-famous Siesta Key Beach.

"It's gorgeous!" her mother exclaimed. "I've never seen the Gulf before."

"Actually, I prefer going down to Manasota Key," Tony said. "You think this is pretty? That's a beautiful beach. Far less developed than here, and quiet. And you can find lots of shark's teeth."

"How far away is that?" her dad asked.

"About an hour south of here. It's worth the trip if you have the time."

Her dad looked at her mom. "Maybe we can do that tomorrow."

"I'll show you on a map how to get there. It's easy to find."

After stopping for dinner at a different place in Sarasota, they dropped her parents back at their hotel. "So what are you kids doing tomorrow night for dinner?" her mom asked.

"'You kids?' Did you really just say that, Mom?"

Karen smiled. "Parental prerogative."

"I was hoping," Tony said, "we could have you over to my place for dinner." He smiled at Shayla.

This was news to her.

"You could pick Shayla up at her place," he continued, "see her apartment, and then you all could ride together to my place."

"That sounds lovely," her mom said before Shayla could come up with a reason not to. "Thank you. What time?"

He looked at Shayla and caught her gaze, winking at her. "Six works for me." She knew that wink. It meant if she didn't get her perpetually procrastinating parents there on time, it would be *her* ass that paid for it later.

The thought of another spanking only made her hornier.

They said their good-byes. Back in Tony's car, Shayla looked at him. "You could have warned me, Sir." She'd caught herself several times wanting to call him Sir in front of her parents.

He laughed. "What fun would that have been?" He held out his hand. "Collar, pet."

She retrieved it from her purse and handed it over. She held her hair out of his way so he could buckle it around her neck. Her eyes fell closed as a sense of peace settled over her.

"Good girl. And I have something else for you." He pulled something from his pocket and held it up.

The amulet necklace from the gift shop.

She gasped. "Sir, thank you!" She threw her arms around him and hugged him. "I wasn't expecting that!"

"I know you weren't, pet. That's why I bought it for you." He draped it around her neck. "I've been wanting to get you a day collar anyway. That was the perfect opportunity. I like it, and I know it's something you like."

She looked at the amulet. The forty-nine-dollar price tag had been out of her range for such a splurge for a piece of jewelry. "I don't know what to say, Sir. Thank you."

He cupped the back of her neck and made her look at him. "Consider this your other collar. When you go out, you wear it. Except for your shower or in the pool, you need to have one or the other of these collars on."

"Or both?"

He smiled. "Silly pet. Yes, or both. But you can wear this one to work and only you and I will know what it really means." He slightly tightened his grip on the back of her neck. "It's as good as if my hand were physically on your neck like it is now. Understand?"

She nodded, fighting the slew of happy tears she struggled to hold back. "Thank you, Sir. I love it."

I love you.

But she didn't say that last part. Although she really wished she could.

Chapter Twenty-Five

Eight weeks seemed to fly by. It felt like Tony had always been in her life, and she refused to contemplate a future where he wasn't.

But he hadn't mentioned changing their arrangement, so she didn't want to rock the boat. She had dropped a few hints here and there over the past couple of weeks, but she didn't know if he was just being a typical guy and not picking up on them...

Or maybe he didn't want to extend things.

Either way, she'd decided just to let things play out.

He picked her up at seven to go to dinner with everyone before they headed to the club. She noticed at one point during dinner he seemed a little quiet, deep in thought. "Are you all right, Sir?" she softly asked.

He smiled, but it looked sad. "Sorry. Preoccupied. Can't quite get myself out of work mode today. Early flight to Denver tomorrow."

"Oh, that's right. Your trip." With every article she'd written, the e-mail response and web hits increased to the point it felt like her entire world revolved around BDSM both professionally and privately.

Not that she minded.

"Two weeks of hell," he said with a smile. "I have a feeling I'll make a few enemies while I'm out there. My staff in Bradenton is used to my management style. I want stuff done the way I say it, when I say I want it done. I don't feel like spending more than two weeks out there because someone gets butthurt over me wanting them to work as hard as I do."

She giggled. "Here's my shocked face." She made an *O* with her mouth.

That finally got a genuine smile out of him. "Keep it up, pet. I haven't put you over the bench yet tonight."

"Maybe that's what I'm hoping for, Sir."

Later, at the club, he took his time with their scene. He ramped her up with pain and pleasure several times, pushing her to her limits, making her cry and sob and plead for more until a final crescendo of cane strokes across her ass. After that, he used the rabbit on her and kept her coming until she wasn't sure she could take anymore when he finally stopped.

With Shayla wrapped in a blanket and curled in his lap on the sofa, he kept his fingers laced through hers.

I love him.

He'd be gone two weeks, though. She didn't want to just dump her feelings on him as he was leaving town for a brutal business trip. She didn't want him to think she'd morphed into one of the clingy drama llamas he despised. She'd wait until he got back, make him a nice dinner, and then tell him. It would be a long two weeks waiting for his return, but then, hopefully, they could write a whole new chapter in their relationship.

She was, however, determined to make one request before he left on his trip. One she hoped he'd take her up on.

* * * *

Shayla's body flew high on endorphins, still deep in subspace as Tony drove her home a few hours later. She hoped tonight to ask him to take that one last step, to rid their dynamic of that one final barrier.

She wanted him to own her. Fully, completely, utterly. Wanted to feel his cock, flesh and blood, fucking her.

When they arrived at her apartment, he took her keys from her and let them in, closing the door behind them. "Here you go," he said, putting them back in her hand.

She didn't understand his sad smile. "Thank you, Sir."

"You don't have to call me that anymore if you don't want to, Shay."

She blinked at his use of her name. "What?"

Before she realized what he was doing, he'd unbuckled her collar and removed it from her neck. Her hand went to her throat, where the cool air brushed against her flesh where seconds earlier the warm leather had cradled her throat like a hand.

His hand.

He cocked his head. "Shay, our time's up. It's the thirty-first. Remember?"

"What?"

He gently cradled her chin with his hand. "You said you wanted our contract to end tonight. That's why I rearranged my schedule so I didn't go out of town until tomorrow. I wanted to be able to take you out to the club one more time." His thumb gently stroked her jaw before he released her and stepped back, the collar in his other hand.

She couldn't process this. "But…" She tried to breathe because even that had become difficult. This wasn't how she'd planned to end their evening!

"I'm sorry I can't stay late tonight. I have to get up at five to make it to Tampa in time for my flight today. Like I told you, we start installs at the new Denver data center early Monday morning. And I still have to pack. Are you all right?"

No! Her brain screamed it over and over again, but she found herself nodding a little. She would be a good girl for him.

She would show him what a good pet she could be.

He'd have more than enough on his plate. She didn't want him to have to worry about her.

He reached out again and palmed her cheek. "Thank you," he softly said. "This has been a wonderful experience. Thank you for placing your trust in me." He leaned in and kissed her forehead. "I'm going to miss you while I'm out there."

Her breath came in short, hitching gasps she knew would end up full-blown sobs if she didn't get herself under control and fast. That wasn't the way she wanted to leave things. "Thank you," she whispered.

Don't you want me? Don't you need me?

Don't you love me?

Involuntarily, she leaned into his touch even as he withdrew his hand and stepped back toward the door. "Go on to bed," he softly said. "Get some rest. I'll try to be in touch with you this week, but I'm going to be slammed and I doubt I'll have cell reception inside the data center building there anyway. I likely won't have many chances to talk while I'm gone."

She nodded a little, unable to move, barely able to breathe.

That smile. That sweet, damn smile of his. "Lock the door after me, Shay."

Before she could process that, he slipped out, closing the door behind him. She realized she was still clutching at her bare throat with her hand as her feet carried her forward. This was not how she'd thought their evening would end.

Far from it.

Finally releasing her throat, she reached out and snapped the deadbolt shut.

Feeling as if her very soul had been ripped from her, she turned and headed toward the bedroom.

* * * *

Tony forced himself to get in the car and start it. It wasn't until he reached the main gate of her complex that he stopped and pressed his forehead against the steering wheel. He took several deep breaths to steady himself.

Still warm from being wrapped around her flesh all night, her collar lay in his lap. He fingered it, something in his heart feeling unraveled and frayed at the thought of her not wearing it.

He'd thought about broaching the subject of them having a real relationship now that their agreement was over, but she hadn't said anything about it.

She's a big girl. She spoke up when she wanted to add oral to the arrangement, I'm sure she'd speak up now if she wanted to keep things going. I refuse to take advantage of her. Especially when she's still deep in subspace. If she wants a relationship, she's going to have to ask for it and tell me that's what she wants. I won't be a douche and take advantage of her when she's like this.

"Fuck." Once he returned from his trip and could think about something other than work, he'd ask her to sit down to talk with him. See if there was any chance for them as a couple. Tonight, as tired and rushed for time as he was, it wasn't the right time to talk about it. Especially when she was in no headspace to have such a conversation.

He'd promised he wouldn't change the rules on her, wouldn't renegotiate on the fly. Considering how he'd narrowly avoided destroying her trust in him with the letter-reading incident, he wasn't about to do something in the heat of the moment that would kill her trust in him and drive her away.

I won't be a douche.

Not to mention, since she hadn't asked him about it before now, he wasn't sure he wanted to face the very real possibility of getting shot down right before what would already be a grueling couple of weeks working out of town.

He laid the collar on the passenger seat and headed out toward I-75 to go home.

He didn't sleep at all. After packing, he tried to lie down for a nap and gave up. Sleep wouldn't come. All he could see were Shay's hazel eyes and the lost look on her face when he uncollared her.

She hadn't protested, though. She hadn't asked him not to.

She didn't beg him to stay, or to at least talk about it.

She didn't ask him to extend their time together. He would have gladly and readily agreed to that without further discussion. It would have bought him more time with her.

It's not like she doesn't know how to ask for what she wants. His mind refused to release that point, chewing on it. She'd asked to include oral sex as part of their agreement. That was a pretty big step. If she'd wanted more from him, surely she would have asked for it before now.

His thoughts kept returning to that, that she could have asked.

That he *wished* she'd asked.

That he wished she'd told him she loved him, the way he knew he loved her.

If she doesn't want to end things, we can talk about it when I get back. I'd rather sit down and have a long talk with her than rush it and fuck it up.

She's worth waiting for, if it's really meant to be. It's only two weeks.

He forced it out of his mind as he drove to Tampa and parked in the airport's long-term parking lot. As he stood in line to board his flight to Denver, he fingered his cell phone.

Maybe I should text her.

But she would likely be asleep until later in the afternoon. Then there was the fact that he would have to hit the ground running and head over to the construction site as soon as he got a rental car to find the manager. They were going to meet to go over the next day's schedule.

With a sigh he turned off his phone and slipped it into his pocket. *I'll text her later.*

* * * *

Shayla stretched out on her bed and cried herself to sleep after Tony left. In the morning, with a throbbing headache and a sick stomach, she curled into a ball and stared at the clock. 11:17 in the morning.

He's in the air already.

And then he would be in Denver, overseeing the installation of the new equipment, for at least two weeks.

I can do this.

The next morning, she burst into tears when she caught herself picking up her phone to text him before leaving the apartment. The thought of calling in sick to work appealed greatly to her, but she had to get the last article finished and turned in.

After washing her face again and forgoing makeup that would run and smear and make her look even worse, she forced herself to drive to work. It wasn't until she was there that she realized she wore her amulet necklace.

She didn't have the heart to take it off.

Loren texted her while she was in the Monday morning editorial meeting, and she ignored it. Until after lunch, when she realized she had three more texts and four voice mails from Loren, each one sounding increasingly worried, along with additional texts from Leah, Tilly, and Clarisse, all asking if she was okay.

She locked herself in the bathroom to cry and respond to her friends. They all got the same generic message courtesy of copy and paste.

I'm okay. Busy day. Will text later.

She pulled herself together. Barely.

With her headphones on and her music turned up as loud as she could tolerate it, she opened a fresh document file on her computer.

When I first started on this journey I genuinely wanted to learn, as both a journalist and as a woman, what appeal the BDSM lifestyle held for so many.

She caught herself fingering the amulet.

Closing her eyes to squeeze the tears back, she took a few deep breaths to steady herself. Then her index fingers came to rest on F and J on her keyboard as she opened her eyes to type some more.

Popular fiction leaves many with a completely erroneous impression of the people who participate in this admittedly alternative lifestyle. I consider it the utmost honor to now call many of the people I met while writing this piece my friends.

I wanted to experience firsthand the things many go through on their journey. If nothing else, so I could accurately write about it.

I never expected to learn so much about myself in the process, or fall in love with it along the way.

Sobbing as quietly as she could, she continued to type and prayed no one came up behind her and spotted her like this.

They say as journalists we're supposed to stay as objective as possible when reporting a story. BDSM is an issue already charged with controversy. It's fine to say that mental health professionals understand consensual sexual acts are normal and healthy behavior for those who willingly choose to participate, even if it is a minority of people.

But the truth isn't nearly as clinical as that. And learning about BDSM changed my life for the better. I learned how to let go and trust and feel things I never before dreamed I would ever experience, much less enjoy...

Shayla's fingers flew across the keys. She refused to censor herself and knew she'd completely sailed into the realm of commentary and editorial instead of a feature news story.

She didn't care.

When she finished the story several hours later, a little after five o'clock in the afternoon, she copied and pasted the text into an e-mail to Loren. She included a brief note at the top of the e-mail.

This is a rough draft so please excuse any typos. Please let me know what you think.

S.

She hit send without reading any of it.

Then she went into the bathroom, locked herself in, and threw up before heading home for the day.

* * * *

She somehow made it in to work Tuesday morning despite the horrible headache pounding in her temples. She hadn't checked her inbox at all after sending Loren the e-mail.

But she'd spent hours cradling her cell phone in her hands and praying Tony would text her.

She couldn't bring herself to send him a text Monday night. Before she went to bed, she wanted to say *Good night, Sir.* Or, *Sweet dreams, Sir.*

Or even, *I love You, Sir.* Get it out in the open.

Her heart ached, empty over the silence from Tony.

No *How are you, pet?*

No *How's My pet?*

Nothing.

Worse, she knew, would be the pain if she texted him and received no reply.

Or worse still, confirmation that it was truly over between them.

I will not *be clingy.*

Grateful there wasn't an editorial meeting Tuesday morning, she stuck to her cubicle and kept her headphones on as she began work on another story due Wednesday afternoon. She checked her e-mail but didn't see a response from Loren.

At eleven that morning, a tap on her shoulders startled her. She wheeled around to see Loren, Leah, and Tilly standing in the entrance to her cubicle. She pulled her headphones off and started to speak, to ask them what they were doing there.

Instead, her tears flowed.

Loren was the closest and enveloped her in her arms as the other two women also surrounded her. "You're okay," she whispered to Shayla. "It'll be okay."

That only made her cry harder.

"Do you want to talk about it?" Loren asked.

She shook her head. Someone pressed a tissue into her hand. She blew her nose and tried to pull herself together even though her soul felt ripped loose and adrift.

"Have you heard from Tony at all?" Leah asked.

"No. I guess I don't expect to because I know he's super busy right now. The data center they're setting up, it's huge. He warned me he probably wouldn't have any cell reception. It's okay." She took a deep breath and sat back as Loren stared down at her.

"We came to take you out to lunch," Loren said.

"I...I can't. I'm sorry. Not today."

"That wasn't a request," Tilly snarked. "Unlike these two, I'm not afraid to get toppy on your ass."

Shayla snorted, which turned into another bout of tears.

"Okay," Tilly said, nudging Loren out of the way. "That's it. No arguing. We go to my house for lunch. I'll text Cris and Landry to scoot their tushies out the door for a couple of hours."

Leah snickered. "I didn't know Landry would scoot his tushy for anyone."

Tilly had pulled out her cell phone. She hit a button on speed dial and put it to her ear. "Yeah, well, he will for me. I'm special."

Loren laughed. "Special, huh?"

She nodded. "Yeah, those two men aren't nearly as scary as they think they are. I'm way scarier. Especially this time of the month."

Minutes later, they'd bustled Shayla down to Tilly's car and were heading south on US 41 toward Tilly's. Shayla sat in back with Loren while Tilly drove and Leah rode up front.

"I think you need to contact Tony and ask to talk to him," Loren said.

"He's busy. I don't want to bother him while he's out of town. He's working."

"You're in a lot of pain, sweetie. I think it'd upset him to know you're hurting like this."

"It doesn't matter. We had an agreement, and he stuck to it. I'm the fucking dumbass that fell in love with him."

"Does he know you're in love with him?" Tilly piped up from behind the wheel. "Men aren't psychic, no matter how good a Dom they might be."

"Love wasn't part of the agreement," Shayla said. "It's my fault."

Tilly let out a loud, barking laugh. "Yeah, believe me, I totally get that. That's how I ended up with Landry and Cris for life. Love wasn't supposed to be part of our deal, either. Yet there I went and fell in love with the guy, and fell back in love with Cris despite him being a total fucking dumbass sometimes." At a stoplight, she glanced in the mirror and made eye contact with Shayla. "Unless you speak up and tell him what you feel, you'll never know if he feels the same way."

"Wouldn't he have told me how he feels before now?"

Leah turned in her seat as far as her seat belt would allow. "You have to understand something. Tony is a very honorable guy. From what you told me, that wasn't part of your original agreement. He might be a sadist, but he's not going to force himself on someone."

"But he wouldn't have been forcing himself on me."

"You might see it like that, but look at it from his point of view. He sees himself in a position of power over you as your Dominant. He will never do anything that, to him, seems like he's abusing that power in any way. Okay, yes, sucky timing that he had to go out of town and you two can't just sit down and talk about this. But you sitting here hurting and not reaching out to him isn't healthy."

"If he'd wanted me I'd think he would have spoken up. He's not exactly bashful. Besides, he said he might be in contact this week."

"Did he say when?" Loren asked.

Shayla shook her head.

"Did he say you couldn't text him?" Leah asked.

"No," Shayla said.

Leah turned to face forward. Shayla saw her doing something and realized she'd pulled out her phone and was sending a text. "What are you doing?" Shayla asked.

"I'm texting Sir Dumbass and telling him to check in with you."

"Leah, wait. Please don't. He's working."

Leah looked over her shoulder at Shayla. "So? I text him all the time when he's at work. He texts me back when he can."

"Please, no. It's okay. Besides, I know he doesn't like clingy women. I refuse to be like that. I can tough it out until he gets back."

"Clingy? One text two days later isn't clingy," Loren said.

"I know what Tony's talking about when he says that," Leah added.

"And believe me, you do *not* fit his clingy definition."

Shayla shook her head. "Please, it's all right. I'll be okay."

After looking at her for a moment, Leah turned to Tilly. "What do you think?"

Tilly shrugged. "I don't know. The Domme and friend part of me says fuck it and chew his ass out. The slave in me understands why Shayla wants to wait him out."

"Which part is winning?" Leah asked.

"I'm PMSing. Is that really a fair question?"

"We don't want his balls removed," Leah joked.

"Or roasted," Loren added. "And no, we're not asking Landry to hold him down for us."

For some reason, that comment made the other three women laugh.

Tilly let out a melodramatic sigh. "You guys are no fun at all." Tilly glanced in the rearview mirror again. "Sorry, Shay. Long story. We'll tell you later."

The women made her lunch, made her talk, and held her while she cried. By the time Tilly finally agreed an hour later to take Shayla back to the office, Shayla did admit she felt a little better after talking to her friends.

They exchanged another round of hugs before Shayla headed back upstairs. "Just text him," Leah said. "Please? It'll be all right. I'm sure the two of you will work this out. It sounds like you two just need a good, long talk."

Shayla wasn't so sure, but nodded for her friends' benefits. But she didn't text Tony.

He's working. I won't interfere with his work. I'm a big girl. I can wait until he's back, unless he texts me.

It didn't stop her from keeping her phone in sight on her desk, next to her computer, and the ringer volume turned up loud.

* * * *

When Shayla's phone rang that night, her heart jumped. Instinctively, she grabbed it and answered without looking at the screen.

"Hello?"

"Shay?"

She frowned and looked at the screen. That wasn't Tony's voice.

The screen read *Rat Bastard*.

Shit. James.

She took a deep breath, her tone immediately U-turning from warm and hopeful to chilly and neutral. "What do you want?"

Apparently the change in tone didn't go unnoticed and caught him off guard, too. "Um, I wanted to talk."

"Why?"

Another moment of silence. "I saw you've been getting my checks."

"Yep."

She wouldn't make this easy on him. She refused to.

He certainly hadn't made her life easy.

Then again, I never would have met Tony.

He sighed on the other end. "Look, I really want to talk to you. I want to tell you how sorry I am."

"I saw the letters. Thank you."

More uncomfortable silence. "I'd like to see you."

"What?" She sat bolt upright, heart pounding. "Look, I have a job. A life. I'm *not* flying back to Cleveland to have a powwow with you."

"No! That's not what I meant. I have to be in Orlando next weekend for meetings. I'd like to get together with you to talk. I looked at the map. I can drive to Sarasota from Orlando in just a couple of hours."

"That's not a good idea."

"Please, Shayla? Just to talk. We can meet at a restaurant, if you want. Somewhere public. I'll buy. Pick somewhere nice."

Dammit. Now she wished she'd never given him her address. *I should've gotten a PO Box.* "That's not necessary." *Why the hell can't I just tell him to fuck off?*

"I'd consider it a favor if you would. I know you don't owe me anything, but I'd really appreciate it. Please?"

Despite how much she hated what he'd done to her, his plaintive tone of voice killed the animosity she felt toward him. Yes, he'd been a dick. But he was trying to make amends. She probably shouldn't piss him off in case he decided not to keep paying her back. "I've got a lot going on next weekend. I don't know if I can change my plans. I'll have to let you know."

He sounded relieved. "Okay, thanks. I appreciate it."

"I have to go." She ended the call and tossed her phone to the other end of the couch. She stared at it, praying James wouldn't call back.

After a few minutes of silence, she relaxed.

Unfortunately, that same silence only emphasized that Tony hadn't called or texted her.

Chapter Twenty-Six

Tony threw himself into his work upon arriving in Denver. He tried to ignore his personal cell phone and the fact that he didn't receive any text messages from Shayla. Tuesday morning, he left his personal cell in the hotel room because all day Monday he'd found himself reaching for it every few minutes despite the fact that he had sketchy cell reception, and everything that could go wrong with the install did. Except for fire, flood, nuclear holocaust, and zombie attack, things that shouldn't go balls-up did just that, requiring every last bit of his attention and energy.

I have to focus on my work.

It irritated him that normally he was a guy who could do just that, stay focused on his work. No matter what was going on around him in his personal life, once he was on the clock, or in work mode, that was it. Nothing blasted him out of that headspace.

Until Shayla.

He had told her he'd be in touch, but he didn't want to smother her. He also didn't want to get into an emotional conversation via text and have it blow up in their faces due to a misunderstanding.

And he didn't want to be left standing there with his dick metaphorically hanging out if she didn't want a relationship with him after all.

It didn't escape his notice that the loneliness he'd felt before Shayla had returned with a vengeance.

* * * *

Shayla forced herself to stick to some semblance of a routine even though her heart certainly wasn't in it. Every day she didn't hear from Tony hurt her heart that much more, but strengthened her resolve not to embarrass herself by texting him.

Besides, she knew he'd be overwhelmed with work, and the last thing he needed was her whiny ass bothering him. She'd have a talk with him after he got back.

The first weekend was even harder than the Monday after he left. She spent her time wondering what he was doing, what they might have been doing had they still been seeing each other…and what she wished they were doing.

It stunned her to realize she hurt worse now than when she discovered James' second round of betrayal.

I love him. I love him and don't even know if I can tell him. Telling him and learning he didn't feel the same would hurt worse than never telling him at all.

She plodded through the second week by sheer force of will, keeping busy and working long hours, going in early and staying late, taking more assignments than she normally would and busting her ass to do anything but think about Tony Daniels. Leah had elicited a promise from her to come to dinner with them on Saturday and go to a club with them up in Tampa, but she decided she didn't have the heart to.

That was why she almost didn't answer her phone when Leah called her as she was getting ready to leave the office late Friday. "How you doing, sweetie?" Leah asked her.

Shayla sighed as she stared at her monitor. "I'll live. I'm going to cancel on tomorrow night, though."

"Aww. Are you sure? You can ride with us. We weren't planning on staying real late. Just going to hang out and watch and visit with friends."

"No, I'm sure. But thank you anyway." She ran her finger over the keyboard. "I'm going to shut off my phone after we hang up and keep it off all weekend. I'm going to spend the weekend drowning my sorrows in Guinness and sinfully dark chocolate, watch cheesy B-movies in my jammies, and start Monday fresh with a new attitude and ready to kick ass and take names."

"Well, call or text me, huh? Let me know you're okay?"

"Nope. James is in Orlando this weekend on business. I don't want to do something stupid like pick up the phone and talk to him if he calls, or return any texts."

"Oh. James as in James the ex?"

"Yep. Him." She shut down her computer and pushed away from her desk. "He called me a couple of weeks ago. Said he wanted to get together to talk while he was down here. The way I feel right now, I'd be too tempted to do something stupid."

"Still haven't heard from Tony, huh?"

"Nope." She let out a sigh. "Look, I know you really want to, but please don't say anything to him, okay?" She swallowed back tears when she felt the prickles in her eyes. "He's made it abundantly clear by his lack of communication that this was just a formal arrangement and not a personal one." She took a deep breath. "I'm a big girl. I've finally got my big-girl panties on and I'm sucking it up and dealing with it. If he wants to talk when he gets back, we will. He stuck to his end of the deal. I'm dang sure not going to be a whiny drama llama."

"I'm sorry, sweetie. I'm going to kick his ass next time I see him."

"No, please, don't. Like I said, he didn't do anything wrong." She closed her eyes, trying to squeeze back stray tears that wanted to force their way out. "I'm the one who fell in love with him. This is my problem. He never led me on. I did that to myself just fine without any help from him. I need to go. I'll talk to you on Monday."

"Okay. Take care this weekend. Call me if you change your mind about tomorrow."

Shayla ended the call and immediately shut off her phone. She'd already decided to leave her laptop at the office so she wouldn't be tempted to check e-mail. She didn't have a landline, so for the weekend she'd be totally off the grid. If she wanted to buy e-books, she could do that through her Kindle without ever getting on the Internet. She'd leave her cell phone shut off and in the dresser drawer in the bedroom and focus on getting this maudlin mental crap out of her system.

Then she could just move the fuck on with her life.

I hope.

She wasn't going to delude herself and get her hopes up that Tony wanted more from her.

Wishing for a happy ending had already got her heart broken with James. She wouldn't embarrass herself like that again.

On the way home, she stopped at the grocery store. She stocked up so she wouldn't have to leave her apartment. Not that she planned on staying sober long enough to drive for most of the weekend. She might have a hella hangover come Monday morning, but that would help take her mind off the pain in her heart and soul, at least.

* * * *

No matter how many problems Tony settled during the install, new ones seemed to crop up every day. Putting the new data center together was like herding severely ADHD cats in desperate need of high Ritalin doses. Tony worked eighteen-hour days, collapsing late every night in his hotel room and getting up early every morning to do it all over again. He left his private cell phone in the hotel room where it eventually shut down due to a dead battery.

He didn't have time to think about Shayla or her absence in his life.

Once the servers and other equipment were installed and booted, and the raised floor panels configured, and all the wiring properly run and labeled beneath them, then came the fun part of making sure everything was online and talking to each other, as well as the data center in Bradenton, and integrated with the telecom departments in both locations.

That went along with putting fires out in Bradenton on a regular basis due to him not being there.

Now I remember why I hate taking vacations.

The first week passed in a blur. He couldn't take an hour off to eat lunch, much less a day off to catch up on sleep or personal email, and worked straight through the weekend. It wasn't until the end of the second week, late Friday night Denver time, when Tony finally took a few minutes to check his personal e-mail before collapsing for the night. A few times during the past several days he'd thought about texting Shayla but decided against it. He'd finally remembered to charge his personal cell phone, but she hadn't texted him the whole time he was there.

Well, I didn't want clingy.

But maybe she was really over it, and him.

He scrolled through his mail, dumping almost everything, and skimming past a message from Leah nearly a week earlier that he almost deleted by accident. Once he had the dreck cleaned out, he went back to read it.

She included a brief message at the top of the e-mail, followed by the forwarded text from a message Shayla had sent her.

You need to read this, you frigging asshat. WTF is wrong with you? Why the hell haven't you texted or called her? I thought you gave a damn about her? She's in love with you and afraid to text you because you'll think she's "clingy." Get your shit together or you're going to lose her.
Leah.

By the time he finished reading the rough draft of Shayla's article, his throat felt dry. He called Leah.

"Well, it's about damn time you picked up a fricking phone, you damn asshat."

"How is she? I just read your e-mail."

"Not good, thanks to you. She thinks you don't give a damn about her. And why haven't you texted or called her yet?"

He rubbed his forehead. "It's been crazy out here. This is literally the first time I've had to sit down and check my personal e-mail. I thought since I hadn't heard from her that maybe she was okay with everything ending."

"No. You apparently did such a damn fine job drilling it into her head that you don't like clingy women that now she's afraid to text you first. And she's convinced since you said you'd be in touch, and you weren't, that you don't care."

"Okay, I'll call her right now."

"Good luck with that. It's early Saturday morning here, asshat. I'm only up because we just got back from a club, and besides—" He heard sounds like Leah had lost the phone.

Then Seth came on the line. "Tony?"

"Hi. What just happened?"

In the background, Tony could hear more sounds, like Leah was trying to get the phone away from Seth. "Um, listen, sorry about that. I'm going to put Leah to bed. She's had a long day."

Tony pinched the bridge of his nose. "No, it's okay. I deserve it. I am an asshat." At the sudden quiet on the other end of the line, Tony thought maybe the call had dropped. "Seth?"

"Yeah, I'm here. I was just trying to decide if I heard you right."

"You heard me right. You can put her back on. Don't spank her."

"Oh. Okay. Hold on."

The phone exchanged hands again, because Leah returned, sounding put out in addition to indignant. "What'd you tell him?"

"That I'm an asshat."

Another surprised silence from Florida. "Oh. Okay. All right then. Glad you see things my way."

"I'll call her in the morning."

Leah sighed. "You won't reach her. I talked to her before she left work last night. She's really sad and going off the grid, as she called it, for the weekend. She's shut off her phone and left her computer at work. She mentioned something about getting drunk and eating chocolate while watching bad movies, and I think she means it. I tried to call her again tonight before we went out and it went to her voice mail. Usually she'll at least text me back, but she hasn't."

If he hadn't felt bad enough already, that added to it. "Oh. Crap. You know what I'm like when I'm buried at work. I get tunnel vision. This was a nightmare install." He rubbed his forehead. "I really screwed up here, didn't I?"

"Uh, yeah. Ya *think*? First thing Monday morning, I'd say your ass better be on the phone to her."

"Well, on the off chance you do hear from her—"

"I will tell her I talked to you and that she needs to try to call or text you and let you know she's got her phone back on, yes."

"Thanks, Leah."

"Hey, Tony?"

"What?"

There was a moment of quiet tension before she asked, "Is she the one?"

He let out a breath he didn't realize he'd been holding. "Yeah," he quietly said. "If I haven't gone and fubared it before we even had a chance, I really do think she's the one."

* * * *

Shayla refused to read any romance novels that weekend. She couldn't stomach the thought of reading about someone else's happy ending when hers had been yanked right the hell out from under her.

She also didn't want to contemplate how in the hell she'd ever meet someone else like Tony. No, she didn't have any official confirmation that all hope was dead in the water, but she was a realist. After having been screwed over with James, it was easier to accept the worst instead of hoping for the best.

Hoping for the best had gotten her over fifteen grand into debt she didn't even owe.

Going back to a vanilla life wouldn't be possible. She'd entered a whole new world, one she knew meant she'd never be satisfied settling for a vanilla guy.

I refuse to think about it this weekend.

Instead, she spent the weekend going around the world via microbrewery beer.

She hoped she had room in her recycling bin for all the bottles and cans.

She also moved her car keys into her underwear drawer. She didn't think she'd be stupid enough to try to drink and drive, but if she got so plastered she forgot that, she'd probably never remember where she put them until she sobered up.

Or had to change her panties.

By Saturday evening she'd severely tested the endurance of her liver. She spent the day watching every stupid movie she could think of that she'd never watched before for the very reason that they were stupid. Beer, however, made everything funnier.

It also made it easier not to think about Tony Daniels.

I'm going to get a cat next week. This is ridiculous. I need a life. I'll get a cat.

When the thought of a Facebook meme she'd seen, of an IKEA cube organizer filled with a cat per space, crossed her mind, she giggled.

I'm not so drunk I want to be a crazy cat lady either. One's my limit.

By Sunday afternoon she'd run out of beer and let herself sober up. She wasn't completely hungover, but she took a couple of ibuprofen as insurance.

Her sadness also returned. As she curled up on the couch with her arms wrapped around a pillow, she allowed herself to cry one last time. *I need to get him out of my system. He's like a damn drug I can't wean myself off of.*

She knew Monday would be hard, but she also knew after what she'd faced with James that she should be able to deal with it.

At least he didn't cost me any money. Just my heart.

Chapter Twenty-Seven

I can't wait to get home. Bone weary, Tony found his car in long-term parking and threw his bags in the trunk before getting in. He didn't have the luxury of sleeping in a little that morning before his flight because of last-minute issues cropping up in the Denver data center. For a couple of hours, it was doubtful he'd even make his flight, until they finally got things straightened out.

Since it was just before midnight on a Sunday, he gave silent thanks there wouldn't be any traffic jams to deal with on his drive home from Tampa.

Although it sucked knowing he had to go in to work the next morning. He had too many backlogged issues to deal with there to even think about taking time off.

When he looked over at the passenger seat, he froze. Shayla's collar still lay where he'd left it that morning two weeks earlier, before he went to Denver. He'd forgotten to take it into his house.

He picked it up and fingered it. The lump welling in his throat surprised him.

Life had felt relatively empty since heading to Denver, and he wouldn't deny it. It wasn't due to the trip, living out of a suitcase in a damn hotel, or not having a moment of free time when he wasn't working.

Leah's harsh words to him over the phone played through his mind.

I am an asshat.

"Dammit." He put the collar down and pointed his car south. He reached Sarasota a little over an hour later. Instead of getting off at his exit at Bee Ridge Road, he continued south, to Clark Road, which would lead him straight to her apartment. His original plan had been to call her first thing in the morning.

He couldn't wait. He'd waited two damn weeks with his heart on hold, and he had to know, tonight, where he stood with her. Or if he even had a chance with her.

At the very least he had to apologize to her for not being in touch.

The complex lay dark and quiet when he pulled in and shut the car off. No lights shone behind the blinds in her unit, but her car sat parked in its usual spot.

He grabbed the collar, got out and locked the doors, and marched up to her door. She didn't have a doorbell, so he knocked.

He glanced around as he waited, but there wasn't any response despite his knocking sounding loud to him. He tried again, this time pounding on the door nearly as hard as his pulse thundered through his veins while he yelled her name.

* * * *

Shayla awoke from a deep sleep and lay in bed, disoriented, trying to figure out what woke her. She'd rolled over and closed her eyes again when she heard the pounding on her door.

She grabbed her cell phone from where she'd left it, off and charging, on the bathroom counter. Grateful for the fact that she'd slept in a T-shirt that night, she silently padded out to the foyer without turning on any lights. A third round of pounding made her jump as she approached the door.

"Shayla! Open up, it's me."

She froze for a moment before scurrying to the door to squint through the peephole, since she hadn't grabbed her glasses. Sure enough, Tony Daniels stood on her front stoop.

Her fingers fumbled at the locks, but she got them open and threw the door wide to stare at him in shock. He stepped in, forcing her back, and closed and locked the door behind him. Walking forward until she was pressed against the foyer wall, he stared down at her.

"I don't want to end this," he said.

She blinked, feeling the air rush out of her lungs. "What?"

He reached behind her, fisted her hair, and gently forced her head back so she had to look him in the eye.

"I'm sorry," he softly said. "I got busy and that's no excuse. I should have been texting you every day and calling you every night. I don't want to end this. I do *not* want to lose you. I *can't* lose you, because you're the best damn thing to ever happen to me."

Then he leaned in and kissed her, on the lips, devouring her with a hunger her soul instantly recognized and returned. Her arms clutched at him, afraid *this* was the dream and that she'd open her eyes to find herself alone again and suffering the effects of some crappy microbrewery swill.

When he lifted his lips from hers, she let out a whimper of protest, not wanting to lose the contact with him.

His gaze searched her face. "I'm not just talking about dating or being play partners. I'm talking I want you as *mine*. My slave. I want to own you. If you want it, too, I need to hear it from you. I won't play games. I'm sorry I didn't say anything sooner, but I didn't want you to think I was pushing you. I didn't want to change the rules on you and break your trust. I thought if you wanted to stay together you'd say something sooner, but Leah told me I apparently gave you the wrong impression. I do not think you are clingy. But I do need you to tell me if you want this or not."

She nodded, so hard she thought her neck might break.

That damn, sexy smile curled his lips. "That's not what I meant, pet."

Her heart exploded at the term of endearment. Tears slipped down her cheeks. "Yes!"

"You have to say it. You have to ask me for it."

"I don't want this to end. Please, I don't want to lose you."

He didn't reply, his brow eventually furrowing. It took her a moment that she blamed on being yanked from a sound beer-induced sleep to realize her mistake. "Please, Sir, I don't want this to end. I don't want to lose you, Sir. I want to be yours, Sir. In all ways. I want you to own me."

That was when his entire face relaxed as if a huge weight had lifted from him. He released her hair and cradled her cheeks with both palms and kissed her on the lips again, gently, sweetly.

Lovingly.

"My sweet, beautiful, pet," he whispered. "God, I missed you."

She realized he held something in one of his hands, and he quickly buckled that something around her neck.

She let out a relieved sob at the feel of the collar encircling her throat. She closed her eyes and buried her face against his chest, where they stood like that for several minutes until he silently led her to the bedroom.

He pulled off her shirt and studied her face in the dim light cast by the nightlight in the hall. "I love you, pet."

"I love you, too, Sir."

He pointed to the floor. She sank to her knees and kissed his feet, the backs of his hands, nuzzled her face against the front of his slacks where his cock bulged.

He held out his arms without another word. Instinctively, she stood and set to work unbuttoning his shirt and removing it. His undershirt, then his slacks after he'd kicked off his loafers. His socks and briefs. And while he was hard, when she tried to kiss his cock, he fisted her hair again and made her stand.

"No," he softly said. "Not tonight. I need to sleep, and so do you. It's nearly two o'clock and we both have to go to work in the morning." He made her get into bed and crawled in behind her, spooning her, his arm draped over her.

"Go to sleep, pet," he whispered against the nape of her neck. "We have the rest of our lives together."

She felt his cock eventually soften from where it pressed against her ass as his breathing slowed and deepened. She thought there was no way in hell she'd be able to sleep as happy as she felt, but then a soft, gentle darkness overtook her.

* * * *

She awoke before her alarm the next morning. When she felt the warm heat of Tony's body pressed against her, the night's events came rushing back with crystal clarity. Craning her head, she saw his eyes were already open.

"Good morning, pet," he said.

She smiled. "Good morning, Sir."

He rolled on top of her, his weight comfortably pressing her into the mattress. He found her hands and laced his fingers through hers, raising them above her head and pinning her there. She felt his cock harden against her as he stared down into her eyes.

"About last night."

"Yes, Sir?"

"Do you still feel that way?"

She thought the smile might split her face in two. "Yes, Sir. I still feel that way. I want to be yours."

"To me a collar means more than a wedding ring. If you ever decide you want to be free, you have to speak up and tell me. I'll never force you to stay with me. But I'd be an idiot to let you go without telling you how I feel. Is this what you want, to be with me? To be owned by me?"

"Yes, Sir."

He leaned down and nibbled on the side of her neck, sending heat coursing through her body. He needed a shave, and the long stubble on his cheeks, combined with his beard and moustache, chafed against her flesh in a pleasant way.

"I did vanilla the first time around," he said. "It didn't work. Our marriage will be that of a Master and slave dynamic. I will own you, and you will obey me. That doesn't mean I won't listen to your opinions or won't let you make decisions. I will never force you to do something against your hard limits, although there might be times I push your boundaries for my own reasons. I will always respect a safeword if you say it. I'm not perfect, as the past two weeks prove, but I promise if I make mistakes, I will own up to them and rectify them.

"You will still work, if you want to. I won't cut you off from your family and friends. But I will own you and you will obey me. We will have protocols in place that will be followed or you will be punished, and I will have the final word on some things even though there might be times you disagree with me. Understand?"

More heat, this time straight to her pussy and clit. "Yes, Sir," she gasped.

"I need to hear you say it. I need to hear you ask me for it."

She clutched at his hands, tightening her grip on his fingers. "Please, Sir, make me yours. I want to be your slave. I want you to own me. I want to wear your collar. I want to be yours."

"I promise as your Master I will protect and care for you. I will never share you with anyone else. I won't want anyone else, and I won't top anyone else unless it's while teaching a class and you're okay with it. I will never abandon you. And if you decide you want to leave me, I won't stop you. But if you want to be with me, those are the conditions you have to accept."

"Yes, Sir. I want to."

He transferred both her wrists to one of his hands. Then with his free hand he reached down between their bodies and found her pussy. Two fingers easily slipped inside her, making her moan. Before she could process it, he withdrew his fingers and replaced them with his cock, sinking hard and deep before falling still.

"My sweet pet," he whispered against the side of her neck before biting down, not hard enough to break the skin but just enough that the pain sent more pleasure streaking to her clit. She moaned and squirmed against him, spreading her legs wider to give him better access.

"Who's my good pet?"

"Me, Sir," she whined, desperate for release.

"Can you come for me like this?"

"I...I'll try."

He chuckled. "Good girl." He raised up on his arms with both hands once again pinning her wrists above her head. Looking down into her eyes, he smiled. "Try very hard, pet." Then he slowly started moving.

Every stroke perfectly glided along her clit, feeling different and sooo much better than any of the toys ever had. Something inside her soul soared, no longer feeling adrift.

He wanted her.

He needed her.

He loved her.

"I love you, Sir."

That damn smile. The one that could instantly turn all her "hell, nos" into "yes, pleases." He smiled down at her. "I love you, too, pet."

He slowly picked up the tempo, never breaking eye contact with her as he stroked his cock inside her. She wondered how long he could last like that when she felt the first tingles of her own release start.

Not nearly as powerful as the orgasms he'd forced out of her in the past with a vibrator or his hands, or even with his mouth, but it felt deeper and more fulfilling to her heart and soul. He must have felt her climax, because he moved faster, fucked her harder, his intense green gaze pinning her soul the way his body pinned hers.

There was a brief second of fear when she thought she'd lost the climb, that it wouldn't happen, but then her climax washed over her, breaking like a gentle wave kissing the sand and soaking just as deeply through the center of her core. She felt the tears start and didn't care. Her back arched as she thrust against him as hard as she could, reveling in the sensation and never wanting it to end.

"Good girl," he whispered. His hands tightened on her wrists and she found herself delightfully helpless as he fucked her until he let out a soft groan of his own and fell still inside her.

Winded, he touched his forehead to hers, still not releasing her wrists. "My *very* good girl," he whispered. "*My* pet."

She closed her eyes and wished this moment would never end. "*Your* pet."

* * * *

Shayla wanted to spend all day in bed, but he had to go to work, as did she. He removed her collar before they showered together, taking their time as they kissed and caressed with soapy hands. She easily got him aroused again, but he wouldn't let her make him come.

"No, pet," he said, gently pushing her hand away from his cock. "We don't have time. Tonight. And the rest of our lives."

She was already horny again and knew she'd spend the day in a perpetual state of arousal as her mind replayed the morning over and over again.

As well as the night before.

He pulled her to him, her face buried in the crook of his neck as the water sluiced over them. "I'm sorry I didn't text or call you," he said. "I was so busy, but then I was afraid you didn't want anything else to do with me. As Leah said, I was an asshat."

"I'm sorry, Sir. I asked her not to call or text you."

"No, don't apologize. It's okay. She e-mailed me the rough draft of the article last week. But I didn't get it until this Friday night. That's when I called her, and by then you'd turned off your phone." He made her look him in the eyes. "And she's right. I was an asshat."

"I didn't want you to think I was clingy."

His thumb traced her chin and along her jawline. "I told you last night, I don't think that about you, pet. I'm sorry I put you through that much distress. No more second-guessing. I love you, and I want to spend the rest of my life with you."

Had she ever felt this happy? She couldn't remember it if she had. "I love you, too, Sir."

"I'm going to have a crazy day at work today," he warned. "I've been gone two weeks, and there's a bunch of stuff I have to take care of. I probably won't get out of there until late. So how about I just leave my bags here? I'll come straight here after work and we'll eat snuggled on the couch before we go to bed."

"You haven't even been home yet?"

"No. I knew I had to see you. I couldn't let this go any longer." He kissed her, taking her breath away. When he broke their kiss he touched his forehead to hers and cupped his hand firmly around the nape of her neck. "But, from now on, unless you're on a plane or something, you *never* turn your phone off unless you ask me first and I give you permission. Understand?"

She breathed a sigh of relief. The freedom of knowing he was once again in control flooded her soul. "Yes, Sir."

"Good girl."

How had she got here? Where those two simple words from him could make her heart stand up and sing?

"So we're good for that plan?" he asked.

"Yes, Sir."

He stroked her cheek. "And yes, this is also a wedding proposal, pet. Although we can take our time planning that. Whatever you want to do."

She felt heat in her cheeks. "It won't be much. I can't afford an expensive wedding."

He made her look at him again. "*I* can. So what's your answer?"

It felt good to be blinking back happy tears. "Yes!" she whispered.

She'd have to give that smile a name. His killer smile. His nuclear smile. Something, because it totally disarmed her.

"This weekend," he said, "we're going to the club and making the first part of it official. I will formally collar you in front of all our friends. Then I'm going to lay you across a bench and put my marks on you the way I've been wanting to. There will be no doubt in anyone's mind who you belong to." As his lips traced hers she let out a soft whimper. She wished tonight was already here.

When he broke their kiss, she gasped for breath. "Any special request for dinner, Sir?"

He grinned as he gently chucked her under the chin. "No, I don't care what we eat. All I care about is that you answer the door naked except for your collar."

* * * *

He left a few minutes before she did. She felt like she couldn't focus, couldn't think beyond what she wanted to make for dinner. *Maybe spaghetti. That's fast and easy. No, maybe I should make pork chops. Argh!*

It was a problem she didn't mind having.

When Shayla got to work, she quickly ran through her accumulated texts and voice mails. James had called twice, and she deleted them as soon as she recognized his voice, before he said more than two words. Leah, Loren, and Tilly had all called to check on her. She saw where Tony had called once over the weekend, but hung up without leaving a voice mail.

She grinned, a little thrill running through her at the memory of the feel of his hands on her that morning, the way he'd pinned her wrists to the bed.

Owned her.

Her hand constantly fingered the amulet. She found herself unable to stop smiling.

Dreams do come true.

During the Monday editorial meeting, Bill Melling finally stopped what he was doing and looked at Shayla. "Is there something you want to share with the rest of the class?" he teased.

"Huh?"

Kimberly laughed next to her and gently nudged her with her elbow. "You look disgustingly happy compared to how sad you've been the past two weeks. Did you get engaged or something?"

The barking laugh burped out of her so suddenly that she clapped a hand to her mouth as she looked around the table. Everyone let out a laugh.

"Well?" Bill said.

Shayla nodded as she pushed her glasses up on her nose. "He got back into town late last night and he proposed this morning."

A round of cheers and congratulations went up throughout the room. Bill grinned. "Our congratulations to the bride-to-be." He grabbed a dry-erase marker and wrote *Exotic Wedding Ideas* on the whiteboard. "Hey," he said with a smile, "I'm not above using your good news to give us story ideas."

Only after the meeting ended did Shayla text Loren. *Guess what?*

A few minutes later, she received a reply. *What?*

Tony's home.

She giggled at Loren's reply. *Do I need to call Tilly to help us hold him down?*

Noooo. :)

Loren called her seconds later. "What's going on?"

"Tony's officially collaring me. And he proposed."

"Shut. Your. Mouth. You better not be lying to me."

"No! He really did!"

Loren let out a squeal of laughter. "Congratulations! What happened?"

"He showed up at my front door in the middle of the night after getting in from Denver. He didn't even go home first. And he said Leah was right, that he was an asshat."

She heard Loren sigh. "That's one of the great things about him. He's not afraid to admit he made a mistake. So give me details!"

"I don't have a lot of details to give. We talked and cleared the air, he collared me, and he proposed this morning. I just wanted to let you know."

"Can I spread the word?"

Shayla smiled. "Feel free. And I've been told we'll be there on Saturday. That's when he's collaring me in front of everyone. I need to get back to work." Shayla ended the call and knew within the next few minutes Loren would have their friends updated.

Sure enough, she was inundated with text messages in the next ten minutes from Leah, Tilly, and Clarisse.

After lunch, Tony called to check on her. "How's my pet?"

She giggled, unable to help herself. "Good, Sir."

"Just wanted to let you know I should be at your place by nine. If I'll be any later, I'll call. So plan accordingly. If you want to go ahead and eat and heat mine up when I get there, that's fine. I don't want to make you wait."

"That's okay, Sir. I'd rather eat with you."

"How'd I get so lucky?"

She closed her eyes and pictured his face. "I'm the lucky one, Sir."

She opted to bake a modified ziti casserole that she used to make a lot when she was in Ohio and had friends over. It wouldn't matter what time he arrived. It kept well and made great leftovers.

She wrote her grocery list while she sat at her desk and tried not to nervously tap her feet. She added *garlic bread* to the list, along with *dessert*.

Although hopefully I'll be the dessert.

She giggled.

The closer the clock crawled toward 5:00 p.m. the slower time appeared to drag. She made it to her car by 5:05 and smiled all the way to the grocery store. By six she was home, showered, and naked except for her collar—all the blinds closed, of course—and had started dinner preparations. She put together a salad and stashed it in the fridge for later. She'd throw the frozen garlic bread in the oven when Tony got there.

Now ready, with the pasta casserole in the oven, she texted Tony.

I'm ready, Sir.

A few minutes later, his reply. *Good girl. I'm trying to finish, maybe there by eight if I'm lucky. I'll text when I leave.*

Her heart raced and she went to watch TV to pass the time. She couldn't help reaching up to her collar, feeling it, reveling in it being buckled around her throat once again.

Remembering the feel of his lips on hers as he fisted her hair and kissed her when he came through the door.

Remembering the feel of his cock inside her that morning as they truly made love for the first time.

Owning her mind, body, and soul.

Finally, at seven thirty-five he texted her again. *On my way. ETA 30.*

She let out a squeal, then giggled when she read his next text. *Be kneeling on the floor by the front door when I come in.*

She felt her pussy throb. Her fingers trembled as she texted her reply. *Yes, Sir.*

A minute later, he texted back. *Good girl.*

She turned up the temperature on the oven to reheat the casserole and tried not to pace around the apartment. Twenty-five minutes later, headlights swept across her front blinds as a car pulled into the spot next to her car.

With her heart racing, she ran to the front door, made sure it was unlocked, and knelt in the foyer.

Her pulse pounded in her ears. It took every ounce of her will to slow her breathing to keep from hyperventilating from her excitement and anticipation.

She startled a little at the sound of his knock and she had to lick her lips before she could speak. "Come in," she called out, then returned her gaze to the floor, hands on her knees.

The door opened. At first, he didn't say anything.

The voice she heard made her let out a scream. "Um, Shay?"

She looked up, shocked to see James standing in her front door. "What are you doing here?" She jumped to her feet and grabbed the first thing her hand landed on, her rain jacket, and pulled it on.

He took a step in. "I...Jesus, Shay, is that a collar? I read your articles, but I didn't think you wanted me to—"

"Get out!" She reached for her umbrella, but realized that wasn't any cover at all and instead brandished it at him.

"I left you two voice mails the other day that I'd stop by—"

"Get out!"

"Look, can we please talk?"

She was aware of another car pulling up in front of her apartment, parking on the other side of hers. "No!" She thrust the umbrella at him. "Get out of here!"

"I just want to talk to you for a few minutes. Didn't you get my voice mails? Are you naked for me?"

"No, none of your fucking business, and get the fuck out of here!"

Tony ran up behind James and pushed his way in. "What's going on?"

She nearly sobbed with relief. "Sir, I thought he was you, I—"

"Sir?" James said, stepping closer to her. "Shay, will you please let me talk to you?"

"James, I told you, get out!"

Tony glared at the man as he stepped between him and Shayla. Tony took the umbrella from her.

"Pet, go to the bedroom. *Now*. And close the door." His calm, even tone of voice brooked no argument.

Even though James called after her, she raced through the apartment and into the bedroom, where she closed the door behind her. She sat on her bed, the raincoat still clutched around her, as she listened to the sound of muffled voices. They grew in intensity and anger until she finally heard the front door slam shut.

Then, nothing.

She jumped when the bedroom door opened and Tony walked in. She stood and started to ask him what happened but he snapped his fingers and pointed at the floor.

Without thinking, she complied, shucking the raincoat and letting it fall to the floor as her questions died on her lips.

He stood there as she stared at his shoes and prayed she hadn't just fucked things up.

* * * *

Tony didn't look at Shayla as she ran for the bedroom. When the man looked like he wanted to go after her, Tony stepped in front of him. blocking his way.

"You set one more foot in this apartment," Tony told the guy, "and you'll leave in an ambulance. She told you to get out of here."

"Who the fuck are you? I just want to talk to her. She's my fiancée, dammit!"

It didn't take Tony long to put things together. "Wrong, asshole. She *was* your fiancée until you screwed things up. She's *my* fiancée now. And I'm not going to do something as stupid as lie and cheat and steal from her." The man's face fell. Tony knew he'd hit the mark and then some. "What are you doing here?"

"I just wanted to talk to her. I left her messages over the weekend." He drew himself up, still two inches shorter than Tony. "Look, she told me to come in when I knocked. She was obviously expecting me."

It took every ounce of his being not to bust out laughing. Shayla *had* earned a spanking—for not verifying who was knocking on her door before allowing them to come in.

"She was expecting *me*. I'd just texted her that I would be here in a few minutes. Whatever you want to say to her, you say to me."

"I have a history with her—"

"You're damn lucky she didn't have you arrested is what you are." He took a step forward, forcing James back toward the door. "You're also lucky I'm not kicking your ass right now." From what little he'd heard about James, Tony suspected he wasn't in as good a shape as he was, although a knit pullover shirt hid the guy's physique.

"You're the guy she wrote about, aren't you? In the articles?"

Tony didn't budge. "That's none of your business. Her life is no longer any of your business."

"I read the whole series." He looked down at the floor. Tony tensed in case the guy was trying to throw him off guard. "I fucked up, man. I fucked up big-time. I know that. I didn't think she'd ever want to do any of that stuff. I'd never tried it in real life before. And now she's collared and calling you Sir?"

"Let me give you a piece of advice. Real men, regardless of whether they're kinky or not, don't go hurting their women the way you hurt her. They don't lie to them, and they damn sure don't run up fifteen thousand in debt in their name."

James nodded. "I know." He pulled an envelope out of his pocket and handed it to Tony. "Here." It had Shayla's name written on it.

Tony finally reached out and took it from him. "What is it?"

"I got a loan from my parents. I got rid of the apartment and moved back in with them to save money. It's everything I owe Shay."

"I'll give it to her." He stepped forward again, and now James was in the doorway. Tony put his hand on the door in preparation to close it.

"Can I say good-bye to her?"

"No. That's not a good idea. In fact, unless she contacts you, I suggest you don't ever contact her again. Not unless you want to deal with me."

"Who are you trying to bullshit? You'll order her not to have contact with me."

Tony shook his head. "Again, it's obvious you don't have a clue what you're talking about. I suggest you leave BDSM to people who have respect for their partners and quit thinking you have what it takes to be a Dominant. You can't even control your fucking Internet perving urges. *And* you're stupid enough to pay for porn? *Seriously? And* you're slimy enough to steal from the woman who loved you and even gave you a second chance when you certainly didn't deserve it? That's just…wow."

He slammed the door shut, forcing James to step back or be hit. Locking it, he stared at the envelope in his hand. It felt like there was more than just a check in it, like maybe a sheet or two of paper as well.

He didn't contemplate opening it. Instead, he put the umbrella down, turned on his heel, and headed for the bedroom. He fought another urge to laugh when he saw the frantic expression she wore as she tried to speak. But when she immediately shut up and dropped to her knees at his signal, it hardened his cock.

She sooo needs a spanking.

Then again, he *had* told her to be waiting for him. He'd never expected anyone else to show up, and she certainly hadn't.

And the smell of whatever she'd made deliciously filled the apartment, making his stomach growl.

He stood before her. "Greeting, pet."

She immediately kissed his feet, the backs of his hands, and then nuzzled his cock where it strained through his slacks.

"Look at me."

She did.

Who am I kidding? I'm in love with her. I can't be mad at her. "In the future, pet, ask who's at the door before telling them to come in. Especially if you're naked."

She nodded, so hard he thought her head might come off.

He held the envelope out to her. "He gave me this to give you."

She looked at it but didn't reach for it. "Are you mad at me, Sir?"

He took a deep breath. "No, of course I'm not mad at you, pet. I am upset that you let someone in without identifying who was at the door. I know it's a coincidence he showed up tonight. He said he left you voice mail messages this weekend. Had I not arrived when I did, I'm afraid of what he might have tried with you."

She nodded again. "I didn't listen to them when I cleared them this morning. As soon as I heard it was him, I deleted them."

"Aren't you going to open it?"

She stared at the envelope without taking it, then looked up at him. "Would you please open it for me, Sir?" she softly asked.

His heart wanted to break for her. He held out a hand to her and helped her stand. He led her to the bed and sat her down on the end of it. Then he inserted his thumb under the flap and opened the envelope.

Sure enough, two sheets of paper wrapped a cashier's check for $13,800. "He told me he got a loan from his parents," he explained as he handed her the check. She gasped in surprise over the amount while he read the letter.

In the long, rambling, handwritten missive, he asked for forgiveness, explained he was in therapy, and begged for a second chance. Including that he'd move to Florida to be with her and would agree to any terms she wanted.

He stopped midway through the first page. "Do you want me to read this to you, or summarize?"

"Summarize, please, Sir. Although I bet he's groveling and begging for another chance."

"My smart pet. Yes, among other things. I haven't finished it yet."

She took a deep breath, then slowly blew it out again. "I don't need to hear anything else. You don't have to finish it." She looked up, meeting his gaze. "You're my Sir. If that check clears, which I guess it will, I don't need to have anything else to do with him. Ever."

"You don't want me to finish reading it?"

She shook her head. "No, Sir. Not unless you want to."

"Do you want to keep it? Maybe to read later if you change your mind? I don't have a problem with that."

She shook her head. "No, Sir. I'm not changing my mind about you."

He smiled. "I meant changing your mind about reading what he has to say."

She shrugged. "I don't care what he has to say. I can't ever trust him again and have no desire to be friends with him."

"No desire to have closure?"

She shook her head. "He burned his bridges with me. He's lucky I didn't press charges against him. The only closure I need is when that check clears and I can pay off all the cards and close them. Please, just tear it up."

He nodded, then ripped the papers into small pieces before taking them into the bathroom and flushing them down the toilet. He returned to the bedroom and pulled her to her feet, sliding his hands down her back to her ass. He dug his fingers into her ass cheeks and pulled her hips tight against his so she could feel how hard he was.

"I think I'm going to give you five good, hard swats for letting someone in without checking first. Not fun—punishment. Any problem with that?"

She shook her head. "No, Sir. You're right."

"Good girl." He ground his hips against her. "Dinner smells delicious. Is it ready?"

A smile finally broke through the look of consternation on her face. "I just have to go put in the garlic bread."

He turned her around and delivered a playful swat to her ass. "Then I suggest you go do it. I'm starving."

* * * *

Shayla hurried out to the kitchen. She shoved the check into her purse before she removed the casserole from the oven and got the garlic bread ready to put under the broiler. It wasn't until she had the frozen pieces laid out on the cookie sheet and had it in the oven that she realized she was crying.

She leaned against the counter and closed her eyes, wishing she could control her emotions.

I'm free.

For the first time in the months since she discovered the true depths of James' treachery, she felt like she could breathe without the pain of stress and loss weighing her down.

The check was actually a little short of what he owed her. There were several hundred dollars in fees and interest that had accrued in addition to the original amount he'd charged in her name, but she wouldn't quibble over that. It was well worth the price to finally be free.

She'd never have to have contact with James again.

When Tony slipped his arms around her waist, she jumped, startled, then turned to face him.

"Talk to me, pet."

She shook her head and cried against him, relishing the feel of his hands stroking her back.

"It's okay," he softly said. "I'm here now. I'm not going anywhere."

When the timer went off, she extricated herself from his arms and removed the garlic bread from the oven. She was well aware of Tony's eyes following her every movement as she worked to plate their dinners.

Before she could pick up the dishes to carry them out to the living room so they could eat on the couch, he caught her hand and drew her close again. He feathered his lips along her knuckles, gently squeezing her hand.

"Talk to me *now*, pet."

She blinked at him. "I'm free," she finally whispered.

He smiled. "Do tell."

She realized how it sounded and laughed. "I meant free from him. From the whole nightmare. In a couple of days, all the debt will be paid off. I'm free."

He pulled her close. "And what about me? How do you feel when you're with me?"

She draped her arms around his neck and stared up into his green eyes. "I'm even freer when I'm with you, Sir."

"Even as my slave?"

"Especially as your slave. I can let go of everything else, every other worry, and focus only on you. I never knew how freeing being a slave would feel."

That damn, playful smile of his. She felt moisture pooling between her legs.

"Welcome to the irony inherent in the lifestyle, pet."

* * * *

Dinner was interrupted again by her cell phone ringing. She started to ignore it when she realized it was her parents' home number.

"Hello?"

Her mom. "I just received an interesting phone call from James."

Shayla groaned and pinched the bridge of her nose. Tony walked over, brow furrowed, obviously wanting to know what was wrong. "I don't want to know what he wanted," Shayla said.

"When I get a nearly hysterical call from your ex-fiancé, claiming you're being held hostage by a guy who's treating you like a slave, I think as a parent I should at least make a phone call to find out what's up."

She groaned again. "Mom, look. James showed up here—"

"I don't want to know anything about you and Tony's sex life," her mother said, cutting her off. "I read the articles. I suspect I know what's going on between you two. I'm not an idiot. But *are* you okay?"

She tried and failed not to snicker as Tony nibbled his way up her shoulder toward her neck. "Yes, Mom. I'm fine. I didn't know it was James at the door. I thought it was Tony."

"He seemed like a very nice guy. We both really liked him when we met him."

"I hope you're talking about Tony."

"I am."

She bit the bullet and closed her eyes. "Good, because he's going to be your son-in-law."

There was a moment of silence on the other end of the line. Finally, her mother said, "Seriously?"

"Yeah. Seriously. He proposed this morning."

Now her mother sounded strident. "And you didn't call us?" she shrieked, making Shayla pull the phone away from her ear.

Her eyes popped open. She met Tony's gaze. He was struggling not to laugh and had stopped mid-kiss. "I was going to call you tomorrow. Tony was out of town for two weeks. It was like after midnight when he got here this morning. We haven't even had time to eat dinner yet tonight. He just got here from work."

"When's the big day?"

"Mom, our dinner's getting cold."

"Screw your damn dinner! I get put through this tonight by your ex-asshole, I deserve a little forewarning. When's the wedding?"

Frustrated and knowing her mom wouldn't be happy without an answer, she looked at Tony. "She wants a date," she whispered in his ear.

He smiled. "We're eloping," he whispered back.

"You said my choice."

His smile widened to a grin. "Yes, I did." He kissed her and took the phone from her. "Hi, Karen. How are you?"

Shayla giggled and rested her head against Tony's chest as he looped an arm around her shoulders and held her close. She reveled in the warmth from his body pressed against hers.

"Yes, ma'am. He showed up here at her apartment unannounced. I took care of him. He didn't take kindly to it... Yes, I proposed this morning." He looked down at Shayla. "I love your daughter and I'm not about to let her go... No, I don't spend money on porn, and yes, I'm still gainfully employed."

"Mother!" Shayla yelled as she reached for the phone.

He wouldn't let go of it and arched an eyebrow at her in warning. "Yes, she did seem a little perturbed by that question... James did leave her a check paying her back in full though... Yes, next time the little bastard calls you, feel free to tell him to go screw himself. It's a cashier's check... No, I don't think he can stop payment on it."

Shayla clapped a hand to her forehead, certain she'd just dropped into the rabbit hole for good this time.

"Yes, she'll call you back tomorrow morning with more details... No, we haven't set a date yet. Haven't thought that far in advance... Thanks, Karen. I appreciate that... Okay, thank you, Mom." He kissed Shayla. "You, too. Good night." He ended the call and placed her phone on the counter.

"Did she really call him a little bastard?"

He grinned again. "No, she called him a little fucker. I thought I'd show some restraint and not repeat that back to her. I don't want Mom to start thinking poorly of her son-in-law before we're even married."

* * * *

After dinner he helped her clean up the kitchen before leading her to the bedroom. He kicked off his shoes before standing with his arms outstretched.

She needed no prompting. She quickly set to work undressing him, carefully folding his clothes and laying them on the dresser. When he was naked, he pointed to the floor.

Her knees folded without hesitation. She rested her forehead on his feet, a soft sigh escaping her.

This is where I want to be. I don't care why anymore. It feels *right.*

"How's my pet?"

"Better, Sir. Now that you're here."

"Good girl. Before we can have fun, you owe me five."

"Yes, Sir." Already she felt her pussy clenching, growing wet. It'd be running down her legs in seconds, no doubt.

"Over the bed, feet on the floor."

She stood and turned to assume her position bent over the bed, her clit throbbing, on fire, aching to feel the first stinging slap across her ass.

He sat next to her on the bed and curled his fingers around her collar, pinning her facedown on the bed. His other hand caressed her ass. "Feet wider, pet."

She scooched her feet farther apart.

"Good girl." His hand stilled on her ass as heat built inside her, waiting to be unleashed.

"You're wet, aren't you?"

"Yes, Sir," she whispered, her face aflame at the admission.

"Such a good girl you are," he whispered, leaning in close, his breath in her ear. "I warned you I would rewire your brain. You were such a good girl to let me."

The silken rumble of his voice flowed through her body, only serving to make her crave his sadistic touch that much more. "Thank you for training me, Sir."

He chuckled. His hand continued caressing her ass. "It was most definitely my pleasure, pet. I look forward to many more long training sessions with you throughout the years." He leaned in even closer, his lips pressed to her ear now, his voice barely a breath. "My next goal is to train you to come just by verbal command. How would you like that, pet?"

She fisted the covers and let out a mewling whine. "Yes, Sir. Please."

"How would you like to feel me fucking your reddened ass, clamps on your nipples and clit, begging me to take them off and then I make…you…come." On the last word he delivered a hard, stinging blow to her ass, probably hard enough to make his hand sting.

She let out a cry that was partly pain, but a good deal of pleasure, too.

"Answer me, pet."

"Yes, Sir!"

"Or we could be in the middle of a scene. Imagine me using a riding crop on that sweet ass of yours and taking you just to the verge of coding and keeping you there. And then I turn the crop onto your vulnerable little clit and begin slapping it until you're ready to code…and I make you *come!*" The second blow, every bit as hard as the first, made her gasp with pain.

But his words also made her clit throb.

"I will train you in the fine art of orgasm control, pet. You will get to the point where you won't be able to come without my command. I'll be able to torture you for hours, keep you begging for relief, making you crave the pain as much as the pleasure so you can *come*." She was glad she didn't have any paddles at the apartment. Blow number three brought tears to her eyes, yet she didn't even consider begging for mercy.

She wanted it. Needed it.

Craved it.

"Is my poor pet horny?" he asked, speaking into her ear, her neck still pinned to the bed.

"Yes, Sir!"

"I can tell. I can smell how wet you are. Did you come while I was gone?"

"No, Sir."

"So this morning was the first time since three Saturdays ago?"

"Yes, Sir."

"Aww, my poor pet." *Slap!*

"One more, pet. One more hard one, and then I'm going to play with you until I'm ready to finish you off. Ready?"

"Yes, Sir."

She barely had the words out of her mouth before he smacked her one last, hard time. She sobbed, relieved it was over and wishing it wasn't.

He nibbled on the shell of her ear. "Playtime, pet." He didn't let her up. He slid the hand on her ass lower, between her legs, and fingered her pussy. "Just as I thought. You're a very wet girl." He lightly slapped her pussy, making her gasp.

"Keep those legs spread," he sternly ordered.

She did, bracing herself. He was more playful than sadistic, however, keeping his slaps on the lighter end of the scale. Relentless, he worked back and forth, between her clit and her pussy, until her whole body was on fire and she began begging for relief.

"Please, Sir," she sobbed.

"Please what, pet?"

"Please make me come!"

"Try coming for me like this, then, pet." His strokes grew more regular, the tempo and force slowly increasing until she wasn't sure she could take it anymore.

Then subspace kicked in. Endorphins flooded her system. She rocked her body in time with his strokes, gasping as she felt her release closing in.

"That's my dirty little pet," he said. "You can do it."

She arched her back, crying out as she hit the perfect angle for his whole hand to make contact with both her clit and her pussy at the same time.

And then it happened. A slow boil that erupted before she realized it. She buried her face in the covers and screamed in relief even as he built to a crescendo that pushed her harder and farther over the edge. When he stopped, she gasped again, startled as the last echoes of her release still rippled through her.

Then, with a hand still on her collar, he stood and stepped between her legs. He lined up the engorged head of his cock with her wet cunt, rubbing the head back and forth between her swollen labia and coating it in her juices.

"Look what my pet did. My pet came from having her pussy slapped." He slammed his cock home, hard and deep and drawing a cry of pleasure from her. He pulled her head up with the collar. "Fuck yourself on my cock, pet. Show me what you'll do for me."

She did, grunting as he bottomed out inside her with every stroke. He released her collar and grabbed her hips. His fingers dug deep into her flesh as he took over and brutally fucked her.

"You are *my* pet," he said, his voice a deep, harsh growl. "Who do you belong to?"

"You, Sir!"

"That's right." He slapped her ass. "Who does this ass belong to?"

"You, Sir!"

"Who owns your orgasms?"

She sobbed, feeling another climax building inside her and wishing it'd break free. "You, Sir!"

He fell still, pinning her to the bed with his body. He reached around her and found her clit. "Come again for me, pet. Come hard." He roughly stroked her clit. She was so swollen and sensitive already, combined with his sexy, throaty growl, that she immediately fell over the edge. The feel of her cunt squeezing his cock inside her only intensified the feeling for her and she tried to fuck herself on him but couldn't because of his weight pressing down on top of her.

"Not yet, pet," he said. "One more from you." He bit down on her shoulder, hard, as his hand sped up.

I can't...I'll never... Those thoughts faded away as another climax ripped through her, the almost painful pleasure making her cry out again.

"Good girl!" He grabbed her hips again and fucked her hard and fast, coming in just a few strokes before falling still on top of her.

They both lay there in silence for a moment until he stood and pulled her up, helping her onto the bed where he curled his body around hers. "Rest, pet."

"Yes, Sir." She closed her eyes.

* * * *

"Oh, peeeetttt." Shayla's eyes fluttered open. Tony looked down at her with a smile on his face.

She let out a yawn.

He laughed. "You fell asleep on me, silly pet."

"I'm sorry. What time is it?" She realized the bedroom TV was now on when it hadn't been.

"After midnight. That's okay. I figured you needed the rest."

She snuggled closer to him and pressed the length of her body against his. It felt so good to stretch out naked next to him.

It felt so right.

"I missed you so much, Sir," she whispered.

He touched her chin. "I missed you, too, pet. I'm sorry you thought I didn't care." He kissed her. "And this isn't exactly the way I planned tonight to go."

"Sorry, Sir."

"*Stop.* Stop apologizing." He kissed her again, on the lips, deeply, sweetly, tasting warm and sweet and so, so good. "I got you something on my lunch break today. Stay here." He left the bed and grabbed his slacks, pulling them on and nothing else. She heard the jingle of car keys, the front door open, then the beep of his car as he unlocked it with the fob.

A moment later he returned, stripping before getting into bed with that damn, sexy smile on his face.

"Close your eyes, pet."

She did.

She felt him take her left hand and he slid something on her ring finger. "Open them, pet."

She looked down, the diamond and amethyst ring winking at her in the light from the TV. Her birthday was February twenty-first, hence the amethyst.

Stunned, she stared up at him. He laced his fingers through her hand and kissed them. "Will you please marry me, pet? I know we settled this, but I realized my proposal the first time around wasn't the best. I'd actually planned to go down on one knee for you after dinner."

She squealed, delighted. "Yes, Sir. I'll marry you and wear your collar and take your spankings and anything else you want me to do."

He grinned and rolled on top of her. "I do believe you are the perfect pet."

Chapter Twenty-Eight

She packed a bag and things she'd need for work and spent the rest of the nights that week at Tony's. She had to speak to her landlord about breaking her lease and getting her deposit back. She could still afford to pay the bills there and live at Tony's if they wouldn't budge, but it would suck.

And living at Tony's was well worth it. Seth, Landry, Cris, and Ross would help them move the rest of her things on Sunday.

But first...

Saturday evening she put on the black sundress he loved, and her strappy sandals.

No panties allowed.

She wore her amulet to dinner with their friends, and all the women nearly yanked her left arm off to get a look at her engagement ring. Even Clarisse, Sully, and Mac had made it down to help celebrate.

But as soon as Shayla and Tony were back in the car, he buckled the leather collar and wrist cuffs on her. He hooked a finger through the front D-ring and pulled her close to kiss her on the lips. "My beautiful pet," he whispered. "Just the way you belong, wearing my collar."

The questions no longer mattered to her. She no longer needed answers. All she cared about was that she'd landed in the safety of this man's arms.

"Thank you, Sir."

"Ready to go?"

"Yes, Sir."

He didn't release her. "Last chance to back out. I'm going to collar you in front of everyone. *This* is the anniversary date I will never forget, and the one we will always celebrate. I don't care what date ends up on our marriage certificate."

"Me, too, Sir."

"Good girl."

He held her hand all the way to the club. She waited while he got their things from the car before she followed him inside.

Apparently, Loren, Leah, Tilly, and Clarisse had been busy. Shayla stopped short when she saw the decorations, special centerpieces on all the tables, and a small gazebo that had been set up and festooned with flowers.

She turned to Tony. "Did you know about this, Sir?"

He smiled. "Yep. Hey, Loren is a fierce party planner. Not even I was going to tell her no."

"Smart man," Ross mumbled as he walked in behind them. "You should have seen what she pulled together practically overnight for Tilly's wedding."

Loren walked in with the other women, grins on their faces. Shayla engulfed them in hugs. "Thank you!" she said, near tears and not wanting to cry.

"Hey, it's your big day," Loren said. "Not every day a girl gets collared by her Prince, eh, Dom Charming."

"By the way," Tilly added, "Loren is a notary. So if you're looking for someone to really make things legal, she's your gal."

"Would you?" Shayla asked her.

Loren grinned. "Of course I will! It'll be my honor and pleasure."

At ten o'clock, the DJ shut off the music and called for everyone's attention. Tony had even brought Shayla's pillow and placed it in front of the gazebo. With her pulse racing, she let Tony take her hand and lead her over to the gazebo. When he pointed at the pillow, she immediately dropped to her knees.

Loren had placed the gazebo strategically in a corner, allowing her to take pictures of the event for them without catching anyone in the background.

Shayla couldn't remember ever hearing the dungeon sound so quiet, even that first afternoon she and Tony played together before his whip class. He had refused to tell her what he planned to say, only that she needed to have whatever she wanted to say as a vow ready to recite when he told her.

She would get free rein with the wedding plans.

He, however, got the collaring.

Tony looked down at her. "Tonight is a very special night. One that, for me, means even more than our wedding day." He looked at the audience.

The Denim Dom

"This woman is my life and my heart, and I stand in front of all of you to demonstrate that."

He reached down, unbuckled the leather collar, and removed it from around her neck. She was surprised by this, but didn't resist. He also gently lifted the amulet from around her neck. "I am uncollaring you, Shayla, so that you are free to make this decision. I stand before you offering to be your Master, your Owner, your Dominant. And yes, your husband.

"If death takes me first, then you are free to find another if you choose to do so. I only want you to be happy. But while we are both alive, I demand you place me above all others in our lives. You will obey me. You will respect me. You will take my punishments and the pleasure I give to you. I will never share you. I will protect you. I will consider your feelings and input, but I am, above all, the final word.

"The lifestyle we live is not always easy. There are many things we can't share with others in our lives. There are times that giving over control is the hardest thing you will ever do. I promise to you I will not waste the gift, if you choose to give it to me, of your submission. I will cherish it and you and never forget what a precious, rare, and valuable thing I own.

"I promise to do my best to never let you down. I swear to own up to my mistakes, and I say this now before our friends and witnesses, that I will always strive to do and be the best person I can so that I can do right by you in all ways."

His voice grew quiet. "I promise to love you, and hold you, and soothe your tears, even when I'm the one who draws them out of you. I promise to be as transparent as I can with you. I promise that even when I cannot physically be with you because of other responsibilities, that I will still always be your Master, Owner, and Dominant and make sure you know how much a part of me you are. I am an independent, complete person. But *with* you I am better. Without you, life is simply breathing. You are the air that makes life worth living.

"If you want to live this life with me, you will have to ask me to be my slave, my pet, my property, my beloved and cherished submissive...and my toy." His mouth quirked in a smile. "I want our witnesses to see you make this choice freely and not through coercion."

He stared into her eyes and she realized after a moment that it was her turn. She blinked, trying not to cry over his heartfelt words.

She started to speak, swallowed, and tried again, hoping she didn't forget what she'd written. "When I met you, I had no idea what was in store for me. You took me and restored my trust and faith. You showed me who I could be, and made me realize who I want to be. I want to be your slave. I want you to own me. I love you and while I'm looking forward to being your wife, I want to first be your slave. I love being your pet. Nowhere else feels right anymore except in your arms or with your hand on my collar. I feel naked without my collar."

She thought for a second, her scripted vow over. "Boy, do I feel naked without my collar." The audience tittered softly. Tony smiled. "I hadn't expected this. Being uncollared." She looked out at everyone before looking back at him. "Please, Sir," she asked, her voice trembling. "I need your collar. I *need* to wear it. I *want* to wear it. I've never been happier in my life than with your collar around my neck. Please collar me and make me yours. Please give me your collar."

Somewhere in the back of the audience, a smart-ass let loose with a Gollum impression. "Give us the precious!"

Loren shot a stern look in the direction of the voice. "Someone put a ball gag in Gilo's mouth!"

Tilly called out, "On it!" She stood and headed toward the offender, who began scrambling away from her.

The audience laughed, as did Shayla and Tony.

She looked up at him. "Yes, Sir. I want your collar and I want everyone here to know it."

He pulled a black leather collar from his pocket, a collar that she hadn't seen before. Supple and soft, narrower than the one she normally wore, it had a locking buckle. A silver tag hung from the ring in front.

He held it up to show everyone. "This is her collar, one I bought specially for her. No one else has worn it. The tag says 'pet, Property of Tony' and her slave registration number." She pulled her hair out of the way while he buckled it around her neck.

When she heard the tiny Master lock click shut on the buckle, she felt a deep peace settle over her soul.

He straightened. "And your day collar." He produced a beautiful gold chain, with a heart-shaped gold tag. "My initials are engraved on the back of the tag," he said as he carefully fastened it around her neck. "Just like you're engraved on my heart."

He kissed her, slow and deeply, before helping her stand.

The club erupted into applause. As everyone gathered around to congratulate them, her only focus was on Tony. He pulled her into his arms and cupped the back of her neck.

"My sweet, beautiful pet," he whispered.

She smiled. "My denim Dom."

* * * *

Eight weeks flew by in a flurry of plans, payments, and Tony trying not to be bored to tears while he sat and watched Shayla, Loren, Leah, Tilly, and Clarisse, when she could make it down, hammer out the plans. Finally, the big day arrived. They'd have their kink-friendly wedding first, at Leah and Seth's, followed by the "real" wedding for family and vanilla friends on the beach.

Tony stood behind Shayla where she sat in Leah and Seth's guest room, his hands on her shoulders, and looked at her in the mirror over the dresser. "Last chance to back out, pet."

She smiled into the mirror, her eyes on his. "No backing out, Sir."

"And you're okay with the fact I don't want children? I am not getting my vasectomy reversed, and I'm not adopting."

She nodded.

"Anything else you'd like to settle before we take our vows?"

She reached up with her right hand and laced her fingers through his. "Yes, Sir."

His heart nearly seized. *Then again, this is why I asked. Better now than later.* "Go ahead."

She took a deep breath. Then, in a soft voice she asked, "Can we get a cat, Sir?"

He didn't want to bust out laughing and hurt her feelings, but his relief spiked through him. He gently squeezed her fingers. "No, pet. We cannot get *a* cat."

Her eyes clouded as her gaze dropped. "Yes, Sir."

He blinked. "You don't want to talk about it or ask me why?"

"If you say no, Sir, then that's it."

He pressed his lips together in an attempt to not laugh. He squeezed her fingers again. "*Pet*," he warned.

She looked up again, meeting his gaze. "Why, Sir?" she quietly asked.

The smile finally broke through. "Because I think it'd be mean to have just one. It might get lonely. I'd rather we adopt two. But not until after we get back from our honeymoon."

Her turn to blink in surprise. She turned to look up at him. "You mean it?"

"Of course I mean it. Silly pet. One of these days I'll beat it into your ass that sometimes I want you to challenge me and to not just roll over."

She grinned. "But maybe I like it when you beat my ass."

He pulled her to her feet and kissed her. "I like it when I beat your ass, too, pet. That's why we're perfect for each other."

Tilly knocked and walked in without waiting for an answer. "You, out!" she said to Tony. "I need to finish helping her with her hair and makeup. You can maul her tonight. Right now, she's ours."

Shayla laughed. "I think she means it, Sir."

"I know she means it. That's why I'm getting the hell out." He headed for what he hoped was the safety of the kitchen.

Seth, Tony's best man, walked up to him. "Ready? We've got everyone gathered outside."

"I think so." He straightened his jacket. Thank god Shayla hadn't wanted formal tuxes. "How do I look?"

"Like you're feeling better than I felt on my wedding day," he said with a smirk. "Lucky bastard."

Tony grinned. "I am definitely one lucky bastard," he agreed.

Leah walked up and playfully poked him in the shoulder. "Hey, I have a message to pass along." At both weddings, Leah would be Shay's matron of honor.

"You do, huh?"

"From myself, Loren, Tilly, and Clarisse."

"And how did you get to be the designated bearer of bad tidings?"

She frowned. "It's not bad. And because it's my house."

"Well?"

She poked him in the chest. "If you ever leave her or break her heart, Tilly volunteers Landry and Cris to hold you down while the rest of us practice a game of Dom Disembowelment on you. *Capisce*?" A smile broke through. She stood on her toes and kissed him on the cheek before reaching up to straighten his tie. Her eyes looked too bright, like she was close to tears.

Happy ones this time, thank god. Such a great sight compared to the depths of her despair just a couple of years earlier.

He laughed and looked at Seth. "Can't you get your damn mouthy slave under control?"

Seth hooked an arm around Leah's waist and pulled her close. "Not until after the last ceremony. It'll smear her makeup and Loren will noogie me."

* * * *

The real wedding went off without a hitch. The men of the wedding party were shoved into one limo while the women gathered in another for the ride to the hotel on Siesta Key where Shayla's parents and brother were staying, and where the reception was being held.

The weather cooperated for the beach wedding redux. Tony whispered in her ear after kissing her for the second time at Loren's instruction. "If you weren't mine before, you're doubly mine now."

She smiled and touched the heart-shaped tag on her necklace. "Triply, Sir," she whispered. "And as many times as I need to know I'm yours."

Seth leaned in. "Lucky bastard," he said with a smile.

Epilogue

Shayla awoke early Saturday morning and pounced on Tony. "Wake up, Sir!"

He slowly peeled one eyelid open to peer at her. "What time is it, pet?" he groggily mumbled.

"Seven thirty."

He groaned and closed his eyes. "Five more minutes. And coffee, dammit."

She giggled. "Yes, Sir. Coming right up." Wearing nothing but her collar and leather wrist cuffs, she bounced out of bed and went to the kitchen to get the coffee started. When she returned to the bedroom five minutes later, she carried his mug of coffee, which she'd prepared exactly the way he liked.

She set the mug on the bedside table before crawling under the sheets and finding his cock. He was already slightly hard from a morning woody. She engulfed him with her mouth and slowly laved her tongue around the head. In seconds, he was fully hard.

Tony let out a groan and rolled onto his back. She smiled to herself as his fingers tangled in her hair and held on, using it as leverage to urge her deeper and faster.

Shayla knew she'd get a spanking for this and didn't care. In fact, she was counting on it.

Deeper, faster, his pre-cum sweetly salty on her tongue, rewarding her efforts. It only took a couple of minutes. She cupped his sac with one hand while encircling the base of his shaft with the other. When she felt his balls draw up tight against her palm, she knew he was close. She went deep, swallowing him and moaning as his fingers dug into her scalp and his whole body tensed. He let out a grunt and then jets of his cum filled her mouth.

She eagerly swallowed every drop. She wouldn't let go after he went soft once again, either, gently coaxing every last drop she could from his cock.

He stroked her head before making her let go. "Good girl," he mumbled. "That's five."

She giggled. "I know, Sir."

He raised the sheet up to look down at her. Waking Sir up without coffee being ready first was five strokes. Cane or hand or paddle, his choice. His sleepy smile warmed her heart.

He threw the sheet back and shoved his pillow up against the headboard. Then he patted his lap. "Let's get it over with, pet."

She practically threw herself over his thighs, head to the left as always so he could spank her right-handed.

As the fingers of his left hand hooked around her collar, she spread her legs a little. His right palm settled over her ass, stroking sweetly.

Then it fell still.

He did it fast and hard, delivering all five blows without drawing it out. It left her gasping with pain and need when he finished.

"Aw, is my poor pet horny?"

She kept her face buried in the sheets. "Yes, Sir."

He laughed and patted her ass. "Over the bed, feet on the floor. I'll be right back."

She assumed the position as instructed, her nipples rubbing against the sheets and causing more erotic friction that didn't help matters any. He'd mentioned taking her to get her nipples pierced. The thought both terrified her and thrilled her at the same time. It was something he'd left the decision about to her, and yet she couldn't make up her mind. Loren swore by hers, said it made sex that much hotter.

She was considering turning the decision back over to him. She wanted to do it, but knew if it was up to her she wouldn't.

She'd rather he make her do it.

She heard him in the bathroom. Then he walked down the hall. Somewhere she heard a door open and close and suspected he'd gone to the playroom.

Her whole body heated. No telling what he'd come back with.

When she heard him return, before he even reached the bedroom door he said, "No peeking. Face down."

She closed her eyes and kept them closed.

She sensed him walk into the bedroom and then the heat from his body brushed against her thighs before he ever made contact with her. When he grabbed her wrists and pulled them behind her back, she heard the *snap* of a clip being attached to them, immobilizing her.

He laid something down on the bed next to her. Then came the feel of his thighs pressing against the back of her legs as he rubbed what felt like an enormous dildo between her legs.

Oh, crap.

He chuckled, apparently reading her body language. "Yes, you've earned the wrath of Khan this morning," he teased. The large dildo was at the upper end of her ability to take. He'd joked that he named it that because of the scream of "Khaaaannnn!" that Captain Kirk let out in the movie.

Tony said it sounded like some of the noises she made when he used it on her.

She whimpered as he slowly began working it inside her. Oh, he was going to really torture her this morning. Usually keeping her on edge for a while. She felt him pause and then heard him sipping his coffee before he set the mug on the table again.

The forward progress continued. Khan stretched her, rubbing all the right places inside her. Halfway in, Tony slowly started fucking it in and out, each stroke a little deeper than the last, until he finally had its entire eight fat inches buried inside her and she felt the strap-on harness pressed against her ass.

Then he stopped.

Her muscles clenched around the toy, her need growing as she realized just how long he might draw this out this morning. "That's right, pet. Might as well practice your Kegels on it for a few minutes. You know what happens when you're too eager and don't have my coffee ready. Feel free to squirm around all you want." He pressed forward, which pinned her thighs against the bed.

With her wrists trapped behind her, all she could do was squirm against it. As she did, he lightly slapped her ass with what she guessed to be a small leather slapper. Barely stingy, it only served to add to her sexual frustration.

"Aww, my poor pet. Are you horny?"

"Yes, Sir."

"Serves you right." He grabbed her wrists and fucked her hard for a few seconds before falling still again and leaving her even more frustrated. He repeated this for nearly half an hour, even turning on the TV to the morning news to watch while she begged for release and her thighs ached from the position.

"Please, Sir! Please, I'll do anything. Please make me come!"

He chuckled and leaned in to nip her ear. "Well, let's see. I'm feeling generous. I think when we go out today, pet will wear the short pink sundress I bought for you last weekend, no panties, and those high, strappy sandals I like. Either that, or another hour of this."

She froze. He never dictated her work clothes. But when they were home, he often played barter games for her to wear what he wanted, making her choose between selecting sexy items he loved seeing her in simply for the sadistic pleasure of knowing how embarrassed it sometimes made her, or torture.

Either way, it was win-win for the sadist.

Truth be told, she considered it win-win for her, too.

"Which will it be, pet? Or it will be both if you don't pick soon."

"Yes, Sir," she whispered, her face burning. She needed to come, right now!

"You'll wear it? We're going out for a late lunch with Seth and Leah, remember. We'll be walking around St. Armand's Circle. It'll be breezy."

Her face burned. "Yes, Sir. I know."

He laughed. "Such a good girl. You make me so proud." He grabbed her wrists with one hand, and then with the other he grabbed something else he'd brought in.

She heard a familiar *click* before the vibrator throbbed to life.

He reached under her and wedged it between her and the mattress, so that her body held it in place and she could rub herself against it.

"Come as much as you want, pet. You'll be here a while regardless." He started fucking her fast and hard. Every stroke shoved her onto the vibrator. The first cries of pleasure rolled out of her and she didn't bother trying to keep quiet. Pain or pleasure, he enjoyed making her lose control and make all the noise she wanted. As orgasm after orgasm rolled through her, she lay there unable to do anything but take it.

The thought of safewording never crossed her mind.

"Ahhhhhh!" She was glad he had her bent over the bed because her legs wouldn't support her any longer.

And still he fucked her, varying the strokes between short, shallow jabs that nailed her right in the G-spot every time and drove her over the edge again and again, to long, slow, deep ones that bottomed out inside her and added delicious discomfort to the pleasure.

Finally, when she was left sobbing and wrung out, her body limp and trembling, he withdrew and pulled the vibrator out from under her. He left her hands cuffed behind her and turned her onto her side so he could pull her all the way up onto the bed. Then he sat in front of her and let her press her face against his thigh as she recovered.

He tenderly stroked her hair. "My sweet pet. A good girl once again. All the bad beaten and fucked out of you for the day."

She smiled. "Thank you, Sir."

"My pleasure." He gently tapped her nose so she'd open her eyes and look at him. "And Khan's pleasure."

She laughed and stared at the strap-on he still wore.

"I think you need to show Khan how much you appreciated it. You got him all wet."

She looked up at him and then slowly climbed to her knees. Hands still cuffed behind her made it hard to maneuver, but she managed. She stared Tony in the eyes as she slowly went down on the dildo, her own taste filling her mouth.

"Such a good girl," he said as he palmed her cheek.

She continued sucking on the dildo for another minute or two until Tony tapped her on the head. "Move, pet. Ass in the air."

She turned and once again pressed her shoulders to the mattress, a smile on her face. Sir always got horny watching her do that. And sure enough, he pulled off the strap-on harness and his own cock was once again hard and ready. He knelt behind her on the bed and fed his real cock into her.

"This will be a quick one, pet. You've had your turn." He grabbed her hips and she loved the feeling of him fucking her, using her, serving him.

Objectified? Absolutely, and she loved it because he more than showed his love for her every day. If this was how he wanted her to serve him?

Hell, yeah.

He dug his fingers in as he fucked her, knowing she loved the feel of that. "Here you go, pet." He grunted as he took a few last, hard strokes inside her. He rested for a moment before withdrawing, a hand on her lower back to balance himself. Then he unclipped her wrists and flipped her over so he could kiss her.

"Who's my good girl?"

She stared up into his eyes, a smile on her face. "Me, Sir."

He kissed her again. "Okay, go wash Khan and the vibrator and put everything away and refill my coffee. Then meet me in the shower."

"Yes, Sir." She gathered everything and his coffee mug and hurried to do what he'd ordered. Five minutes later, she was in the shower with him.

"No panties all weekend, pet," he said with a smile. "Remember—"

"Panties are a privilege, not a right," she recited with a laugh. "Yes, Sir. I know."

* * * *

They'd been back from their honeymoon for a week. After catching up at work all the previous week, today was like a mini-vacation for them both. Naked except for her wrist cuffs and collar, which she'd put back on after the shower, Shayla fixed them a quick breakfast. If she didn't feel good, or it was cold, she could wear clothes without permission. Otherwise, she was always to be naked in the house when they were alone.

She'd gotten over her self-consciousness about that the second week they'd lived together. Now, it felt like habit.

Less than an hour later they were in his car and heading to their destination. She suspected her face would be permanently blushing the entire time they were out. The hem of her dress hit at lower thigh when she stood, but sitting or bending over, or a stiff breeze, were different.

He held her hand as they walked inside the building and talked to the volunteer on duty. They had them fill out forms before they took them back to the cat area.

"Remember," he whispered in her ear. "Your choice, but I would prefer two who maybe were brought in together, or two littermates."

"Yes, Sir."

They spent an hour looking at cats. She wanted to take them all home and knew she couldn't. She finally decided on an older pair of cats, male and female, brother and sister littermates that were five years old. Their older owner had died and no family members took in the cats. The male, a black and white tuxedo, was already named Bagel. His sister, mostly black except for a white spot on her tummy, was named Cream.

Tony held Bagel. The cat rubbed his head against Tony's goatee. "I guess we have our kids picked out," he said.

She stroked Cream. "I don't have the heart to change their names."

"Neither do I," he agreed.

While the shelter workers filled out all the adoption paperwork for them, Tony went out to the car and retrieved the two new cat carriers they'd purchased earlier that week. An hour later, their two cats were busy exploring their new home, including the six-foot-tall cat tree, complete with assorted scratching posts, ledges, and boxes, that now sat in front of a window in the living room.

"They aren't allowed in the playroom, pet. Remember that."

"Yes, Sir." She threw her arms around him and hugged him. "Thank you, Sir."

He slid her sundress up over her ass and patted her bare rump. "You might not be thanking me later. Let's go meet up with Seth and Leah."

She let her hand rest on his thigh as he drove. He laced his fingers through hers. "Whatcha' thinkin', pet?"

She smiled. "That considering how dominant cats are by their nature, I think you just got nonconsensually relegated to the role of a switch."

His laughter roared through the car.

THE END

WWW.TYMBERDALTON.COM

ABOUT THE AUTHOR

Tymber Dalton lives in the Tampa Bay region of Florida with her husband (aka "The World's Best Husband™") and too many pets. Not only is she active in the BDSM lifestyle, the two-time EPIC winner is also the bestselling author of over forty books such as *The Reluctant Dom*, *Cardinal's Rule*, the Love Slave for Two series, the Triple Trouble series, and many more.

She loves to hear from readers! Please feel free to drop by her website and sign up for her newsletter to keep abreast of the latest news, views, snarkage, and releases. (Don't forget to look up her writing alter egos Lesli Richardson, Tessa Monroe, and Macy Largo.)

http://www.tymberdalton.com
http://www.facebook.com/tymberdalton
http://www.twitter.com/TymberDalton

For all titles by Tymber Dalton, please visit
www.bookstrand.com/tymber-dalton

For titles by Tymber Dalton writing as
Lesli Richardson
www.bookstrand.com/lesli-richardson
Tessa Monroe
www.bookstrand.com/tessa-monroe
Macy Largo
www.bookstrand.com/macy-largo

Siren Publishing, Inc.
www.SirenPublishing.com

CPSIA information can be obtained at www.ICGtesting.com
Printed in the USA
LVOW08s1232030216

473459LV00027B/565/P